BETWEEN A ROPE
AND A DEAD PLACE

I dangled on the rope for an instant with ocean up to my knees. Then I got my feet against the sailboat's side. A foot lashed out and grazed my head, but I could only duck. I needed both hands for hanging on.

I got a toehold on the bottom rung of the jointed ladder at last and tried to grab one of Giulio's ankles, but he kicked at me again and hauled himself onto the deck above and came to his feet.

I didn't like what I saw. He was dragging the gun from his waistband—and there was no way I could possibly reach him in time . . .

The Revengers

Donald Hamilton

FAWCETT GOLD MEDAL • NEW YORK

Published by Fawcett Gold Medal Books, a unit of CBS Publications, the Educational and Professional Publishing Division of CBS, Inc.

ISBN 0-449-14487-9

First Fawcett Gold Medal Edition: November 1982

10 9 8 7 6 5 4 3 2 1

CHAPTER 1

ONE national cemetery looks pretty much like another at burying time, from Arlington on down—this one happened to be located in Santa Fe, New Mexico. In my line of work we get accustomed to, if never quite hardened to, losing a fellow worker now and then; and since many of us have worn uniforms in the past, the final rites often taken place on government ground. As a result, although appearing at such funerals isn't very good security, we bend the rules often enough out of respect for our dead that the scene tends to become familiar if never exactly comfortable.

There are always the rows upon rows of identical white headstones marching across the green lawns in strict military formations. There's always the sad, somber, and rather untidy little funeral party—no military formations here—almost lost in the great tidy fields of the dead. Sometimes it rains, but not always. It's only in the movies that the scene is always misty and dismal, punctuated by picturesque black umbrellas the prop departments must obtain from a special source, since I haven't seen that many black ones all together in years except on the screen; in real life these days they're mostly either transparent or brightly colored.

But today, in real life, there were no umbrellas. The sun was shining brightly in spite of the fact that we were burying Bob Devine with a back full of buckshot—rather ironical considering the fact that he'd been retired a few years back, at a fairly early age, due to a heart condition, after surviving innumerable dangers that should have killed him, a few of which I'd shared. He'd married and settled down to a peaceful life in my old home town, probably because I'd painted it in such bright nostalgic colors during one of those times that come in our business, when you have nothing to do but kill time, preferably by talking about matters of no importance, since you've already settled everything involving the mission at hand. So Bob Devine had retired and let his guard down and the past had sneaked up behind him with a shotgun. If it was the past. That remained to be seen.

There was a little snow left on the Sangre de Cristo peaks above us; but the small wind was off the desert, warm and dry. It stirred the short dark hair of Martha Devine, beside me, and tugged at the black dress she was wearing that looked a bit too festive for the occasion, with pretty black ruffles encircling neck and wrists and hem. It was obviously a party dress but if people didn't like it, her attitude said, to hell with people. It was black, wasn't it? There were tears in her eyes, weren't there? What did they want, blood?

I guessed that she had picked the dress simply because it was the only long-sleeved black dress she owned and she hadn't seen any point in buying a new and less frivolous one. It wasn't as if she buried husbands often enough to justify investing in a special funeral costume. She was a moderately tall girl, perhaps a bit too big for dainty, little-girl ruffles, even in black; but I remembered that Bob had liked his girls ruffly and feminine. I found myself recalling for some reason the time in a certain Colombian house of ill repute, to use the old-fashioned designation, long before he married the girl beside me. We were there together in the line of duty and it was necessary for us to behave in a manner appropriate to our surroundings or we would never, of course, have dreamed of sampling the merchandise and charging the experience to Uncle Sam. Bob had skillfully maneuvered to get himself, of the two willing ladies who'd adopted us as we came in, the rather attractive one in the fluttery summer dress, leaving me the skinny one in the skintight pants. It could have created a real problem for me since ladies in pants do very little for me and I'm not enthusiastic about the idea of sex as a business proposition anyway. Besides, at the time, I wasn't at all certain that the dangerous characters we were tracking through that part of South America weren't hanging around in the hope of taking advantage of our preoccupation in a rather lethal way, a consideration that also tended to inhibit my virility.

As it turned out, my girl was a bright and observant kid who was just as happy to earn her money in conversation as in copulation, laughing at my atrocious Spanish all the while; and the information she gave me led to the swift completion of the assignment that had brought Bob and me to that part of the world. Funny. I hadn't thought of Rafaelita in years.

But this was hardly the time to be thinking of whores and whorehouses, or my sexual quirks, either. Or even Bob's. Particularly Bob's, now that it was time to say goodbye to a pretty nice and competent guy whose luck had not been good, bringing him first the treacherous heart and then the fatal shotgun; a guy whose wife now stood beside me registering an emotion that was only partly grief. There was anger, too; not unnatural considering the way Bob had died.

She'd apparently been willing to go along with her husband's frilly preferences, at least where her party clothes were concerned; but that was largely, I knew, because clothes didn't mean much to Martha Devine. Unless a few years of matrimony had changed her drastically, she was a slacks-and-jeans girl at heart. She was wearing no hat and to hell with custom and tradition. The black dress was custom and tradition enough. She even had stockings on, and high heels, for God's sake. She was decently and respectably attired; and you had to draw the line somewhere. She'd never gone in for lady-type hats—Stetsons and fishing caps don't count—and she wasn't going to playact her grief now by masquerading ridiculously in some fancy black millinery complete with mourning veil. She wasn't Scarlett O'Hara, dammit, she was Martha Devine.

3

"It's . . . rather a private matter," Mac had told me in his Washington office, with a hint of hesitation that was unusual for him. He wasn't normally a hesitating man. "Well, it concerns us professionally, too, of course; the violent, unexplained death of any agent, even one who is retired, requires investigation, but . . . it's impossible for me to leave Washington at the moment, and I think my daughter may need some help. At least, let us say, some support; and I don't like to send a complete stranger. You remember my daughter, Martha, don't you, Eric?"

Matthew Helm is the name I was born with, or at least acquired shortly after birth; but Eric is how I'm known around that office and in a number of government files, maybe because it's a Scandinavian name and I have Scandinavian ancestors. That's just a guess. Exactly how he picks the code names has never become clear to me, even after working for him longer than I care to remember. (Bob Devine was Amos in the files, don't ask me why.)

Mac seemed to be looking at me a little harder than necessary; and his question was strictly rhetorical. He knew perfectly well that I remembered his daughter, Martha. His expression wasn't clearly visible to me at the moment because of the bright window he always liked to have behind him; but I didn't need to see him clearly. I knew what he looked like; a lean, gray-haired man with heavy black eyebrows, in a neat gray suit and conservative tie. He looked like a banker, perhaps, or an investment broker, or a highly placed business executive; and the last was close. (He's an executive all right, and a good one, but his business isn't making money or providing goods or services. At least the service he supplies—we supply—is not generally offered on the open market.)

His surname isn't Mac-anything; the Mac is derived from his middle name. His real name is Arthur McGillivray Borden, but I'm not really supposed to know that, nobody is, and knowing it I'm supposed to forget it. But he was making forgetting difficult today, reminding me that he had a daughter whom I'd once known—known rather well, if only briefly—as Martha Borden. As I say, he was looking at me a little too hard, as if to let me know that he was quite aware that I'd slept with the girl, his little girl; but she hadn't been so damn little even back then, and what the hell had he expected when he sent us on a dangerous cross-country expedition together in the service of our country? At least my goals had been simple and professional and maybe even kind of patriotic; hers as it turned out had been slightly more complex and confusing, all mixed up with youthful crusading idealism. But that had all happened several years ago. Now she was the wife, or widow, of Bob Devine.

"Yes, sir," I said. "I remember your daughter, Martha."

"As I say, it's my private affair to a degree, a family affair, and I'll understand if you prefer not to—"

"Support?" I said. He was just going through the polite motions of giving me an out we both knew I wouldn't take. I went on, "Do you mean protection, sir? Is there any indication that the guy who got Bob may be gunning for his wife?"

Mac shook his head. "No. They were together at the time, leaving a restaurant side by side. If the assassin had wanted Martha, too, all he'd have had to do was shoot twice. And perhaps support isn't exactly the right word. In fact, come to think of it, it's exactly the wrong word. The word I should have used was restraint."

I grimaced. "I'm slow today, sir. You'll have to spell it out for me."

He said, "My daughter is normally, as you may recall, a very gentle and humanitarian person with strongly non-violent principles. One might say she even makes a career of it, probably as a protest against me, if I may indulge in some amateur psychology. Most children, it seems, are in rebellion against their parents these days, and everything their parents stand for."

"Not only against you, sir," I said. "She didn't like any of us very much. In fact she thought we were all pretty horrid people; and, if anything, I was the horridest of the lot. She had no hesitation whatever in saying so. I've never figured out how she came to marry one of us in the end—

5

not that Bob wasn't a hell of a nice guy. Well, for somebody in this line of work."

Mac gave me a sharp, questioning look with some impatience in it; we were wandering away from the real subject he wanted to discuss. But he answered carefully, "Amos was a sick man when they met, sick and hopeless, the way a strong man can become who has never before experienced a real illness—"

I said, startled, "Hell, Bob had put in as much hospital time as any of us."

"For damage incurred in the line of duty." Mac made a sharp gesture. "Irrelevant, Eric. Certainly, Amos was prepared to accept injury from without; that's a risk any agent must face. He could have coped with the crippling result of a bullet or knife wound, or even deliberate torture. What he could not endure was the knowledge that this disabling blow had come from within; that his own body had weakly betrayed him. . . . Martha gave him something to live for, to fight for. I suspect that, on her side, there were other considerations as well, that you should understand better than I."

He gave me that meaningful look once more. I had an uneasy feeling that he was under the impression that his daughter and I had once achieved, if only fleetingly, a great passionate understanding. . . . Actually, the girl had used a bed only to gain my confidence, that old Mata Hari routine, never mind her complicated, idealistic motives. When it was all over, she'd made it perfectly clear that no matter how much innocent, or guilty, fun we'd had together, no matter what clever, sexy games we'd played in pursuit of our different goals, her basic opinion of me hadn't changed a bit. As far as she was concerned, I still belonged way out in Transylvania, somewhere on the bloody far side of Count Dracula.

But that wasn't anything I cared to explain to her sole surviving parent, who happened to be the man I worked for. After a good many years together we understood each other pretty well, but not that well.

It was better to get away from this phase of the subject

6

altogether, and I said, "Anyway, she did cherish some fairly sentimental notions, I agree. Up to a point."

"Precisely," Mac said. "Up to a point. But as we both recall, regardless of her peaceful principles, she once took rather drastic action in order to save her own life, and yours."

We seemed to have discarded, somewhere, the notion that I might have casually erased his daughter, Martha, from my memory. As a matter of fact, I remembered very clearly the drastic action to which he referred. After all the deceit and trickery, when it had come down to a simple matter of survival, she'd fired a flare gun, the only weapon available to her, into the face of a man who was about to shoot me very dead, first, and then turn his gun on her. The results had been spectacular, ugly, and effective.

"Yes, I still owe her one for that," I said. "Of course, it made her very sick to her stomach and she carried a load of guilt around for days, maybe for years. I wouldn't know about that. I haven't compared notes with her lately. In fact, I haven't heard from her at all since I said goodbye to her down there in Florida, shortly afterwards. Except for the wedding announcement she sent me; and maybe that was Bob's gesture toward an old comrade in arms."

"Nevertheless," Mac said, "guilt or no guilt, she might be capable of . . ." He stopped, and went on, "What I am trying to say, Eric, is that gentle theoretical principles are all very well; but as we have seen, they don't often survive a practical, life-and-death situation. The question is: would they survive seeing a spouse practically cut in two by a shotgun blast?" He cleared his throat. "To put it differently: my daughter has demonstrated that she is capable of acting violently to save her own life, not to mention yours. Could she also do so to avenge her husband's death? As it happens, the answer is of considerable importance at the moment."

"I see." I frowned. "You think she may go after the guy responsible?"

"Something like that. It's a possibility we have to keep in mind. Of course, she has no facilities for locating the man

7

who actually pulled the trigger, or even of determining his identity. The police are working on that. However, it is not as if he had committed a serious offense like smoking marijuana or allowing his dog to defecate on the pavement, so I am not too hopeful of their success." He said this without expression. I wondered how, two thousand miles away, he had come to the same conclusion about the forces of law and order involved that I had reached living there for years; but maybe he was simply disillusioned about modern law enforcement in general. He went on, "But I rather doubt that my daughter's anger—if I'm judging her correctly—is directed at the man who wielded the shotgun. She's an intelligent girl and, for one thing, she must know that she has neither the experience nor the organization necessary to track him down. For another, she probably realizes that hating a man like that is as senseless as hating the brand of firearm he employed. At least, it seems fairly certain from what we know that the murderer, like his weapon, was merely a tool."

I shook my head, puzzled. "As another mere tool in a different toolbox, I fail to see. . . . Oh, you mean somebody set Bob Devine up for the man with the blaster? And Martha knows who that person is?"

"Good," Mac said mildly. "I'm happy to see some small signs of returning cerebral activity. Yes, at the moment I think my daughter is feeling both guilty and betrayed— assuming that my information is accurate and I judge her reactions correctly. She is feeling guilty because in a way she is probably at least somewhat responsible for Amos's death; there are clear indications that she told too much to the wrong person. And betrayed because that person was somebody she considered a friend, somebody with whom she went to college, somebody she trusted implicitly and talked with freely, as girl to girl or woman to woman. Somebody who then made profitable use of the information Martha let slip. . . . Well, you will see how when you read the file I'm about to give you." He patted an envelope on his desk. "You will also see why, if my daughter is considering any kind of vengeful action, she must be stopped. So get out there right away; the funeral is tomorrow. The young lady downstairs has your tickets ready." He shoved the envelope toward me. "You can examine this on the plane. When you have read it, you will undoubtedly see further steps that should be taken to protect us, after you've prevented Martha from creating problems for us. Use your judgment. Good luck."

CHAPTER 2

THE grave was modestly concealed by a large plywood box covered with indoor-outdoor carpeting in a shade of green that was, I suppose, intended to blend with the grassy surroundings. But enough raw dirt showed around it to hint at the waiting hole underneath. The box was apparently designed to support a full-sized casket—it was the right size and shape—but today there was only a small receptacle placed on top of it, containing the cremains, as the funeral director had called them. It had taken me a moment to realize that by this term—cremains, for God's sake!—he was referring to the cremated remains, ashes to you, of the dear departed, who was now being described by the minister in very flattering terms.

I did not recognize my tough, reliable, ruthless, but somewhat oversexed, partner on a number of long-ago assignments in the description I was hearing. However, I suppose this was hardly a suitable place to boast—if the minister was even aware of these facts, which I doubted—that the late Robert Devine had been acceptable with a rifle, passable with a pistol, moderately good with automatic weapons, tops with knife and club, great at unarmed combat, and hell on wheels with women. Although, come to think of it, maybe Big Bob would have liked it better that way.

I felt a hand find my arm and squeeze it hard. I glanced at the black-clad young widow beside me and saw that her head was reverently bowed. A wing of her hair had fallen between us like a curtain, but I knew her features as well as I knew her father's, which was odd, I realized, since I saw Mac fairly often, but it had been some years since I'd last seen Martha, until this morning. But I guess I'd never really forgotten the tomboy face with the slightly upturned nose, the intelligent gray eyes and the heavy dark eyebrows.

I'd had some uneasy moments when I'd approached the house earlier—would I really recognize the damned girl after all this time?—and I'd been prepared to proceed cautiously rather than make an embarrassing mistake if one of the cars parked in front had been driven there by a helpful female of approximately the right size and age. However, when she opened the door herself, I knew her at once and was surprised that I'd had any doubt. She recognized me, too, although that was not very surprising. Mac's office had let her know I'd be there in time for the ceremony, if only barely—the girl downstairs had had to scramble, she'd said, to get me the right connections or any connections at all—and bony gents six feet four aren't all that common. Now Martha was gripping my arm fiercely and I realized that she was having a hard time holding back the hysterical laughter. I covered her hand with mine and pressed it in a conspiratorial way. We stood there studying our shoes soberly and listening to the man of God describing a hilariously saintly citizen named Robert Devine whom neither of us had ever known.

Then there was a moment of silence and a sudden crash of sound that caught us both by surprise: that damned military salute. I heard Martha gasp. Her fingers dug into me convulsively and I felt her sway. I knew she was remembering a time not long ago when she'd been subjected to a similar loud noise and the weapon involved had not been aimed at the sky.

"Easy," I whispered without turning my head.

10

"I'm all right. Can we go now?"

"Slowly. You're supposed to drag it out just a little for the condolences, if you can manage."

"God! All right, coach. Gotta win this one for ole daddy in Washington, right? And . . . and the poor guy in that crazy can over there. Matt."

"Yes?"

"Don't go away, damn you. Stick around for a change."

"I'm right here."

Then it was over and, shortly, I drove my rental car into the driveway, now empty, that looped up to the house through a bit of tricky desert-type landscaping involving rocks and gravel and cacti, and back down to the street again—actually a gracefully curving development-type road. This was one of the new mushroom suburban heavens with which I was not acquainted, moderately expensive, set in the rolling arid ranch country outside Santa Fe, where lots were measured in acres—well, at least fractional acres—instead of square feet. We do collect substantial danger pay and apparently Bob had saved a reasonable percentage of his and spent some of it to house his young bride and himself.

The lot was okay, with a spectacular view down the Rio Grande valley. The house itself, however, was fairly small and not very imaginative; a low, brown, flat-roofed, two-bedroom, cinderblock dwelling done in the pseudo-adobe style common out here in the dry southwest where the mudbrick hut is the ancient standard of architecture by which everything else is judged. There was the usual stylistic confusion between the old-fashioned round vigas, roof timbers to you, that stuck out picturesquely in true pioneer fashion, and the big modern picture window that would have given a true pioneer the shakes—think of trying to defend a window like that in an Indian raid!

Out here there was pretty good separation between the houses; and what with the hilly terrain and the winding road, or street, only a few of the neighboring residences were visible from where I parked the car directly in front. Getting out, I was aware that a tall blond woman in a pale

11

green, long-sleeved blouse and well-fitted green slacks was watching us from the front door of a house directly opposite that seemed to be almost a duplicate of the Devine domicile. She did not wave a greeting; she simply watched. I couldn't quite make out her face at the distance, but her drawn-back hair was smooth and bright and her figure was adult and interesting. I went around to help Martha out. She stood for a moment beside the car, breathing deeply as if she'd just come up for air after a long dive into cold water.

"Well, I guess that's that," she said. "Where are your things?"

"I've got a suitcase in the trunk," I said. "I figured the timing was going to be close so I wore my one dark suit and didn't take time to find a motel."

"Bring your bag inside."

I glanced at her quickly. "Is that such a good idea?"

"You don't want to spoil her whole day, do you?" Martha's head did not turn and her voice was quite even. "If you don't give her something to gossip about, she might bite herself and come down with rabies. Bring it in."

I said carefully, "Sure. If you know what you're doing."

"I know what I'm doing; I'm doing her a favor. She's been looking for a good reason to despise me and I'm giving it to her, okay?"

"Why should she want to despise you?" I asked as I opened the trunk of the car.

"That way she doesn't have to despise herself." Martha glanced across the street at last, and at me. "I thought you knew Bob pretty well."

"Oh."

She laughed. There was a little malice in the sound, but not enough to be disturbing; she was not really sneering at, or hating, the dead.

"Precisely, as Daddy would say. I gave him back something he'd lost. The coronary had undermined his confidence in himself, if you know what I mean. It really shook him very badly. He was afraid . . . afraid that since one important muscle had suddenly and inexplicably betrayed

12

him, another might. I . . . I helped him determine that that did not seem to be happening at all. If you know what I mean."

I said carefully, "It's my impression that the organ in question isn't basically muscular, but I get the general idea."

She laughed again, a wry sound now. "And then, of course, having married him and made a new man of him, I assumed that he was *my* new man entirely. But I was wrong. I mean, I don't have to tell you he was a damned nice guy in many ways; but I don't have to tell you, either, that he had a compulsive need to prove himself. In every way. And after the scare he'd had, it wasn't enough, in the end, for him to prove himself to me. With me. He had to check it out elsewhere, too."

I slammed the trunk and joined her, suitcase in hand. "Um," I said. "Like across the street?"

Martha nodded. "And since she's slept with my husband, naturally our suburban Lorelei over there wants a good reason for hating me so she doesn't have to feel cheap and guilty about her little neighborhood affair. So bring your suitcase along like a good boy and show her what a promiscuous worthless bitch I am, beneath contempt really; a wanton young wench who hauls another man into the house almost before her husband's cold in his grave." She took my arm, leading me toward the front door. "Just relax. It won't hurt a bit. You're doing your good deed for the day, okay? You're soothing the poor bruised conscience of Mrs. Roundheels back there; you're making it easy for her to live with herself again after her reckless fling at passion with the wonderful, exciting, dangerous married man across the street whose young tramp of a wife never appreciated or deserved him. . . ." The door closed behind us. Martha's voice stopped abruptly. After a moment she said in totally different tones, "Phew! How's that for prattling vivaciously? You didn't know I was a compulsive chatterbox, did you, Matt? Just leave your bag right there. How about a drink?"

The inside of the house was pleasant enough if you

didn't take your interior decoration seriously. I mean, the furniture made no particular statement, it was simply comfortable-looking with a sprinkling of the heavy, dark, Mexican-style pieces that are nowadays produced on both sides of the border. There were some pretty good Indian rugs on the floor and some pretty standard prints on the walls, mixed up with a few original landscape paintings by our local artists specializing in aspens. I guess in New England it's the birch with its gleaming white trunk; here in New Mexico it's the aspen with its golden autumn foliage. Well, I'm old-fashioned enough, artistically speaking, to prefer a good aspen or birch to a bad cube or tetrahedron. Leaving my suitcase in the front hall, I followed Martha into the living room. There was a small bar of sorts in the corner. She gestured toward it.

"Martini, right?" she asked, and when I nodded, she said, "Maybe you'd better make it yourself. I open a mean beer but I don't guarantee my mixed drinks. And a little Scotch for me. I'll get some ice."

Then we were sitting down with our drinks. It seemed as if I'd been going at a dead run ever since leaving Mac's office, but of course it was nothing to what she'd just been through. From the massive Mexican armchair I watched her settling into a corner of the husky Mexican sofa, discarding her gracious-young-widow act like a used Kleenex, letting the strain show at last, unconcerned now about the ladylike disposition of her limbs or the graceful arrangement of her dress. I noticed—her careless posture made it obvious—that she was wearing sheer black panty hose; and I realized that it was permissible for me to notice this now that Bob Devine was properly interred. Permissible but, perhaps, premature. She saw me looking, and gave me a small, amused grin. She flicked her pretty black dress down to where, propriety said, it belonged. Okay, premature.

"Thanks for the helping hand, Matt," she said calmly. "I didn't really know if I was going to survive today. It's been pretty grim. I was afraid I'd make an awful spectacle of myself before it was over. Thanks for helping to preserve the brave image." She sipped her Scotch, watching me over the glass. "But now tell me what you're really here for."

It was a little frightening. The girl had grown up. Not that she'd been painfully juvenile when I'd last seen her; but there had been a hint of baby-softness to her figure, and more than a hint of brash and youthful cocksureness in her attitude. Now she was a mature young woman with a calm assurance that came, not from a lot of self-righteous theoretical beliefs, but from a practical awareness of her own abilities. She'd had some tough years, but she'd used them well. She was leaner, smarter, and more experienced than the girl I'd once known; she was also considerably more attractive.

"What are friends for," I asked, "but to rally around in times of trouble?"

She laughed. "Bullshit. You've acted as if Bob and I had the plague for three years—or is it four now? I forget. Bob was even kind of hurt; we'd hear you'd been in town but you never came around. What kind of a friend is that?"

"You didn't used to be stupid, doll," I said.

"What . . . oh."

"I didn't know the situation," I said. "I didn't know how much you'd told him; I didn't know how you wanted to run this marriage of yours. When I finally heard of it. I was off somewhere when it happened. And if he'd seen us together, he'd have known, wouldn't he? There's no sure way of hiding *that*, ever, not when it happened so recently. Not from an observant guy like Bob. We're neither of us good actors. I didn't know all your special problems, but it just seemed better to stay the hell away."

Martha nodded slowly. "All right. Sorry. I'll buy that. As a matter of fact I didn't tell him. He . . . we had enough to handle without comparing old loves and old lovers. So it could have become a sticky scene and you were right not to risk it. But I still don't believe you came here today just to hold my trembling hand and wipe my runny nose."

"Maybe not," I said. "But before I answer the question, there's something I'd like to know. Why the hell did you marry him in the first place?"

Her eyes wavered. "Well, he was sick—"

"Cut it out, Martha," I said. "Your Florence Nightingale complex isn't that strong. And even if it were, you could have found a worthy invalid to marry who hadn't spent all those years working for your daddy in an organization whose purposes and methods you detest."

She licked her lips. "Well, it was your fault, really. On that crazy trip we took. You turned everything upside down for me. Everything I believed in. And after you were gone I discovered a dreadful thing. All my past was filmed in dull black and white, except that part of it we'd just been through. That was recorded on my memory tapes in living, vibrant color, as they say. And it stayed that way. Am I making sense?"

I grinned. "Hell, it's the only part of your lousy little life you'd spent alive. Hunting and being hunted. Loving and being loved, if I may dignify our tricky relationship with such an important little word. What did you expect? All the rest of your girlish existence, like everybody else, you'd spent trying to be safe and secure and comfortable the way you'd been told since childhood your beautiful life was supposed to be. Jesus! A whole damn nation brought up to do nothing but be *safe*! No wonder it needs a few nasty unsafe guys like Bob and me to protect it. So you got your lovely comfortable safe security back and it didn't feel so lovely any longer. Big deal."

She made a face at me. "Maybe you're right. Maybe when you've run with the wolves—hi, wolf—you kind of lose interest in cocker spaniels, bright and docile and well-trained though they may be. I kept meeting all these wonderful spaniel-men who bored me stiff. I kept thinking, if you'll excuse it, how every damned one of them would have shit his pants full if they'd been where you and I once were with people shooting at us." She shook her head. "And then Daddy took me to see Bob in the hospital and he was a mess, but he was not a spaniel, dammit. And he was a nice guy and he needed me and . . . and I knew what he'd done in the past but that was over. He was out of it now, so I didn't have to reconcile his lousy work with my conscience. And I was lonely and I needed him, too, I really did. So I married him and it was rough for a while, while he was getting well, but then it was very good for a while. *Very* good. And then he disappointed me badly, hurt me badly; badly enough that I did something I'll spend the rest of my life wishing to God I hadn't. I spilled it all girlishly to somebody I trusted. I was a weepy little creep with too many drinks inside her, whining because her man had gone astray. My God, I knew the kind of guy I was marrying, didn't I? Hell, you could tell just by looking at him that he could be relied on in every way but that way. Did I expect him to turn into a goddamned monk just because . . . Matt."

"Yes?"

"Did they tell you how it was?"

"You mean the shooting? Not in detail."

She drew a long, ragged breath. "We were hating each other, you understand," she said. "Now we both had reasons: his roving eye and my blabbing tongue. So we went out to dinner hating each other but trying to be civilized, trying to retrieve something very important to both of us that had gotten lost; but cold, cold, cold. No real give on either side. And we came out of that restaurant without touching each other—you know the place on the Trail with the parking lot in back—and, as we headed for the car, there was a sound in the alley. I saw Bob start to throw himself down and aside. He could have made it, I think, he was very quick; he could have been safe on the ground behind a parked car. But he remembered me, the wife he hated, the wife who'd tattled about things that were none of her damn business, still standing there dumb and paralyzed. I guess I was thinking of my nice slacks and my pretty blouse and how dirty the ground was and how silly I'd look if. . . . He checked himself and took time to give me a great big sideways push that sent me sprawling. And the shotgun fired." She cleared her throat. "When a guy does that for you, thinks of you first at a time like that, you kind of forget whom he slept with that he shouldn't have." She cleared her throat again. "Your turn."

After a moment I said, "I'm here to help you if I can, of course. But I'm also here to see that you don't take any embarrassing action."

"Action?" She glanced at me and laughed, but her eyes were not quite candid. "You mean, like revenge? But how in the world could I? . . . I mean, even if I wanted to, even if I were capable of . . . I only caught a brief glimpse of the man in the alley. I wouldn't have the slightest idea of how to go about finding him and I wouldn't recognize him if I saw him. He was just something moving in the dark."

I said, "We weren't thinking of the man."

She shook her head quickly. "Really, Matt, how melodramatic can you get? You know me. You know how I feel about . . . about guns and violence. Even now after what's happened. You mean, little nonviolent Martha taking the law into her own hands and making some kind of a stupid vendetta? How could you, or Daddy, think I could possibly . . ." Her voice trailed off. I didn't say anything. I waited. At last she licked her lips. When she spoke her voice was almost inaudible. "All right. I'm not fooling anybody, am I? But it's necessary, Matt. You must see that it's necessary. Nobody can be allowed to do what she did to us. To me. Nobody. Oh, publishing it, if she'd found it all out somewhere else, all right. She was supposed to be my friend, but I guess she has a job to do, so all right. But coming here and accepting our hospitality and taking what I told her in confidence when I was all broken up like that, using it like that. . . ."

There was a little silence. A car went by outside. Daylight was fading from the picture window.

"Have you got a copy handy?" I asked. "I've got one in my bag but I haven't had a chance to do more than glance through it."

"It's right here. I wouldn't be without it. I'll treasure it the rest of my life. Maybe it will teach me to keep my damned mouth shut." Her voice was grim. She opened the little black purse she'd put on the cocktail table and took out some stapled-together and folded-up magazine pages and held them out. "Here. I don't have to read it again, actually. I know it by heart."

I took the pages she held out and unfolded them. There was the standard dramatic closeup picture of a giant hand holding a giant gun aimed directly at the reader, supposedly threatening; but those magazine people don't ever know anything about guns. They don't realize that a Colt .45 automatic isn't really much of a threat until you cock it. The hammer was down. And the old .45 is too bulky and clumsy and noisy for our purposes, anyway. But the page had a lot of impact if you didn't look at it too closely or think about it too hard.

THE U.S. MURDER MACHINE
by Eleanor Brand

Case History #1: He is a husky, rather handsome man with bright blue eyes. He is married to an attractive, dark-haired girl, considerably younger. They live together in a conventional home in a conventional development outside Santa Fe, New Mexico; but Robert Wilson Devine is not really a conventional man. Until he retired with a heart ailment a few years ago he was a top professional assassin in the employ of the United States of America. . . .

CHAPTER 3

I have two culinary specialties. I'm a good guy to have around at breakfast time; I'm handy with bacon and eggs. (On the other hand, I don't recommend my coffee to the connoisseur; I'm lazy and go the instant route. I've slurped down too many strange brown concoctions under conditions of considerable stress to make a religion of coffee.) At the other end of the day, if you've got some

19

leftover steak or roast around, and a few boiled potatoes, and some onions, I can whip up an exotic dish my Scandinavian ancestors called *pytt-i-panna*. A very loose translation is put-it-in-the-pan. Put any damned thing in the pan. Hash to you.

I was in my shirtsleeves with my funeral necktie off, concentrating on the latter delicacy, when Martha entered the kitchen after a half-hour absence. It had hit her suddenly while we were discussing the Eleanor Brand article, triggered by nothing in particular: an uncontrollable case of the weeps. She hadn't wanted any sympathy or comfort from me. She'd apologized tearfully for being so goddamned stupid and told me to have myself another drink while she retired to chastize this dumb blubbering female severely. Now her face was washed, her hair was combed and the slight misty pinkness of her eyes was almost imperceptible. She was minus her high heels and funeral dress, and plus a pair of sandals and a long, loose, striped blue-and-green garment with the irresistible sex appeal of an umbrella tent.

"You don't have to do that!" she said quickly. "I'm perfectly capable—"

"Sure you are," I said. "The question is, am I? Let's see how it turns out."

"It smells good . . . Matt."

"Yes."

She hesitated, and I saw that she was uncomfortable about something. "I hope . . . I mean, what I'm trying to say . . . I didn't mean to give you a wrong impression, if you know what I mean, dragging you inside like that. I was just putting on an act for her. I mean—"

I grinned. Her embarrassment made it quite obvious what she meant. "You mean you don't really want to fuck tonight."

She gave me an honest-to-God blush. "If we have to be so goddamned explicit, yes. I mean, no. There should be a little . . . a little respect, shouldn't there? A small period of . . . of mourning. Anyway, I'm pretty damned tired and morbid." She giggled abruptly. "You wouldn't want me to break into tears in the middle of it, would you?"

I said, "Actually, I wasn't planning on laying the widow-lady right on top of the just-filled grave. But since I'm to be deprived of sex, maybe I'd better have a little more booze to console me. I think there's some left in the martini pitcher. And then you can set the table. No heavy conversation. We'll analyze the situation some more after we eat."

The hash turned out quite well, if I do say so myself. The secret is a cast-iron frying pan hot enough to turn everything brown and crusty instead of merely warming the mixed-up mess; some dexterous stirring and turning helps. Martha ate hungrily and I managed a second helping myself. The last food I'd had, if you want to strain the definition of the word, had been on TWA. Martha stopped me when I started to clear the table.

"No, leave the dishes alone, damn you. And I'll do the coffee. Whose house is this, anyway? You go out into the living room and sit."

I followed orders and started to reread the Brand article but I found it hard to concentrate. I was very much aware, in a sexless way—well, an almost sexless way—of the quiet, comfortable, undemanding house and the starry New Mexico sky outside and the pretty girl making busy noises in the kitchen. I'd had this once, even to some offspring asleep in the rear of the house. I wondered how the kids were doing and if Beth was still happy in Nevada with her rancher-husband, a pretty nice and competent guy. I don't check on them very often. I don't like to leave a trail that way. There are people around who'll use almost anything against you.

But this is a very good specimen, Mr. Helm. A little young for you, perhaps, but bright and brave, from durable and intelligent heredity, on the one side you know about, at least. Attractive to look at and, the record shows, quite a pleasant companion in bed and elsewhere. An unfortunate compulsion to save the world, perhaps, but even that seems to be subdued nowadays. Maybe she's outgrown it. Too bad in a way, the world certainly needs it, but more comfortable to have around. All in all, a quite acceptable candidate, already well tested under rigorous conditions. And it would be pleasant to have a place like this to come back to and somebody like this to come back to, for as long as you manage to make it back at all, which presumably won't be forever.

But you tried it once, you gave it a good long try, and it didn't work then, so why should it work now? And she's a hell of a nice kid who ought to do better for herself than a sick gladiator retired from the bloody arena, or even a healthy one not yet retired. And there's always the danger that somebody wanting to hurt you will take it out on anybody you allow to become too important to you. So you just leave her alone, hear? Anyway, he's all right to work for, he's very good to work for, but would you want him as a father-in-law, for God's sake?

I watched her come in with the coffee tray, the loose striped garment swirling around her. She set the tray down on the cocktail table, poured a cup for me and one for herself, and gave me mine. Then she settled down in her sofa corner with her feet tucked under her. We're all supposed to be perfectly equal these days, male and female, but girls' arms still aren't hinged quite right to throw a baseball properly, and their legs are still articulated in a manner that allows them to assume strange catlike positions that would have a man screaming in agony in a very few minutes. It makes one wonder what other built-in inequalities women's lib has overlooked.

I said, "This Brand female must not be harmed, certainly not by us or by anybody who's connected to us in any way. You can see why, can't you? To have the publicity she's giving us is bad enough, but we can probably live through that; we've done it before. But if there's ever a suggestion that an American government agency or anybody associated with an American government agency— and you're damned well associated, both by blood and by

22

marriage—would take violent retaliatory action against a respected American lady journalist for something she'd published, then the people who believe as a matter of faith that all spook shops are evil and should be abolished would have a lever handed to them that would probably destroy us."

"She killed my husband," Martha said softly. "Worse, she got me to help her kill him."

"Maybe," I said. "We won't know that for sure until we learn who the hit man was and who gave him his orders. If we ever do."

"Come *on*, Matt! I hope you're not trying to convince me that a man with Bob's background got himself shot down by a casual maniac—right after the publication of an article describing his career and giving his home address almost to the street and number. How coincidental can you get?"

I said, "Everybody who matters already knew all that. I mean, we've got dossiers on practically everybody in the business; and everybody in the business has dossiers on us, at least those of us who've been around for a while. Do you think Moscow's going to waste a good removal agent's time on an opposition operative with a heart condition who's obviously settled down harmlessly to spend the rest of his life working in his cactus garden and fishing for trout? Or Peking?"

"Somebody he injured in the past in the line of . . . of duty, then," Martha said stubbornly. "Somebody vengeful who'd been looking for him but might never have found him if I hadn't opened my big mouth and Elly hadn't printed what I said. Somebody who read that lousy article and knew that the . . . the end of the hunt was at hand."

"Again, maybe," I said. "But there's not a lot of that going around. We don't make a practice of carrying on blood feuds, and neither does the other side, or sides. It's the luck of the game; some live, some die. We do make a note of people *outside* the undercover community who interfere gratuitously. We make a point of dealing with them

23

if and when it's convenient. As your father once said, they have to learn not to monkey with the buzz saw when it's busy cutting wood. But within our tight little profession, no."

She shook her head irritably. "Pretty soon you'll be telling me Bob didn't die at all, I just imagined the whole thing." She drew a long, ragged breath. "Anyway, I'm not a member of your lousy professional community; I'm just a wife wanting to get even for something awful that was done to her husband. And to her." She grimaced. " 'Get even.' It sounds so childish, doesn't it? How can one ever get *even*? That would mean setting the clock back; and it doesn't run backward. But goddamn it, Matt, she can't go around trading on friendship and hospitality like she did and not have somebody kick her ass up between her ears."

I said, "Hell, if all you plan to do is boot her in the tail, be my guest. I thought you had something serious in mind."

"You mean . . . you mean like *killing* her?" Martha laughed heartily. "Matt, you must be kidding! I mean, really, do you think I'd go around with a *gun* chasing somebody down like an *animal* even if . . ." She stopped and made a face at me. "God, I'm such a lousy actress, and I'm so damned tired. Let me go to bed and stop making a fool of myself. You can find the guest room; it's down the hall. Second door to the left. Bathroom, first door. Leave the dishes; I'll get them in the morning." She rose, and I rose, and she hesitated, facing me. "If you really . . . I wouldn't want to think of you *suffering* or anything. After all, it's not as if we'd never done it before."

I grinned. "Therapeutic, you mean? Thanks, I'll survive."

"Don't say that so positively. I might get the idea that I'm not irresistible. Good night, Matt."

CHAPTER 4

I carried my jacket, tie, and suitcase back to the room she'd indicated. As a pro, I like to case the terrain in advance of the operation if possible, even if the operation only involves going to bed. I laid out my pajamas for future reference and got out the file Mac had given me, for immediate study. The room was small, with a small bed, and a good-sized loom set up against one wall along with some auxiliary equipment I didn't understand; apparently Martha had taken up weaving as a hobby. It's a recognized Santa Fe syndrome. We're all frustrated artists or artisans here.

I checked out the little hall bathroom on the way back to the living room, and used it. The plumbing worked. As if in answer I heard her flush another, similar device elsewhere in the house. It gave me a cozy and companionable feeling. In the living room I laid down the file, picked up my coffee cup, carried it to the picture window and parted the curtains to look out. It was a quiet night in the moderately high-class development known as Casa Glorieta. No traffic at the moment. There were lights in the house across the road but the picture window was covered and no sleek blondes were visible. A sturdy, four-wheel-drive vehicle was now parked in the wide driveway in front of the double garage: the fancy Jeep station wagon called Wagoneer. Well, most two-car families out here have at least one tough vehicle for hunting, fishing, or just taking the kids to school on a snowy day. There was probably something more civilized in the garage for the lady of the house to drive to the grocery and bridge club when the weather was good.

The sight of the husky vehicle reminded me of my own personal transportation, another hefty station wagon on a Chevy 4WD half-ton-truck chassis, known as a carryall. I told myself that for the sake of the government that was paying the bills I ought to get it out of storage and turn in the expensive rental job I'd grabbed for my dash up here from Albuquerque. The airlines don't fly to Santa Fe; you have to drive the last sixty miles or take the bus. (Not even the Santa Fe Railroad goes to Santa Fe; the town is serviced by a spur from the main line at Lamy.) I soothed my conscience by telling it that I probably wouldn't be staying long enough for Avis to break the expense account.

I let the window drapes fall back into place, took my cup into the kitchen and refilled it. I carried it back into the living room, sat down and dumped the contents of my big envelope onto the cocktail table. The Eleanor Brand article, my copy, was on top. I'd read the piece once, hastily, on the plane, and once more here with Martha watching me; now I settled down to give it a careful study without distractions. It was a thorough job. The girl reporter had dug up a lot of stuff, more than Martha could possibly have told her about. Active or retired, well or ill, Bob would never have confided in his wife to this extent; and Mac was certainly not one to whisper state secrets into his daughter's ear. Obviously, Martha's information had simply been used as a springboard for further research. Well, Freedom of Information is the name of the game these days. There was even a brief description of that ancient South American safari on which I'd made the useful acquaintance of chatty, friendly, little Rafaelita. My name was mentioned with a hint that I was an interestingly murderous chap whose gory history would be presented in detail in a later installment of this startling and revealing series.

So Miss Eleanor Brand, or Ms. Eleanor Brand as she undoubtedly called herself these liberated days, was a skillful researcher, a pretty fair writer, and an indignant lady who'd grabbed, so to speak, the torch of nonviolent idealism from Martha's faltering hand. She was also, it seemed,

26

a fairly ruthless bitch who didn't give a damn whom she betrayed or hurt or got killed in pursuit of her journalistic career. Well, considering the nature of my own career, I was hardly in a position to criticize.

There was a picture of her down in one corner of the first page, and a small biographical blurb. Ms. Brand was twenty-seven years old, a graduate of Smith with a master's in journalism from Columbia. She'd worked for a number of publications I'd heard of and some I hadn't. She'd won some kind of a prize that meant nothing to me since it wasn't either the Nobel or the Pulitzer. Currently she was down in the near-Caribbean acquiring a suntan and doing research on a projected article on the Bermuda Triangle.

I frowned at that. It didn't seem in character. I'd been exposed to that Triangle legend myself in the course of one assignment, and it didn't seem like anything for this competent and cynical young woman to get her sharp little teeth into. I mean, hell, either you proclaim breathlessly that it's all true, true, true, and there are sinister and unearthly forces at work here beyond our comprehension— and that's been done. Or you announce coldly that careful scientific research proves conclusively that it's all a lot of melodramatic superstitious crap—and that's been done, too. This was a girl who obviously liked to find shocking new grist for her typewriting mill. Why was she wasting her valuable time on a bunch of old missing ships and disappearing airplanes that had already been exploited to the puking point and beyond?

Studying the photograph, I decided that the original family name could not really be Brand or even Brandt. It was not an Anglo-Saxon or Germanic face. The head was brachycephalic rather than dolichocephalic. In other words, it was wide and short from front to back rather than long and narrow like, for instance, my own Scandinavian skull. She wore her straight darkish hair quite short, parted on one side and combed across to the other. Her face was wide and flat with a long thin mouth, a short bony chin, and a low snub nose. The eyes were set well apart but the sparse brows and lashes didn't do much for them, and she

27

obviously didn't take the trouble to prettify them in any way.

There was no way to describe her and make her sound particularly attractive. Her features, at a glance, were unspectacularly shaped and uninterestingly arranged. It was the pushed-in face of a clever and determined female monkey rather than the shining visage of an intelligent and lovely girl. Still, I had an uneasy feeling that if Ms. Brand ever came to the conclusion that you were worth it personally, or particularly if she thought you had something she wanted, or knew something she wanted to know, you might suddenly find yourself deciding that you had nothing against female monkeys after all—that, in fact, they were really rather charming creatures in an offbeat way. . .

Well, that was a lot to read into a photograph hardly larger than a postage stamp; and enough of Eleanor Brand. She wasn't the only researcher around. I found a copy of the police report on Devine, Robert, deceased. The shotgun had been fired at slightly under thirty yards. A single twelve-gauge Magnum case had been found nearby—the short two-and-three-quarter-inch Magnum, not the long three-incher, which requires a specially chambered gun and is more shell than most hunters need. It had originally been loaded with Number One buckshot, a pretty good choice for a target the size of a deer or a man, although it's Double-Ought buck that gets all the glory. Fourteen pellets of the load of twenty had struck the body. Eleven had been found in the course of the autopsy. The other three had been peripheral or glancing hits that kept on going after leaving their marks. Well, eleven solid hits with practically anything would certainly do the job. I once knew a man, hunting quail during deer season, who jumped a good-sized buck and dropped him dead with a fairly light load of fine birdshot. I frowned at the report for a while and glanced at an accompanying photograph, taken at the scene—Mac had apparently pulled strings to get total police cooperation. But it wasn't a picture I cared to study at any length; it had nothing to do with a guy with whom I'd once visited a Colombian cathouse.

28

I put all the materials back into the envelope and sipped my cooling coffee thoughtfully. Martha seemed to be asleep; I'd heard nothing from her room for half an hour. I picked up the coffee tray and carried it into the kitchen and, like a good house guest, rinsed off all the dinner dishes and loaded them into the washer while she was unavailable to lodge a protest. Besides making me feel virtuous, it killed some more time. Then I went into the guest room and, with a regretful glance at my pajamas, changed my clothes. I got into jeans, a navy-blue turtleneck and a pair of soft, rubber-soled shoes. I dug the little five-shot Smith and Wesson out of the hidden compartment of my suitcase, checked the loads, and tucked it into my waistband, letting the shirt hang down over it. The metal was cold against my skin. I checked the little knife I always carry. I turned out the guest room, weaving room light, went back to the kitchen and started the dishwasher. The rushing and rumbling sounds of the machine apparently did not disturb Martha at the other end of the house; at least she did not come running to complain about my presumption in doing her dishes in her home. I set the latch of the kitchen door so I could get back in, and slipped outside with the noise of the washer to cover my stealthy exit.

It was a damfool notion, of course. Obviously a wild-goose chase, a blind stab in the dark. Nothing could possibly come of it. I was grasping at straws, chasing ghosts, tilting at windmills. Who the hell did I think I was; Sherlock Holmes, Nero Wolfe, Hercule Poirot, Lord Peter Wimsey? I didn't even know for sure if the man I was after existed. I'd never seen him. I didn't know his name. Still, there had been some odd discrepancies in the accounts I'd heard and read of Bob Devine's death. The gun wasn't right and the behavior of the man who'd used the gun wasn't right, not if said murderer was the kind of professional everybody seemed to assume. It was a long-odds gamble that would cost me nothing but a little sleep to check out.

It was a clear night without a moon. The stars were

much brighter than they'd been in Washington, D.C. Well, we were seven thousand feet closer to them, up here in the foothills of the Sangre de Cristos, the Blood-of-Christ mountains. This was not a community of walls and fences, and I slipped over the low rise behind the Devine house and found myself at the back of somebody else's couple of acres. I sneaked on down past the lighted house that was there, to the road. So far, so good. Once on the road, I started to jog. It used to be that a running man either created a panic or was picked up by the white-coated boys with the butterfly nets. Nowadays, the best way to turn invisible is to proceed at a steady lope, just another health nut flushing the stale air from his lungs.

I had some trouble with the gun and considerable trouble with my breathing. I'd just come up from sea level and it takes a week or two to get used to the altitude. I took the first crossroad to the right. This brought me back to the road on which Martha lived, known as Navajo Drive. I crossed this and went on to the next, labeled Ute Road, turning right again. With the last of my failing breath, I made it to a spot opposite my starting point but a block over, if this elaborate countrified community dealt in such conventional urban divisions as blocks. I stole between two of the scattered houses here and followed a fold of ground back toward Navajo Drive, finding myself at last on a hillside from which I could see the house from where I'd come, across the street. The bedroom wing where Martha slept was dark; the living room and kitchen were lighted as I'd left them. Directly below me was the house with the Wagoneer in the driveway, although the vehicle was now hidden from my vantage point on the hillside behind the house, by the garage. I sat down to catch my breath by a dark desert juniper against which, I hoped, my own dark shape would be invisible if anyone should look.

Nothing happened. A neighboring house went totally dark. An occasional car drove by. A distant yapping sound that I hoped was a coyote—we used to hear them regularly, back when I first lived in Santa Fe as a married man—turned out to be merely a yapping dog, soon answered by another. They'll fix that soon. The noise is bad enough, but obviously no dogs must shit in our immaculate future cities, and no pigeons must crap in them, either. Clean, silent communities and empty skies. Well, deep philosophy is always a good way of making the time pass on watch; but it was getting on toward midnight now and I couldn't see spending the whole night sitting under a bush. Apparently they weren't about to turn out the lights below me and go to bed; and while a man or woman aroused from a sound sleep is at a useful disadvantage, I could do without that edge, I hoped.

There were two doors to cover: the kitchen door at the rear of the house, and a small door in the side of the garage. There were, of course, the big garage doors facing front, away from me, but it seemed unlikely anybody'd go to the trouble of raising those just to look out. There was also the front door, but I remembered that the light was on there, making it impossible for anybody to slip out inconspicuously that way. I made my way to an ornamental pine tree at the corner of the garage, took up station beside it, picked up a handful of small stones and started pitching them into the ornamental bushes beneath the lighted windows at the rear of the house, making interesting rustling sounds. I made a couple of them clatter lightly against the house wall.

Nothing happened to tell me whether I was playing to an empty theater or standing room only. I sighed and found a good-sized rock after groping around in the dark. I stepped away from the house and turned and pitched my missile through the nearby garage window. It made a fearful crash in the quiet night—the distant dogs had ceased their canine dialogue. I moved back into my ornamental evergreen shelter. After a while, he came.

I was kind of sorry about it. It meant I had him figured right as the kind of man who trees his own coons and stomps his own snakes; and that's practically an endangered species these helpless days. Of course, if I had him figured right there was no chance of his calling the police. He wouldn't want the cops around, under the circumstances. But even under other circumstances he'd feel quite capable of protecting his premises himself, thanks. It's an attitude I admire, so I regretted what had to be done now; but unfortunately the guy had gone too far and we do have the policy of teaching outsiders, as a matter of principle, not to monkey with the buzz saw. It was too bad about blond Mrs. Roundheels, as Martha had called her, that suburban Lorelei, and Bob Devine should certainly have remained faithful to his own wife and let other people's wives alone, but a shotgun was carrying things just a little too far.

The broken window was a help. When he stumbled over something, sneaking through the garage—probably the rock I'd thrown—and swore softly, I heard him clearly and knew where to expect him next. I was ready for him when he opened the side door and stepped outside, the long-barreled weapon he held gleaming faintly in the starlight. When, scrutinizing his property warily, he swung away from me, I stepped around the corner of the building.

"Easy, friend," I said. "There's a thirty-eight looking right up your backside." He stood quite still, frozen, and I went on, "If you're thinking of trying to swing that cannon around, don't. You'll never make it. Lay it down gently, now."

"Who are you?"

"Lay it on the ground, please," I said. It always disconcerts them when you're polite. "We can talk afterward. No hasty movements. . . . That's fine, now you can straighten up, but don't turn around. There's nothing for you to see but a man you don't know and don't want to know."

"Who the hell *are* you?"

I said, "Just a guy with a gun. What's the matter, friend, are you stupid or something? You read the article, didn't you? Hell, everybody in Casa Glorieta has read that article, I'm sure. 'Hey, did you *see* the story about that new family over on Navajo Drive, the big guy with the nice young wife, did you *read* about him, hey?'" I paused and went on, full of menace now to see what I could shake loose. "Why'd you do it, amigo? Do you make a habit of feeling under rocks for rattlesnakes or skiing past avalanche-warning signs just for kicks? If you've got to shoot somebody, why pick on a man with friends and associates like that? Did it never occur to you that we might take care of our own even after they're retired? I know, he probably had it coming in a way, but the unwritten law doesn't work any longer, friend. Sorry. Up against the wall now, please." I stepped forward and picked up the weapon he'd laid down. "So this is the gun."

It was exactly what I'd expected, exactly what it had to be from what it had done: a long-barreled autoloading shotgun eminently suitable for ducks and geese, not so hot for quail, and clumsy and unwieldy for homicide. I couldn't read the barrel markings in the dark, but I would have bet a considerable sum that it was bored full-choke to throw tight patterns for long-range shooting—the spread of the shot can be controlled, like the stream of water from a hose, by the amount of constriction in the end of the gun barrel. It had to be fully choked if I had it figured right; besides they don't usually make thirty-inch barrels in any other configuration.

The man in front of me, call him Mister Lorelei for purposes of reference, stirred and said, "You'll never prove. . . ." Then he stopped.

"Sure," I said. "A load of buckshot out of one shotgun —or birdshot for that matter—looks just like that out of another. Who can tell anything from a bunch of little round pellets? But you didn't stop to pick up the fired case. That's the trouble with these autoloaders from the criminal standpoint—they toss their empties from hell to breakfast. Yours is in the hands of the police; and a fired shotgun shell *can* be traced to the gun that fired it. The firing-pin indentation is unique, and there'll be other markings for the ballistic geniuses to drool over. Of course, twelve-gauge shotguns are a dime a dozen out here in the Southwest. The police could hardly stage a house-to-house search of Casa Glorieta to locate the murder weapon, particularly since the crime occurred in town and it was thought to be a professional hit anyway, because of Bob Devine's past history. But if somebody gives them the idea of checking up on local motives and they come looking. . . ." I hesitated. "Why didn't you get rid of it?"

Still facing the wall, he shrugged his shoulders. "I do a bit of hunting; everybody knows I have a shotgun. If it turned up missing it would be as good as a confession, wouldn't it? At least *she'd* have known. . . But she found out anyway from the way I was acting; I couldn't help it."

I said, "I'm not up on local mores, but I didn't think who slept with whom was a killing matter these days."

"You don't understand," he said. "We were doing all right at last. We had it made at last. Goddamn it, my wife is not a tramp, she just gets . . . a little bored and restless sometimes. And drinks a little too much sometimes, or used to. But we had it licked, she had it licked, and everything was fine; and then *he* came along and that damned magazine story: the big dangerous fascinating man with the intriguing disability, tragic really, a great handsome virile guy like that with a time bomb ticking away in his chest. And what with all the tension and guilt and . . . and excitement of carrying on an affair like that, she started doing it to herself again, poisoning herself again. Destroying herself again. I *had* to. . . ." He stopped and moved his shoulders once more. "All right. I don't mean to sound too altruistic. I was jealous, sure; and I hated the good-looking bastard for what he was doing to us after we'd worked so hard to build something together; but goddamn it, it wasn't even as if he loved her and wanted what was best for her. . . ."

He stopped. A car went along Navajo Drive but the headlights did not reach us where we stood. I said, "You hesitated, there behind the restaurant. He had time to start one way, and change his mind, and come back the other. You had a clear shot—"

"Hell, I didn't want to hurt his wife, I had nothing against her," he said. "That's a tight-shooting gun, but I had to wait until they were separated enough so I could be sure she wouldn't get sprinkled; even one buckshot can do a lot of damage. Is that how you knew?"

34

"It had to be a full-choke gun or Mrs. Devine would have been hit, regardless," I said. "But a pro wouldn't have lugged around a long piece of field artillery like that. He'd have used a short, wide-open, sawed-off weapon that he could hide under his coat; and it would have sprayed lead all over that parking lot. No matter how hard and fast her husband pushed her, she'd have picked up a few stray pellets, regardless. And the shot concentration in the body wouldn't have been nearly as great if a sawed-off had been used." I drew a long breath. "And then, a pro wouldn't have given a damn about the wife. He wouldn't have taken any chances with a trained man like Bob Devine who might have been carrying a gun. He'd have shot instantly and to hell with who else got hit. If that made it a double killing, too bad." After a moment I said, "Okay. I had to know for sure, but okay. This is as far as I go, friend. I'll report it as a private matter, of no concern to us. The fact that you took time to see that Mrs. Devine wasn't hurt earns you a break from me. For whatever it's worth now."

"Yeah," he said, softly and bitterly. "For what it's worth now. I—"

Abruptly, the garage lights went on and a woman's voice called out, "Hey, where the hell are you? What are you doing out there? What's taking you so long? Whatsh . . . what's going on out there, anyway?"

I'd worked the shells out of the shotgun as we talked; now I set the empty weapon against the wall and stepped over into the shrubbery as she appeared in the lighted doorway, an unsteady silhouette with a glass in its hand.

"Whawash . . ." Her voice was slurred. She realized that she wasn't transmitting clearly and tried again, "What was that awful noish . . . noise, anyway?"

"A kid with a rock, I guess," the man said. "He got one of the garage windows."

"And you couldn't get a shot at him? How too, too bad!" There was a cold savage hatred in the voice that, for a moment, sounded almost sober. "You couldn't drop him as he ran, like a rabbit? What the hell kind of a loushy . . . lousy hunter are you, anyway?"

She stepped away from the door, turning to see her husband more clearly. The light caught her as she turned; revealing that her appearance had undergone a shocking transformation since I'd seen her watching us from across the street. I'd gotten a clear impression then, even at a distance, that Bob Devine's partner in adultery was a handsome woman who dressed nicely and took good care of herself—but that had been this afternoon.

She must have been drinking hard ever since. Now, at midnight, the sleek shining hairdo I'd admired from afar was falling apart into wisps and loops of lank blond hair. The crisp, pale green blouse hung limp and untidy and half-unbuttoned, one crumpled shirttail dangling. The expensive, smoothly tailored, pale green slacks had succumbed to careless wear and the soft warm pressures of her mature body, becoming almost embarrassingly creased and shapeless. It was hard to understand how, in just a few hours, she'd managed to get them looking as if she'd slept in them for a week. She swayed dangerously on her high heels, standing there; and liquor spilled down her clothes as she tried to drink from her unsteady glass. She did not seem a bit concerned about the state she was already in or the further mess she was making of herself; she actually seemed pleased by the effect she was creating, peering down to admire the dark, wet splotches as if she thought they added a final artistic touch to her ruined costume, as of course they did.

I realized belatedly that, instead of fighting it as in the past—if her husband's account was correct—tonight this woman had deliberately given herself over to the booze she knew she could not handle. She was quite aware of, even perversely proud of, what it was doing to her. She was taking malicious pleasure in showing her husband how little he'd gained by murdering her lover. All he'd gotten for his crime, she was saying, was this stumbling, slovenly and drink-stained creature, really quite worthless. After the ghastly unforgivable thing he had done, she would never again, could never again, be any more than this to him. It was her revenge on him, and on herself.

"You see," the man murmured without turning his head. "You *see* what he's done to her? She was doing fine before he came!"

It didn't seem fair to blame it all on Bob Devine, the basic problem had obviously existed long before he arrived on the scene, but he certainly hadn't been altogether blameless. There were too many confused and violent emotions here; and there was really nothing for me to do here, anyway. I'd learned what I'd come to learn. If punishment was needed, these two people seemed to be dispensing it quite adequately themselves, without my help.

"Go on," I whispered. "You'd better get her to bed if you can. Good luck."

The man's voice was soft and bitter. "Good luck? What's that?"

Then he moved forward hastily as the glass dropped from his wife's hand and shattered on the concrete walk. A startled look had come to the woman's blurred but still-handsome face as she realized abruptly that in her anger she'd gulped down just a little too much too fast of the stuff that was poison to her. She had not intended to carry her self-destroying vengeance quite so far tonight; and now she was making a shaky effort to regain the shelter of the house and, no doubt, the bathroom. He reached her in time to catch her as she faltered; he steadied her and led her out of sight inside; but they didn't make it all the way through the garage. I heard her become violently ill in there. The sound of her retching spasms followed me as I sneaked away.

Martha was in the lighted kitchen as I slipped into the Devine house by the back door after some cautious detours that were probably unnecessary; but you get into certain habits in this business, if you survive.

"I made you some fresh coffee," she said, turning from the stove.

"You're supposed to be asleep," I said.

"Well, so are you," she said with a grin.

After what I'd just seen, she looked very good, very reassuring, in her long loose kaftan or dashiki or whatever

37

the hell it was called. There was still some hope for the human race. I even liked the bare feet peeking innocently out from under the hem of the garment, although I'm not really a freak for barefoot girls; I find heels and nylons a lot more stimulating. But stimulation was not the game tonight. We were just two people who'd come to know each other pretty well and were now surprisingly comfortable with each other, which had not always been the case in the past. There was a question in Martha's gray eyes, but she did not ask it aloud. I answered it anyway.

"The guy across the street shot Bob," I said. "The husband. You can probably figure out a motive if you try hard. That article by Eleanor Brand had nothing to do with it, so except for a personal grievance for the way she abused your trust, you have no reason to look her up with intent to do grievous bodily harm, as the saying goes. She's not responsible for Bob's death in any way."

That wasn't quite true, of course. The buildup given Bob in the magazine story had apparently intrigued the bored and unhappy, temporarily ex-alcoholic, Mrs. Lorelei, making easy the seduction from which everything else had come, but I saw no reason to split hairs at this point.

Martha nodded. "All right, Matt. I guess I'm glad in a way. It was something I felt I had to . . . just a kind of compulsion, I guess. But if it wasn't her fault, or mine, that he was killed, I guess I can forgive her for the rest." She was silent for a moment, and went on a little stiffly, "So you've done your job here, the job Daddy assigned you. You've very skillfully prevented me from causing any trouble. Where do you go next, Mr. Troubleshooter?"

I started to answer, and stopped. A siren was wailing in the distance, coming closer. I went into the living room and watched through the curtains as a car with a flashing light-bar on top pulled up across the street. I wondered if the wife had gotten to the phone over there without the husband's knowledge and turned him in, as part of her destructive vengeance, but I didn't think so. It was unlikely that she'd been in any condition to telephone after being so deathly ill; but he would have known that his position was no longer tenable. He'd tried to do what was best for her, but some of what he'd done had gone very badly wrong, disqualifying him from further efforts on her behalf. It was time for him to leave her to others who might be able to give her the assistance she so badly required.

I doubted that, even at her sober best, she'd ever been a woman who could have aroused a great tender passion in me; but my tastes and preferences were beside the point. *He* had loved her, a little too much for his own good; he still did. So he would have helped her gently out of her bedraggled clothes over there, and cleaned her up and made her look as nice as he could. He would have put her carefully to bed and maybe even kissed her goodbye if he thought it would not upset her too much the way she felt about him now. Then he would have gone to the phone himself and looked up the police number and made that call and another to a friend or neighbor whose wife could come over and look after her, after he'd been taken away. It occurred to me that I'd never seen his face, or heard his name.

"Here's your coffee," Martha said, behind me. "You didn't answer my question. . . ."

CHAPTER 5

IN many ways Florida is about as distant from New Mexico as you can get. There's a two-thousand-mile geographical separation, for one thing, and a seven-thousand-foot difference in altitude. There's also close to a hundred percent difference in humidity: nothing ever rusts in New Mexico, nothing ever stops rusting in Florida. They are both popular resort and retirement areas, but the people who gravitate to the high Southwest are not the same type of people as those who gravitate to the low Southeast. The artists and intellectuals and screwballs who tend to choose Santa Fe have very little in common with the conventional businessmen who generally vacation or retire around Miami.

But the biggest difference is perhaps in the field of recreational transportation. In New Mexico it's horses and off-road vehicles. In Florida it's boats, boats, boats. Unfortunately, the nautical scene, although I've been exposed to it fairly often in the line of duty, is still something of a mystery to me. After considering the situation carefully myself, and having some checking done by others, I decided to consult a professional nautical expert before deciding what to do next—more specifically, how to approach the problem that concerned me next. The problem and the person.

The fact that the person in question was known to have consulted the same nautical expert—not just once but twice—was, of course, a factor in my decision.

From Albuquerque, where I gave the red-clad Avis lady back her car, I got a flight to Dallas that connected after a fashion with one to Miami, where a courier met me with some materials I'd requested. Then I picked up the DC-3 that flutters uncertainly down the Florida Keys to Key West with one stop at Marathon. Another rental car awaited me at the little Marathon airport.

The Faro Blanco Marine Resort hadn't changed much in the years since I'd last been down there. It was still a palmy refuge from the hot-dog-and-hamburger atmosphere of the nearby Overseas Highway, as it's called—the crazy string of bridges and causeways, linked by stretches of beatup pavement, flanked by motels and filling stations, that connects the Keys with each other and the mainland, replacing the long-ago railroad built by a guy named Flagler that blew away in a hurricane. I drove past the office and down through the park-like grounds with their scattered little resort cabins, to the waterfront. The marina hadn't changed much, either. Even many of the boats seemed to be the same. The *Queenfisher* still had the same

40

slip among the charter-fishing boats along the sea wall. Harriet Robinson—Cap'n Hattie as she was known locally —was down in her engine room as usual. I might never have been away.

"*Queenfisher*, ahoy!" I called.

She surfaced in the cockpit with a smudge of grease on the side of her nose, a tall handsome woman in oil-stained khakis, about whom I knew more than probably anybody else around. She had once lived considerably farther north and had a lot more money and an ineffectual husband she didn't think much of. Her name hadn't been Robinson then, or Harriet, either, but never mind that. A forceful person with very strong opinions, she'd gotten herself mixed up in something violent and moderately unpatriotic she shouldn't have, something that concerned us. She'd been obliged to disappear in the end as an alternative to going to prison; and now she was down here in the Keys without wealth or husband, but with a boat she loved and handled very well, that made her a pretty good living.

We'd originally played on opposing teams, but more recently, tracked down, she'd reluctantly done me a considerable favor, like saving my life. In payment—although she'd asked no payment—we'd done our best to wipe out the criminal past for her, although there are limits to what can be done along those lines by an organization such as ours. But legally, she was no longer the grand lady I'd first met. She couldn't be, since that rich dame—wanted by the police—had officially drowned in the tail end of a Chesapeake hurricane. The woman who faced me was now, as securely as we could make her, just tough Cap'n Hattie Robinson with a new and phony but moderately serviceable past, and grease on her nose.

"You again," she said, as if I'd spent the past few busy years just hanging around.

"Your face is dirty," I said.

"What's my face to you?" She rubbed herself clean with a corner of the rag she was holding. "One of these days I'm going to have to put new diesels into this old bucket."

"How's the fishing business?" I asked.

"Don't ask unless you really want to know. It'll take about three hours for me to give you the high points. Do you know what it costs me nowadays just to fire up these mills?"

"Buy you a drink?"

She hesitated, obviously remembering that we'd been enemies, reluctant allies, even hasty lovers once when the situation seemed to call for it, but never exactly friends. It was a strange and uneasy progression I seemed to be making, from Martha Devine to Harriet Robinson; and I guess you could say that I was revisiting the scenes of old conquests, except that in both cases there had been considerable doubt about just who had conquered whom.

Harriet shrugged. "Hell, come aboard. I've got a bottle somewhere; I think I can find it if I look real hard."

I said cautiously, "The last time we parted, as I recall, you told me in effect to get the hell off your goddam boat and stay there."

Harriet laughed, and glanced toward the marina cocktail lounge and restaurant across the road, then at her clothes. She said, "I'm too dirty to appear in public; and that was too many years ago. Come on. I don't stay mad this long, even at you, even if you did con and blackmail me into helping you that last time. Just wait a minute while I wash my hands. . . ."

Five minutes later we were relaxing in *Queenfisher*'s comfortable deckhouse. On the cabin table was a bottle it hadn't taken her very long to find. There were well-iced glasses in our hands. One thing about sportfishing boats, you seldom lack for ice, but if they've kept bait in the box you may find yourself drinking some slightly fishy whiskey.

"I've missed you, you bastard," Harriet said fondly. "When I think of all the years I spent hating you for what you'd taken away from me . . . and don't get stuffy and tell me I did it all to myself—I had plenty of help from you! Anyway, I do miss that lovely hate. I was going to really enjoy killing you the next time I saw you; and then you tricked me into saving your lousy life instead!" She took a healthy slug of whiskey; and I reflected that it was nice to be with a lady you knew could carry her liquor like a gentleman. She asked, "What's on your mind, Matt? Last time you were brooding about some disappearing millionaires you wanted me to find for you. Don't you ever do any work yourself? What are you looking for this time that I'm going to have to lead you to like a helpless little boy?"

"Some disappearing ships," I said, watching her.

"You mean that old Terrible Triangle crap?" she asked casually, but I was watching her eyes and I knew I'd come to the right place. I wasn't the first person who'd questioned her on this subject.

"Maybe," I said. "That is, I'm not so much concerned about the ships as about somebody who's investigating them; and she claims to be doing research on that legendary Triangle. Our information is that she's visited you twice, once well over a year ago and once quite recently. Here's the girl in question." I passed her the Eleanor Brand article. "Go ahead, read it if you like."

Harriet laughed. "Don't be stupid, Matt. I've got a copy right over there. Why, your name is in it. Would I pass up the chance to read all about the man and the organization that stripped me of everything and turned me from a fine society lady into a lousy working girl at the mercy of a pair of broken-down diesels? Anyway, I had a special interest in that series of articles: she was working on it the first time she interviewed me. She'd learned about that old mission of yours—of ours. She wanted all the gory details. I'm afraid I wasn't a great deal of help. Something about reporters does weird things to my memory."

"And the second time she was down here, just the other day? What did she want, Harriet?"

Harriet was watching me, her eyes steady on my face. She shook her head minutely. "No, my dear. I won't do it. I won't help you do it."

"Do what?"

She shook her head again, almost irritably. "Dammit, I know what you do, remember? I didn't like her particularly; but she's a professional woman doing a professional job, and I can respect that. I didn't finger you for her. I'm not going to finger her for you, Matt."

I said, "You're kind of a dumb broad, aren't you, Hattie?"

It was rather exciting to see her draw herself up haughtily at the insult, suddenly regal and arrogant despite the unbecoming work clothes she was wearing. She had the kind of face you don't often see these pretty-pretty days, with a bold nose and good strong cheekbones; a dark-haired hawk of a lady—I'm told the lady hawks are bigger and tougher than the gents—lean and tanned, with little squinty sun-wrinkles at the corners of her fine dark eyes.

"As you reminded me just now, I kicked you off my ship once," she said softly. "Are you plugging for boot number two?"

"Be your age," I said. "Don't believe everything you see on TV."

"What are you trying to say?"

"If we wanted the woman dead, all we'd have to do is sit on our hands. The rough, nosy, inconsiderate way she operates, somebody's bound to take her out eventually. I don't know exactly what she was after here—I'm hoping you'll give me a hint—and I don't know what she's looking for wherever she's gone from here; but she could make those deadly creatures from outer space kind of mad at her, poking around their private goddamn Triangle the way she's doing. And on the other hand, if she's just using that Triangle nonsense to hide what she's *really* looking for, which is my guess, she could put herself in even greater danger."

"And that worries you?" Harriet's voice was dry. "According to that magazine piece, the next installment in her series is going to blow your cover sky-high."

I sighed. "Hattie, Hattie! Don't talk like an I-Spy girl. I was in this business long before you and I met, and that is already quite a while ago. Do you really think my opposite numbers in other countries don't know me by now? I've been blown for years, in that sense. Against real professionals with access to the dossiers, there are very few places where I can operate secretly anymore, so mostly I don't. A young lady recently called me a troubleshooter, and she got it exactly right. And one trouble we do not need, Captain Robinson, is a girl reporter getting herself brutally murdered right after publishing a story exposing our wicked agents and their sinister plots. No matter who does a job on Miss Brand right now, you know damned well we'll get the credit. Like you're doing, everybody'll assume we simply terminated her with extreme prejudice— as the boys out at Langley like to put it—because we didn't like the nasty things she wrote about us. We're having some trouble already because of the publicity she's giving us, my chief tells me; but it can be kept under control, he thinks. But that kind of a violent incident we couldn't possibly survive, so it must not be allowed to occur."

Harriet studied me thoughtfully. "You're very convincing, darling. But then, you always were."

I said, "Hell, as far as her story about me is concerned, she's doing me a favor. If it says what I think, I couldn't ask for a better PR job, could I? Once that piece is published, I won't even have to carry a weapon. Everybody'll know what a terrible, dangerous fellow I am; they'll tremble in their shoes when they see me coming. They'll all straighten up and fly right without my even having to threaten them. One piercing look from my murderous blue eyes will do the job."

She looked at me for a moment longer, and shrugged minutely. "If you're not going to do anything constructive with that damned bottle, slide it this way."

Taking the bottle I moved within her reach, she poured some whiskey into my almost-empty glass and then gave herself a moderate refill. The boat rocked gently from the wash of a large cruiser leaving the harbor.

I said, "As far as Miss Brand's revelations are concerned, naturally we'd like to find out if she's going to expose any of our people who are still unknown to the opposition, particularly any who are off on dangerous business at the moment. At least that way we can yank

45

them home before somebody lowers the boom on them. And naturally, we'd like to persuade her nicely to soft-pedal the names of a few agents whose usefulness might actually be impaired. . . ." The woman beside me had stirred uneasily; now she threw me a sharp glance. I said irritably, "Damn it to hell, Harriet!"

"What's the matter?"

"You didn't always have such a cliché mind. When I say persuade I mean persuade; I'm not talking about the pincers and thumbscrews."

"Well, you can hardly blame me for—"

"You're reacting like a TV-crazy kid. Snap out of it," I said harshly. "Years ago you killed one of our people, or you had a henchman do it for you. You're still sitting here alive and healthy, aren't you? With a shiny new past provided by us. We don't go around casually massacring or torturing crazy ladies who just don't happen to like us. You should know that if anyone does."

There was a little silence. Then, deliberately, she reached out a long, slim hand—she hadn't gotten it entirely clean, but that was irrelevant—and turned my face toward her and leaned forward to kiss me lightly on the lips.

"I'm sorry, my dear. When you live with corny people, you develop corny reactions. You should drop around more often to keep me sensible." She grimaced, and seemed to become aware of her unromantic appearance. She retrieved her hand abruptly. "Well, tell me what you want so I can finish up my work and take a shower. Essence of Diesel Number Two seems to be the perfume of the day."

"As I said, we'd like to persuade her to cooperate a little," I said. "My clever idea, cold-blooded, I admit, is that a gal whose life you save is likely to be grateful to you and may even be talked into getting her publisher to delete a name or two you'd rather not see in print. But that's pretty iffy. It may not break that way at all, and even if it does, Miss Brand seems to be a girl whose gratitude—or friendship, or loyalty—you don't want to rely on too strongly if her work is involved. So my chief concern is simply keeping the dame alive. If we can cash in on it afterward, so much the better, but we simply can't afford the suspicions that will be aroused if somebody kills her right now. After her series on us is published, and people have had time to forget, she can lie down and croak for all we care; but at the moment, her life is very precious to us."

Harriet laughed softly. "Well, that's clear enough, brutally clear, but it doesn't really tell me what you want from me."

I said, "I want to make sure she's not sticking her long snoopy nose—well, her short snoopy nose, judging by her picture—into anything dangerous—"

Harriet shook her head quickly, and I stopped. She said, "You'd better not count on that, Matt."

"I see. Thanks. That's one thing I needed to know. So we plug in Contingency Program Number Two; and as official troubleshooter I'll roll up my sleeves and prepare myself to protect the inquisitive bitch from whatever trouble she manages to stir up. Can you tell me where it's likely to come from?"

The woman beside me hesitated. "How much do you know about what she's doing?"

I said, "Well, I didn't take that bloody Triangle nonsense of hers too seriously. I figured she was using that to hide behind while she probed away secretly at something else. So what was she likely to be investigating while she pretended to be collecting fascinating data on the Mysterious Sea of Missing Ships? What made her pick that particular cover story, to cover the story she's really working on? It came to me in a flash; and I had Washington crank up the computer and find out if there had been any *new* cases of ships going mysteriously missing of late. They sent me a bunch of clippings and some other stuff, very interesting. Inside and outside the Deadly Triangle, folks have been polluting the sea bottoms with busted-up vessels in a most reprehensible way, racking up well above the normal run of collisions and storm losses and groundings. The computer kicked out over half a dozen it thought deserved special

47

attention—I haven't gotten around to reading them all—
and that doesn't count the most recent one that was in the
newspaper I read on the plane coming east. Come to think
of it, I've got that one in my pocket. Here."

I dug out the torn-out piece of newsprint and laid it on
the cabin table. Harriet turned it so she could read the
headline above the picture of a neat new ship proceeding
peacefully across a placid ocean.

"TANKER SINKS," she read aloud. "Date and so forth.
. . . Four lives were lost when the tanker *Fairfax Constellation*, shown above on its maiden voyage in 1963, went
down off the Bahama Islands in moderate weather after
reporting an explosion and fire on board. The remainder of
the crew was picked up etc., etc. . . . . The twenty-five
thousand ton ship was registered in Monrovia, Liberia.
After taking on a full cargo of oil in Aruba, it was proceeding towards Wilmington, North Carolina, when the disaster
occurred. The cause of the explosion has not been determined. . . . It!" she said explosively.

"What?"

"*It*, for God's sake!" Harriet made a face at the clipping.
"I'm getting goddamn sick and tired of these Libbers man-
gling the goddamn language. A ship is not an it, goddamn
it! A ship is a *she*, and has always been a *she*. As a woman
I simply loved having hurricanes named after me; it's bad
enough now when they call a nice, big, beautiful blow
'David,' for God's sake! It should have been 'Danielle,' or
'Dorothy,' or 'Dora' or something, a real credit to our sex.
But when they have the gall to deprive us of having a
lovely thing like a ship, even a seventeen-year-old flag-of-
convenience rust-bucket like that, referred to in the feminine! . . ." She grinned abruptly. "Did you hear about that
big whirlpool off Norway? You're now supposed to call it
the Personstrom, or the equal ladies will have your hide.
Instead of the Maelstrom—*Male*strom—get it?"

I said, "Lady, you need another drink. Ugh!"

She laughed and said, "I gather you're convinced that all
these recent sinkings are related in some way."

"Wasn't Eleanor Brand? Isn't that why she came to see

you a second time, remembering from the previous interview that you know a hell of a lot about anything that floats?"

After a moment, Harriet nodded. "You're a good guesser. Yes, that's why she stopped by on her way down to the Caribbean; but I couldn't give her much help. Big ships aren't really in my line. Anyway, you'll have gathered I wasn't very fond of Miss Eleanor Brand; and, of course, there were . . . reasons why I didn't particularly want her hanging around asking questions."

"Reasons?"

"Now who's being stupid?" she asked. "Naturally, I don't want her putting me into an article or giving me any other kind of publicity. And I certainly don't want to get her interested enough in me to start checking up on my past, do I? And when a conscientious reporter gets important information from a certain source, he starts checking that source for reliability, doesn't he? Or she?"

"So you were careful not to give her any important information," I said. "What important information?"

She hesitated and looked oddly embarrassed. She spoke too quickly, "I didn't mean . . . I was just speaking generally. What I meant was that I simply brushed her off as fast as I could; the last thing I wanted was her calling attention to me by quoting me as her tame nautical advisor."

"Sure," I said. "What about me?"

"What do you mean?" Her voice was guarded.

"How about being my tame nautical advisor, Hattie? I'd like to have some idea of what this gal is getting herself, and me, involved in. You must have done a bit of thinking about this recent rash of ship sinkings, and even if big ships are out of your line, you know a hell of a lot more about them than I do."

She started to speak quickly, and stopped. There was a brief silence; then she said, "I'm afraid I can't be much help to you, Matt." She wasn't looking at me; and her voice sounded strangely uncertain, for her. Then she drew a deep breath and turned to face me a bit defiantly. She said, "No, that's not true. I won't lie to you. I simply don't want to be much help to you, any more than I wanted to be much help to Eleanor Brand. For just about the same reasons."

It shocked me a little. It was not what I'd expected from Captain Harriet Robinson, as she now was; even though it was a perfectly sensible attitude.

I said, "You still feel pretty vulnerable, even after all these years, is that what you mean?"

She nodded. "I . . . there could be something rather peculiar going on, Matt; but if there is, I don't want to be mixed up in it in any way. Please try to understand. I mind my own business, ashore and on the water, and I let others mind theirs. Cap'n Hattie is deaf and blind and very, very, dumb, in a bright sort of way; and everybody knows it. I don't ever see anybody smuggling drugs although it takes a lot of concentrated not-seeing. I do my fishing legally and if somebody else does it some other way you can never prove it by me. Everybody loves me and nobody hates me and I want to keep it that way. I don't want to make anybody mad. I don't want to give anybody reason to start asking questions about me even if you did fix up my records so nicely, for which you have my thanks. But I earned that, in a way, didn't I? I don't really owe you for that."

"You don't owe me a thing, quite the contrary," I said.

She was looking out the cabin window, again refusing to meet my eyes. "*Please* understand. I'm still an easy mark for anybody who wants to make a real project of digging into my past. Even if you want to, you can't protect me beyond a certain point, can you? Not if they learn the truth and take it to the proper authorities. There are still some old charges that could be revived if it's learned that I'm alive; charges I doubt even your big man in Washington has pull enough to do anything about, if the information gets into the hands of an eager official—prosecutor?— who feels compelled to act on it. Accessory to murder is only one; they could call what I did up there conspiracy, or even treason, couldn't they? I . . . I was so goddamn proud

50

and cocky in those days, Matt, and so goddamn stupid! And I don't intend to go to prison, my dear; I couldn't endure that. It's bad enough being . . . being exiled like this. . . ." Her voice stopped. We sat silent for a moment; she seemed to be listening to a replay of her own words. I felt her shudder beside me. She whispered, aghast, "God, listen to me, Matt! What's happened to me? I sound like a sniveling coward hiding in a dark cave!"

I said quickly, "It's all right. I shouldn't have—"

"No, goddamn it, it's not all right!" Her voice was fierce. "That's no way to live, what the hell am I thinking of? I *have* picked up some hints—"

"No," I said. "You really don't owe me anything, Harriet. The debt runs the other way. I shouldn't have come." I got up. "Thanks for the drinks. I'll be on my way. It's been nice seeing you."

She said harshly, "You goddamn spook, park your ass and listen. Sit *down!*" There was a resonance to her voice; the ring of command. I sat down. She said, "I'll give you a reference and a name; what you do with them is up to you. The reference is COLREGS Rule 18-a-iv. The name is George Winfield Lorca. And I did not give any of that to Miss Brand, why should I stick my neck out for her? But if you want to use it, directly or for trading purposes, be my guest."

I asked, "Why should you stick your neck out for me?"

She smiled and reached out to touch my lips with a silencing forefinger. "No questions. You got what you came for. Now you can go."

There was a hint of challenge in her voice, a go-to-hell inflection that made me look at her sharply. After a long moment I asked, "Did I?"

"Did you what?"

"Get what I came for?"

She drew a long breath, regarding me intently. After a little, she said very softly, "Hey, spook, I think we have a problem."

I cleared my throat. "I don't know about *we*, but when a skinny seafaring dame in greasy khakis begins to look good to me, I know I have a problem. A skinny seafaring dame who kicked me off her boat with curses when last met."

She smiled slowly. "But who hadn't been too hard to talk out of her dress and shoes a little earlier."

I cleared my throat again. "As I recall, that's all you were wearing at the time, a dress and shoes."

She asked, "Well, how do you want me tonight, quick or pretty?"

I told her I preferred my ladies gift-wrapped, if that was what she meant and if she truly wished to be my lady. She said for me to have another drink and start the clock when I heard the shower stop, let it run five minutes, and I should be right on target.

I was.

CHAPTER 6

EARLY morning is usually a good time in the Florida Keys, calm and clear. I slipped out of the double bunk in the wedge-shaped stateroom up in *Queenfisher*'s bow—the big berth, set at a slant with respect to the boat's centerline in order to take advantage of the oddly shaped space, pretty well filled the little forward cabin—and carried my clothes up into the deckhouse, leaving her asleep. I couldn't shave or change into anything clean until I got my suitcase out of the car, so I simply hauled on shorts and pants for the time being. Shoeless and shirtless gents cause no particular comment around a Florida marina; but I had to admit that my torso was kind of fish-belly pale by local standards.

An early-rising fisherman was heading out of the marina in a small outboard-powered boat; otherwise everything was very quiet as I stepped ashore. The little vessel's

V-shaped wake traveled silently across the glassy water of the harbor, but made small, surging, hissing noises when it encountered the sea wall, and sent a ripple of movement through the docked boats. I padded along the sea wall to the pay phone across the road from the lounge and restaurant, now closed and silent. If you want to buy breakfast in that resort, you have to hike or drive up to their coffee shop on the highway; but most of the cabins have kitchen facilities. Waiting for my call to Miami to go through collect, I admired the boats, now lying still once more, and the motionless palms, and the clear blue Florida sky. I hoped for a pelican to appear—the ugliest bird in the world and the most beautiful flyer—but they're getting scarce down there nowadays and none showed.

"Eric here," I said when a voice spoke in my ear. "Report."

"The Paradise Towers Hotel, Nassau."

"What the hell is she doing in Nassau? I thought she was down in the Virgin Islands somewhere."

"The location is our business, friend; the motivation is yours."

I grimaced at a flying seagull, who didn't seem to mind. "Well, that pretty well confirms my guess about what she's really after; she must be checking up on that last ship that went down, but she reacts fast . . . *Fairfax Constellation*," I said. "Twenty-five-thousand-ton tanker, Liberian registry, out of Aruba, recently sunk somewhere off the Bahamas. It was in the Miami papers yesterday; probably others as well. Get what details you can and locate the surviving crew for me, will you? Although I have a hunch all I have to do is keep Miss Brand in sight and she'll lead me to them."

"Request noted."

"Who's our man in Nassau these days, Freddie?"

"Fred is still our man in Nassau, yes."

The voice was expressionless; but there are very few secrets in the organization and I had a hunch that our man in Miami, a young standby agent named Brent with whom I'd worked in the past, was quite aware that there had been friction between Fred and me the last time I'd operated in the Islands. Fred thought I was a racist bastard and he was perfectly right. I am highly intolerant of black men who are slow pulling the trigger when my life is at stake; and the last time we'd worked together he'd been damned slow. Of course I'm also intolerant of white men, blue men, red men, and green men who display similar dilatory characteristics under similar circumstances.

I said, "Can you set me up for the flight and the hotel?"

"Already done, friend. Get yourself up to Miami today; you've got a room for the night at the Airport Hotel. You take Eastern out tomorrow morning at eight-oh-five and land on New Providence Island at eight-fifty. Your reservation at the Paradise Towers is waiting. The subject is in room four-oh-five. She has company along; male, blond, husky, handsome. Ostensible occupation, photographer, but I wouldn't trust him to cover my wedding if I were getting married, which I'm not. More muscle than art, I'd say. Name, Warren Peterson. Room four-oh-seven. I believe there are connecting doors."

"I'm jealous already," I said. "But that's real service; I'll mail you a gold star for your report card. A couple more things. Please find out for me what the hell is a COLREGS. Cee-oh-ell-are. . . ."

"The latest International Regulations for Preventing Collisions at Sea were promulgated in 1972 by the United Nations Inter-Governmental Marine Consultative Organization. They were updated recently, I believe in 1977. They are now known as COLREGS—Collision Regulations, get it? In case you're interested, the organization itself is known as IMCO. Just as a seagoing toilet is nowadays known as a Marine Sanitation Device or MSD, a life preserver is a Personal Flotation Device or PFD, and a pump or bucket is a Dewatering Device or DD—well, I don't vouch for that last contraction. All courtesy of the fun-loving linguistic jokers of the United States Coast Guard known as USCG. What part of the rules?"

"Rule 18-a-iv."

"I don't have it on tap but I can find it."

"It's a relief to learn there's something you don't know offhand. I thought for a moment I might be hooked into our omniscient friendly neighborhood computer. Well, look it up and get it to me care of Fred, will you? Also a copy of an old article in Travel Times entitled 'Kiruna Today,' by a lady named Louise Taylor." I gave him the date and waited while he wrote it down. He read it back to me to make sure he had it right. I went on, "I'd also appreciate it if you'd send somebody down here to keep an eye on Captain Harriet Robinson. You remember Cap'n Hattie. I have a hunch she knows too much to be perfectly safe." There was something I had forgotten, but it came back to me. "Oh, and check on a name for me, please. George Winfield Lorca."

I heard a soft whistle. "Watch yourself, friend. That name packs a punch."

"I'm just an ignorant desert dweller," I said.

"I'll send you what I can get in an asbestos envelope. Tell Fred to have his fire tongs handy."

"I get the message," I said. "I'll wear my bulletproof union suit known as BVD when I land in the British West Indies known as BWI. Only they aren't that any longer, are they?"

"No, they're pretty much an independent nation now. Good luck."

"Eric out."

As I stepped out of the booth I saw that one lonely brown pelican had, after all, put in an appearance. He was sitting perched on top of one of the dockside pilings I had to pass, in the stump-like way they have, long beak tucked in close to long neck. He gave me a baleful look as I approached and spread his wings and glided away, instantly transforming himself from a figure of fun to a creature of remarkable grace. Even the outsized bill looked right when he was flying.

I walked gingerly over to the rental car in my bare feet, got my suitcase out of the trunk, and returned to the boat. There was no sound from the forward stateroom as I shaved in the diminutive cubicle called a head, utilized the apparatus known as MSD, and made myself reasonably respectable; shoes, shirt, and the works. I hoped Harriet had fewer protective and possessive feelings about her galley than Martha had about her kitchen, although that was not exactly a comfortable thought. My life seemed to be getting a bit complex with regard to the opposite sex. Risking displeasure, I fired up the stove, which operated in normal fashion on butane gas, a relief. Some boat cookers use alcohol or kerosene and require priming; and while I was checked out at an early age on Coleman gasoline camp stoves, which operate similarly, my rustic-stove techniques had become pretty rusty of late.

I started heating water for instant coffee—Harriet seemed to be of my own persuasion in this respect—and found bacon and eggs in the small boat refrigerator; also some canned orange juice, which always seems unnatural in Florida. All those citrus groves and you're supposed to drink it out of a *can*, for God's sake? But the last time I got real, fresh-squeezed, breakfast orange juice handed to me in a restaurant, I recalled was in a motel in a little Mexican mining town with the odd name of Heroica de Caborca, where they were too far from civilization to know any better. The galley was very neat and tidy, but it was a sailor's neatness, not a cook's neatness. There was nothing to indicate that cooking was anything but just another boat chore to the owner, like polishing the fittings or scrubbing the decks. There were no intriguing, specialized, culinary implements in evidence, or oddball spices. When the deckhouse table was set and the bacon was draining on a paper towel, I went downstairs—oops, below—to wake my lady.

She was kind of breathtaking lying there asleep, tanned and lovely; she had always been a spectacular lady. She had declared war upon the United States of America because of the arbitrary way its bureaucracy had condemned some land she'd owned and loved for purposes of which she did not approve—it had been part of a sizeable estate she'd inherited up there in Maryland. I could have sympathized with her angry feelings if she hadn't picked her allies

56

so badly, disregarding their motives and political beliefs in her desire to strike back at the establishment that, she felt, had robbed her of an important part of her birthright—and if, as I'd reminded her the night before, she hadn't caused the death of one of our people in the course of her vengeful operations.

She'd come close to killing me, or having me killed; and in the end only the breaks of the game had prevented me from killing her or sending her to prison. Despite our differences, however, I'd been relieved when she'd made her escape in the end, diving overboard from her wrecked schooner yacht in the storm in which she was now officially listed as having drowned. It had pleased me to know for sure, later, when she was found living down here under a different name and in considerably different circumstances, that she hadn't drowned after all. Not that I'd considered it much of a possibility. She wasn't an easy girl to drown.

So the long rough game between us had started there up north, where I had thus won Round One by frustrating her plans and those of the foreign associates she'd been angry enough to choose, making a fugitive of her. The second round, however, had been hers, down here, when in the course of a different assignment I'd received information from her that had saved my life, obligating us to do our best to make her secure in her new existence. One and one. Yesterday the bell had rung for Round Three; but as I looked down at her sleeping face I found myself entertaining strong emotions I did not care to identify. Their mere existence, however, indicated that some time during the night it had ceased to be a game. . . .

She became aware of my presence, and opened her eyes a bit warily; then she turned lazily onto her back, remembering, and smiled to see me standing there.

"Hey, spook."

"Breakfast is served, Captain Robinson, ma'am. The dining room steward wishes to be informed if you want your eggs fried or scrambled."

"How about poached, shirred, or coddled?"

"We can only serve what's on the menu, ma'am. No special orders."

She sat up and shook her tousled dark hair into place—it was short enough that it needed no more to discipline it—swung her feet to the cabin sole and restored a vagrant satin ribbon, pretending to be a shoulder strap, to its proper functioning position. It made her shoulder look very smooth and brown. I'd asked for a gift-wrapped lady and she'd given me one. The nightgown was white, long and graceful, with some discreet lace top and bottom. It was neither wantonly provocative nor innocently bridal; it was simply a handsome and becoming gown that raised the whole man–woman business to a much higher plane than simple, crude, nude copulation. Naked dames have their place, no doubt, and I'm not knocking nudity; but there's something very special about being allowed the privilege of discovering, and lovingly uncovering as far as necessary, a beautiful woman within a decorative garment she's put on specifically for the purpose of having her body admired and explored, and in the end, fully exploited, by you.

Yet there was a sadness, too, in seeing her in her expensive gown. It was obviously something she'd bought on impulse, in a moment of weakness, to remind herself of what she had been and no longer was. It did not belong to her present incarnation as a tough female sportfishing captain living under rather Spartan circumstances on a forty-foot boat. When I kissed her I felt her cling to me for a moment, as if she needed the reassurance of some affectionate bodily contact even though we'd finished with passion for the moment. I'd never before thought of her as someone who might need reassurance and the idea disturbed me; but after a moment she laughed softly and freed herself.

"Two, over easy," she said.

"Yes, ma'am. Coming right up, ma'am."

I was just placing our breakfast on the table, about to call her, when she appeared in the deckhouse wearing jeans, a short-sleeved jersey and brown leather boat shoes with white patent soles, the kind with the squeegee pattern that supposedly won't slip on any deck no matter how slick and wet. I couldn't see the pattern, but I knew the shoes; they're worn everywhere around the docks. She looked lean and competent. The soft, clinging female in the fragile, lacy gown might never have existed.

"What, no toast?" she said, seating herself. "You'll have to snap into it, steward, we run a taut ship here."

"Toast being served, ma'am."

We batted it back and forth like that for a while, with variations, but there were tensions here that had not existed as long as we were below in each others' arms. Now that the hint had been given me I could see that she had changed, and I could realize that what had been so very good about last night was the fact that she'd needed me desperately; me, or at least the assurance I could give her that she was still an attractive and important person— Harriet Robinson, formerly Robin Rosten, who'd never needed anyone before in her life. The evidence had all been there but I'd preferred to ignore it.

When I'd last seen her she wouldn't have dreamed of worrying how she'd be received in the cocktail lounge, any cocktail lounge, after working on her engines; in fact, she hadn't. She'd considered them damned lucky to have her even in baggy pants with grease on them. She'd never have referred to her present existence as an exile; and she'd certainly never have thought of buying some frivolous and expensive lingerie to remind her, in secret, of the gracious life she'd left behind forever. Nor would she have considered holding her tongue about anything for timid and sensible reasons of self-protection. Back then she'd been playing the part of Captain Harriet Robinson to the hilt and enjoying it immensely; but now, I could see, the enjoyment had faded and regret and caution had taken its place.

I could look at her clearly at last and know that she was lost. She was a lovely lady and she was breaking and there wasn't a damned thing I could do to help her. This rather primitive and, in many ways, humbling life—a charter

59

boat captain, male or female, has to take a lot of guff from a lot of slobs—was wearing her down, not to mention the fact that despite our best efforts she was still legally a fugitive with the ultimate horror of prison still hanging over her. But mainly she was remembering everything she'd given up. She was realizing that she wasn't really made for this, she was being wasted here, and the waste was irretrievable. I had a momentary sickening picture of another woman I'd just seen who'd been totally degraded by pressures too great for her to bear. I did not think that Harriet's break, when it came, would take that form—it was an unbearable thing to even consider—but she was obviously no longer holding her own here and the end, some end, was inevitable.

"Tell me about the girl," Harriet said abruptly.

"What girl?"

She laughed. "Your girl, Matt. The one you so nobly left unloved for her own good." She reached out to cover my hand with hers, briefly. "I don't mind, really I don't, but do you think a woman doesn't know when she's being used as a substitute? You came down here to the Keys needing somebody to make love to very badly, my dear, obviously because you'd just been with somebody you would very much like to have had, whom you couldn't bring yourself to touch for, no doubt, the highest reasons in the world." She studied me shrewdly. "Of course, there's a possibility that she simply rejected you, but I doubt it. If you'd just had your face slapped, you wouldn't have been such a little bundle—well, big bundle—of iron self-control, all done up tight in self-tied knots until we. . . ." She stopped and a little color came into her face. She said quickly, "Steward, my cup is empty again. A little service here, *if* you please!"

I was glad of the excuse to leave the table and the dark eyes that saw too much; but there was a strong impulse to laugh ruefully, too. While I'd been considering her sad case, she'd been considering mine; and, of course, she was perfectly right. I had found it very pleasant to be with Martha Devine in the home she'd made with Bob. There had been a strong temptation to stay and build upon the comfortable relationship we'd achieved; and bed had certainly been one desirable goal that had occurred to me. I'd been aware that, if I used reasonable restraint and consideration and patience, that goal and maybe others were probably not unattainable. But I'd come here instead, not really knowing why; and it hadn't been very fair to Harriet Robinson.

"Am I right?" she asked when I sat down again.

I nodded. "All the way down the line. I'm sorry—"

"I hope not!" When I looked surprised, she said, "My dear man, only one thing is totally unforgivable, and that is being sorry afterward."

I grinned. "All right. I'm not sorry."

She laughed, and sipped her coffee thoughtfully, watching me. "What's the big obstacle, Matt? You're an attractive scoundrel, in a gruesome sort of way; and the work you do should be no problem unless the girl is a very timid type. Most women are attracted to dangerous men, even if some of them don't care to admit it."

I said, "Nothing like a little analysis at breakfast."

"Well, you were analyzing me, weren't you? I could see you. Is it a strictly masculine prerogative now?"

I said, "The young lady in question is . . . well, fairly young. At the moment she was mourning a just-dead husband and did not feel it proper for me to move into his bed with him so recently buried."

"That's what she said, but did she mean it?"

I shrugged. "It doesn't matter. She's practically a kid, she's had one not-very-good marriage with a guy in my line of work, and the last thing she needs is another superannuated mercenary just stopping by the house occasionally between wars. What she needs is to boot us lousy spooks out of her life altogether and make herself a real marriage with some gentle and civilized young fellow who faints at the sight of a gun."

Harriet studied me for a long moment, and shook her head sadly. "I don't know how the hell you've lasted so long in the business you're in. I wouldn't think being a nice guy had a lot of survival value. And, of course, you're wrong. Spooks are habit-forming, like heroin. Once you're hooked on them, life is very dull without them. She's not going to settle for a handsome insurance salesman now, or a nice doctor or dentist."

I said, "I was obliged to give her the chance. What she does with it is up to her."

Harriet was still watching me steadily. "So now it's your turn, Matt," she said. "What conclusion did you come to about me?"

It was no time for hesitation or diplomacy. "That you weren't doing so well here any longer," I said bluntly.

She nodded. "That's right. I'm a snob, you see. Hiring myself out to find fish for a bunch of beer-swilling peasants and enduring their vulgar pleasantries, living in a space hardly larger than a respectable closet, never looking nice or meeting any nice people—except occasionally as a kind of servant-employee—well, it was fun as long as I could kid myself I was being very clever and putting one over on the world and it wasn't going to last forever. . . ." She stopped abruptly and cleared her throat. "But it is," she said very softly. "I keep realizing that's all that's left now. Forever."

"I'd pass the crying towel if I knew where you kept it," I said deliberately.

I was going to have to watch it, I warned myself. It was always a temptation to do it to her, to watch the quick-flashing anger burn away all her doubts and uncertainties and bring her fine head up sharply and put that arrogant, hawk-like gleam into her splendid eyes. She glared at me for a moment; then she threw her head back and laughed heartily.

"Thanks, spook," she said. "I was getting a bit soggy there, wasn't I? Matt. . . ."

"Yes."

"Will you be back? There's . . . no obligation. I would simply like to know."

"I'll be back," I said. It was a commitment. Nobody ever

makes it quite alone. Perhaps, after all, we could both make it, together.

The following morning I was in Nassau.

CHAPTER 7

FRED was at the airport when I arrived. I spotted him at once standing beside his cab as I came outside after the customs-and-immigration bit, even though he'd exchanged the big blue Plymouth I remembered for a smaller taxi—red and shiny and new—in line with current fuel-conservation trends that may be ecologically and economically terrific, but tend to ignore the physical requirements of long-legged passengers six-feet-four.

Although it had been some years, I recognized the rather tall and muscular gent with the cheerful black face that became somewhat less cheerful when he saw me, so I knew old resentments were still operative. However, they did not prevent him from maneuvering skillfully so that, with the help of a little judicious stalling by me, we got together at the loading curb; but then some other passengers for the same hotel were put aboard with me, so we couldn't talk. Fortunately, a great deal of conversation wasn't needed at this point. When he unloaded my suitcase in front of the hotel, he set down beside it a handsome attaché case that apparently didn't belong to anybody else in the cab. Paying my fare, I wound up holding a small key that presumably fit the case.

"Thank you, sir," Fred said politely. "I hope you will enjoy your stay in Nassau, sir."

"It doesn't seem to have changed much?" I said, turning the statement into a question.

"Ah, you have been here before, sir? No, there have

63

been not so many changes. I think you will find it quite familiar."

The last time I'd been in Nassau I'd stayed at the British Colonial Hotel, a fine old landmark of a building right on the harbor, with probably the worst service in the world. The Paradise Towers, out on what is now known as Paradise Island—formerly Hog Island—was a step down architecturally, looking like any tall modern confection of glass and chrome and concrete; but the desk crew did condescend to look up my reservation with reasonable dispatch, and the bellboy even thanked me for the tip, which would never have happened at the British Colonial. The room was small, soulless, and expensive; but everything worked.

I locked my room door, laid the attaché case on the bed, unlocked and opened it. It contained a large assortment of paper materials, from pamphlets to clippings to file folders. It also contained a .38 Special Smith and Wesson revolver with a two-inch barrel, ammunition for same, and one of our standard little drug kits, which I pocketed. I loaded the weapon, but did not conceal it on my person since I did not believe firearms were indicated, at least not yet. Instead, I hid it with the remaining ammo in the secret compartment in my suitcase—well, it's secret unless somebody who knows how to look, looks for it hard. I hoped that, if I did have occasion to use the unfamiliar weapon, it would shoot somewhere close to where it pointed. Not that these snub-nosed little artillery pieces ever manage any spectacular accuracy, if only because the sight radius is just too damned short.

I examined the other contents of the attaché case hastily. Our efficient young man in Miami had done a hell of a job in the short time at his disposal; everything I'd asked for seemed to be there. I would have liked to sit down and study all this new material carefully, but Fred had indicated that there had been no significant changes locally, meaning that the lady in whom I was interested was still where last reported, in her room. I wanted to catch her before she took off somewhere for the day or perhaps, her work in Nassau done, checked out for good. I added the stuff I'd been handed earlier to the papers already in the attaché case, closed and locked the case, and stood for a moment frowning thoughtfully; but I could see absolutely no reason to be clever. I had to make contact with Ms. Eleanor Brand somehow. The simplest method was to walk up to her hotel room door and knock. Taking the attaché case with me, I did just that. A little silence followed my knock.

"Just a minute."

It was a female voice, somewhat muffled by the intervening door. Another lengthy pause followed. I heard another door close somewhere beyond the one that faced me. I heard crisp feminine footsteps approach, and the voice I'd heard spoke again, closer.

"Who is it?"

"My name is Helm," I said. "Matthew Helm."

"What do you want?"

"Bob Devine is dead," I said. "I'd like to tell you about it."

After a moment, the lock rattled. The door swung open and there she was, not quite as big a girl as I'd expected; and somehow that made a difference. What's plain or even ugly on a large horse of a girl can look merely unusual and intriguing on a female constructed on a smaller and daintier scale.

Not that she was diminutive. There was a reasonable amount of woman there, say five-three, say one-fifteen. I saw that the offbeat monkey face I'd studied in a black-and-white magazine reproduction was really not bad-looking in living color. Her complexion was good, her short straight brown hair was clean and smooth, and there was a touch of lipstick on her long and mobile mouth. She had a small scar on her lower lip, I noticed, not too recent but not dating back to childhood, either. I wondered idly if she'd been slugged by somebody who'd got mad about a story she'd written; but more likely she'd bumped into something in the dark or been involved in a minor car accident. Her figure was as unfashionable as her snub-nosed face, slender enough but rather long in the body and short in the legs for this era of long-stemmed lovelies; but the legs were quite good and she was smart enough to make the most of them in high heels and nylons. She was built and shaped all wrong according to modern beauty standards for the breed; her conformation was simply terrible as the dog show people would put it; but she projected a strong impression of one Eleanor Brand, a unique person; and uniqueness is hard to find these copycat days.

Whether or not she was aware of it, and it seemed unlikely that she was, she'd taken the direct route to my heart by wearing a neat suit with a skirt, not pants. It was nice for a change to meet a lady who did not feel that the new feminine freedom was best displayed in old masculine trousers. The suit was a light summer number in brownish chambray, if I have that slick cottony material properly identified. There was a little white blouse with a round collar. Her eyes watched me with wary speculation. They were hazel eyes in which a hint of apprehension lurked, but she had no intention of giving in to it.

"Come in, Mr. Helm," she said, stepping back. "I know you, of course. I mean, I know about you."

The room was larger than the one to which I'd been assigned. A double bed protruded from the wall to the left. The wall to the right had two doors, the nearer one of which stood open to reveal a bathroom. The farther door was closed. A table and a couple of chairs stood in front of the windows straight ahead. A rather fancy camera bag, equipped with a heavy strap with a rubber shoulder pad, held the place of honor on the table, with a woman's purse playing second fiddle. I closed the hall door behind me and set down the attaché case.

"Yes, you know all about me, I gather," I said as I straightened up with what I hoped was a friendly and reassuring grin. "And you're not a damned bit reticent about what you know, I'm told."

"Is that what you're here about, Mr. Helm?" She was still studying me cautiously. "You mentioned Bob Devine; was that just to get me to open the door for you?"

I shook my head. "I'm a friend of Martha's, as you undoubtedly know, among all the other things you know about me. I was just out there to see her. I thought you'd be interested in hearing about her husband's death."

"I've already heard about it, thanks," Eleanor Brand said a little defiantly. "Am I to understand that you consider me to blame for it?"

"Martha certainly did at first," I said.

She drew a long breath, and her face was troubled. "Yes, I know. I'm very sorry about that. I'm afraid Martha simply doesn't understand that professional considerations must always take precedence over personal relationships."

I grinned at her. "A fancy way of saying that you'd doublecross your own mother for a scoop, not to mention a friend who trusted you."

She'd gone a little pale; she obviously found the conversation difficult, as she was meant to. She raised her head in a nice haughty way that reminded me strangely—since they were such totally different women—of Harriet Robinson, and said, "I don't really think you're in a position to criticize, Mr. Helm. Have you never sacrificed your personal feelings to your . . . your professional work?" When I didn't answer at once she said, "Anyway, scoop is a pretty corny and obsolete word."

I said, "As I told you, Martha did blame you, at first. However, I did a little detective work when I got out there. I determined that your magazine piece had nothing whatever to do with Bob's death. He'd been playing around, as you know, and a jealous husband took a shotgun to him. So your conscience is quite clear, Miss Brand. I thought you'd like to know."

She looked at me for a moment. I saw that her eyes had become oddly shiny; and she turned abruptly and walked to the window and stood looking out. After a little, I went over to stand behind her. When she spoke, her voice was almost inaudible.

"I don't understand."

"About Bob Devine? He was a good man, a brave man, a tough and loyal partner where masculine relationships were concerned; but he always had a wandering eye. Some men can't help being like that."

"No," she said, "that wasn't what I meant. It hasn't been . . . very nice, thinking that I might be responsible for his death even though I didn't like him very much; I thought Martha was throwing herself away on a man like that. But I certainly didn't want him killed because of something I'd written about him, and I don't understand why you should take the trouble to come all this way to . . . to let me off the hook."

"You mean," I said, "because you're a nosy writer-lady who's written a nasty piece about me, too; so why didn't I simply let you stew in your own guilt even if it was mistaken guilt?"

She turned slowly to face me, the light behind her. Her shadowy mouth spoke to me quietly, "You're a surprising man, but of course I learned that when I was researching you. But that's what you're deliberately working at right now, isn't it? Surprising me and keeping me off balance?" There was a little pause and I reminded myself that, on the record, this was one of the least stupid ladies I was likely to meet in a long time. She went on in the same gentle voice, "What do you want from me, Mr. Helm? What are you hoping to gain by coming here? The article about you, the second in my series, will be published very shortly, you know that."

"I know," I said.

"Well, then, if you know anything about publishing, and I know you do, you know it's already too late for them to make any changes, let alone drop the piece completely. Even if I should ask. Even if you could persuade me to ask, or coerce me into asking. All you can do now to stop the truth about you from being read by everyone, all your hush-hush organization can do, is confiscate and destroy that whole issue of the magazine, if you have that much power and influence."

I said, aghast, "My God, lady! What do you think we live in, a police state or something? We wouldn't dream of fracturing the first Amendment or challenging the power of the press. Really, Miss Brand, what an outlandish idea! You must have some other government in mind, and some other organization, like maybe the KGB." I jerked my head toward the door nearby that, presumably, led into the adjoining room. "And talking about spies and spooks and snoops, don't you think it's about time to invite Junior to join the party? He must be getting lonely in there all by himself, eavesdropping on the grownups having fun next door."

She hesitated briefly, and turned her head. "All right, Warren," she said.

The door opened and the man I'd already had described to me came in. He was blond, all right, curly blond, and big, almost as tall as I and considerably wider. He had a big, tanned, blue-eyed, boyish face and he was wearing a blue-checked gingham sports shirt—or whatever chemical concoction passes for gingham these days—very snug white slacks, and white moccasin-type shoes of roughed-out leather, very sporty. He was carrying a pistol built around the same size hole as my recently acquired S and W but somewhat more substantial, with a four-inch barrel, manufactured by the competing firm of Colt Firearms, Inc. You can call it a handgun if you like, but to me that's still an old in-term used only by real shooters under some circumstances; otherwise by phonies trying to sound knowledgeable about guns who don't really know much about guns. To me they're all pistols. If the magazine, or cylinder, goes round and round it's a revolving pistol—the original old-time term—or revolver; if the magazine works up and down it's an automatic pistol or automatic.

Anyway, he had a gun. I watched him come, and stop a judicious distance away. The gun changed everything as it always does. It was too bad. She'd seemed like a fairly reasonable girl and for a little I'd hoped to be able to present my proposition in a civilized manner and persuade her to go along with it. I made a final try.

"Ask him to put it away, Miss Brand."

"Warren—"

The blond man shook his head quickly, and aimed his

weapon at me. "Not until I've made sure he isn't armed, Elly. Don't interfere. You asked me to come along for protection; now let me do it my way, please." He jerked the gun upward. "Up with the hands, you. Over against the wall so I can check you out."

I drew a long breath. "I'm going to reach into my inside coat pocket very slowly," I said. "I'm going to take out a small leather folder, the contents of which identify me as an agent of the United States Government. You are welcome to shoot any time. Fire away."

Moving very deliberately, I brought out the fancy ID we're given to use if it becomes necessary to impress some law-enforcement officials we happen to encounter, and maybe an occasional civilian as well. I flipped it open, laid it on the table by the window and gave it a little shove so it slid toward him. He glanced at it and shook his head.

"That means nothing," he said. "We know what you people really are, government or no government. We know what you're really here for, don't we, Elly? We've been kind of expecting you. That's why I came along, to protect her, not just to take pictures for her. Up with them, I said!"

He did some more pistol-waving. I was happy it was a double-action revolver he was holding, and that the hammer was down. Cocked, the weapon would already have fired, the sloppy way he was handling it. He could still fire it by means of the self-cocking mechanism, using a long, strong pull on the trigger, but he would have to mean it.

I was suddenly very tired of Mr. Warren Peterson and his menacing, careless weapon; Mr. Peterson who'd never learned the first lesson of practical pistolry, to wit, that you never point one at anything or anybody you don't fully intend to shoot right now. I was even getting weary enough of him to do something very foolish about him.

I told him softly, "Listen carefully. I am now going to walk right up to that thing you're waving at me, amigo. Pull the trigger any time you feel like it. Please note that my hands are quite empty. I am not carrying a gun. If you want to shoot an unarmed man, be my guest."

"Mr. Helm—" That was Eleanor Brand. Her voice was strained.

"Too late, Miss Brand," I said without looking her way. "You can always remember that I asked you nicely to stop this; and that I have displayed no weapons whatever; and no hostility, either."

"Warren, please—"

But I was already in motion and Warren Peterson was watching me approach and trying to make up his mind; he paid her no attention. His face was pale and his knuckles were white, holding the gun; except those of the trigger finger, which did not move. Then I was there. The muzzle rested against my chest. I reached up very slowly and carefully. I grasped the barrel and guided it gently to a point on my shirt slightly left of center.

"Any time, friend," I said, looking into his pale, uncertain face. "You're right on target; you can't miss. Fire at will . . . no? Okay, now I'm going to back away from you very slowly, holding your gun barrel firmly against me, just like this. You have a choice. You can continue to hang on, in which case we'll have a nice little tug of war and the gun will fire and you'll have a loud noise and a bloody dead man to your credit. Or you can simply let go." I watched his uneasy blue eyes. "Ready? Here I go. Backing away now. Make up your cottonpicking mind."

It really was no contest. I should have been ashamed of myself. He was one of the no-kill kids produced by the current spate of anti-firearms propaganda; I'd sensed it and taken advantage of it. Some of them can't even bring themselves to shoot in combat when they're being shot at. Morally speaking the attitude was to his credit, I suppose; but what the hell was he doing, then, with a gun? But of course he'd never thought it out; they never do. It had never really occurred to him, when he picked up the weapon, that somebody might actually—Heaven forbid!—make him shoot it. To him it had only been a symbol of power, a magic scepter with which a lady was to be protected, not a real weapon capable of producing noise and blood. After a moment of agonizing hesitation—agonizing for both of us—he opened his hand reluctantly and the revolver was mine.

I reversed it, hit the latch, swung out the cylinder, and shook the cartridges out onto the carpet. I closed the cylinder and took the weapon by the barrel once more, and held it out to him as if to return it. When he reached for it instinctively, quite bewildered now, I stepped in fast and clubbed him with the gun butt—and the hardest thing I've done in my life was to hold back just enough. I don't think I've ever wanted anything as badly as I wanted to smash the big stupid bastard's skull and then slug him a second time with all my strength just for personal satisfaction, as he went down. But I managed to hold back, and I stepped back to let him fall without hitting him again; but the frustrated desire was probably still on my face as I turned.

Anyway, Eleanor Brand looked suddenly startled by whatever sinister expression it was she saw, or maybe it was the sight of her amateur bodyguard lying limp on the floor. She tried to run for the door. Dropping the empty revolver, I caught her in three steps. I got the right grip and applied the right pressure at the right point, so that she sighed and went slack in my arms. I carried her to the big bed and dropped her there, not too gently. I got out the drug kit, pulled up her rumpled skirt a little farther and gave her a short dose of unconsciousness in the thigh, right through her nice sheer panty hose. Then I went back to the unconscious man on the floor and gave him the full four-hour prescription in the arm; and he was damned lucky I didn't use the stuff out of one of the other vials in the kit, the effects of which are permanent.

I didn't start to shake until they were both taken care of. Iron Man Helm.

CHAPTER 8

THERE had been enough in the needle I'd given Eleanor Brand to keep her under while I spread the materials from the attaché case on the window table—after setting aside the camera bag and purse—and glanced through them to see just what I'd been handed and how it all hung together, if it did. I was aware of her on the bed, of course, and of the fact—facts—that her hair had gotten badly disordered, her suit skirt wasn't quite where it should be; and that those all-in-one nylon nether garments aren't quite as visually impenetrable as they might be. However, having found adequate sexual release with a considerably more spectacular lady quite recently, I wasn't significantly aroused by this minor immodesty involving a young woman who wasn't exactly a sexpot. I decided that, even moderately disheveled as she was, lying there, she would prefer not to have a strange male person adjusting her clothes on a phony pretense of tender gentlemanly solicitude.

The man on the floor didn't bother me a bit. I could hear him breathing, apparently quite normally, but if his brains started leaking out his ears, it was just too damned bad. There would hardly be enough of them to damage the carpet; and he'd never miss them anyway since he'd made no use of them when he had them.

I was aware when she woke up. I was pleased by her first move as she very, very cautiously started working one foot around to where she could reach it and slip off her high-heeled shoe, the only weapon readily available to her. She obviously intended—second move—to leap out of bed and clobber the overconfident creep from behind as he sat at the table reading, sadly underestimating Ms. Eleanor

Brand. In this topsy-turvy world where policemen actually discourage law-abiding citizens from resisting or obstructing criminals as they go their illegal ways, where helpless hostages have even been known to fall abjectly in love with their terrorist captors, I found her healthy, hostile reaction quite refreshing.

"You'll never make it, Elly," I said, without turning my head.

I heard her sigh softly and relax and lie back on the bed. After a while she asked, "Warren. Is he all right?"

She was doing very well. After first exploring the possibility of immediate and effective action, just as she should have, she'd next demonstrated her concern, commendably, for her assistant or associate or lover or whatever the guy was to her.

"Is it important?" I asked.

There was a little pause, as if I'd shocked her. "He's a human being, Mr. Helm."

I shook my head. "The world is made up of friends and enemies, Elly. Friends are human. Enemies aren't. I'm a very friendly guy, normally. I love everybody until I'm given a reason not to. I might even have managed to love that muscle-bound creep, with an effort; but he saved me from straining my good nature to the limit by pointing a gun at me and making himself an enemy—not human. Open season. His choice, not mine."

"That's a terrible way to think!"

I kept on talking rather pedantically to give her time to get herself fully oriented after her short drugged sleep, "A colleague of mine once pointed out that in this new over-populated world we're eventually going to have to overhaul all our old humanitarian standards. We can't afford to preserve everybody any longer. There's simply not that much room. We've got to make this crowded world a pleasant place for those who are willing to behave in a reasonable and considerate manner toward each other by promptly disposing of those who aren't, one way or another. I do not consider pointing a gun at me reasonable and considerate behavior. I feel morally entitled—maybe

74

even morally obliged—to improve the world, at least my part of it, by eliminating the man who does it, since he's made it quite clear that he's willing to eliminate me."

"Warren wasn't *really* . . . I mean, he'd never have pulled that trigger, you know that."

"If he's not going to shoot it, what the hell is he doing with a gun in the first place? But in answer to your question, respiration seems to be normal. He should wake up in three hours or so." I waited. It was time for her to try to learn what I was planning for her; but she was even better than I'd thought. She'd thought it all through, and she'd decided not to demean herself by asking frightened questions that would obviously be answered in the normal course of events. She could wait and see. Okay. A bright and proud and gutsy little girl; and one it would be a pleasure to keep alive, if I could persuade her to let me. I said, "COLREGS. Rule 18-a-iv. Does it mean anything to you?"

She hesitated briefly, obviously tempted to ask if I'd slipped a cog or something; but she contented herself with a minimum answer, "No."

"Let me read you the pertinent section. Page 20, Coast Guard Publication CG-169, of May 1, 1977. Rule 18, responsibilities between vessels. Except where Rules 9, 10, and 13 otherwise require: a) A power-driven vessel underway shall keep out of the way of: (i) a vessel not under command; (ii) a vessel restricted in her ability to maneuver; (iii) a vessel engaged in fishing; (iv) a sailing vessel. Does that cast any light on the subject?"

"I don't even know what the subject is," she said. "I think you're crazy. What's this all about?"

I said, "I've been doing a little of your work for you, at least what I think is your current work. Somebody I asked, somebody fairly knowledgeable, considered this rule relevant and important. You can see no connection between this and anything you're doing?"

There was a little pause. "May I sit up?"

"You may even stand up, and pull your socks up and your skirt down, if you like," I said. "Hell, you may run

75

out that door and yell for help, if you like. But I don't think you will."

"Why in the world would you think that?"

"Because you're a newspaper woman," I said. "A reporter. A journalist, and I understand a pretty good one. And if I have some information you need—and I think I do—you're not going to run away from me screaming just because I'm a nasty man you've given some reason not to like you."

I turned to look at her at last. She was on her feet, and she'd rearranged her clothes tidily but her hair was still mussed from our recent struggle. She shoved it back from her face and said, "For better or worse, my piece on you is finished and in the production line. What information could you possibly have that could interest me now?"

"You can learn that best by looking at it."

She stood there for a moment longer, and rubbed the pressure point on her neck that was probably a bit sore, and scratched her thigh absently through her skirt. Realizing what she was doing, she looked down briefly, puzzled. She lifted her skirt unabashed to investigate, finding the tiny spot of blood on the smooth nylon underneath.

"What did you do, give me an injection?" she asked. "Oh, of course. I remember the stuff you use. Since I woke up, that would be your Injection A, wouldn't it?"

"Right," I said. "And remember, there are two others."

She said evenly, "Injection B, which kills instantly but leaves traces. Injection C, which takes a little longer but is undetectable in the body after death. Very unpleasant. Why should I remember them?"

"Give it some thought," I said. "I could have used either of them, hung a DO NOT DISTURB sign on the door, and been out of the country before you and your friend were discovered in here—if I'd come to kill you. But I think you'll admit that I've displayed no homicidal symptoms whatever. All I've done is deal in what I consider a commendably restrained fashion with a dangerous situation that you precipitated by sicking an armed man on me."

"I didn't know Warren was going to. . . . All right, I suppose I was responsible. I brought him along and I knew he'd arranged to get himself a gun. So your motives are pure and shining, Mr. Helm. So what?"

I said, "Hell, I had you at my mercy, wench, and I didn't do a damned thing to you except put you to sleep for a short cooling-off period that I hoped would enable us to talk sensibly. And if you were to comb your hair with a comb instead of your fingers, you'd look almost respectable."

But she came forward instead to kneel beside Warren Peterson, and checked his pulse in an almost-expert manner. I noticed that her watch was a businesslike stainless steel number with a sweep second hand, probably designed for nurses. Its efficient appearance seemed in character.

"You're sure he'll be all right?" she asked, looking up.

"I don't guarantee a thing," I said. "Beating people on the head is always risky. There could be damage to the brain, but considering the brain, it wouldn't be much of a loss, would it?"

She rose indignantly. "You're too damned callous to live!"

"No, just too damned callous to die," I said. "As I would have died if the stupid jerk had been brandishing a cocked automatic with the safety off instead of an uncocked revolver; and he probably doesn't even know the difference! And why should you go into hysterics about my reprehensible attitudes? You've already done a large amount of research on me, so they can't come as a terrible surprise. Go comb your hair and take a leak so we can talk like civilized people."

She started toward the bathroom, hesitated, and looked back, wryly curious. "How did you know?"

I grinned. "That you need to go? After what you've just been through, it would be abnormal if you didn't." I kept on talking as she disappeared into the bathroom, raising my voice to carry through the door she closed between us. "One thing. About your gofer. I'm not going through that again. Assuming that he does wake up healthy, as I think

77

he will, the next time he makes a hostile move I'll take him out for good. He's had all the breaks from me he's going to get. Keep him in line or lose him. Understand?"

She didn't answer. I had time to wonder if she was going to spoil her perfect record by locking herself in like a panicky TV-ingenue; then the john flushed in there, the door opened, and she emerged with her short hair showing the marks of the dampened comb she'd used to put it into order. She stopped in front of me and said, as if there had been no pause, "You're rather incredible, aren't you? You really mean it."

"First I was merely surprising and now I'm incredible," I said. "Goody, I seem to be gaining on it. Whatever it is."

"You're also a fairly brave man," she said. "To do what you did with that gun. Or *really* crazy."

I said, "I had no choice. Living in a world where a moron like that can wave a gun at me like that is not a prospect I care to contemplate. Much better to die courageously trying to remedy the situation. If it should come to that, which it didn't."

She studied me for a moment. "If that's the way you think, it's a wonder you've lived so long."

I shook my head. "No. The most dangerous thing in this business is to let somebody, anybody, get the impression that you're afraid to die. If that ever happens, they'll cut you down instantly. Whether I really am afraid or not doesn't matter. As long as I can kid everybody that I'm crazy enough—or brave enough if you want to be so flattering—to go for broke every time, regardless of consequences, I'll probably survive. Nobody really wants to go up against a guy like that. And maybe I'm not even kidding. They don't know, you don't know, and maybe I don't know, either."

She licked her lips. "Maybe I *should* try to revise that forthcoming article a little before it comes out, after all. I'm afraid I didn't get the picture quite right." She shrugged resignedly. "Of course, you never do, quite. What is it you want me to look at here?" But when I started to pull out a chair for her, she hesitated and looked down at the unconscious man on the floor. "Would you mind if we put him on the bed? I'd feel better."

I shrugged. "Whatever makes you happy. Grab the feet and we'll tuck him in pretty."

"This is really kind of weird," she said after we'd lugged him to the bed and laid him out neatly. "A weird interview or whatever you want to call it. What are you really trying to accomplish, Mr. Helm?"

"Hell, I'm bucking for a job, Miss Brand," I said, and went on before she could speak, "Isn't it obvious? I've carefully demonstrated that my intentions are not violent; I could easily have killed you and didn't. I've demonstrated that your current protection is totally incompetent as protection. Now if you'll come over here, I'll show you that I can even take better pictures than he can. Also that I have sources of information for your story that he can't begin to touch. In fact, I'm a very desirable employee in every way. Over here, please." Back at the table, I held a chair for her and sat down beside her. "Look this over, first."

She took the stapled-together tear sheets I handed her. " 'Kiruna Today,' " she read aloud. "By Louise Taylor. Photographs by Matthew Helm." She glanced at me. "Of course. I came across this old article before, when I was digging into your background. You were kind of a professional photographer at one time, weren't you?" She frowned at the pages. "Kiruna, that's the big mine way up north in Sweden, isn't it? Who's Louise Taylor?"

I grinned. "You're supposed to be examining those pix with a critical eye, not asking irrelevant questions about irrelevant dames. She was in your line of work for a while, but over in Europe. I heard she got married later. We only worked together that once."

It was a strange, almost eerie, business. I seemed to be stumbling over the past wherever I went. Bob Devine and Martha, Harriet Robinson, and now Lou Taylor. I found that I remembered her quite clearly; dark and rather thin and intense, with that odd hoarse voice she'd gotten as a result of a bullet fired from the same submachine gun that had killed her first husband, in the hands of a sentry who'd had special orders given him by a foreign gent I'd finally taken care of. Strangely, that had ended it between Lou and me. She hadn't liked the way I'd done it, even though it had avenged her husband and saved her life. Well, I hoped she'd found a very gentle man to marry who suited her better.

"Not bad," Eleanor Brand said judiciously, studying the photographs. "Not very imaginative, but competent."

"You mean he's fired and I'm hired."

She turned to look at me. "You *are* serious, aren't you?"

"Very serious."

"Tell me why."

"Figure it out," I said. I was glad I'd laid it all out once for Harriet; it made the words come more easily now. "Think about it hard and you'll realize that we can't afford to let you get hurt as long as that article series of yours is running. Your life is very precious to us, Elly. And we can't trust an incompetent beach boy like Junior to preserve it properly. So, Sir Matthew at your service, my lady."

She stared at me a moment longer, taking it in at last. Her laughter, when it came, was unrestrained and infectious.

"You mean," she gasped at last, "you mean you people feel compelled to protect·me because you're afraid that if I'm hurt somebody may think *you* . . . that's really kind of beautiful, isn't it? Ironical and beautiful."

I grinned. "Every five years at the crack of New Years', somebody discovers what a terrible outfit we are. I mean, in between lambasting the CIA and the FBI and various other dreadful, brutal, and snoopy government organizations. We're hardened to that; we'll survive it. Even an expert hatchet job like yours." I stopped grinning. "But if it were suggested that we actually go around murdering pretty young U.S. journalist-ladies to hide our sins from the great American public, that could make things really tough for us. And it's exactly what would be suggested if anything happened to you right now."

80

"But why should anybody *want* to hurt me? Except you?"

I shook my head sadly. "Elly, you're a big disappointment to me. Somebody or something is sinking ships out there, right? And you're investigating it, right? And people have gone down with those sinking ships, which adds murder on the high seas to all the other nautical crimes involved—and Miss Brand can see no reason why somebody might want to stop her from looking into it? If that's what you really think, you don't need a bodyguard, you need a keeper."

"I see." She licked her lips. "Not only surprising and incredible, but intelligent, too. How did you figure out what I was really working on? I thought I'd covered myself pretty well."

"That Bermuda Triangle nonsense?" I shook my head again. "It just wasn't your subject. You're not a cheap sensation-monger. Or let's say that while you're happy enough to monger a sensation, it's got to be a genuine sensation, like a bunch of wicked assassins lurking in the halls of government, not just a lot of phony supernatural and outer-space bullshit." I grimaced. "So I looked for another, more likely subject. And if I can figure it out, so can somebody else."

She said, "There have been no attempts on my life, sir. The worst that has happened is that a big goon forced his way into my hotel room and yanked my skirt up and stuck a big needle into my tender flesh; and Heaven only knows what he did to me while I was unconscious." She grinned. "And how the hell he got my panty hose back on so neatly afterward, I . . ."

She stopped abruptly; and something odd and frightened happened in her eyes. I could see that she was cringing inwardly at what she'd just said, wondering how she could have been so stupid and tasteless. Even though her comments might have been considered slightly off-color by some, it seemed like overreaction for a girl who'd been around; but I sensed that basically she found the whole subject of sex distasteful and regretted very much having brought it up. It was too bad. She was quite a girl, but I guess everybody has hangups somewhere.

She looked away from me quickly. "All right, say I'm trying to make sense of these sinkings, what have you got that's supposed to help me?"

I slid a fairly thick file folder toward her. "This is supposed to be pertinent, but I haven't made the connection yet." Actually, I hadn't had time to give it more than a glance. "I hope you can," I said.

She looked at the tab. "George Winfield Lorca. What in the world is he supposed to have to do with it?"

I knew a small cold feeling of apprehension. It seemed incredible that Harriet Robinson should have more information about these ship sinkings than the girl beside me, an experienced investigator who'd been studying them carefully. Or perhaps it was not so incredible. Cap'n Hattie operated her boat daily in a busy shipping area off some islands that had once been a hotbed of piracy and still teemed with drug smugglers and other latter-day buccaneer types. She was known to be a lady who made a point of keeping her mouth shut. Furthermore, I reminded myself, she was a lady with a secret, who might be vulnerable to pressure; and she'd been in a disturbed and disturbing mental state when I'd seen her, depressed and uncertain and insecure, not the Harriet Robinson I'd known.

I said, "You haven't come across this name at all in your investigations?"

Eleanor shook her head. "I know who he is, of course. As a matter of fact, I did a piece on him just before the last election."

I thought irritably that everybody seemed to know who George Winfield Lorca was, of course; everybody but me. But I had no time to say it. The telephone rang. Eleanor Brand picked it up, listened, looked a bit surprised, and held it out to me. I took it and identified myself.

"Priority Red," said a woman's voice I recognized. I'd never met the woman who went with the voice; but she'd given me instructions before, here in Nassau. "Priority Red. Fred's cab is waiting for you at the door. There's a plane warming up on the field. All clearances have been waived. Priority Red. Execute."

Fun and games. All these standby people must have been waiting eagerly for years for the chance to show how well they could execute a red priority mission, which means drop everything and don't ask questions, just *go*. Now they felt like real secret agents.

All I felt was fear. After enough years in the business, you don't ask yourself where you're going on a hurry-up emergency deal like that, or why you're going there, because you'll be told soon enough, and the answer is never good.

CHAPTER 9

NOT the Keys, I thought, please not the Keys.

After the breathless telephone summons, the actual operation had turned out to be fairly undramatic. In a movie, of course, they'd have had the latest needle-nosed jet fighter waiting for me on the strip, and they'd have suited and helmeted me on the run, practically, and strapped me in and clapped down the canopy or however they do it, and I'd have hit the wild blue yonder with after-burners screaming, or whatever the hell it is that makes all that racket. The catch is that I don't know what buttons to push to make those things go; and being less than a couple of hundred miles from the U.S. I didn't need a thousand-knot airplane to get me back there. What I got was some kind of an executive four-place Cessna with two nice old-fashioned propellers, a middle-aged pilot with a bushy moustache, and a cruising speed of about one-sixty, judging by my passenger's-eye view of the dials.

Not the Keys, I thought. How about it, Up There? Miami or Fort Lauderdale or Saint Augustine, okay; but please not the Keys.

I didn't think it out beyond that. I could have figured it out all right, why I didn't want to go there, why I didn't want to find myself being dragged back there hastily under a hot priority red indicating that something drastic had happened there, something that concerned me, but why crowd it? If I didn't bring it out into the open and admit the possibility existed, maybe it would go away. I couldn't read the compass clearly from where I sat, so I watched the sun instead—we had a nice clear day for flying. A little past noon would put the sun a little past south; and it steadied just forward of the port beam or whatever you call it in an airplane. Course west or a little south of west. So we were heading too far south for Augustine or Palm Beach or Lauderdale; but it could still be Miami, I told myself. I didn't have the geography that clearly in mind.

I watched the green-green islands of the Bahamas pass below, and the blue-green water of the endless shallows of the Great Bahama Bank, and the blue-blue water of the deep Gulf Stream. Then land again, and a dome of pollution-haze well off to starboard that was Miami, and we were flying down along the Keys on a closing course. Well, I've never had much luck with prayer. I should either practice it harder or give it up altogether, I guess.

The moustached gent who was driving the plane had nothing to say and neither had I. He had his thoughts, no doubt, and I had mine. He brought us in to the Marathon strip from seaward in a sweeping curve and put us down very gently and expertly. Brent, our young man in Miami, was there with some guy from customs or immigration or both, who didn't give a damn about me, he had the word on me, but he felt obliged to do his stuff with the pilot and plane. I told the pilot goodbye and thanks and we left them to it.

Brent hadn't changed much since the last time he'd come out of his standby Miami existence, whatever it was, to give us a hand—the last time I knew about, that is. He was a few years older now, of course, we all were, but he was still a compact youthful-looking redhead with crisp curly hair and sideburns, who kept himself in good shape.

I'd gathered that his specialty was the underwater stuff with the mask and fins but he was good with boats, too. He was wearing jeans and a T-shirt. He didn't tell me anything and I didn't ask. I knew approximately what I was here for now, I knew what it pretty well had to be, to necessitate my being brought here, only the details were lacking; and talking about it wouldn't help it any. It was lousy and it was going to stay lousy, talk or no talk.

We got into Brent's car—at least I assumed it was his, since it looked like private transportation—one of the sporty Datsuns designated by a number ending in Z. He drove us along the island and over to a house, mostly glass, on a man-made inlet on the ocean side, one of the concrete-lined canals that have taken over most of coastal Florida. You dig a ditch and use what you get out of it to fill in the sea marsh on either side, carefully ignoring the screams of the ecologists. Instant waterfront property. In the canal was a dock and at the dock was a boat that was more like it. The movies would have loved it, a long and rakish speedster with a small padded cockpit and an endless deck aft with big hatches hinting at monstrous power plants lurking underneath.

"Anybody'd think we were in a hurry," Brent said. "They tell me it'll do over sixty, which is moving for a boat. I'll take their word for it."

I didn't offer to help with the docklines. He knew what he was doing and I didn't, really. I can handle simple powerboats in an amateurish fashion, but I don't know the stylish way of doing the nautical bit, so mostly I just leave it alone if I can manage without seeming pointedly unhelpful. I just parked myself in the cockpit, knowing enough to stand up and get a good grip on the bar they give you to hang onto. At speed, those things will break your back coming off a wave if they catch you sitting, and I didn't have too much faith in Brent's leisurely attitude. Horsepower is almost always addictive. But he took her out very gently, down the canal and out the channel between the mangrove islands beyond. Reaching open water he just put her up on plane and let her run easily, setting no records. I got myself oriented. We were heading back up the Keys with the sun behind us, still well up in the sky; and it had already been one of the longer days of my life.

It wasn't too long before Brent spun the wheel and we cut through some pretty shallow water past the end of a sandy key and there was the boat I'd been hoping not to see. It told me that my subconscious had been right all along, but that was no help at all, being right.

"Bonefish Harbor," Brent said. "One of the better anchorages along this coast."

Queenfisher was anchored in the little bay, lying very still with the anchor rope showing no strain and the tall tuna tower casting broken reflections in the slightly rippled water. A man sat in the cockpit, fishing. At least he was holding a fishing rod and dangling something in the water. He reeled in his line and laid the rod aside and fended us off as we slid alongside. We climbed aboard the larger boat and left him to secure the smaller one.

"Where?" I asked. It was a silly question. A forty-footer isn't all that big.

"Up forward," Brent said. "Go on. I'll wait out here."

I entered the familiar deckhouse. It was spotless and tidy except for a sheet of paper on the table on which I'd served us breakfast yesterday morning, apparently a letter, held down by a small green box of cartridges—.22 Long Rifle Hollowpoint. Remington, if it matters. Winchester-Western uses yellow. Federal uses red. I didn't stop to read the letter. It could wait.

She was in the double berth forward. She'd done it nicely, as nicely as such a thing can be done. She'd fixed her hair and colored her lips discreetly and even done something to her eyes, although even as a fashionable lady up north she'd never been one for a lot of eye makeup. She'd put on her pretty nightgown, the one I'd seen; and she'd gotten into the big bunk and done it from the far side, using a quick-expanding little hollowpoint bullet so there would be no chance of total penetration, an ugly exit wound and a big mess in her boat. Or maybe that was just the ammunition she'd happened to have handy, but I didn't think so. She'd never been one to leave things to chance. At first glance she seemed to be just lying there peacefully asleep with the .22 Colt Woodsman on the pillow beside her. There was very little blood.

One of the longest days of my life and one of the worst; I should have sensed how terribly vulnerable she was and taken much greater precautions. But there were a few things to be done before I could stop and think—feel—just how bad it really was. I examined the gun as carefully as I could without disturbing it, and there was nothing wrong that I could see. She was right-handed, I remembered; and she had used her right hand here. And it was right for her, as right as such a thing can ever be. Nobody setting it up could possibly have gotten it so right: gown, makeup, hair, everything. There were no jarring discrepancies, there were no psychological impossibilities, there was nothing out of character here. It was her goddamned life. She would live it as long as it was worth living, and then she would put an end to it cleanly, and to hell with you and your moral or religious scruples, which she'd thank you to keep to yourself.

I went back up into the deckhouse and read the letter. It was very short. Actually it was a carbon copy of a letter— to the States Attorney of the State of Maryland, Annapolis, Anne Arundel County, Maryland. Be advised that the fugitive Mrs. Robin Rosten wanted for conspiracy to commit etc., etc., is presently residing in Marathon, Florida, under the name Harriet Robinson. Signed, Concerned Citizen. Across the top had been written blackly with a felt-tipped pen: ORIGINAL MAILED THIS DATE. And yesterday's date.

I wondered how many times she had read it before making the decision, but that was stupid. She would have made that decision long ago. Probably she had made up her mind from the start that she would never submit to the indignity of being dragged in handcuffs back to her former home and friends for a lurid trial even if, particularly now after so many years, there might be some question about the outcome. Once in the hands of the law, she would have lost her freedom of choice; and it was a risk she could not take.

I don't intend to go to prison, my dear, she had told me, *I couldn't endure that.* She had visualized clearly the grimy humiliations and degradations to which she would be subjected there. She had known that, the privileged kind of person she had once been, the protected way she had been brought up—accustomed to receiving respect and consideration and courtesy from everyone—she could not possibly survive intact the treatment that would be visited upon her in such a place. The exile years had tempered her to some extent, but not, she knew, enough. Prison would either kill her—in which case why not do it decently now and get it over with?—or, worse, it would simply break her, finally and completely. One day she would wander out of there fully, at liberty again but uncaring, a gray shell of a woman, beaten and prideless; and that could not be allowed.

I went back down and stood by her for a while. She had, of course, been born out of her time as the saying goes. She should have been up on the ramparts in velvet gown and wimple, or whatever they wore back then, calmly supervising the preparation of the boiling oil with which she would greet the attacking miscreants when the dumb gents in the iron pants failed to keep them off the castle walls. The fierce, undisciplined pride that had driven her to her ruinous rebellion against authority in this century would have done her no great harm back then; it was expected of people like her in those days. Some gesture was needed, and I touched her hair lightly—goodbye, Milady—and got the hell out of there.

"Tell me," I said to Brent, in the cockpit.

Brent gestured to the other man. "This is Marco. He'll tell you."

Marco was dark-faced and black-haired, with a big nose. "I kept an eye on her as ordered. She had a visitor in the afternoon. Not a visitor, just Benny with a letter or something for her. Maybe that one in there."

"Benny?"

Brent said, "Benjamin Crowe. Works around the marinas. Not too bright. I have the details."

"Go on," I said to Marco.

"After Benny had gone, about half an hour after, she took her boat out. I had my own boat ready with the boy aboard—he's waiting around the point to pick me up now. Didn't want too many boats cluttering up this anchorage, attracting attention. Anyway, she took this one out. No customers. Alone. Way out into the Stream, no land in sight. Stopped and watched a school of dolphins. Seemed to be just playing around out there with the boat. Run a little and drift, just sitting up there on the bridge, looking around. Came back in and anchored here about sunset. Had a drink in the cockpit, just the one that I could see, ate, worked on the boat. Engines, too. Looked like she wanted to get it all in good shape for something. Took a short swim in the dark, showered; calm night, I could hear it running across the water. Then sat in the cockpit, just sat there. All night, what was left of it. Sunrise, she watched the birds a little, they fly good here in the early morning. Went below. Half an hour. Small noise, like a stick breaking; but I know a .22 when I hear it. Went aboard, saw her, made my report. That's it." He looked at me for a moment and made a defeated gesture. "Sorry. Don't know what I could have done to stop it."

"There's no blame," I said. That wasn't quite true, of course; but any blame there was, was mine.

"Nobody came near her," he said. "I would have moved in, on that."

"I know," I said. "She had her mind made up. She was just saying goodbye to her friends out here on the water. To everything out here."

Brent looked at me. "You're satisfied?"

"I'm satisfied," I said. It wasn't the best possible way to put it, you could hardly call it satisfactory, but I knew what he meant.

"You can get the police on it now," Brent said to Marco, and to me, "Let's go."

Try that on your J. Edgar Hoover some time, or whoever's taking his place over there this week. A priority mission laid on just to let an agent say a final goodbye to a lady with whom he'd spent the night. So he keeps his people and they don't wander off to the big glamor agencies where they'd be docked just for taking time off to attend the funeral. Of course there was more to it than that. There had been a small debt. I'd just kept his daughter from getting herself, and maybe him and us, into trouble.

And then, of course, there was the simple fact that he runs us direct from Washington without any intermediate field representatives, case officers, controls, or whatever the jargon is; and he knows us. He would have known that without this, I wouldn't have been much use to him for a while. I wouldn't have accepted suicide if I hadn't been allowed to see it. I'd have had to get to work and dispel all doubts; and it would have taken time and might have caused trouble. Because—and he would have known this, too—there was guilt involved here as well as sentiment. After all, right or wrong, justified or unjustified, I was the one who had driven her into exile as she'd called it; and I was probably the one who'd brought this last trouble to her, or at least activated a trouble she'd already had.

I don't want to . . . help, she'd said when I told her what I needed to know, *I don't want to make anybody mad.*

But driven by her own stiff pride she had helped, and I had let her, and somebody had got mad, or scared. Somebody who'd known her well enough to know how she'd react to that letter. Somebody who had just made a serious error. Killing her would have been bad, but it's a commodity in which I deal myself upon occasion, so I don't feel entitled to take a high moral stand on the subject. But breaking her with the one threat she really feared, forcing her to do it to herself, that was not acceptable. I wondered if the man who had done it to her now considered himself safe, having done it so cleverly without getting, as he thought, any blood on his hands. But he would have been much better off with the straightforward murder, if he felt she had to die. Now he would never be safe

90

again, because when you do it like that, unacceptably, there will always be somebody coming after you.

Somebody like me.

CHAPTER 10

BUT first there was an obligation to be discharged and a job to be done. The fact that Mac had gone to considerable trouble and expense to bring me here and let me see it for myself and satisfy myself that it was genuine, meant that I was now obliged to concentrate on the mission at hand, briefly interrupted for morale and information purposes. I could play Nemesis on my own time, later. Anyway, I wouldn't help a dead woman much by letting a live one get killed; and there was even a possibility that the job of keeping Eleanor Brand unharmed would lead me, in the line of duty, straight to the man I wanted, which would certainly be the most convenient way of doing it.

"Have I still got a plane?" I asked Brent as we cruised easily back down the coast in the sharp-nosed speedster.

"Standing by. You want to get back to the Bahamas right away?"

He sounded, not exactly surprised, but a little relieved. I realized that Mac must have discussed with him over the phone my possible reactions to Harriet's suicide; this was obviously the preferred one. I wondered what Brent's instructions had called upon him to do if I'd announced my intention of staying here and, for instance, beating hell out of a guy named Benny to learn from whom he'd gotten the envelope he'd delivered to *Queenfisher* the previous afternoon. But that would have been a waste of effort. If the man I wanted was stupid enough to be traced so easily, I'd have no trouble catching up with him later, when I had time to put my mind to it. I didn't think it was going to be that simple.

I said, "I asked Fred to mind the store while I was gone, but I don't like leaving him alone too long."

"Fred's a good man," Brent said. I liked him for saying it, knowing as he must that Fred and I hadn't always gotten along as well as we might. It showed he wasn't intimidated by my stratospheric seniority.

"I know," I said, "he's competent enough, but this isn't really his line of work. And that blond pistol-packing gofer Brand has with her, Peterson, is strictly nothing." I glanced aft, but *Queenfisher* was no longer visible astern. "You'll see that . . . everything is taken care of, won't you?"

He nodded. "What about family?"

I said, "Maybe. They've been thinking she drowned years ago, but if that letter is made public they may want to do something. Or maybe not. Just so it's done right by somebody." I seemed to be involved with a lot of funerals lately. Well, just two, but that's a lot when the people being buried are people you'd liked.

Brent nodded. After a moment he said, "I'll check out Benjamin Crowe, but I doubt that'll get us very far. Our man's probably too smart to trip himself up that way; and the police will grill Benny about the letter anyway."

"That's my feeling." I drew a long breath and glanced at him, patting the instrument cowling in front of me. "Look, can we thrash this thing a bit?"

He grinned. "I thought you'd never ask. Buckle up or she'll toss you in the drink." When we had fastened the straps, he said, "Okay, you're the throttle man, go for it."

I reached for the knobbed levers and eased them forward. He'd been handling them with one hand, steering with the other, but you don't work wheel and throttles simultaneously when one of those things really starts to go; each is a full-time job. Soon the big mills aft were talking loudly, then roaring, then screaming. Brent cut out of the coastal channel known as Hawk Channel and over the reef out into the violet-blue Gulf Stream, where a southeast wind was kicking up a chop. I had to watch the seas coming at us and play the throttles accordingly; and there was no more time for regret or guilt. Finally I missed one badly, she came off the wave flying and landed with a crash that would certainly have cracked a vertebra or two if anybody'd been sitting down, unable to cushion the shock with the knees.

She stuck her nose right through the next one and a tidal wave sluiced down the foredeck and exploded against the rudimentary windshield, half-drowning us both. I pulled the levers back hastily and we stood there laughing. It had been a release of sorts and, having gotten rid of something black and violent, I probably wouldn't kill the next clumsy sonofabitch who jostled me on the street.

"Can you keep after it?" I asked Brent later as we were driving away from the glass house with the dock, leaving the boat as we'd found it. When he glanced at me questioningly I said, "After all, this is supposed to be just spare-time stuff for you, isn't it? You've got other things to do."

He grinned. "Actually, to answer the question you were so careful not to ask, I'm a lawyer. Low man in the office, bucking for a partnership; but they know I have a mysterious sideline connected with law-enforcement that takes me away occasionally. They don't mind. A little practical experience is good for the image, and police and government connections don't hurt the office, either." He glanced at me, and grinned again. "And to answer another question you didn't ask, like how did a nice girl like you etc., etc., well, the way it happened was, I did some work for a guy when I was just out of law school. Legal work, but it led me into some rougher places than it was supposed to. He really should have got some rent-a-cops on it, but he wanted it kept very quiet, just between the two of us; and I guess he was satisfied with the way I finally worked it out by myself. Apparently he mentioned me to somebody he knew in Washington and one evening I got a phone call. . . . Well, you know how it goes."

As a matter of fact, I didn't know how it went. I'd

never had the standby experience; I'd come up by a different route, full-time all the way. But on our agency budget we can't afford to keep permanent employees stationed all over the world like those well-heeled people out in Langley; and I suppose it brings a little excitement and money into the lives of the conventional citizens, carefully screened, who contract to keep themselves available to help the mysterious stranger in black with the tied-down guns when he moves in to clean up the town.

Brent seemed to be a pretty high-class specimen of the standby breed, I reflected; more than just an underground switchboard operator. He'd handled a boat for us at least once that I knew of, when the navigation had been very tricky. Anyway, I always have more faith in those who are clearly in it just for the kicks with maybe some thought for the fact that they could be helping their country, than in those who do it strictly for the cash.

"As for your original question," Brent said. "I knew the lady too, remember? I don't like what was done to her, either. What do you want me to work on?"

"First, I want you to check the pay phone on the sea wall near her boat, just opposite the marina restaurant," I said. "Get somebody to look for bugs who knows how; let's hope there hasn't been time enough for it to be removed. I doubt she went out of her way to tell anybody she'd spilled the beans, so how did they know? She had a plug-in phone on her boat, but I was careful to use the booth when I called you—at least I thought I was being careful. But maybe somebody was even more careful and bugged both instruments, just to know what she was up to. *And* her stupid goddamned guests."

Brent said, "I think I know a local man who can handle that. What else?"

I shook my head ruefully. "I can't give you a good directive. I'd say boats and strangers. Did she stumble on something peculiar out on the water and was she seen doing it? Did she notice somebody hanging around who didn't fit and get curious? I don't know. It doesn't agree with her policy of minding her own business; but if she felt herself threatened in some way, maybe . . . damn it, *some-how* she got hold of the information she gave me; and the people involved knew she had it. They checked on her and learned about her hidden past and used it to keep her quiet."

"Maybe," Brent said, "but that's a lot of guessing, isn't it?"

I shook my head again, irritably. "It's got to be like that. She was a changed woman, amigo, so what had changed her? They leaned on her and it killed her a little to go along with them, but she couldn't bear the thought of the alternative. But it made her feel less than a woman, it destroyed things for her, everything she'd built up here, her whole new identity. The hard and competent Captain Harriet Robinson, what a phony! She lost faith in herself, learning that she could be blackmailed like that; that she wasn't strong enough to tell them to publish and be damned. That wasn't the proud, brave picture of herself she'd carried all her life; and then I came along—a man out of her past—and saw how much she'd been, well, damaged by yielding to their threats. She realized how she looked to me now, timid and insecure, and that was more than she could stand. So she got mad and blew the whistle on them and to hell with the consequences. But what did she see she wasn't supposed to? Whom did she see who didn't want to be seen?"

Brent said, "Boats and strangers. I'll check it out as well as I can."

I said, "Watch your back. Somebody could be prepared to fire off more than correspondence and carbon copies thereof, if you know what I mean." I grinned. "This is kind of funny work for a legal eagle."

"Listen to who's talking. It's even funnier work for an ex-camera-jockey," Brent said. "Incidentally, I got you a basic photo outfit; it's in the plane. Anything I forgot, you can pick up in Nassau, probably cheaper."

I said, "You'll make some woman a damned fine husband, or have you already? No, that's right, you said you weren't married."

He shook his head. "Would I be sticking my neck out for a bunch of spooks if I had a family to think of?"

"Well, watch that neck," I said, wishing I could send him out to the ranch in Arizona for a quick course of training. He was very good material, but there were too many things he didn't know that could get him killed.

A couple of hours later, with darkness falling, the taciturn moustached pilot set me down on Providence Island light as a feather, and I headed for a taxi to take me in to Nassau. I was halfway there before I realized that I still didn't know his name, but maybe he wanted it that way. They often do, in this business.

CHAPTER 11

IT was just as well that I was tired and preoccupied and therefore a bit slow, because when I let myself into my room with my key, the light was on and an unfamiliar black gentleman in shirt-sleeves was pouring liquor into two glasses on the dresser. An unfamiliar black lady was emerging from the bathroom wearing jeweled, glittering evening sandals with high slim heels, and dark panty hose. She was quite a handsome lady. Her naked breasts were magnificent and so was her poise as she reached calmly for a not very opaque red negligee thrown over the back of a nearby chair.

"And who might you be?" she asked, wrapping the thin bright garment about her without haste.

"Get the hell out of here," said the man.

I glanced at the key I'd carried all day, and at the door. The numbers matched. "I was under the impression this was my room," I said.

"Suppose you go down to the desk and get your impressions corrected," said the handsome black lady.

"Yes, ma'am," I said. "I will certainly do that. My apologies."

"Accepted," she said. "Conditionally, contingent upon a speedy withdrawal."

"Yes, ma'am," I said.

Back in the corridor, I pulled the door shut behind me and stood there for a moment breathing deeply, because it had been too damned close. If the woman hadn't come out of the bathroom in that disarming state of undress, if the man had been off to the side instead of straight in front where I could see him clearly, and if he had made a hasty move as he might well have done, I could not have helped reacting violently to a strange and apparently hostile character coming for me in a hotel room I knew to be mine. We don't survive by waiting for formal introductions under such circumstances. I settled the Smith and Wesson, that I'd half drawn, back where it belonged, and grinned. She certainly was a spectacular person with a fine command of the English language. As I headed back toward the elevators, Fred came hurrying toward me, breathless.

"Damn, I had one of the other drivers stationed to catch you at the front door and head you off while I took a phone call, but he must have blinked," he said.

Strangely, I didn't resent the goof, although it could have had serious consequences. People make honest mistakes and to hell with it; it's being almost killed for their highfaluting humanitarian impuses—as I'd once almost been killed for one of Fred's, involving a pretty little girl he couldn't bear to shoot, even though she was about to kill me. That gets a bit trying.

"What goes on?" I asked. "Who called?"

"Brent was calling from Marathon," Fred said. "I'm to tell you that you were right about the phone booth, whatever that means. The shipboard phone had received the same treatment, he said."

I thought that over without pleasure. What it meant was that I was the one who'd carelessly tipped off the adversary

97

about what Harriet had told me, which wasn't nice to think about, not nice at all. The fact that I hadn't realized that I'd entered a combat zone where wartime precautions applied was absolutely no excuse; we're supposed to anticipate things like that. And the fact that the pay telephone near *Queenfisher* had been bugged, as well as the instrument on the boat itself, meant that I was up against somebody pretty thorough. It seemed hardly likely that I'd make it unless I hauled up my socks and started operating in a careful and professional manner for a change.

"Okay, thanks," I said. "And what's the story on my hotel room? I just took a very expert reaming from a lovely lady in *deshabille*, as the French call it—or is it *dishabille*? —who seemed to think she and her husband, if that's what he was, had established rights to the premises in some way."

"Yes, I'm sorry," Fred said. "They must have rented the room right after I moved you to four-oh-seven in accordance with instructions from our subject. She's waiting for you in the dining room. When the pilot called to report you were taking off from Marathon, I let her know you were on your way and mentioned a tentative ETA. She's one or two ahead of you by now." He reached out for the camera case I was carrying. "Suppose I take this and put it into your new room for you, so you can get right down there? She's not a patient lady. I'll leave the key at the desk for you."

"Sure," I said. "Thanks, and you might as well turn in this one, too." I gave him the key I'd just used, or misused, with some regrets; it had not been an altogether uninteresting experience. I said, "And this time let's set some indicators, both doors, bottom; I guess it's time to start being careful. You know the routine. Any hostile activity noted?"

He shook his head. "Calm as summer."

"To hell with that," I said. "That's hurricane season around here, isn't it?"

When I entered the dining room, Eleanor Brand was holding down a table for two along the wall. She was wearing a short-sleeved white silk dress with big black buttons that marched down the front as far as I could see from the soft open shirt-like collar. She sat there smoking a cigarette and making notes on a pad in front of her and frowning thoughtfully at what she had written. Her hair was neat and businesslike and the cool white silk of the dress made her skin look smooth and warm. She looked up as I stopped at the table, and made a show of glancing at the stainless watch she still wore.

"Punctuality is part of the job, Mr. Helm," she said with straight-faced severity. "You may sit down. . . . But I was informed that you would arrive half an hour ago, and laid my dinner plans accordingly. You have kept me waiting, a heinous crime."

"Sorry, ma'am." I spoke with equal formality as I seated myself facing her. "Headwinds, you know. Do I gather that I may consider myself employed, ma'am?"

She grinned abruptly. It was a big grin I hadn't seen before and it lit up her entire face. It couldn't make her beautiful, but she certainly wasn't unattractive.

"Yes, damn you," she said, "and, as a matter of fact, I'm very glad to see you. You really know how to spook a girl. I've been expecting a bullet in the back all day. Your man Fred is nice and conscientious, but he isn't mean-looking enough to inspire real confidence."

I laughed. "Am I supposed to take that as a compliment?"

She laughed also, and said, "I hope you don't mind that we moved you in next door to me. I thought, since you were going to play bodyguard, that was what you'd want."

"It's fine," I said, "but what happened to the previous incumbent?"

Her expressive mouth went suddenly thin and firm. "Let's not talk about that," she said; and I was rather sorry for Warren Peterson, who'd first been badly humiliated by me and then, obviously, sent packing by the girl facing me without, I had a hunch, too many concessions to diplomacy. I guess my feelings showed on my face because she felt obliged to add, rather stiffly, "Mr. Peterson seemed to be slightly confused about the nature of our relationship. I had to . . . to straighten him out." She looked at me hard. "Which brings us, Mr. Helm, to certain conditions governing your employment."

She was cute as a monkey when she grinned, but that moment was past; and I reminded myself that I already had reason to know that this was a fairly ruthless and cold-blooded little girl.

I said, "Don't worry about it, Elly. I won't presume upon our nonexistent friendship, if that's what you're driving at."

She sat perfectly still for a moment, her eyes steady on my face. "ESP, too?" she murmured.

I said, "My job is to keep you alive and, incidentally, take some pictures for you. For that, friendship, or any other form of emotional involvement, is not required. Satisfactory?"

She frowned slightly. "Of course, but now you're mad at me. Why?"

I said, "The poor dumb sonofabitch was doing his level best for you with a pistol he didn't even know how to handle. He thought he was going up against a bunch of murderous government characters super-trained in the arts of killing, him and his silly little .38; but he was willing to give it his best shot, to protect you, because he liked you." I grimaced. "I saw what you did to one of your good friends out west; now I've seen you deal with another. Don't worry, Elly, the last thing I want is your goddamned friendship. It doesn't seem to be a very rewarding relationship."

Her face had paled. Her hazel eyes were still fixed on my face. I waited for an angry outburst, but it did not come. Instead I saw her relax slowly. She said a strange and totally unexpected thing.

She said, "I'm sorry. You've had a bad day, haven't you? I should have realized."

It startled me, and scared me a little. There was much more woman here than met the eye. I said harshly, "We should get along just fine, Elly. I'm hard on my friends, too. I've just come from one. Somebody sent her a message she couldn't bear, so she put on her prettiest nightie and got into bed and fired a bullet into her brain. And I knew she was in trouble; and if I'd just taken a few more simple precautions. . . . Ah, to hell with it!" I cleared my throat. "So we seem to have a lot in common, everything except drinks. Does only the management drink around here and not the hired help?"

"It's coming," she said, and suddenly a waiter was placing a stemmed glass in front of me although nobody'd given the order; apparently it had been prearranged. She smiled faintly at my expression. "Martini, right? I'm the girl who wrote an article about you, remember?"

I took a stiff slug and drew a long breath. "Phew! That helps!" I looked at her across the table, feeling a little ashamed of myself. Warren Peterson's problems were his own, after all; and she was not to blame for mine. I said, "Sorry. Like you said, a bad day."

"We all have them." She hesitated. "Is it . . . relevant? Am I allowed to ask about it?"

I told her about it; although it got a little awkward, trying to explain to this strange young lady the long and complex relationship that had existed between Harriet and me. It was a relief to get away from such intimate matters and try out on her the theories I'd already expounded to Brent in Marathon.

"So you think she was driven to suicide to keep her quiet," Eleanor said at last.

"Something like that," I said. "But since she'd already spilled some of the beans, perhaps most of them, it was also a matter of punishment. And I wouldn't be a bit surprised if our man got some mean satisfaction out of taking the fine lady down a peg—taking her all the way down to the bottom, in fact, to prison or to death. So we begin to get a picture of an arrogant man who expects to be obeyed, uses blackmail to see that he is, and retaliates savagely when he isn't; a man who's also small-minded enough to resent any indication of superiority—that lady-of-the-manor manner you referred to."

"Small-minded," she said. "Thanks a lot."

101

"Present company excepted, of course," I said.

"Of course," she said dryly. "What else do you think Captain Robinson could have told you if she'd lived?"

I said, "What she gave me was pretty much the meat of what she had to tell: who and why. But she could have speeded things up for us quite a bit, probably, by telling us exactly what it meant, how she'd found it out and perhaps even where to look for confirmation. The man was obviously buying time when he silenced her, or got her to silence herself. He didn't expect to achieve perfect security; he'd already lost that."

"Buying time for what?" Eleanor asked.

I said, "Time enough to kill me, and now you, before we can take what Harriet told me any further. But I see no reason why we should help him out by voluntarily starving ourselves to death. . . ."

The food arrived within a reasonable time and was reasonably edible. Afterward, well fed and comfortably relaxed for the first time since I'd caught the plane from Miami that morning—I seemed to have been shuttling between the U.S. and the Bahamas all day—I tasted my cognac appreciatively and watched Eleanor take out a fresh cigarette.

"You don't mind?" she asked, startling me a little as I held a hotel match for her. I guess I'm way behind the times, still living in the era when only the gentlemen apologized when they broke out the smokes.

"Puff away," I said. "As far as I'm concerned, your lungs are your own business; and in my line of work, I don't really expect that when I expire it will be from a little smoke drifting across the table from somebody else's cigarette."

She laughed. "Well, you're a welcome relief after all the anti-emphysema crusaders. Warren was forever trying to save me from myself." She drew a long breath. "But enough stalling. Now that we're well fed and pleasantly alcoholated, we'd better get down to business."

I said, "Yes, do tell me all you know about George Winfield Lorca."

CHAPTER 12

GEORGE Winfield Lorca, she told me, was a re-formed character. He made no bones about the fact that he had once been an evil man, very evil; but he had seen the light of righteousness—although he would admit wryly that said light had to be kind of smashed over his head before he would accept it. In other words, he'd had a brush with death that had left him with a dramatic scar; there had been a long and terrible time when nobody thought—including George Winfield Lorca to the extent that he was then capable of thinking at all—that he would ever leave his hospital bed; or that if he did leave he could ever move, or be moved, any farther than the nearest institution providing special care for people who were badly damaged upstairs and incapable of caring for themselves. But while he was a hard-nosed guy who didn't believe in mystical experiences, he had to admit that something had happened to him in that hospital bed that he could not explain: the way out of the darkness had been shown to him. Later he had paid his debt—he was a man who always paid his debts—by dismissing his wicked companions and mending his wicked ways.

"Of course he could afford it," Eleanor said dryly. "He'd made a pretty damned good pile working for the syndicate; the corporation as they sometimes call it. And after being shot in the head like that—well, a man with a half-paralyzed arm, not to mention a slight speech impediment is pretty well disqualified from the strong-arm business that used to be his specialty. But you've got to hand it to him. He fought like hell to come back from the limbo into

103

which that bullet had sent him; and he made it. And it gave him a good excuse to pull out of the rackets and spend more time with the wife and kids—well, kid. Usually they don't get to retire comfortably until the boys are good and ready to let them go."

She reached for another cigarette and I started to do my gentleman bit with the matches; but she lit it quickly, nervously, from the butt of the first, girl-reporter fashion, movie version, stubbing out the butt in the glass ashtray. Some uneasy questions were stirring in my mind. It was far-fetched, but I'd once encountered a high-class syndicate muscle gent who'd got shot in the head; and although his name, the name he'd been going under at the time, had not been Lorca, it had been Spanish, not usual in an organization originally imported from Siciliy. But the man I was thinking of was dead, or was he?

Eleanor was speaking again before I could frame my question. She said, "What some of us media geniuses are wondering, Matt, is now that he's entered politics. . . . Well, it seems to us the boys were just a little too ready to let him go, bad arm or no bad arm. And then they were just a little too tolerant of all the mean things he said about them during the recent campaign. Hell, they must know things about him they could have used to keep him quiet. He spent a good many years in a rough business; and repentance, even sincere repentance—if it is sincere—does not confer legal immunity. And as I said, he has a wife and child, who aren't bulletproof. Lorca's ex-associates aren't known for being bashful about putting the pressure on somebody who talks out of turn. But Mr. Lorca's cars never blow up when he turns the keys. His daughter goes driving and riding and sailing just like any normal girl— well, there was a bit of an uproar there for a few days, at one point, but it turned out that the kid had simply managed to capsize her boat in a storm while out cruising with a friend; she was picked up after drifting around for a while in a life raft. You can believe it was checked out, and it checked. And Mrs. Lorca visits the bank and the beauty parlor without a bodyguard in attendance, just as if her husband hadn't been bad-mouthing his former colleagues all over the newspapers and TV screens and promising, if elected, to use his special knowledge to clean up this cesspool of corruption once and for all as a way of atoning for his own past sins. He was good all right, he used his scar and his handicaps to good advantage, and the people lapped it up. Senator George Winfield Lorca; and he's been keeping a pretty low profile in Washington up to now, but fireworks are expected at any time. It's rumored that the party's even got its eye on him for the Number One spot eventually if he can keep the sparks flying—what the hell, he's not the only potential candidate who ever had a cloud on his record, and at least Lorca's frank about his. Well, you must have seen or heard him. It was a pretty spectacular show, like an old-time religious revivial, except that it was crime that took a beating instead of sin. As I say, he's been keeping pretty quiet lately; but at the time he got more election coverage than anybody else in his part of the country."

I shook my head. "I'm a very poor citizen. All the time the political fate of the nation was being decided, I was either out of the country or up in the mountains communing with a trout, recuperating from a very rough trip, never mind where." I frowned. "Lorca. I never heard the name before, except for a Spanish playwright I remember vaguely from college."

Eleanor said, "I think he's of mixed Spanish and Anglo-Saxon ancestry. George Winfield Manuel Lorca de Sapio, something like that. I can never get those endless Spanish names quite straight. I believe in his younger and more active days he was sometimes known as Kid Sapio or The Sapper, maybe because of his favorite weapon. . . . What's the matter?"

It was Old Home Week, goddamn it; and I didn't like it a bit, the way the past kept coming at me lately. I said, "Hell, a syndicate character calling himself Manuel Sapio died down in Baja California, Mexico, on a bluff overlooking a deserted cove called Bahia San Agustin, except that it wasn't deserted when I was there. There was a boat in the cove and there were people all over that cactus coastline and they all had guns, including Sapio and me. It was a smuggling deal with ramifications and Washington had an interest beyond drugs, never mind the details, although it would have made very interesting material for your article, Miss Brand, the one on yours truly. Or maybe it's in there? If so, you know that I put Sapio out of action myself, but some other folks moved in and got the drop on me and executed him while he was still unconscious, with a bullet in the brain. . . ."

Eleanor said, "My God, I didn't know you were involved in that; you really get around, don't you? I thought I'd done a pretty good investigative job on you, but. . . ." She shrugged resignedly. "Anyway, that's the man, all right; but the execution didn't take. Lorca wound up in a San Diego hospital with the skull doctors working on him in shifts around the clock."

"When I knew him as Manuel Sapio, he was a very tough specimen," I said. "I'd be very much surprised if a hole in the head had mellowed him much. Of course, you're supposed to be able to turn a tiger into a pussycat if you sever the right aggressive connections up there; but I'd want somebody else to check that the transformation was genuine before I stepped into the cage." I grimaced. "Except that we both seem to be in the tiger cage whether we want to be or not. Well, it just shows."

"What does it show?"

"That it doesn't pay to be soft-hearted. If I had executed him when I had the chance, instead of just putting him to sleep in my gentle humanitarian fashion and leaving the job to somebody else, he'd have stayed executed." I frowned. "Let me get this straight. Your theory and that of some of your journalistic friends is that this repentant Mr. Lorca is a phony, is that what you're trying to say?"

"Yes, but I wouldn't say it very loudly, or to anybody I didn't trust. That's another thing we noticed, a straw in the wind so to speak. Strange things seemed to happen to people who got in the way of Lorca's election campaign.

Oh, no black sedans with tommy guns poking out the windows. No skullduggery in dark alleys. Just . . . things."

"Sure," I said. "Things. What you're suggesting is that organized crime, whatever you want to call it, instead of just buying up a ready-made politician here and there as in the past, has now constructed one of its own, who's ridden to power—and will presumably continue to ride—on the current wave of anti-crime feeling, as a man who really knows the evil but has rejected it in favor of the good. As a confessed, reformed sinner who hates the sin he's renounced and knows how it should be dealt with better than anyone. And then?"

She shrugged. "Oh, then, as soon as he feels himself secure, we'll see a lot of underworld fall guys falling to make Mr. Clean look good. There'll be a lot of sacrificial goats and chickens offered up on the anti-crime altar. But in the meantime . . . well, with a truly powerful secret friend high up in national politics, who knows how far the syndicate can go? They already control a lot more of our country than people are willing to believe."

"And what," I asked, "has all this got to do with ships sinking up and down the Atlantic coast?"

After a moment, Eleanor shook her head. "I don't know. As far as I was concerned there was no connection; not until you came along. I was working on a different story entirely. You're the one who brought in George Winfield Lorca, you and your lady charter-boat skipper. I didn't know that he had anything to do with what I'm investigating now. I still don't, really."

"Yes, you do," I said. "You know that Harriet Robinson took the sacred Lorca name in vain, in this very connection; and was instantly punished for it. That can't be coincidence. So the connection must exist. All we have to do is find it."

She hesitated. "The Lorca dossier you brought is still in my room where you left it," she said a bit reluctantly. "Maybe we'd better go through it together and see if we can spot anything significant."

Ten minutes later, we were emerging from the elevator

on the fourth floor, having signed the dinner check—her obligation as head of this journalistic partnership—and picked up my key at the desk where Fred had left it. I was aware of her walking silently beside me in her nice white button-down-the-front silk dress and her neat high-heeled pumps that made no sound on the hall carpet; and I knew she was aware of me, too. I hadn't missed her poorly concealed reluctance to suggest a conference in her room, at this hour of night.

"Matt," she said.

"Don't give it a thought, Elly," I said. "We got those emotional involvements all taken care of a couple of hours back, remember? That goes for physical involvements, too. Just business, business, business all the way, okay?"

She said stiffly, "Don't try to read minds; you're not very good at it. All I was going to say was that I'm pretty tired. That dossier can wait until morning, can't it?"

"Sure," I said. "Whatever you say, Boss."

"Matt."

"Yes, Elly."

She looked straight ahead as she walked. "You're jumping to conclusions. I'm not really the shy ingenue type; and normally the idea of holding a late consultation with a man in my hotel room and having him sleeping next door wouldn't bother me a bit. I . . . I'm just trying to avoid a situation that could be very embarrassing for both of us. I can't explain. But I'd appreciate it if you'd stop acting like the experienced man of the world being so damned patronizingly considerate of the timid little girl from the sticks with her silly sexual hangups. I'd appreciate it very much."

We'd stopped in front of my room, since I had that key still in my hand. I looked down at her for a moment; and she met my look steadily.

I said, "My mistake. I. . . ." Then I saw what was lying on the carpet at her feet. I grabbed her and felt her body react with instant, violent panic. "Easy, easy!" I breathed in her ear, after drawing her close in spite of her struggles. "Listen! Get the hell out of here, fast. Call 23572 from a

108

booth in the lobby. Tell them where you are and stay right there until they come for you. 23572. Now scat."

I released her and shoved her away and saw her, after a moment's hesitation, turn and tiptoe away. Hoping our brief scuffle had been heard, I spoke more loudly.

"Hey, baby!" I said hoarsely. "Hey, sweetheart! You almost had me fooled with that cool professional look. So, all right, let's move the meeting inside where we can give the subject serious consideration. . . . What the hell did I do with my key?"

Perhaps I was making a fool of myself, but if there was no audience it didn't matter. I glanced again at the telltale Fred had set on my door, now lying on the floor nearby. Well, it could have been the maid coming to turn down the bed, but if so why hadn't she entered Elly's room as well? That telltale was still in place.

I fumbled with the lock long enough to make them nervous in there, if they were in there. Then I hit the door hard, slamming it back against the wall, and went through it. . . .

CHAPTER 13

I'D figured he probably wouldn't send anybody to do the job alone. If he was the man I thought he was, he knew who I was and what my business was. You don't send a lone soldier after an experienced professional in my line of work, not unless your boy is very damned good; and with all due modesty, the fact that I'm still around in spite of arousing a certain amount of hostility here and there over the years, would seem to indicate that there aren't many boys available that good. I could name you a

109

few who might qualify, or who might think they qualified, but they aren't in private employ.

So he wouldn't send just one. And he wouldn't send three. That would be giving me undue importance and suggesting that I was really somebody to be afraid of; and that could not, of course, be admitted publicly by a man in his position. Besides, three men tend to get in each others' way when the going gets rough, particularly in a confined space like a hotel room.

So there would be a two-man team inside. One man would be posted right in front of the door facing me, armed, to attract and hold my attention the instant I entered; while the second would be waiting on one side or the other—to my left, in this case, since the door swung right —to get the drop on me from behind while I stood gawking at the first, all shocked and bewildered and scared.

I caught a glimpse of the decoy gent in front of me, but safely back out of my reach, gun raised, as I crashed inside; but he would keep, I hoped. I swerved sharply left and the second man was there, all right, taking aim; but he'd been expecting to have my helpless back to aim at as I came to a screeching halt, a steady target. He didn't get it. He got my front instead, coming at him; and I took advantage of his moment of paralyzed surprise to slap the gun from his hand—it was as easy as that—and grab him by the lapels of his gaudy sports coat. His shirt was equally dramatic, I noticed.

I was between the two men now. The one in the center of the room had a clear shot at my back but of course he didn't take it. I mean, if you're a man with a gun who's had any training at all, you don't take any hasty shots toward your partner's position. You get the permissible sectors of fire clearly set in your mind first thing; you remind yourself firmly that shooting in *that* direction is simply not allowed. Just as the AA guns on a warship are blocked, or were back when they used that kind of rapid-fire guns—for all I know they use lasers now—so that the ones aft can't blow the heads off the guys serving the ones forward if somebody gets excited, so each member of a good hunting partnership, whatever the quarry, establishes certain limits for himself beyond which he *must* not fire, at least not without thinking it over and being very, very careful. It was possible that the man over by the bed could have shot me hoping that his teammate was not quite in line or that my body would stop the bullet; but the warning signals were screaming in his brain—*danger bearing, danger bearing*—and with the klaxons going off in there and the red lights flashing he took a moment to think it over and wait for a safer shot. I swung the other guy clear around by his bright coat and slung him straight at the gun and heard it fire.

The sound was muffled between the two bodies. I saw the man with the gun step back, aghast, as the partner he'd shot went to his knees on the carpet feeling behind for the place that hurt, that he could not quite reach. Before the standing man could recover, I had his gun. I sent him reeling back with a blow to the windpipe, not as hard as it might have been. Nevertheless, he grabbed for his throat, strangling, fighting for breath.

"Should I close the door?"

I whirled, stepping aside quickly so I could cover the two men and the doorway as well. Eleanor Brand was standing there. She seemed to have lost some height. I saw that she was in her stocking feet, holding one of her sharp-heeled white pumps at the ready.

I said harshly, "I told you—"

"I know what you told me," she said calmly. "Just a minute, let me get my purse and my other shoe." She disappeared into the corridor, and returned after a moment, and closed the room door. "All clear," she reported in the same calm voice. "The noise wasn't really very loud; it sounded kind of muffled. Nobody seems to have noticed." She bent down to set the shoes neatly before her, and stepped into them. When she straightened up, I saw that her face was suddenly quite pale and a little shiny; reaction was setting in. "That was. . . ." She swallowed hard, and cleared her throat. "That was really very neat. What are you going to do with them?"

"Cut their throats and put them out with the hotel garbage," I said.

"No," she said. "You're just kidding me."

"Yes," I said. "I'm just kidding you."

"If you'd really wanted to kill them, you'd have used your own gun."

I said, "We're here to do a story, remember, not to argue with a bunch of Bahamian cops. Guns cause a lot of trouble, particularly in foreign countries. I can never understand why. You can kill a man with anything from a baseball bat to a knitting needle and nobody really minds; but if you shoot him with a firearm, people get all excited. Why did you come back?" Then I shook my head quickly. "Skip it, temporarily. Let's get rid of the trash before we go into all that." I turned to the standing man, leaning weakly against the bed, a heavyset gent in white slacks and another gaudy sports shirt. He was gradually managing to pull in enough air to survive on. "You," I said. "I don't know who sent you, not really, but if you should happen to meet a gent named Lorca, alias Sapio, give him a message from me. Tell him that he'd better try to remember a bay in Baja California and what I told him one night on a bluff overlooking that bay. That was before I put him to sleep along with his four henchmen. They were really rather pitiful, no problem at all, just like you two clowns. Now haul your ass and your friend to hell out of here and don't let me see you again. Next time I might get mad and hurt you."

The standing man tried to speak, but nothing but a rattling sound came out of his bruised throat. He bent over his teammate, who groaned as he was lifted but managed to stay on his feet once he was put there. I nodded to Eleanor, who opened the door, looked out cautiously, and gave me a nod in return. She stood well back as the two stumbled out; then she closed and locked the door behind them.

"Do you . . . do you think he'll live?" she asked. "The one who was shot, I mean?"

I shrugged. "I told you once, Elly, there are friends

112

and enemies. What happens to the enemies couldn't concern me less. Just so he doesn't do his dying in here."

She said, "You're so damned tough and your hands are shaking. Do you keep any booze in here?" Then she saw it on the dresser and uncapped the bottle and tried to pour and spilled some. She set the bottle down helplessly. "Oh, Jesus! It seems to be contagious." She stood there for a moment, steadying herself against the dresser. She spoke without turning her head. "What did you tell Lorca/Sapio that night in Baja?"

"To leave my girl alone."

"What girl? Another one?"

"This one was very cute," I said. "Silver-blond, slinky, a tall, slim, Hollywood-starlet type. You wouldn't think she'd be much good in bed, no more hips than she had, but you'd be wrong. Now that you're mad, can you pour the whiskey, or do you want me to?"

She looked at me for a moment. "Why should I be mad because you slept with a starlet?" But she managed to pour the drinks and handed me one. "You're crazy, you know that," she said softly after taking a good swallow from hers. "You're just . . . well, *crazy*. How do you keep living, doing things like that?"

"By knowing when to quit," I said. "That's it."

"What do you mean?"

"You can get away with that sort of dumb thing once or twice at the beginning of a game; but now we start playing for keeps."

"Why didn't that man shoot, the one by the bed?" When I explained it to her, she said, "And you staked your life on a thin theory like that? Crazy! What happened to the platinum Hollywood type?"

"She wasn't really," I said. "She was a very serious girl, really. Too serious. She decided I should be reformed, led into gentle paths of nonviolence. I decided I shouldn't be. I haven't seen her since. How did you come to decide to do a story on us, Elly, or series of stories?"

Her eyes wavered. "I can't tell you that. Professional secret."

113

"Sure," I said. "Do you mind if I make a phone call? You're welcome to listen. In fact, I recommend it."

"Why should I mind? I'll just take the bottle over to that chair and get quietly drunk while you chat. Don't bother to pour me into bed. Just let me sleep it off right there."

I sat down on the bed, got the phone and got the Washington number. It took a little while to get through to Mac, but he's never too hard to reach, even at night. Suddenly he was on the line.

"Eric here," I said. "We have some reconsidering to do, sir. I'm afraid I've been a little stupid; I should have caught on sooner."

"Caught onto what, Eric?"

"Do you know the whereabouts of Roberta Prince?"

"I don't recall the name . . . oh. Yes, of course."

"Five-ten, slender, silver-blond hair, blue eyes, last seen in Mexico heading north for the U.S.A. Anyway, that's where she was last seen by me. Like with Harriet Robinson, we erased a few dubious items from Miss Prince's record, as well as we could, in return for services rendered; but that was several years back. Do we have any recent information?"

"I'll check—"

"Just a minute, sir. While you're checking, please get hold of Martha and find out the name of the man who was living across the street from her; and where he can be reached now, if she knows."

"The man who shot Amos? That information I have. Some of it at least. His name is Elliot, Roger Elliot. He's out on bail awaiting trial. I should think there would be a good chance of catching him at home."

I said, "Bail? For murder? He must have a good lawyer."

"He does. But I don't have his telephone number here."

"That's all right," I said. "It was Navajo Drive, Casa Glorieta, wasn't it? I'll get it from Information. I'll call you back."

Eleanor was smoking one of her cigarettes; the girl was a human chimney and the Cancer Society would take a dim view of her. She was curled up in the big chair and I

114

thought she looked kind of pretty like that; but I guess any girl looks pretty who's willing to tackle a couple of armed men with nothing but a high-heeled shoe, in your behalf. She raised an eyebrow when she saw me looking her way, but she asked no questions. It took me a while to get Santa Fe, New Mexico, on the line; then a male voice I remembered spoke in my ear. It occurred to me that I still didn't know the face that went with the voice. I only knew his shoulders and his shotgun and his blond, unhappy, unfaithful lush of a wife.

"Mr. Elliot?"

"Yes?"

"We met a while back, in a manner of speaking."

There was a brief silence. "Yes, I thought you sounded vaguely familiar. What do you want?"

"The answer to a question. What gave you the idea?"

"What do you mean?" But there was more defiance in his tone than there should have been.

I said, "Did you catch them in flagrante delicto, if that's the way to pronounce it? Or did she boast of her infidelity and tell you she'd found a better man? What sent you on the warpath with a loaded twelve-gauge?"

After another pause, he said, "I don't think I want to answer that."

I said, "I suggest that it didn't happen that way at all. I suggest that you got an anonymous letter or phone call."

More silence, then his voice came again, "If you know, why ask?" When I didn't speak, he went on softly, reminiscently, "I didn't know. I had no idea. I didn't believe it, at first. I didn't want to believe it. Everything had been going so well, I thought. And then, when it became quite obvious. . . . Well, I just flipped, I guess."

I asked, "Letter or call?"

"Call."

"Anything that might identify the person at the other end?"

"Nothing. Except that it was a woman."

That surprised me a little. "You're sure?"

"Of course I'm sure. The voice was kind of deep and

115

husky—I guess you'd call it a contralto—but it was definitely a woman's voice."

"Thanks," I said. "It's none of my business, of course, but how are things going now?"

"She's . . . in a place. She lets me come visit her. It's funny, she hated me so much until the police. . . . Now, I don't really think she wants to see me convicted. We'll see how it works out."

"Well, good luck," I said.

"You said that once before," he said. "Keep trying."

When I'd hung up, I glanced toward Eleanor, but she just gave me the quizzical-eyebrow treatment and remained silent. I got Washington again, after a minor struggle with the Bahamian telephone organization; but nothing serious, nothing like trying to get a call out of, for instance, Mexico.

"It's not good," Mac said.

"I didn't think it would be," I said. I cleared my throat, remembering certain things. "Dead?"

"She got married four years ago," Mac said. "Somebody she met in Hollywood. One child, a boy. Recently they went sailing out of Marina del Rey; they had a small sailboat there. A speedboat ran them down. The man survived. He claimed the speedboat turned back and made another pass—the girl was pretty badly mangled by the propellers—but nobody really believed him; he'd taken a bad blow on the head. The child was never found."

I'd seen, once, what a fast boat's whirling props could do to a human body; it wasn't nice to think about. I thought of a pretty, bright, and rather brave young woman who'd wanted peace and nonviolence and had almost made it when the past, in which I'd played a part, caught up with her. Mac was speaking.

"What did you say, sir?" I asked.

"How did you know?"

"It was logical," I said. "Once you considered it all as a single calculated program instead of a number of unrelated events. I just talked with Elliot, the man who killed Bob Devine. He was triggered by an anonymous phone call. And Harriet Robinson killed herself as a result of an anonymous letter. And I just had a couple of anonymous visitors with guns. And a certain lady journalist did a series of damaging exposés on us and won't say what gave her the notion. Somehow I get the idea that somebody doesn't like us very much. He's doing everything in his power to embarrass and destroy us, from sicking a jealous husband onto a retired agent of ours who happened to be married to your daughter, to setting a muckraking female journalist on our trail." I winked at Eleanor, who maintained a careful poker face. I went on, "It's too much, sir. I should have seen it sooner. It's got to be a deliberate campaign, not just a run of bad luck."

Mac said carefully, a thousand miles away in a different country, "We must watch out for paranoia, Eric; it's an occupational disease. And Roberta Prince, Roberta Hendrickson as she became, was not one of ours."

"No, but she was involved in a certain operation of ours down in Mexico; and at the time I carefully warned a certain gent to lay off her. He'd want to deal with her, not only because he felt she'd double-crossed him by helping me, but to show me clearly what he thought of my warning. In a way you could say I bestowed the kiss of death on her by standing up for her like that."

"I see," Mac said softly. He was silent for a moment. "He calls himself Lorca nowadays, doesn't he? I would very much prefer not to have to deal with him, if it's at all possible. He's in a position of considerable power these days."

"You have no choice, sir," I said. "We have no choice. He's obviously involving himself with us as a matter of revenge, very systematically."

"Very well. Do what you consider necessary."

I said, "It was a woman with a contralto voice who informed Roger Elliot of his wife's infidelity."

Mac said, "That's very interesting. Roberta Hendrickson's husband thought the driver of the speedboat was a dark-haired woman, but he was not quite certain, since there is no longer a strong correlation between length of hair and sex. I'll see what the possibilities are. Eric."

"Yes, sir."

"Be discreet. What with Miss Brand's recent article on Amos and other articles forthcoming, we are not in a very strong strategic position at the moment."

"Discreet," I said. "Yes, sir. Discreet."

I hung up and sat there for a while. Eleanor Brand lit another cigarette from the butt of the first, and waved the smoke aside.

"So that's how the death sentence is passed," she said. "Discreetly."

CHAPTER 14

SHE said she'd done an election piece on Lorca while the recent campaign was still news.

"I used a number of sources," she said. "They weren't all reliable, of course. In a situation like that there are always people with axes to grind. You've got his PR people trying to build the guy up, and you've got the other guys' PR people, plus his natural enemies, trying to tear him down. You've got to evaluate the information you get very carefully; that's part of the job, maybe the most important part of the job. But even a doubtful source will often give you a useful quote, or lead you to a nugget of real information you might otherwise have overlooked. And sometimes other lines of inquiry open up as you dig, and suggest ideas for new articles. . . . Well, I don't have to tell you. You've been there and done it, although more with a camera than with a notebook and tape recorder." She gave me a quick, almost embarrassed glance. "It's funny. When I wrote that story on you, it didn't seem likely we'd ever be sitting like this having a friendly drink. . . . Ooops, sorry! I forgot;

friendship has no place here, the man said. It's all strictly business, right? Where was I?"

"You were evaluating sources," I said.

Eleanor stubbed out her cigarette in the hotel's ashtray. "Yes, well, one day a man who'd been feeding me some tidbits of Lorca dope told me he had something that was totally irrelevant to the election story I was working on, but maybe I could use it anyway. He'd been looking for somebody to tell it to and he'd decided I could be trusted to keep him out of it no matter what. That was all he wanted, protection. He had this material and it scared him and if certain people knew he had it his life would be in terrible danger. He gave it a big buildup."

I grinned. "I suppose those certain ferocious people were us."

She nodded. "He claimed he was a former government employee discharged under a cloud—strictly a frame-up, of course; he was really quite innocent; they always are— who'd once stumbled across this information that had been on his conscience ever since: information about a terrible secret government organization that really should be exposed for the good of the country. He had quite a bit of material and he was able to tell me where to look for more. When he mentioned that the chief of this deadly agency had a daughter named Martha, who was married to a retired agent named Devine, I knew where I could find still more. After the Lorca piece was wrapped up, I went to work on it." She glanced at me sharply. "And please don't lecture me on my sneaky low-down methods, Mr. Helm. You used that Hollywood blonde for your own purposes, didn't you, even after sleeping with her; and in the end she died of it. I don't think that leaves you much room to criticize."

"I didn't say a word," I said mildly. "But didn't it occur to you that your timid source might have hidden motives for setting you on our trail? Or that somebody might?"

Eleanor laughed. "Don't be naive, little boy," she said. "Of course it occurred to me. They always claim to be snitching for the sakes of their pure, patriotic, public-

119

spirited consciences; and deep down they're always trying to get even with somebody who's been mean to them. So what? A leak is a leak is a leak. I cross-checked the information and it was all solid. So maybe the guy was avenging himself on the government that had fired him, or one particular branch of it. Or maybe he had other motives. What was that to me, as long as he handed me valid data? And now it turns out that maybe somebody else was using him, and me too, to get even with you, and to hell with that, too. Show me where they sneaked one false item past me and I'll apologize all over the place; but I was pretty damned careful and I don't think you can do it. And as long as my story is accurate, as the old saying goes, chuck you, Farley. If you don't want stuff written about you, don't do stuff worth writing about."

I thought maybe she was protesting a little too much; but on the other hand, they always do get carried away when they get on any subject relating to the freedom of the press.

"Down, Lady, down," I said. "Nobody's going to hurt you, so let's not have all that defensive growling and snarling, there's a good doggie."

After a moment, she drew a long breath and grinned. "I haven't been called a bitch so nicely in a long time," she said.

"And Harriet Robinson, how did you get onto her?" I asked.

Eleanor shrugged. "Not from that source. Her name came up in the course of my further researches on you and your fascinating operations; so I went to interview her, as I told you. She wasn't much help as far as you were concerned. To hear her tell it, she hardly remembered your name. But that was back when the first ship sinkings were in the news and we talked about them casually. She was a mine of nautical information; she really knew her stuff. When I got the idea of going to work on that story, later, after I'd finished up with you and your outfit, I remembered the knowledgeable Captain Robinson; but when I went back to see her, she clammed up completely.

I thought at the time it was just a personal thing, you know we didn't really get along too well; but I guess there was more to it than that."

I said, "Yes, I guess by that time she'd managed to get herself mixed up in it somehow, so she was afraid to talk. And you know something? I have a hard time buying the idea that at just about the time you interviewed Harriet about me because you'd been given a lead to me by Lorca, she just accidentally stumbled onto a totally different branch of Mr. Lorca's mysterious operations." I frowned thoughtfully. "You weren't particularly careful how you approached her, I suppose."

"Careful? How do you mean?"

"You didn't take any precautions to avoid being followed? Anybody interested could have learned that your investigation into my nefarious past was leading you to a certain charter-boat skipper down in the Florida Keys?"

Eleanor said rather defensively, "You're the secret agent around here, Mister. I'm just an innocent journalist; I don't keep looking over my shoulder to see if people are trailing me around." After a moment, she asked, "Do you think they were? Do you think I . . . led them to her?"

I nodded. "I'm afraid so. You called her to their attention and then I paid her a visit. Between us . . ." I shrugged. "With friends like us, who needs enemies? Not Hattie Robinson."

"You're just guessing."

"Not really. It's apparently a systematic campaign to find our weak spots and take advantage of them. Hell, if they were watching Bob Devine closely enough to learn that he was playing around, and that it might stir things up a bit for us, in an embarrassing way, if they broke the news to the husband of the lady in question; why shouldn't they keep an eye on Harriet to see if she might prove useful, once she was brought to their notice? Only it's my hunch that in this case the strategy back-fired to a certain extent."

"How?"

I said, "Harriet was not an innocent journalist lady like you, with nothing on her conscience. She had a past that could catch up with her at any time; she was on the alert for that, always. Also, she was a sailor; and she could spot a landlubber ten miles off on a misty day, even if he was all dressed up in Topsiders and sunglasses and nice, white slacks. It wouldn't take her long to spot some mysterious city slickers tailing her around trying to act salty. She might put up with it for a while, but she was not a patient lady, and after a little she'd just naturally get mad. If they were cops, why didn't they move in with the handcuffs and get it over with? If they weren't, who the hell were they? Eventually, fed up, she'd try to backtrack the lubberly jerks to learn something about them. She could do it, too. She was in her territory and they were out of theirs. My hunch is that they got careless and led her to something or somebody they shouldn't have. So they called the boss and confessed their sins because they were scared not to. Lorca had collected enough information about Harriet's past by this time that he was in a position to threaten her with exposure to keep her quiet. Which he did."

"But we still don't know what or who she saw," Eleanor said. "It doesn't seem likely that she stumbled upon George Winfield Lorca himself firing torpedoes at an innocent freighter or tanker."

I said, "It looks to me as if he's got two separate operations running. One is a revenge mission: he blames us, particularly me, for what happened to him down there in Baja, and now that he's the powerful and invulnerable Senator Lorca he's exacting secret payment for that hole in the head. That's straightforward enough; but the piratical bit still doesn't make much sense. It certainly can't be aimed at us, me. We've got no interest in any shipping lines. But there's got to be a connection between these two different Lorca activities, because Harriet found it. It's up to us to find it, too. Or up to me."

"Us," Eleanor said. She looked at me curiously. "As a matter of fact, I don't quite see why you're so interested in that phase of it. I mean, all you need to do is nail him for murder, if you're going to be so law-abiding about it. He's responsible for at least three deaths already—"

"Prove it," I said. "Harriet killed herself. Bob Devine was shot by a jealous husband. Bobbie Prince died in a boating accident, at least nobody seems to have proved otherwise and it seems unlikely that anybody will. And the word is discretion, remember?"

She frowned. "I don't understand."

"A popular new Senator gets into a feud with a not-so-popular old government agency; who's going to get the best of that argument? With your articles running to show what a mean, sneaky bunch we are? We haven't got a chance in the world of doing anything about him because he's been mean to us. It will be a simple popularity contest, which we can't possibly win. No, we've got to get something else on him, something that doesn't concern us at all, like these sinking ships of yours."

She licked her lips. "Of course you could . . . just shoot him. That's what you're trained for, isn't it?"

I said, "Assassination isn't all that simple, ma'am, or all that effective."

She laughed abruptly. "If it were, I'd be dead for what I've written about you, wouldn't I? Instead of having a secret agent all my own, supplying me with booze and protection." She yawned, and rose. "Well, I think that's enough for one day, Mr. Bodyguard. Anything we've overlooked will just have to wait until tomorrow."

"Let me check your room before you go in there," I said. When I returned, I said, "Don't open the hall door for any reason without waking me. And any strange noises you hear in the night, I want to hear about right away."

"Yes, sir, Mr. Helm, sir."

I looked down at her for a moment. It had been a long day, but she didn't really show it. The only indication of how much she'd drunk was that she looked softer and prettier tonight than when we'd met that morning. Or maybe that was an indication of how much I'd drunk.

"I'd like to leave the connecting door open," I said carefully, "if it doesn't bother you."

She said coolly, "It won't bother me if it doesn't bother you. Suit yourself. Goodnight, Matt."

"Good night, Elly."

She was an odd, contradictory little girl—I couldn't help remembering her panicky reaction to my touch, when I'd grabbed her outside the door. But she was perfectly self-possessed now.

I had no trouble going to sleep, so the open door between us couldn't have bothered me very much.

CHAPTER 15

I came out of bed fast on the side away from the connecting door, gun in hand. I didn't know what had awakened me, but if you wait to find out you may not live to find out. As I crouched there warily, sheltered behind the bed, the sound came again: the gasping, sobbing sound of a woman suffering unbearable pain and terror. Barefoot in my pajamas, gun ready, I moved swiftly to the doorway.

"No, I *won't*!" I heard her gasp. "No, you can't, oh you *can't* . . . damn you, damn you, damn you I'll kill you for . . . oh God, oh God, oh God, no. . . . Ahhh!"

I knew just about what I had to deal with, then. I pushed the half-open door gently aside and stepped past it. There was, of course, nobody in the room beyond; nobody except the girl in the big bed. She'd thrown off the covers and she lay on her back on the white sheet as if crucified there, helpless and vulnerable, her arms flung wide. She was more or less covered by a long disordered nightgown of some kind of printed stuff, but I couldn't make out the pattern or color in the dim light from the window. Although without sleeves, it seemed to have much more material elsewhere than it really needed, spread out about her like a shroud.

124

Eleanor Brand was breathing very deeply and audibly, lying there, dragging in each lungful of air as if it might be the last before rationing was imposed. Her eyes were closed.

"I'll kill them," she whispered. "I'll kill them, kill them, kill, kill, kill them, but oh God, oh God, why did they have to. . . ."

Abruptly her eyes opened and she sat up with a start, staring at me. Her hair was matted and untidy; she reached up mechanically to push the damp strands out of her face. Then she drew a long breath and switched on the bedside light and looked at me again.

"Don't shoot, Mister," she said in a normal voice. "Just a little old nightmare. Everybody's got them. Go back to bed. Sorry."

"Sure," I said. I noticed that the loose sleeveless gown had slipped from one shoulder; and that it was a rather nice shoulder. Well, a girl you comfort in the middle of the night is supposed to have nice shoulders; it's in the rules. She pulled the garment straight while I laid the pistol aside and picked up the fallen bedclothes and reorganized them for her. She drew them up over her knees, sitting there. I asked, "How did it happen?"

She didn't pretend she didn't know what I meant. She merely shook her head. "I don't want to talk about it. There's nothing to talk about. Hell, it's a perfectly normal occupational hazard for young lady reporters who stick their noses where they don't belong."

"Whatever you say," I said. "Have you seen a shrink?"

"I don't need a shrink. I'm perfectly all right. I just have these dreams, but I'll get over them. Go back to bed." After a moment, when I didn't move, she said, "All right, if you have to be nosy, get me a cigarette, damn you. Over there on the dresser. I didn't really think it could happen to me."

I got the package for her, but the fingers with which she tried to extract a cigarette were clumsy, so I got one out for her, placed it between her lips, and lit it. I laid the package on the table beside her, put an ashtray handy, and sat down on the edge of the bed.

"They never do," I said.

"Don't be corny," she said. "Look at me."

"I'm looking."

"Well, what do you see?" Her voice was impatient. "I have a face right out of the primate cage in the zoo, right? I've got a crazy, skinny, short-legged body with a couple of dumb little breasts stuck on it anyhow. My ankles aren't bad but who's going to get their gonads in an uproar about a pair of ankles these days?" She waited for me to speak, but she didn't really want me to speak. She was busy tearing herself down and she wanted no interference from me, thanks. She went on, "With all the pretty girls around to violate, who's going to bother with an ugly little monkey with a notebook? At least that was the way I had it figured; and anyway, you can't spend your life being scared of things, not if you're going to get any work done. I had to have two teeth capped afterward and you can still see the scar where the big one hit me in the mouth, here."

"It doesn't show much," I said.

"Nothing *shows* much," she said softly, "but they spoiled me, damn them, they really spoiled me, even if it hardly shows any longer. They spoiled everything. It's not the same world any longer and it's not the same me."

"Physically?"

"Oh, all the pieces are still there. I had a checkup later and some tests to make sure they hadn't . . . hadn't given me anything, biological or pathological, if you know what I mean. But the pieces don't work right any more. I've got these goddamned Victorian-old-maid reactions now. Not that I was ever a flaming sexpot—with my looks, who gets the chance?—but I was at least reasonably normal about it when it was offered, or mentioned. But now I can't even talk about it normally. I can't bear to be touched. Well, you noticed. I saw you notice."

"But you're perfectly all right and you don't need a shrink," I said dryly.

"What's one of those creeps going to do for me?" she

126

demanded. "He can't turn the clock back; he can't make it not have happened. They were waiting by the car when I came out of the place, kind of a low-down dive in a low-down part of town, but nobody bothered me inside and the man I'd come to see was very polite and even bought me a beer. But they must have seen me go in and they must have been very hard up for it or something. They were laying for me when I got back to the car, a big one and a little one, real loose-lipped types. I tried to run but they caught me and dragged me around the corner of the building into a dark vacant lot and did it to me, beating hell out of me first when I tried to resist." She drew a ragged breath. "It's the unbelievable helpless humiliation of it, you know, as much as anything. They don't leave you anything. When they're finished with you there's nothing left of your dignity as a human being, let alone your dignity as a woman. . . ."

The hotel was silent around us. She wasn't seeing me any longer. She was no longer talking for my benefit. She was revisiting the scene of her agony, deliberately putting herself through her ordeal again to test how much it still hurt after the time that had passed; to check how far the healing process had gone, how far it still had to go. Her voice was wickedly soft as she reminded herself of how it had been,

"Sobbing in the dirt afterward among the cans and weeds and beer bottles, naked except for the shredded stockings down around my ankles and the grimy sweater up around my neck they hadn't quite managed to rip all the way off me. Hurting all over, afraid to move at first and learn just how badly I'd been beaten; then terrified that somebody would come along and see me like that. Like a nightmare, bare-ass naked in the middle of the city with car lights going by only half a block away, finding my shoes and purse, and some useless scraps of nylon—well, I used them to scrub the stuff, you know, off my legs. Finding at last what was left of my skirt. Pinning the crazy rag around me, blubbering stupidly as I tried to do something with the hopeless wreck of my sweater, stumbling to the car like a falling-down drunk—and back in the automatic, thank God, hotel parking garage avoiding the elevator and hauling myself up the endless empty stairs and staggering to my room without meeting anybody; safe at last with the door locked behind me, turning on the light and coming face to face with this *thing* in the mirror, this crazy, tattered, filthy, bloody *thing* with its slitty little eyes all squinched up in its swollen fright-mask of a face, and its ghastly, mangled, broken mouth. . . ." Her voice rose hysterically. She stopped and swallowed hard and spoke in normal tones, "I guess I hadn't really grasped until then what they'd done to me, what they'd made of me, how thoroughly they'd spoiled me inside and out."

She stared at me, blind and dry-eyed. I reached out, took from her fingers the cigarette she'd forgotten, and extinguished it in the ashtray. She shook her head minutely, as if in answer to a question only she had heard; she drew another long, uneven breath and licked her lips.

"Okay," she breathed. "If I can talk about it I'm getting better, aren't I? Okay."

"Elly. . . ."

"Just one thing," she said. Suddenly her voice was hard and steady. "Before you get too sentimental about the poor innocent little girl all ravished and ruined by two dreadful big men, I'd better tell you that I fixed them afterward." When I looked at her sharply, she said, "Well, did they think they could do *that* to somebody and not pay for it?"

"Tell me," I said.

"I just told you!" Her voice was impatient. "I fixed them. They held them down for me while I did it with a knife I'd gotten in a hardware store, you know, one of those little two-bladed stockmen's knives. I'd read up on it in a book on cattle and horses I'd found in the library there in Miami. The librarian, nosy bitch, was kind of curious about me, the crazy way my face was, reading up on a dull subject like animal husbandry. How to do it without losing a single head of livestock to hemorrhage or infection. They do it all the time to cattle and horses, you know, a very simple operation. Actually, when it came right down to doing it, it got to be kind of a ghoulish scene and I was sick in the bushes afterward, but I couldn't ask anybody else to do it for me, could I?" She looked at me long and hard. "*Now* you can start the poor-little-ravished-girl routine."

The strange thing was that she looked so small and defenseless in the big bed, telling me about it. I hadn't really expected anything like that, I hadn't been braced for it, but I managed a grin to live up to my character as the tough secret agent, Superspook himself.

"What am I supposed to be, shocked?"

She shrugged. "I'd decided I'd better not kill them after all," she said in conversational tones. "It wasn't really worth spending my life in jail for; although why anybody should have to go to jail or even stand trial for . . . I mean, goddamn it, it should come under the heading of public service, shouldn't it? But the crazy way things are, whatever the verdict it would have been a mess, a public mess, and I didn't want that. I didn't want people knowing and looking at me funny and feeling sorry for me. I told everybody later, when I got back home to Chicago, what I'd already told them in Miami, that I'd been in a car crash and got thrown against the windshield. Doing it that way and not killing them, I figured there'd be no trouble with the police; they wouldn't want to advertise what had been done to them, either. And I was right, nobody squawked, and it's all taken care of now. I can forget them now. My mind can forget them. But my stupid body can't forget them."

"Who did you get to help you?" I asked.

"Somebody big and unpleasant in Miami Beach I did a favor for once, or he thought I did. I learned something and didn't print it. Actually, it had nothing to do with what I was working on at the time so I had no reason to use it, but later he let me know he owed me. So as soon as I'd figured out what to do and researched how to do it, as soon as I could get around without crippling along like an old lady—to hell with how I still looked; that would have

129

taken too long, actually it took months longer with the dentist and everything—I called him and said I needed three husky men and he sent them and we found them and fixed them and he doesn't owe me any more, if he ever did. But I guess now you think I'm pretty horrible." She said it quite flatly, watching me.

"Horrible," I said. "And ugly, too. Don't forget ugly."

After a moment she laughed shortly. "It's funny, I never told it to anybody else except those three musclemen who were helping me, who had a right to know why, and were guaranteed to keep their mouths shut. I even made up some story for the doctor; not that he really believed it, but I picked one who'd mind his own business. I don't know why the hell I'm babbling it all to you."

I said, "That's easy. I'm one of the few people you know who's in no moral position to get self-righteous because you gelded a couple of jerks who raped you." I studied her for a moment. "But you'd better make up your mind, Elly. What's really bothering you, your guilt or your traumatic frigidity? Better concentrate on one or the other."

"I don't have any guilt," she said defiantly. "They got exactly what was coming to them. I just . . . feel kind of dirty for having done it, that's all; I find myself wanting to wash my hands whenever I think of it. But after what they did to me, what's a little more dirt?"

I said, "I know, you were all soiled and spoiled already."

Anger flashed in her eyes. "Damn you, I don't know why I picked a callous creep like you for my midnight confessions!" She stared at me with calculated malice. "And I most certainly don't need Dr. Helmstein's sure cure for traumatic frigidity, thanks just the same, you *macho* bastard!"

I grinned. "Now you feel better, having gotten that out, don't you?"

"Well, it's what you were thinking about, sitting on my bed, isn't it?"

"Naturally," I said. "Wouldn't any man, sitting on a lady's bed at two in the morning? Do you think you can sleep now?"

"I think you're a phony," she said. A sly look had come into her eyes. "Always boasting about fucking all these women everywhere. Hell, you're probably impotent, really."

I said, "You're not ready to play that game, Elly. And you don't know me well enough."

"What game?"

"Actually, you'd kind of like for us to try it to see if maybe, just maybe, it will work now; but you're scared for us to try it because it'll be so lousy if it doesn't. So you think if you insult me and make me mad I'll grab you and make up your mind for you, like shoving a parachutist out of the plane who's scared to jump."

There was a little silence. I saw her breasts lift sharply with her breathing, under the flowered stuff of her nightie.

"Instant diagnosis by Dr. Helmstein?" she murmured, but now there was no malice in her voice. "I'm sorry. I guess I'm pretty obvious, aren't I? It's . . . such a lousy way to be crippled. I keep thinking if . . . just once with somebody I could really trust. But there's no reason I should trust you, is there?"

"Not any," I said. "I'm the most untrustworthy guy you're apt to meet. Did you trust Warren?"

Her breath caught. "Damn you, that's not any of your . . ." She stopped, nodded ruefully, and went on in a different tone, wryly amused, "The poor guy didn't know what hit him. The lady's signals were perfectly clear, he thought; and then suddenly he had this shrill, panicky wildcat in his arms. Oh, Jesus, it's an awful way to be! I'm just telling you so you'll be warned."

"Sure," I said. "I've got a capsule if you want one to put you to sleep, but it's not really a good idea on top of the booze."

She shook her head. "It's too damned easy to get into the habit. If I ever start that, the way I'm feeling these days, I'll never stop. I'd better just sweat it out without. Matt?"

"Yes?"

"I'm sorry. I'm just a bitch. I can't help being nasty about this."

"Sure," I said, rising to look down at her, and retrieving the gun from the bedside table. "A horrible, ugly, nasty bitch. But you're wrong about one thing. It's not just your ankles. Your shoulders are kind of pretty, too. Good night, Elly."

The light went out behind me as I passed through the connecting door without looking back. Back in my own room I stood for a moment looking out the dark window, thinking it was a damned unnecessary complication to an already tricky assignment and tricky relationship. I had a sudden unwanted picture of a small girl with a swollen and discolored face and a couple of broken teeth bending over a pinned-down man, wielding a bloody knife. Nightmare stuff. But would I rather play bodyguard to a dainty tender-hearted wench who'd call me a beast because I'd hurt those poor little fellows who'd been waiting for us in here with loaded guns? I'd had that experience, thanks; and in a pinch I'd take Eleanor Brand any day, Elly with her ruthless attitude toward her work, her terrible self-loathing, her vengeful anger, and her ready high-heeled shoe. To hell with all the sweet unresisting females—and sweet unresisting males, too—everybody thought were so great these supposedly nonviolent days.

I didn't sleep nearly as well the second half of the night as I had the first half; and when I finally did start sleeping soundly, the telephone woke me. I looked at my watch and saw that it read almost seven o'clock.

"Room 743," said the female voice that had given me the red priority message yesterday.

"What's there for me?"

"He'll be there and he wants you there on time."

"I'm always on time," I said. "What time?"

"I was supposed to wake you exactly one hour early . . . Mark."

"Right. Where's Fred?"

"Unavailable at the moment. Meeting his special flight at the airport and running some errands afterward. You'll continue to cover the subject yourself for the time being. I'm to tell you to be very careful."

"Message received and understood."

I hung up and looked up to see the subject in question standing in the doorway between the rooms, yawning, looking childish and innocent in the flowing nightie that left her arms bare. I'd already determined that the stuff was cotton, or a good modern imitation, and that the pattern had a lot of little red flowers among a lot of little green leaves. There was some demure lacy white stuff around the neck. She had, I noticed, rather small and pretty feet. I didn't like noticing that; I seemed to be getting a thing about female feet lately. And why the hell did my mind keep dredging up memories of Martha Devine?

I told myself to forget about Elly's pretty feet. All I was required to do, I reminded myself firmly, was to keep this weird little knife-wielding dame alive until she could do us no harm by dying. I didn't have to like her.

"We've got an hour to dress and eat," I said. "The big boss is coming to Nassau. Big deal."

"I'm sorry about last night," Eleanor said.

"*De nada,* as we say in our fluent Spanish."

She grimaced. "I let it all hang out, didn't I? My God, I told you stuff I didn't think I'd ever tell anybody; and the funny thing is I hate people who moan and groan about their sad fates. So a couple of creeps beat me up and raped me in a vacant lot, so what? Forget the whole gooey performance, will you, please?"

"Did it help?"

She looked a little startled. "Well, I slept like a baby the rest of the night, so I guess it did help. Thanks." After a moment she said, "Matt?"

"Yes?"

"Why did you say that, last night?"

"What?"

"About my shoulders. That's kind of silly, isn't it? Ankles, legs, okay. Tits, ass, cunt, swell. But who cares about *shoulders*, for God's sake?"

I said, deliberately deadpan, "Maybe I'm a shoulder freak. Anyway, a girl with a face like a mud fence ought to have a little encouragement. Even if it's only shoulders."

The quick anger came into her eyes and she started to speak hotly; then she gave me her special, big, engaging grin instead. "You bastard. You've got it all worked out, haven't you? Keep the girl off balance and she'll follow you anywhere. I'll be ready by the time you've shaved."

CHAPTER 16

SHE wore her neat little chambray suit again with the same or another round-necked white blouse. As we left the table after breakfast, I noticed that her ankles really were quite attractive, set off by her nice sheer hose and slim-heeled tan leather pumps. I told myself again to cut it out. She'd make an intriguing project for somebody who liked intriguing rehabilitation projects—there was really too much good stuff there for her to be allowed to go around forever thinking of herself as ugly and spoiled—but it wasn't my line of work; and it was hard to forget what she'd done in retaliation even with the best, or worst, provocation in the world. On the other hand, I told myself, considering my own violent profession, it hardly became me to be squeamish about a little thing like that.

She glanced at me, almost shyly for her, as we waited for an elevator. "Now I wish I hadn't told you," she murmured. "It did help, but you're looking at me differently. That's why I never told anybody before. I didn't want their lousy slushy sympathy."

"It's not that," I said. "I'm just wondering where you keep that damned knife. I've heard of castrating-type women before, but this is ridiculous."

After a startled moment, she laughed and took my arm

to enter the cage. "Are you always so blunt, or is this your idea of therapy, Dr. Helmstein?"

I said, "Oh, I can be diplomatic as hell when I want to be."

"But you can't quite remember the last time you wanted to be." She flashed her big grin at me, and stopped grinning. "Talking about wanting, are you sure I'm wanted at this high-level conference, whatever it is?"

I shrugged. "You're wanted by me. I'm supposed to protect you, remember? My instructions specifically said to be very careful, and since we're always supposed to be very careful anyway, the fact that it was mentioned in the orders would seem to indicate that there's something special to be very careful about. So until Fred is available, you don't get out of my sight; and I don't plan to trust even Fred too far if the going gets rough. If I were supposed to park you somewhere and come alone, the orders would have been worded differently." Riding up, we had the lift, as the British call it, to ourselves; and I regarded her approvingly and said, "I thought lady journalists were all strictly trousers types."

She glanced at me, again rather shyly for her, and hesitated a bit before she said, "When . . . when you're not very pretty, you've got a choice, Matt. Either you say to hell with it, you're obviously a total loss anyway, so you might as well look like a complete slob in dirty jeans, what have you got to lose? Or you say to yourself, honey, if you had a face like an angel you could get away with dressing like a tramp, but since you've got nothing else going for you, you'd better be careful to look as good as you can." She made a wry face at me. "Anyway, you haven't seen me in slacks, let alone jeans. I look positively deformed—well, even more positively deformed than usual."

It was very revealing and, I suppose, rather touching; but I forced myself to say deliberately, "I don't mind ugly girls, but ugly girls who keep talking about it all the time kind of bore me."

She turned on me sharply; then she drew a long breath

135

and said very softly, as if speaking to herself, "A sense of humor is supposed to help. And a *very* thick skin."

"You're the one who said it," I reminded her. "An ugly little monkey with a notebook, you said."

We stepped out of the elevator on the seventh floor, checked the room numbers, and started in the right direction, but Eleanor touched my arm and came to a halt facing me.

"Look," she said, "look, do you really have some kind of crazy therapeutic theory about me, is that why you keep needling me like this?"

I said carefully, "I've got to put up with you in the line of duty, Elly. And you'll be a lot easier to put up with if I can kid you out of this nonsense about what a revolting freak you are. The other, what happened to you, you can't help. Okay. So I have to listen to the lady's nightmares; I don't have to listen to her daymares, too. What's the matter, did you have a pretty little sister your daddy loved better than you?"

We were walking again. Looking straight ahead, she said rather stiffly, "No, but I had a pretty little mother who wanted a pretty little doll-baby to play with and got something that looked like a junior-grade female chimpanzee instead. Well, what did she expect? Daddy wasn't the handsomest man in the world; he was just smart and rich which was why she'd grabbed him in the first place. But if she wanted pretty babies she should have married a movie star." She paused, and a funny little smile tugged at the corners of her mobile mouth. "You haven't told me I'm *not* a revolting freak."

"Hell, I told you you had pretty shoulders, didn't I? I'll get around to reporting on the rest of you eventually, don't rush me. . . . Hold everything!" I caught her arm and pulled her to a halt.

"What is it?"

We'd turned the last corner, and the room numbers were going the right way and getting close, and there were two men waiting outside a door down the hall ahead. When

136

they saw us, they stopped talking and moved apart—and I knew at once that it was wrong.

These were not just a couple of lower echelon escort-type gents waiting for the big shots inside to finish their business, meanwhile chatting casually about football or baseball or women, and pausing in their talk to open the door for some honored and expected guests, after which they'd just resume their interrupted conversation. These were men waiting to carry out a prearranged plan, taking up prearranged positions. I knew from the way they moved a little too stiffly, a little too carefully, that they were feeling somewhat tense, the way you always do before the action starts—even though it shouldn't be too damned difficult to deal with just one man and a girl, all unsuspecting.

"Back to the elevator," I said, swinging Eleanor around. "If I say run, run like hell. Do you remember the number I told you last night?"

We were walking away now. They didn't follow us, at least not while I had them in sight, but that meant nothing.

"23572?" She must have had questions, but she didn't ask them.

"Good girl," I said. "If anything happens and we get separated, you get clear, all the way clear and call that number. Somebody'll come for you."

The elevator was before us now and we were in luck: the door was opening. Two well-dressed young black men stepped out, talking with soft Bahamian accents, paying us no attention. I took us back down to the fourth floor. There was nobody in the hall except a black maid shoving a cart, who didn't give us more than a casual glance. The room doors showed undisturbed. Apparently the maid hadn't got to us yet; more important, nobody'd been in to set a trap since we'd left. I let us into my room and locked the door behind us.

"Okay," I said. "So far so good. That was what he meant by being very careful, apparently. Now we wait for Phase Two."

"What is it, Matt?" she asked. "What's happening?"

I shook my head. "Let's not waste time guessing. Sooner

137

or later somebody'll let us know what's up. Open your purse."

She glanced at me curiously but obeyed. I pulled one of the guns I'd liberated yesterday from the depths of my suitcase—it was Warren Peterson's, I noted—and showed it to her.

"Do you know how?" I asked.

"Just a little." She studied the weapon carefully and said, "At least I know it's a revolver and doesn't have a safety."

"Hell, you're a ballistics genius," I said. "A lot of people who write books about the damned things don't know that much."

"It's the kind you don't really have to cock, isn't it? You can, but you don't have to."

"Correct. A long, strong pull on the trigger will do it all."

She licked her lips. "What do I shoot?"

"When I tell you to point it at somebody," I said, "you point it at him. And when I tell you to shoot him, you shoot him. And keep on shooting him until I tell you to stop shooting him. Not after lunch or tomorrow or next month. Now."

She grinned briefly. "Yes, sir, Mr. Helm, sir."

I checked the loads and snapped the cylinder back into the frame. I stuffed the weapon into the big leather purse that matched her shoes.

"One more little detail," I said. "I don't really care who you blow away, as long as it isn't me. But be kind of careful about that, huh?"

She nodded, sober now. "Yes, I know. I'll be careful." She touched the weapon lightly, before closing the purse. "I wish I'd had that, that night."

"Best purity-preservation medicine in the world," I said. "That's one of the things it was invented for. But nowadays they seem to figure, better ten lovely innocent virgins deflowered than one lousy rapist shot. Well, it's a funny world full of funny people. . . ."

The telephone interrupted my foray into social philosophy. I glanced at Eleanor and picked it up. A familiar voice spoke in my ear.

"Matt?"

"Yes, sir," I said. "I was reporting at the specified location at the specified time, but I didn't like the looks of the welcoming committee."

"I'm afraid you're getting a bit jumpy, Matt." Mac's voice was cool. "As soon as we finish here we should consider another visit to the Ranch for rest and re-evaluation; don't you think?" The Ranch is the place in Arizona where I'd wanted to send Brent for training, the place where they also patch up the damage from the last mission and make you ready for the next. I didn't take the suggestion too much to heart, since Mac was talking for public consumption, as indicated by the fact that he was carefully and repeatedly employing my real name instead of my code name, the warning signal. He went on, "Our colleagues of the OFS are quite harmless, I assure you."

"Yes, sir," I said. "Will you ask them to be harmless inside the room, please? Back from the door where I can see them all as I come in. The door unlocked and nobody behind it or near it. No weapons in sight. I've had trouble with somebody in this hotel already, two somebodies—three somebodies, come to think of it—and I'm responsible for the young lady's safety. As you say, I'm jumpy as hell. If anybody waves a firearm at me with whatever motive, or comes at me from an unexpected direction, no matter who, I won't be responsible for my jumpy reactions."

Mac said, "It all seems quite unnecessary and even slightly paranoid, but if that's the way you prefer it, I will ask Mr. Bennett to instruct his men accordingly. Incidentally, he's very interested in said young lady. He thinks she may be able to provide him with valuable information about a nautical terrorist problem with which his organization is concerned. He's very anxious that she should be delivered here promptly so that he can interview her. As a matter of fact, he finds the delay quite annoying, although I have explained to him that your instructions require you to take all possible precautions where Miss Brand is concerned."

"Yes, sir," I said. "I'll bring her along. Matt out."

I laid down the instrument and sat for a moment, running the conversation back in my mind to determine just what he'd really been telling me, that didn't necessarily correspond with the words he'd been speaking. Eleanor was silent. The girl had an endearing habit of keeping her mouth shut and saving her questions until the time was right for them. At last I looked up at her where she stood, waiting.

"We've both got trouble," I said.

"Tell me."

"Mr. Bennett of the OFS wants to interview you. That's polite for taking you over and, presumably, freezing us out. The OFS, as you undoubtedly know better than I do with your Washington experience, is the Office of Federal Security, formerly the Federal Security Bureau, formerly . . ."

"Yes, I know."

"Whenever somebody complains too loudly about their high-handed methods they get themselves reorganized under a different name; they change their name almost as often as they change their shirts, and they're very meticulous about their button-down shirts. A very high-class bunch of spooks, far above us low peasants laboring sweatily, and sometimes bloodily, in the undercover vineyard. The takeover kids. If there's publicity involved they'll grab it, no matter who was on the job first. Strictly in the public interest, of course. Right now they seem to have a terrorist problem at sea and think you can help them, which means they must have come across a political angle to all these sinking ships of yours. . . . What?"

Eleanor was shaking her head. "No. It's not political and it's not terrorist. I don't know what it is, but it's not that."

"What makes you so sure?"

"What made you so sure those men were waiting in this room last night, Matt? I'm a pro; it's my business to know. Take it from me, whoever thinks that, is wrong." She grimaced. "It's just the sort of simple-minded answer those

140

officious jerks of the OFS would grab at. They've got two pat answers for everything, and if it isn't drugs, it's just got to be terrorism. But they're full of shit, if you'll pardon the phrase."

I nodded. "I guess you've done quite a bit of work on this story already."

"Enough to get the feel of it. There's a crazy random feeling to it, Matt, a kind of *amateur* feeling, if you know what I mean. Did you ever come across a case where you just knew that when you caught up with the guy he wouldn't be a trained agent on a mission, or even a dedicated revolutionary following his stern political principles? You could just *feel* that you were dealing with a poor damned jerk who'd grabbed a gun and started shooting people, simply because somebody creamed his new car or hurt his girlfriend."

"I know what you mean," I said.

She said, "Look, the ones that go down are mostly kind of slob ships, if you know what I mean; flag-of-convenience vessels that are getting on in age and aren't too well managed or maintained. Cheapo ships, you could call them. Exactly the kind of beatup old buckets a terrorist would scorn; he'd make his big political statement by sinking some shiny new freighters or container ships or preferably giant supertankers, wouldn't he? Lots of publicity. Important losses that would make the shipping world sit up and take notice, and pay up promptly when the price was stated. But this has been going on for a couple of years already with no demands that I've heard of; and I've listened very closely, I can tell you."

"Any other kind of pattern?" I asked.

She hesitated. "Well, there's something funny about the crews. I've been interviewing all the survivors I could trace; that's what I'm doing here in Nassau. Some of the men off of the last ship sunk are in the hospital here and I've been talking with them. I was there yesterday questioning a young officer, the third mate, who was on the bridge when it happened." She frowned. "Matt, the funny thing is, he's hiding something."

141

"What?"

Eleanor shook her head. "I don't know yet; but he took refuge in being too sick to answer—he was pretty badly burned—when I started asking too many questions about how it happened. Damn it, I know when an interviewee is trying to keep something from me; it's the first thing you learn in this racket. And I've hit some others like that from the other ships, usually officers. They just don't want to talk. I don't know what it means yet. Some kind of collusion? Barratry? A giant industry-wide insurance swindle involving ancient ships that are worth more to their owners at the bottom of the sea?" She shrugged. "I don't know, but I hope to go back to the hospital today, if this business of yours doesn't take too long, and see if I can't pry it out of this one. He's pretty young and I think he's having a hard time living with it, whatever it is."

I said, "You can't have it both ways, Elly. If it's a giant criminal conspiracy of some kind, it's unlikely to be an amateur production."

She shrugged. "I can't help it. But I know damned well it's not a terrorist caper; I've dealt with a few of those and they smelled altogether different." She grinned abruptly. "Hardly evidence I could present in court, right?"

I asked, "How do you feel about sharing your information with the OFS?"

"Stupid question number one thousand," she said. "How do you think I feel? It's *my* story, goddamn it. What's the matter with these law-enforcement freaks, anyway? The information is there. The sources are there. If they want to know something, why don't they do a little simple investigative work and find out for themselves, instead of trying to hitch a free ride on our coattails? Then they can go ahead and cheerfully betray their own informants instead of trying to force us to betray ours—and see how far their next investigation gets, after word gets around they're not to be trusted!" She shook her head grimly. "Like this boy in the hospital. Obviously, what he knows is discreditable to him or he wouldn't be hiding it, would he? And obviously, he's not going to tell me unless I swear to him that his name will never come into it; that I'll only use his information to help me learn what's going on and nail those responsible, not to crucify him. That I'll cover for him all the way, even if it means going to jail and telling the judge chuck-you-Farley." She grimaced. "What the hell kind of a law is it that tries to make people break their sacred goddamn oaths to people who've trusted them?"

I grinned and said, "It's a great speech and you may need it in court, but we'd better not take any more time to practice it now."

She drew a long breath. "Sorry. Push the Freedom-of-the-Press button and out it comes. If that's my trouble with the OFS, what's yours?"

I said, "Whether or not to give you to them."

She frowned at me. "Have you got a choice? They're pretty big and powerful and claim all kinds of jurisdiction, aren't they? Don't they?"

"Claim is the word," I said. "There are ways of dealing with their claims. My chief made certain I'd remember that I'm here to take all possible precautions where you're concerned, not to oblige Mr. Bennett of the OFS. I figure that means I've got discretion: your safety comes first. For strictly selfish reasons, of course. We can't afford to have you killed, at the moment."

She smiled. "I like dealing with a man who's all heart."

I said, "Anyway, what it amounts to is that if I think you'll really be safer with Bennett's boys, I'm presumably authorized to turn you over to them; but if I don't think they could protect a dimestore wedding ring locked up in Fort Knox, I'm allowed to keep you for a pet, all my very own."

There was a little silence. She was watching me steadily. "Well?" she asked at last.

I said, "Hell, it's up to you, Elly. I can only protect you if I have your full and happy cooperation, which I obviously won't have if I bully you in my usual crude fashion and keep you away from that nice Mr. Bennett and his handsome cleancut agents very much against your will."

143

A smile touched her lips and went away. "But can you really buck them?"

I said, "Lady, a man with a gun can buck anybody—as long as he lasts."

"How?"

"Don't ask if you don't really want to know."

She licked her lips. "I want to know."

I said, "Well, it'll be the biggest goddamned circus you ever saw, a real Wild West show. Billy the Kid and Wild Bill Hickok and Wyatt Earp in one neat economy package. My chief will try to quiet me down, of course, he always does; and I'll tell him where he can go and stuff himself with what, I always do. We've worked this crazyman routine before; we know all the moves. Bennett doesn't really have any authority over us; but he's got power enough to make things uncomfortable for us unless I give my chief an out, which I will do, and which he will take. And that will put it strictly up to me, and you. All I ask is that you don't let me get clear out to the end of the limb and then hand them a saw to cut it off with. Make up your mind. Either we go all the way together or we don't start. What's your choice?"

She picked up her heavy purse and took my arm. "It sounds like fun. I like circuses. Shall we go?"

The first thing I saw, as we entered the seventh-floor room, was the man whose Adam's apple I'd clobbered in my own room the evening before.

CHAPTER 17

IT was apparently the sitting-room part of a suite, with the sleeping facilities next door. It was Old Home Week in spades, I thought sourly. Not only was one of my last night's playmates present—I'd had to rearrange my thinking about that incident when I learned the OFS was involved—but also the pair I'd seen in the hall this morning, all lined up on the sofa like pigeons on a wire. Warren Peterson was there, too, for reasons yet to be determined. He was looking grim and handsome and as stupid as I remembered him, in his blond beach-boy fashion. If I'd left a lump on his skull it didn't show. He had a big chair to the left of the only man in the room I didn't know by sight, another boldly handsome gent—if you overlooked the fact that he had no hair to amount to anything. Nature had harvested the crop on top and he'd mowed the rest to match. I didn't like that. It's an affectation I'd met before; let's call it the skinhead syndrome. It almost always spells trouble.

It used to be that the ones with lots of hair were making a statement about what free and independent spirits they were. In those days, the crew-cut joes were the conventional ones. Nowadays, hair is square, and it's the self-made baldies who are making the statement, generally about how tough and virile they are, as opposed to the lace-pants sissies with the flowing locks. Bennett had a long, big-nosed face with the nose thrusting downward, straight and bony, from a point well up between the eyebrows. The eyes were brown, and as a good blue-eyed transplanted Swede, I don't trust brown-eyed people much—I have never claimed to be particularly tolerant—but I wouldn't have trusted this one if he'd had eyes like a summer sky. He was wearing a light suit of the kind that used to be called Palm Beach before they started making them out of petroleum. Completing his costume—well, aside from a few odds and ends like shirt and shoes—was a little bow tie, undoubtedly another significant statement in this age of four-in-hand neckwear or no neckwear at all.

It was too bad. The problem wasn't that he was tough; the problem was that he thought he was tough—he thought about it all the time. The really tough ones can be reasonable; they've got nothing to prove. They know what they are and to hell with you. But this guy with his goddamned statements, obviously wasn't quite sure. But he'd die or kill you rather than let his doubts be known.

He looked at his watch with a flourish. "Helm? You were ordered to report here at eight o'clock sharp."

I paid that no attention. I wasn't his man and my orders and my punctual execution thereof, or lack of punctual execution thereof, were no concern of his. I glanced at Mac who'd been seated at Bennett's right, but had risen courteously at Eleanor's appearance, the only man in the room to do so. He was dressed in one of his customary gray suits, one of the lighter ones as a concession to the Bahamian climate. He's got them, it seems, in every weight from tropical to arctic. Maybe he's making a statement, too, but after all the years I'd worked for him, I wasn't going to worry about its meaning now. His smoothly shaved face seemed impassive; but I saw an eyelid flutter almost imperceptibly. It was about as much of a wink as he ever manages, equivalent to a contorted grimace on another man's face. It said that he knew what I had in mind, what I must have in mind under the circumstances; so put the gaudy show on the road. I turned to the heavy man whose conversational apparatus I'd damaged the night before, now dressed neatly in suit and tie. Apparently the sports shirt outfit had been a disguise.

"Up!" I said. "Get the lady a chair, slob!"

Shocked, the man started to answer angrily; but Bennett cut in, "I give the orders around here, Helm!"

I wheeled on him. "Then give them, for Christ's sake! A room full of healthy male creeps all parked on their fat rumps; what happened to manners, anyway? And what's this muscle-bound dodo doing here?" I glanced at Warren Peterson and back to Bennett. "If he's on your payroll, you must really be scraping the bottom of the barrel!"

Bennett said stiffly, "Mr. Peterson had certain information that seemed relevant. He claims that the lady and he were attacked by you; and that you must now be using certain drugs—you used some on him, he says—to dominate and control her."

I said, "Hell, the stupid bastard threatened me with a

gun, so I took it away from him and hit him on the head with it. If that's a drug. Then I gave him a mild sedative so he wouldn't come awake violent and force me to kill him. As for Miss Brand, she's quite capable of speaking for herself, so I won't bother."

Eleanor said quickly, "I'm not under anybody's domination or control thank you very much. And I asked Mr. Peterson to go away and mind his own business. I have no idea what he thinks he's doing."

Peterson cleared his throat. "Long before that, you asked me to help you and protect you, Eleanor. I feel it's my duty to continue to do so, even though you seem to have fallen under the spell of the very man you hated and feared. . . ."

"You're being very silly," Eleanor said. Her voice was sharp. "And what you're really doing is getting back at me because I kicked you out of bed."

There was a brief silence in the room. Warren Peterson turned bright red, a real honest-to-God blush that would have done a Victorian maiden proud. Bennett cleared his throat.

"All right, Lawson. Please get the young lady a chair."

I looked at Mac. "Just what are we supposed to be doing here, sir? I came because those were your instructions, but I'd like the record to show that I'm acting under protest."

"Matt, there's no need for hostility—"

"Tell them that," I said. "Just how much of their hostility do I have to put up with before I produce a little of my own? Two of the men in this room, and one somewhere outside who belongs with them, have pointed guns at me within the past twenty-four hours. I consider that fairly hostile behavior, don't you, sir? Two others were laying for me in the hall when I came up here half an hour ago. It's, well, kind of an effort for me to be polite to them, or their boss, under the circumstances. What's supposed to make it worth my while, sir? Our while?"

"Inter-agency cooperation—"

"Cooperation, my ass!" I said crudely. "What the hell were a couple of OFS characters doing in my room last

147

night with loaded firearms, cooperating? You know damn well what they were doing. You know what they were doing out in the hall this morning. They were going to get the drop on me, they thought, and disarm me neatly, after which they'd have it all their own way, with the lady they wanted safely established under their 'protection' instead of ours. Cooperation, hell!" I wheeled as the heavyset man called Lawson turned away, after ungraciously shoving forward a straight chair for Eleanor to sit on. I said, "Here, catch." He turned hastily and fielded the revolver I tossed him. "That's your sick pal's," I said. "Here's yours." The second weapon came too fast for him and, still busy with the first, he fumbled and dropped them both. I said, "Don't get nervous, amigo. I took the bullets out of them. Us pros generally call them cartridges, but I suppose you amateurs call them bullets like in the lady-type detective novels, so we'll keep the terminology simple for you." I turned back to Bennett. "You'd better instruct him not to load them in here. He keeps shooting people accidentally."

Bennett said, tight-lipped, "A loud and impressive performance, Helm. Well, at least loud. Now if we can get down to business. . . . I'm sorry, Miss Brand. No smoking in here."

I looked at him for a moment, unbelieving. At least I pretended to be unbelieving; actually, from him, I'd have believed anything. I turned to Eleanor and took her arm, urging her off the chair onto which she'd just settled.

"Come on, baby. Let's get the hell out of here."

Again she asked no questions; she simply rose and turned with me toward the door.

"Helm!" That was Bennett, behind me. When I gave him no answer, he snapped, "Lawson! Burdette!"

The two men came off the sofa and moved to block the door. Then they stood very still, looking at the snub-nosed revolver in my hand.

I said, "Elly."

"Yes."

"Now's the time. Your gun, please. I have the one on the left. You take the one on the right. When I shoot mine,

148

yours is all yours. . . . Ready?" Under my breath I said, "I told you it was going to be a goddamn circus."

"I'm ready, Matt." Her voice was quite steady, and so was the weapon she'd produced from her purse.

Behind me, Bennett's voice said sharply, "I must ask you please to control this madman of yours!" Obviously he was addressing Mac.

I said, "Sir."

"Yes, Matt."

"Warn them, please. They may have some strange notion that I'm bluffing. Tell them. If a gun shows, if there's a single shot. Tell them what will happen."

Mac's voice spoke calmly, "There was a barge on the Fraser River, up in Canada; a houseboat of sorts. There was a meeting—you'll be interested, Bennett—of a certain terrorist group. Ten people were present. Two departed; eight remained, including my agent here, a prisoner. There was some shooting. Eventually Mr. Helm walked out. He had in him two metal-jacketed 9mm submachine gun bullets, one soft-nosed .38 caliber revolver bullet, and three double-ought buckshot pellets, but he walked out. Nobody else emerged from that floating shack alive, except for one young terrorist who was carried out on a stretcher, whom the doctors eventually managed to save. I would not be too hasty with the firearms, gentlemen."

After a moment, Bennett said, "Order him to put his gun away, then."

"I do not interfere with my agents in the field," Mac said. "I simply give them their assignments and allow them to carry on as they see fit. You seem to have antagonized Mr. Helm. He's been attacked with lethal weapons. Traps have been set for him. Oddly enough, he does not seem to consider this appropriate behavior for the members of co-operating agencies. Oddly enough, neither do I. You made the problem, Bennett, now deal with it."

He was departing from the standard script which, as I'd described it to Eleanor, requires me to take all the heat while he dissociates himself, and the agency, from my violent antics. Apparently he had no great fondness for, or fear of, Mr. Bennett; and he saw no reason to encourage the man's high-handed tactics.

There was a hint of shrillness in Bennett's voice. "But what does he want?"

Mac's voice was impatient. "Why not ask him?"

"What do you want, Helm?"

I said, "The lady has been entrusted to my care. I feel responsible for seeing that she is treated with courtesy, respect, and consideration. Her personal habits are not open to criticism. If she wants to pick her nose, she'll pick her nose, and there will be no comments. If she feels like smoking, she'll either smoke here or I'll take her where she can smoke, and I doubt there's anybody in this room who can stop me. If somebody wants to try, let's get on with it."

There was a little pause; then Bennett laughed lightly and I knew it was over, at least for the time being; but he would have to be watched from now on. He would want to avenge this blow to his pride and he would certainly have to be watched. But I would have had to do that anyway.

"All this fuss about a mere cigarette!" he said easily. "I do most humbly apologize, Miss Brand, I didn't realize how much tobacco meant to you. Of course you may smoke. Lawson, an ashtray for the lady, *if* you please."

"Okay, Elly," I said. "You can put it away now."

Warren Peterson's voice spoke shrilly, "You see? He's established power over her somehow, just like I told you. Why, she's even willing to kill for him now!"

Nobody paid any attention to this nonsense. As Eleanor seated herself once more, her lips moved almost imperceptibly, "If you're Wild Bill Hickok, what does that make me, Calamity Jane?"

"She was even uglier than you," I murmured. "But then, she was lots bigger. Handled a twenty-mule team like a pair of ponies, I'm told—"

"Miss Brand."

Eleanor threw me a wicked glance, and said, "Yes, Mr. Bennett."

Bennett cleared his throat. "Now that we have all the

dramatics and melodramatics out of the way, I hope, perhaps you'll be good enough to tell us about the journalistic project upon which you're presently engaged."

I saw Mac wince. "Presently," employed in that way offends him almost as much as "contact" used as a verb. The proper usage, according to him, is "at present."

Eleanor said brightly, "Oh, you mean my piece on the Bermuda Triangle? Well, I'm afraid I haven't really come up with a lot of new material yet. You know, of course, about the flight of military planes that disappeared from Fort Lauderdale, and the private yacht *Revonoc* that shoved off from Key West and was never seen again."

"Please, Miss Brand. We're aware that you've used, shall we say, a little misdirection to hide the true purpose of your research—"

I said quickly, "But the people with whom she's dealing may not be aware of it yet. I thought they were, when we ran into that ambush last night, but it turned out to be a friendly cooperating agency just having a little friendly cooperative fun. . . . Incidentally, how's the casualty?"

Bennett said stiffly, "I wondered when you'd get around to showing some interest. His condition is stable; it looks as if he'll make it all right."

I said, "About people who wave guns at me, Mr. Bennett, and get shot as a result, my interest is very limited. Even when I shoot them myself; and in this case I didn't. But I'm happy for Mr. Lawson's sake that his victim is going to survive."

The heavyset man said angrily, "Goddamn it, if you hadn't—"

"It's rough," I said. "In a couple more generations we'll have bred us a nice gentle race of citizens that'll never fight back, and disarmed them totally for good measure. Too bad you were born too early, amigo. You'd have loved it in a docile society where nobody had guns but you."

Mac cleared his throat. "I think that's enough, Matt."

"Yes, sir," I said. "As I was saying, it may be that Miss Brand's misdirection is still working; and before we go on here I'd like some assurance that it's going to stay working

151

as long as possible. Just because Peterson seems to have spilled the beans to you, Bennett, about what she's really investigating, doesn't mean it has to be broadcast all over the waterfront."

"I assure you, we're well aware of the importance of security," Bennett said coldly. "As it happens, in this case the point is already moot, as you'll see in a minute. However, I'll take the opportunity to assure Miss Brand that nothing of what she tells us will be divulged unnecessarily." He looked at Eleanor. "Now, please. How much information do you have about these terrorist activities?"

Eleanor hesitated. I knew what she was thinking; but we'd already made the point that we weren't going to be pushed around for anybody's convenience. She was smart enough to see that there was no sense in overdoing it. However, she did feel obliged to make her attitude clear.

"I'm not aware of any terrorist activities," she said. "I have been investigating some recent ship losses along the coast, but I haven't been able to determine what's behind them. I have found no evidence that would lead me to call them acts of terrorism."

"Perhaps we have a little more information on the subject than you, Miss Brand." Bennett's voice was smug. "Nevertheless, we would appreciate it very much if you would share with us whatever information you have."

There was an angry glint in Eleanor's eyes, but she made her report in a crisp and businesslike fashion, "I went back five years. I listed all the possibles; collisions, groundings, storms, fires, explosions, etc. I discarded a large number of incidents I was sure were simply normal seagoing accidents. I set aside a few doubtfuls; generally cases where a ship went missing but nobody, even among the survivors if any, seemed to know exactly what had happened. I was left with a small category of what I consider practically certains. Five ships, six with this last one. They all had similar characteristics. The damage was always forward. The ship had apparently hit something that either exploded of its own accord or caused an explosion on board. Well, that's one theory. Another is that the bow blew up due to sabotage of one kind or another, although why a saboteur would pick the same location on every ship isn't easy to understand. These incidents, it turned out, all took place within the past two years."

Bennett nodded. "We will want all the names, Miss Brand. And all the associated information you have. In particular, it's my understanding that you have interviewed a number of the survivors. I'd like transcripts of those interviews."

"I'm sure you would," Eleanor said dryly. "What's wrong with doing a little interviewing of your own?"

"Even if we could afford to waste our time duplicating your efforts, it would be impossible in the case that concerns us most at the moment."

Eleanor frowned at him. "You're leading up to something. Spring it, please."

"The man in question was named Jurgen Hinkampf. He was third mate on the *Fairfax Constellation*, the tanker that recently sank off the Bahamas. He was smothered in his hospital bed last night, with a pillow. The murderer has not yet been apprehended."

Eleanor's face was pale. "Oh, the poor kid!"

"You spoke with him in the hospital yesterday, I understand."

"That's right. But he clammed up on me. I'd . . . hoped to be able to question him again today."

"Obviously that will not be possible," Bennett said. He glanced at me and went on, with some malice, "That is what I meant when I said the question of security is moot in this case. Obviously, somebody is already quite aware of the true purpose of Miss Brand's research, fairly obvious once she started looking up and interviewing these survivors. Apparently this individual or organization is trying to frustrate her efforts by eliminating her sources of information." He looked back at Eleanor. "You were under the impression that this Hinkampf was holding something back?"

She nodded. "But I haven't any idea what it could be. We didn't get that far."

153

"How far did you get?"

"He'd been telling me what happened," Eleanor said. "He said there was a violent jolt and a loud noise and he rushed out onto the open wing of the bridge—it was his watch—just as the whole bow of the ship went up in flames, like a great fireball that rolled aft toward him. He was badly burned as he tried to get back into shelter; so badly that he pretty well ceased to function. Some of his shipmates apparently helped him into the lifeboat."

"Your description makes it sound as if the ship were carrying gasoline."

"No, crude oil," Eleanor said. "But that's the whole works, you know, light and heavy stuff, just the way it comes out of the ground. And the light stuff is practically gasoline—it *is* unrefined gasoline—and can form an explosive mixture if the right precautions aren't taken. Apparently, they weren't taken on the *Constellation*. She was a fairly old and decrepit tanker, and whatever went bang up forward just set off the whole damned cargo." Eleanor hesitated. "I suppose the Bahamian authorities will want to talk with me, since I saw him shortly before . . . before he was killed."

"Yes, you're requested to pay them a visit this afternoon. I'll give you directions to the office. We can arrange transportation if you like."

I said, "I'll arrange transportation."

Bennett shrugged. "Suit yourselves. Miss Brand, you say Hinkampf told you all this? He wasn't reluctant to describe the actual disaster?"

"Oh, no. It was when I tried to . . . well, I wanted a clear picture of the situation on the bridge at the time of the explosion, but when I tried to establish exactly what he'd been doing, and the seaman who'd been on watch with him, just before hell broke loose, that was when he suddenly decided that he was too sick to do any more talking."

"Do you have any theories as to what he may have been hiding?"

She shrugged. "Just the obvious ones; that he'd been doing something he shouldn't, or not doing something he should. Maybe just goofing off while the autopilot steered the ship; and reading a comic book, or Immanuel Kant or whatever. It happens. Those ships practically run themselves, even the older ones. Anyway, he was too eager to tell me all about the pretty fireworks and too reluctant to discuss the technical details of his midnight watch. I think he knew that he'd done something wrong, something that, as the officer in charge, made him at least partly responsible for the loss of the ship. . . ."

"Guiltily responsible? Criminally responsible?"

She shook her head quickly. "If you mean, was he part of a plot to blow her up, I doubt it very much. From the way he told it, I'm sure that the explosion itself came as a terrible surprise to him. He wasn't expecting anything of the sort and he had no hand in arranging it; I'd swear to that. But I do think he was aware that he'd made a professional blunder or oversight that had at least contributed to the disaster. Something he didn't dare let anybody know about, particularly a nosy female journalist who'd turned out to know a little more about shipboard routines than he'd expected when he agreed to be interviewed." She smiled faintly. "I spent a week on a freighter, you know, just learning my way around a ship, before I started this investigation."

"You mentioned another man on watch, a seaman. Have you questioned him?"

"He's not around to be questioned," Eleanor said. "Jurgen didn't know exactly what happened to him; but he's not listed among the survivors."

"If there was some collaboration with the terrorists who arranged the sinking, that could be the inside man so to speak, taken off secretly and whisked to safety."

Eleanor said, "It's an interesting theory, but I don't believe it's very plausible, Mr. Bennett. With the tanker on fire and burning oil spreading over the sea all around it? Personally, I think that man went down with the ship, but if you want to hunt for him, his name was Einar Kettleman." She hesitated. "And I really don't believe it was the work of terrorists."

Bennett gave her his slow, smug, malicious smile. "Then it's very strange that we should have a note in our possession demanding a large sum of money in the name of a certain undercover organization, and threatening to sink another ship if the cash is not forthcoming by a certain deadline. Don't you think so, Miss Brand?"

CHAPTER 18

"BULLSHIT," Eleanor said. She turned to face me. "That's what it is, you know just fancy blue bullshit. I don't give a damn what kind of menace notes that bald bastard claims to have gotten hold of. It's not that kind of an operation. I can feel it."

It had been a hard day after our long session up on the seventh floor, which itself hadn't been easy; but she didn't show it. It was evening again and we were back in my fourth floor room in the Paradise Towers after dinner, having spent the afternoon going through the police bit together. That had involved a lot of waiting around, in between dealing with a large number of dumb officials and a smaller number of bright ones, both types hard to take in view of the differences of race and nationality.

A long hard day, but her suit and blouse—we'd gotten back so late she hadn't taken time to change for dinner—still looked fresh, her fragile stockings remained smooth and whole, and her businesslike hairdo had stayed obediently in place. A durable girl, but I thought I would have preferred a few wrinkles and smudges and straying locks. Her compulsive neatness was a little frightening. I guessed that she was fighting it very hard, rejecting anything that reminded her of a certain night when her tidy, disciplined image of herself had been brutally destroyed. I put a glass into her hand and raised mine.

"To terrorism," I said. "If Bennett wants to believe in it, why worry? Having him off chasing phantom fanatics may just keep him out of our hair."

But she was thinking of something else. "Matt," she said. "Matt, this morning, would you really have shot that gun? That man?"

I looked at her for a moment. "Nosy, aren't you?" I said.

"I was involved, remember. I think I'm entitled to know."

I watched her closely. I asked, "Would *you* have fired?"

She hesitated, and shrugged minutely. "I think so. If you'd told me to. I mean, if I go to a physics expert for advice, I don't argue with him about the validity of $E=mc^2$. And if I consult a weapons expert and he tells me it's necessary to make some loud and lethal noises with a firearm, who am I to contradict him? Yes, if you'd given the word, I think I would have fired. I would have assumed you knew what you were doing. But would you really have done it?"

I remembered that this was the tough little girl who had exacted payment for certain injuries received in a very unpleasant manner. Well, one gets tired of dealing with sentimental nitwits, and she certainly wasn't that.

I said, "There are three men alive today who would be dead if I hadn't exercised considerable forbearance yesterday, and run considerable risk. I had all the excuses I needed to defend myself violently, meaning lethally; but I passed them up. I told you that was the end of it. They've had all the breaks from me I can afford to give them. I've wasted all the luck on them I intend to. Let's put it this way: I don't wave firearms at people for fun. If I had really decided to leave the room and they had made a real effort to stop me, there would have been shooting. If any one of them points a gun at me again, or threatens me with any other weapon, I don't care who he is or whose orders he's carrying out, he's dead. Does that answer your question?"

She nodded, and started to ask a further question, but thought better of it. After a moment she said, "The Sacred Earth Protective Force, for God's sake! A million-buck ransom or another ship goes boom! A hell of a funny way to protect the sacred earth, by blowing up ships and blasting oil all over her sacred oceans. I tell you it's all wrong, Matt. I'm sure of it."

"Which," I said, "means that you're not quite sure, doesn't it?"

Then I was sorry I'd said it, because she stared at me oddly for a moment. I saw her face kind of crumple and her body kind of slump with the weariness she'd been trying to ignore. She looked around helplessly for a place to sit down. I pulled an upholstered chair closer for her. She sank down onto it and took a big gulp from the glass I'd given her—holding it in both hands—and shuddered. She spoke without looking up at me.

"You're getting too smart about me, damn you," she said softly. "Much too smart. Yes, I'm not quite sure. No, I'm not quite sure. Before . . . before it happened to me, I would have been. I was very bright and confident back then. I had it all figured out, always. But I was wrong that night, wasn't I? I was quite certain I'd be safe there and I wasn't. So what other mistakes have I been making in my cocky, cocksure way?"

I pulled another chair around and sat down facing her. "Well, I can think of two," I said. She looked up sharply; and I went on, "Two coincidences that you seem to be accepting that just can't be. I'm very sensitive to coincidences, Elly. In my racket you can't afford to pass anything that even looks like a coincidence. Too many people have died that way."

She drew a long breath, and reached down to slip off her shoes. She set them neatly side by side on the carpet and curled up comfortably in the big chair, giving a couple of quick, expert, feminine touches to her hair and clothes.

Suddenly she was the tidy, untiring lady journalist again, just relaxing—well, slightly—with a friend.

"What coincidences?" she asked. Her voice was a little stiff. "I wasn't aware that I'd overlooked . . . oh, you mean Lorca being mixed up in this sea business, is that it?"

I nodded. "That's number one. Let's take a look at it once more. After doing an election piece on George Winfield Lorca, now Senator Lorca, you then washed your hands of him, you thought, and took on a totally different subject for your next article, well, series of articles. Us. Only it now seems very likely that the idea had been fed to you by a guy on Lorca's payroll, right?"

She said, "To hell with where it came from; I told you I checked it out very carefully—"

"No criticism intended," I said hastily. "But look what happens next. You finish up that job, us, and start on still another one, ships. And by God, there's Senator Lorca in the middle of that one, too, if Hattie Robinson knew what she was talking about, and she usually did. I can't believe that just happened, Elly. I won't believe it, coincidence-shy as I am. There's got to be a connection somewhere."

Eleanor frowned. "You can't think Lorca planted that idea on me, too! Getting me to investigate you, to make trouble for you, that figures, the way he feels about you; but it hardly seems likely that he'd set me to investigating himself. And then smother people when they start to talk to me, that doesn't make sense! Anyway, I told you; I got the idea talking with your Captain Robinson."

I said, "That was the first you'd heard of these sinking ships, when you interviewed Harriet the first time? It came as a great revelation to you? An inspiration from the journalistic muse, so to speak?"

Eleanor made a face at me. "You know it doesn't work like that. I get lots of story ideas and I try to jot them all down, even though I know most of them will never get any further than my notebook. But every once in a while, one will kind of open up. It may have been lying around in my head and notebook for months. Then I'll read something, or talk to somebody, like Harriet Robinson, and suddenly the subject will take some kind of workable shape, if you know what I mean. And I'll wind up what I'm doing and tackle this new project. As I did."

"So you had some notes on it already, before you visited Harriet?"

"Yes, of course. It was a possible article and one that would be fun to do, if I could sell the idea to somebody. When I realized how much she knew about boats and ships, I remembered this nautical problem I'd been kicking around. I pumped her about it after I'd finished asking her all about you. And by that time she was very happy to get away from all my snoopy questions about you and her and what mysterious things the two of you had been up to along the coast of Cuba, and tell me about ships instead. Of course, the next time I came around to confirm what she'd already told me, she wouldn't give me the time of day."

I frowned. "But you don't really know where your story idea came from in the first place."

She said, "My God, Matt, you've done a bit of professional writing yourself; you know how it goes. No I don't know where it came from. Something I read in the papers, maybe; something somebody said—"

"Who?"

She started to speak angrily and checked herself. "All right," she said after a moment. "All right. You may have something there. I do seem to remember . . . Serena."

"Who?"

"Serena Lorca. The daughter. I was interviewing Lorca's family: wife, Janine; daughter, Serena. The kid seemed to be hipped on the Bermuda Triangle, and wanted my opinion on whether the latest sinking—there had been only two at that time—could logically be connected with all the other outer space stuff. I said, hell, I didn't believe any of it; but afterward, I got to thinking. . . ."

I said, "So it was this young girl, Serena Lorca, who got you to thinking about this project. Actually lined the whole thing up for you with camouflage story and everything."

Eleanor shrugged. "Well, if you want to put it that way. But it doesn't seem likely she did it on purpose, does it? And she's really not that much of a kid. She's a fairly husky young lady in her early twenties. I can't really feel it's terribly significant." After a moment, she asked, "What's the other coincidence?"

"That you just happened to get yourself kind of accidentally raped while doing an article on George Winfield Lorca. That, my dear young woman, is not within the realm of possibility."

Eleanor said sharply, "I'm not your dear young woman, and it happened, didn't it? I didn't dream it, goddamn it!"

"I'm not saying it didn't happen; I'm just saying it couldn't have happened like that, accidentally and coincidentally." I leaned forward. "Look, Elly, here's a guy who had one pretty lady chopped up by a boat's propellers for the sake of an old grudge. He sent a death message to another because she'd had the temerity to step out of line a bit. In between, he casually instigated, or had instigated, the shotgunning of a guy he didn't know merely to embarrass some folks he did know and didn't like. Just yesterday, he arranged for a young fellow who was talking too much to be terminated with a pillow. At least we have to go on the assumption that Lorca is behind all this; it's the only safe assumption we can make. You don't really think Jurgen Hinkampf was killed by one of the doctors at the hospital because he pinched the fanny of one of the nurses, do you?"

"No, but—"

I said harshly, "No, but you trustingly believe, it seems, that a sharp female journalist just happened to get herself clobbered, sexually and otherwise, by two wandering sadistic thugs with itchy pricks at just the time she was investigating this dangerous gent. Mama, tell me the one about grandma and the wolf!"

Eleanor licked her lips. "But . . . but what would be the point, Matt? They'd been very cooperative, Lorca and his PR people; why would they suddenly send somebody

161

to? . . . Anyway, those goons didn't threaten me, or tell me to lay off or anything. No menacing speeches about how they'd get me even worse next time, like dead, if I didn't drag my poor battered, tattered carcass home quietly and forget all about George Winfield Lorca. No warnings or ultimatums at all; just beat the dame into submission and . . . and strip her and screw her and run."

"No words at all? Total silence throughout?"

She swallowed and said, "This isn't fun for me, you know."

"You're not here for fun. And much as I enjoy your company, I'm not here for fun, either. We've both got jobs to do and we can't do them blindfolded. What really happened? What was really said? Tell me about it. Play by play. Word for word."

Her face was pale and stubborn. "But I did tell you about it. I poured it all out to you last night, like a hysterical little ninny——"

I shook my head. "Last night you told me about afterward. Tonight let's hear about before. All I know is that it was terribly humiliating and did awful things to your dignity as a woman."

She whispered, "Damn you, Matt, what are you doing to me?"

I said, "Damn you, Elly, you've overlooked something. Missed something. Forgotten something. Tucked something away that you can't bear to look at. You've pretended to take this so-called casual rape for granted. Just a normal occupational hazard, you said; but was it? Come on, let's have it without all the maidenly reticence. Hell, I helped haul one girl agent out of a Central American jungle after a whole revolutionary army had used her as a plaything for weeks; am I supposed to be impressed by your little one-night, two-man stand?"

"You bastard!" she breathed. "Oh, you lousy bastard!"

"Words," I said insistently. "They talked, didn't they? You're the great investigative journalist, aren't you, trained to recall conversations verbatim? So let's investigate one Brand, Eleanor; or are you supposed to be sacred or something? Can you only dig up dirt on other people? Just your best friend who trusted you, a government department that's doing its poor damned best according to its simple lights, and a young ship's officer who was murdered in his bed for talking to you, but not you? Come on, Miss Front Page! There wasn't just a lot of punching and fucking and heavy breathing. Let's have the details, please. There were words. I want to hear those words."

She drew a long breath as if preparing to scream abuse at me, but she let it out again soundlessly. She licked her lips. " 'Just be good to us, baby, and you won't get hurt, much,' " she whispered tightly. "There are some words, goddamn you! How do they help?"

"And then?"

"Then I fought them the best way I could, breaking free and getting caught, getting knocked down, getting to my hands and knees half-dazed and catching a contemptuous kick in the rear that sent me sprawling again, rolling aside and getting up and trying to run, getting caught and hit and knocked down and casually kicked around some more, getting up. . . . I didn't really hope to escape, I guess; I was just trying to delay it a little longer, to keep it from happening a little longer. And they weren't really trying to smash me, break me, kill me; they were just playing with me, getting a big bang out of . . . of mussing me up and tormenting me before they. . . . But then I got my nails into the big one's face and he got mad and took a real swing at me and I felt my teeth go like that—my mouth all numb, and a sickening jagged gap in front, and dreadful little bloody broken bits that I had to spit out so I wouldn't choke on them. Details, Mr. Helm? Actually, I thought there was more damage than there really was. I had a horrible vision of . . . of having them all knocked out if I kept on struggling; and spending the rest of my life like a little old toothless lady taking my dentures out at night and putting them in a glass of water. I couldn't bear that. So I quit and just sat where I'd landed with blood running down my chin. . . . I do hope this is all detailed enough for you, Mr. Helm!"

"You're doing fine," I said.

Her eyes hated me. "You really are a bastard, aren't you?" She sucked in a deep uneven breath. "Then the big one hauled me to my feet and held me and the little one did some gloating. . . . Words? Okay, words. He said something like, *now* look at the proud little lady with her pretty face all messed up and her pretty clothes all dirty and her pretty stockings all torn just because she wouldn't condescend to be nice to us peasants. Then he grabbed the neck of my sweater to rip it off but it wouldn't rip, just the shoulder a bit. He got mad and got out a big knife that went click and tried to cut it, but it wouldn't cut, not really, it was too soft and yielding and the knife wasn't very sharp. He just made a crazy droopy mess of it, all holes and rags, a brand new cashmere sweater, oh, and it was pink before it got all stained and dirty, you did want the details, didn't you? The big one said for him to stop horsing around and get on with it before somebody came. So the little one sawed through the waistband of my nice tailored beige skirt, well it had been tailored and nice before I got knocked down in it so many times—more details for you!—and he gave a big yank and tore it off and threw it away. He reached up under my sweater-rags and grabbed the front of my slip and jerked hard and hacked with the knife until he had that all off me, too. He started to toss it aside but stopped to admire the lacy stuff, all ripped and slashed as it was; there was enough light from the nearby street for him to see a little. He said. . . ." She stopped abruptly.

"What did he say, Elly?"

She hesitated. When she spoke, the bitter resentment in her voice had been replaced by an odd note of apology. "You've got to understand, Matt. I shut it all away afterward. I closed the door on it completely. I wouldn't let myself think about it. This is the first time I . . . I've allowed it to come back. I *couldn't* let myself think about it. It made me all sick inside, remembering." Her anger returned. "It still does, damn you!"

"What did he say?"

"He said . . . he said I sure dressed pretty, even underneath, expensive like a princess; they must pay me plenty for being a lousy snooping muckraking little. . . ."

"Little what?"

She shook her head. "The big one told him to shut up and get on with the lousy job. That's what he said, the lousy job. So the little one tossed my slip aside and—you wanted all the details—he made a funny, funny thing of, well, kind of operating on my panty hose with his knife, he really got a charge out of that, you can imagine. Then he laughed and laughed at the dumb way I looked with the ragged stocking-parts he'd left me sagging down my legs after he'd sliced away the main . . . well, the panty part. I do hope you're enjoying these details, Mr. Helm." She swallowed hard. "But he didn't put his knife away, although now I was . . . was stripped enough for all p-practical purposes. Exposed enough. He stared at me kind of funny and I knew he was thinking of other things he could cut with it, stick with it. Fun things. More fun than nylon and wool and polyester. He put the point against my naked stomach hard enough so a trickle of blood ran down but the big one behind me, still holding me for him, told him to quit it now. He said for him to put the goddamn slicer the hell away; he told him to remember that they weren't supposed to spoil me too badly. I guess that's where I got that word. I didn't realize it before; I was trying so hard *not* to remember."

There was silence in the room, but somebody walked down the hall outside. She waited for the footsteps to die away, before she went on, speaking very steadily;

"And then they just threw me down and did it to me, that's all. I think you can probably supply those details from your own experience, Mr. Helm. They weren't very original about it, thank God; it was a pretty standard sexual exercise." After a moment she continued softly, "Oh, and you'll like this final detail, I'm sure. All naked and bruised and hurting like that in the weeds and dirt, my stupid body responded numbly, like a damaged mechanical doll. And I let it, Mr. Helm. I was afraid that if I didn't give them some satisfaction, some response, they'd get mad and hit me in the mouth again. I didn't really care what I did by that time. I just wanted to save what was left of me, what little was left of me. Isn't that a lovely detail, Mr. Helm? I thought you'd like that, you bastard. Get me a drink."

When I returned with her refilled glass she didn't see me at once; then she reached up and took it from me. I stood there a moment.

"Elly—"

She said tonelessly, looking at her drink, "We're really going through this stuff, aren't we? We ought to go into the movies; the old hard-drinking reporter-private-eye routine." She was silent for a little and went on softly, "Don't say it, Matt. Don't apologize for being rude and crude. You proved your point, didn't you? They *did* know who I was; it wasn't just a casual pickup rape. And they had their orders, they were supposed to . . . to spoil me but not too badly, meaning, I suppose, not too permanently, not enough to raise a stink just before election time."

"I had to blast it loose even if it hurt."

She said, "Yes, and tomorrow or next week I'll probably be very grateful to you for making me face it all at last. It'll probably turn out to have been very good for me. But tonight I don't like you very much, so let's get this over with so I can take a shower. I feel dirty all over just from talking about it."

I sat down facing her once more. I said, "The man you were talking with in that joint, before they caught you outside, the one you said was very polite and bought you a beer—what did you go to see him about?"

Eleanor shrugged. "His sister. She used to be a girlfriend of Lorca's in his wicked past he has now renounced. A pretty blond kid who thought she could sing, named Arlette Swallow. Her brother, Pete Swallow, was setting it up for me to interview her."

I said, "It could be that Lorca didn't want her interviewed. Maybe he thought an old mistress was bad for the image."

166

She shook her head quickly. "These days? Don't be naive, little boy. Hell, even presidents sleep around and nobody thinks a thing of it. Anyway, I doubt the magazine would have used it. There seems to be a kind of gentleman's agreement about this political stuff: you lay off the bedroom dirt unless it's just too irresistibly dirty. So even though I'm not a gentleman, I didn't really expect to get much mileage out of the fact that Lorca had slept with a cheap little nightclub nightingale occasionally, particularly since it had happened well before his miraculous and well-publicized conversion to righteousness. Now he was a devoted family man with a pretty wife and daughter he wouldn't hurt or shame for the world. But the name had cropped up. . . ."

"How?"

She hesitated. "Well, it had been whispered to me in confidence by somebody who had good reason to want to embarrass the Lorca campaign. I didn't think it would prove all that embarrassing even if the information was straight; but I thought I'd better check the girl out anyway. At least I could get an idea of how Lorca had looked from her viewpoint, to add to my other worms-eye views of the great man."

"Did you?"

"Well, as a matter of fact, no. The brother was supposed to call me, but I guess he didn't. . . ."

"You guess?"

"Matt, for God's sake!" Her anger had a defensive quality. "I could hardly get out of that damned hotel bed the next day, and what I saw in the mirror wasn't worth getting up for anyway! I gave the hotel people my auto accident story and stayed in my room except for. . . . Well, I told you. Until I could show my face without causing a riot. In the meantime I just beat on the damned typewriter and tried to forget how much I hurt and why."

"Writing what?"

She made an impatient gesture. "The Lorca election piece, of course! What's the matter with you, anyway? Why the crossexamination?"

I said, "The Lorca election piece without the girlfriend. Because the brother never called back. And you hurt too badly to bother finding out why he never called."

"Damn you, Matthew Helm! . . ." She stopped. There was a lengthy silence, while a little flush came to her face. At last she nodded reluctantly. "Yes, damn you. The Lorca piece without the girlfriend. Yes. Because I hurt too damned bad to remember I was a reporter, and damn you for pointing it out. Yes. I just wanted to get the lousy article out of the typewriter so I could lie in bed and count my aches and explore my crazy new mouth with my tongue and wonder how long it would be before I looked human again, well, as human as I ever look." She grimaced. "Yes! I just knocked the piece out with what I already had in my notes and sent it off to the magazine. There were some minor changes they wanted, but we took care of those over the phone. So I guess Mr. Pulitzer is just going to have to find somebody else to give his prize to. Even if it were offered, I'd be morally obliged to turn it down, wouldn't I? A journalistic false alarm like me?"

"Don't be too hard on yourself."

"Hard?" Her voice was savage with self-contempt. "I didn't hurt *that* badly. I didn't hurt too badly to see a doctor and a dentist and read up on animal husbandry, did I? But I never once asked myself *why* did it happen to me just then, and *what* could *who* gain by having me . . . well, disfigured, demoralized, partially disabled, at just that point in my research. The smooth sly bastard! If there had been threats I'd just have got mad and stubborn, but the way he did it. . . . No threats, no warnings, just go out and spoil the wench a little! Give her something else to think about, the nosy bitch!" She drew a shaky breath. "And I did what he obviously hoped I'd do. In spite of everything they'd let slip they obviously weren't supposed to, in spite of the way they'd betrayed themselves, I crawled back to the hotel just cursing my lousy luck at accidentally meeting up with two cruising sex freaks. And then hauled myself out of bed just long enough to knock out a nice innocuous Lorca article

168

and to hell with making any more efforts to check out mysterious girlfriends and their secretive brothers. I didn't even ask myself why the brother was so secretive; why the sister was so hard to interview. Did you ever since Garbo hear of a performer who made it tough for a reporter to find her? My God, usually you can't keep them out of your lap!"

I nodded. "So you have no idea why Pete Swallow never called you as he'd promised."

Eleanor shook her head. "No. As I keep saying, I just shut that whole ghastly evening out of my mind; it was the only way I could continue to function. But I'd better do a little checking right now, hadn't I?"

I said, "It can wait until morning. You ought to get some sleep."

"Go to hell," she said. "You worry about your goddamn health and let me worry about mine. I may need a bodyguard but I don't need a male nurse." She frowned. "I'll see if I can get hold of Spud Meiklejohn in Miami. He probably can't do much tonight, but he owes me, and he'll get what's to be got as soon as things open up tomorrow."

"Don't have him send it here. We'll pick it up over there."

She glanced at me sharply; then she grinned. "You're supposed to be guarding the body, Mister; not pushing it around. But what's the plan?"

I said, "What's left for you to do here in Nassau? The man you wanted to interview is dead. The police gave you clearance; best to get the hell out before they change their minds and think of more questions they want to ask you. And I want you to introduce me to somebody."

"What somebody?"

"That big man in Miami Beach who lent you three thugs when you needed them."

"Velo? What do you want with Giuseppe Velo?"

"Is that his name? I presume he has syndicate connections."

"None better. He *was* the syndicate down there for

many years; he's kind of semi-retired now. A very tough old buzzard, and I do mean buzzard. That's just the way he looks."

"Good. Just the man I want."

"But does he want you, Matt? And do I want to be responsible for bringing the two of you together? Velo is a good man to do a good turn for, but I wouldn't want to do him a bad one without a very good reason."

I said, "Hell, I can do it on my own, Elly. I know some names, too. But if you've got a pipeline to a big local guy like Velo it's easier. You might as well do that first. There's the phone over by the bed. Tell him to check with Otto Rentner in Milwaukee about the man from W who was with Heinrich Glock, known as Heinie the Clock, when he died with a twelve-gauge shotgun in his hands."

She looked at me for a moment. "What's W?" she asked at last.

"You should know that, after all the research you did on us. That's what they call us in the syndicate. W for waste."

She shivered a little. "And I don't suppose you mean garbage. No, I never came across that. It's very . . . picturesque; I could have used it." She hesitated, and went on, "Well, all right, I guess you know what you're doing. But run that past me again, please, slowly. . . ."

It took an hour. There were the two calls to the U.S. and then a wait for the first party called to call back. At last the phone rang and she picked it up.

"I see," she said. "Yes, of course. For lunch. Yes, I know where it is. Please thank Mr. Velo very much." She put down the instrument and looked at me. "It's okay. Apparently you checked out okay. He's seeing us for lunch at his place tomorrow."

"Thanks, Elly. It'll all become clear eventually. I'm trying to get the kiddies off the street, that's all."

"If I'm supposed to understand that," she said, "you'd better repeat it in the morning when I'm thinking clearly again. My God what a day! Who makes the plane arrangements?"

"I do," I said.

"Well," she said, "well, I'll let you have your phone." But she didn't move at once, sitting there on the edge of the big bed, my big bed. She seemed to have dismissed the natural hostility she'd felt toward me for the way I'd goaded her into unearthing all the buried ugly memories of her ordeal. She looked rather small and vulnerable, sitting there; and there's nothing more dangerous to virtuous masculine resolutions than the natural masculine feeling that, no matter what the lady's sexual hangups may be, no matter how they might have been incurred, you're just the guy sent by Fate to cure them. By the traditional method, of course. She looked up at me and smiled faintly, rising. "No, dear," she murmured. "The patient is not yet ready for the Helmstein Treatment."

"Madame will inform me when she thinks it is the proper time?"

"Proper is hardly the word, Herr Doktor," she said. "But Madame will certainly inform you. Goodnight, Matt."

"Goodnight, Elly."

CHAPTER 19

IN the morning, inevitably, there were afterthoughts. Breakfast was a remote meal. Psychologically speaking, socially speaking, the distance across the table could have been measured in rods, even miles, instead of feet. Although I'd been aware of no nightmares, she'd obviously spent an unsatisfactory night; her eyes looked bruised and tired.

I knew she must have relived the whole dumb evening; hating every stupid revealing word she'd uttered, herself for uttering it, me for bullying her into uttering it and then sitting there listening avidly to her recital of the awful indignities that had been inflicted upon her. Now I was the

171

man who knew exactly the abysmal depths of humiliation to which she'd been brought. I even knew her ultimate degradation—that she'd probably intended to tell to no one, ever—the fact that in the end she'd deliberately allowed herself to give some satisfaction to the men violating her in order to save herself from further injury. Her cold defensive attitude this morning made it clear that she'd decided that I must now consider her very soiled and damaged goods indeed; and a lousy little coward to boot.

Well, I guess there are men around who deal only in perfect, unblemished dream-girls; just as there are other men around who deal only in perfect, unblemished stamps that lose most of their value if they're used, certainly if they're damaged in any way. Of course they must all, girls and stamps, be sheltered and protected very carefully to preserve their perfect purity, their pure perfection. Well, dream-girls are nice to dream about; and I suppose every man has at least one dream-girl in his past—I was married to mine for a while—who meant a great deal to him at the time but didn't prove very practical when the going got rough. I mean, there's a limit to how far you can go to shelter a woman from reality.

Then there are the real girls who've been dirty and hurt and maybe even a little broken at times, who've done what was necessary for survival no matter how distasteful it might be, and who've picked themselves up afterward and washed themselves off and patched themselves up and gone on with the business of living. You don't have to save them from use, they expect to be used, they like being used; they know that's what women, like men, are for. While you'd like to protect them from harm, it's not a tragedy if you fail a little. They don't lose their value so easily. This one was getting very close to becoming a very real girl, at least to me; and I wasn't at all sure I wanted her to. Dream-girls come and go, but real girls can be forever; and there's no good place for forever girls in our line of work.

"When do we catch the plane?" Eleanor asked, glancing at her businesslike watch.

"Whenever you say," I said, getting to my feet. "It's waiting on the field."

She rose and started to move away, but her innate fairness made her pause and look back. "Well, there's something to having a high-powered bodyguard after all. Private air transportation, yet. Very nice, Mr. Helm." She hesitated and glanced down at herself a bit self-consciously and went on, "It's not a deliberate act of hostility, Matt."

I looked where she'd been looking, and grinned. "Oh, you mean the slacks."

"I know you said you don't like women in pants and I don't like me in them either; but I was just too damned tired to wash out a blouse last night and this is all I had clean in my suitcase. I've been moving around too fast to get any laundry done the past week or so." She grinned. "Anyway, Seppi Velo just loves trousered ladies; he's always got at least one blonde around in skintight pants. I think he likes to pinch them where they're tightest. At his age, it's probably all the excitement he can stand."

"In those," I said, "you're going to wind up with your ass black and blue before Velo ever gets a crack at you. My fingers are itching already."

But that was going too far; I was taking unfair advantage of her moment of friendliness. She looked at me coolly. "I think we'd better get moving if we're going to be in Miami Beach in time for lunch," she said.

I watched her walking briskly ahead of me in her high-heeled blue sandals, crisp white linen slacks and a thin little navy blue sweater with a round neck and short sleeves. The slacks weren't really outrageously snug, they just fit as well as they should; and I thought that, some day when we were friends again, I'd have to tell her that in addition to having very nice shoulders and ankles she had a very nice little bottom. When we got to the airport I saw a couple of young men in greasy coveralls look up from their work to watch her go by on her way out to the waiting plane, not the prettiest girl in the world, perhaps, not the most beautifully proportioned body in the classic sense, but a neat, taut, youthful figure, unique and unmistakably feminine, a specimen any girl-watcher would be proud to add to his private collection of attractive memories. I didn't at all mind being the man fortunate enough to be her escort and thereby earning their brief envy. It seemed too bad that she was psychologically incapable of recognizing and enjoying their admiration.

It was the same two-propeller, four-person plane with the same silent moustached pilot. We got into the rear seats although Eleanor indicated that she wouldn't really mind if I sat up front where my long legs would be more comfortable. Apparently she wasn't yearning for my companionship; but as we took off I felt her fingers find my arm and tighten briefly. It was nice to know that planes still scared her a little, even after all the traveling she must have done. They scare me, too.

When she removed her hand, I glanced at her, and saw that her face was faintly pink. "Only the little ones," she murmured. "I can take the big ones, but the little ones still bother me a little. I'm never quite sure they'll get all the way off the ground."

"I know," I said.

She hesitated, and looked at me directly. "I'm a bitch," she said.

"So what else is new?"

"No, let me apologize. I just felt so . . . naked this morning. Now you know everything about me."

"Well, you know a hell of a lot about me, too, so I guess we're even," I said.

We sat for a while, listening to the motors and watching the colorful islands of the Bahamas pass below.

"Matt."

"Yes?"

"That girl," she said, looking straight ahead. "The one in the jungle?"

"What girl in the jungle?" I asked. "Oh, *that* girl."

"The girl agent you said you rescued." Eleanor gave me a sidelong glance. "Sheila Summerton was her name, wasn't it? That was one of the operations I did get some

174

information on." After a little she said dryly, "The record wasn't clear on the point, but I bet you slept with her, too."

I remembered the starved and abused scrap of female humanity we'd brought out of the jungle, all bones and eyes, and the slim, big-eyed, haunted girl she'd become. We'd managed to lay to rest a few of her ghosts eventually, if you'll excuse the phrase. But it hadn't worked out in the end. She'd been too gentle for the business. Her gentleness was what had betrayed her in the first place, when she'd been unable to pull a trigger that needed pulling badly. Later, her gentleness had almost got me killed. She'd left us and I hadn't heard from her, or of her, since.

I said, "As you add up my sex life, Miss Brand, you might keep in mind that you're referring to a handful of ladies encountered over a considerable number of years. It's not quite as if I'd serviced them all last week."

She shook her head quickly. "Please don't get mad. That girl . . . she'd had a hard time, too. Can't you see that I might be interested?"

I said, "Yes, ma'am. Since you ask so nicely, I did sleep with her. Later, after fattening her up a bit. She was pretty skinny when we got her out of there. I felt, well, a bit guilty about it, considering everything, but she laughed at me and said that after going through all that why shouldn't she go to bed with a man she liked for a change? I realize that didn't say much for her taste in men, but otherwise it seemed like a healthy attitude."

Eleanor was silent. Maybe she didn't think it was a healthy attitude; or maybe she felt it was a little too healthy for a girl who had, after all, been through considerably more than she, Eleanor Brand, had. Maybe she thought I was making comparisons, not altogether in her favor. As a matter of fact, I had spoken without really thinking how it would sound to her. I was just a bit stale on Miss Eleanor Brand's psychosexual problems this morning. I had a few problems of my own, like just what to say to that Miami Beach godfather type, Giuseppi Velo.

But before I could get that problem solved, and it wasn't

175

really solvable until I'd gotten some notion of Velo's attitude, we'd landed in Miami and had another problem presented to us, or at least a distraction. Airports with all those strangers running around aren't good places to be if you have somebody to protect, and I was doing my best to pick up possible hostile blips on the radar screen as I followed along behind Eleanor, aware that she, too, was looking for somebody; the difference being that she knew who.

He turned out to be a tall man with cynical eyes and wild sandy hair, who handed her a large manila envelope, kidded her briefly about some past incident or assignment they'd shared and took off, never having spoken to me. I didn't belong to the inner journalistic circle; I was just part of the view. I was watching him move away and making another sweep of the premises when I heard Eleanor make an odd strangled sound that had me whirling and reaching for my gun instinctively. By using a private plane we'd short-circuited the hijack-scanners, so I hadn't had to go through that firearms-shuffle again.

But Eleanor was standing there unharmed. Her face was very pale, however; and I reached for the photograph she'd been staring at. She shook her head quickly.

"No, look at this one first. Arlette Swallow."

It was a stock eight-by-ten-inch glossy glamor photo of a pert, pretty young woman with fluffy blond hair, an interestingly inadequate costume, and a big guitar. I gave it back to Eleanor and she handed me the second print.

"Arlette Swallow."

It would have been worse if I hadn't already seen her reaction to it; but it was bad enough. The girl in this picture was dead. It was a police photo and, although the features had not been damaged by whatever had killed her, there was hardly enough resemblance to let me recognize her as the same girl. The blond hair had darkened and looked as if it had been stringy and uncared for even before death. The pert nose had become oddly flattened and a little crooked; but the cutie-pie mouth was the feature that had changed most. The upper lip was marred by a

176

great slashing scar, like a badly repaired harelip. There was another ugly scar across the right cheek. I cleared my throat.

"Standard beer-bottle job," I said. Eleanor glanced at me. I said, "Okay. Chivas Regal. Piper Heidsieck. But the one I saw on a man was a good old Budweiser operation. He got it busted across his face and then he was chopped up with what was left. Looked worse than this, but then he hadn't been very pretty to start with."

Eleanor shivered. "And I've been making a big deal of how terribly I suffered with a couple of black eyes and a couple of chipped teeth! The poor kid! All she had was her pretty face, really; and he got mad or drunk and . . . spoiled it for her. And wouldn't even get her to a good surgeon who could, at least, have minimized the damage! No wonder she got bitter enough to want to hurt him publicly, seeing *that* in the mirror every day."

"What are the other ones?" I asked.

She licked her lips. "Brother Pete, of course. Pre- and postmortem, also. They were both killed in the same auto accident the day after I got . . . worked over."

I said, "And if you swallow that accident, we'll try you on the Easter Bunny. And I'd say that was a deliberate job of face-wrecking, not just an ugly-drunk act. My hunch is the girl was dumb enough to play around and Lorca/Sapio caught her at it. It would be his early Sapio style, to fix her so no man would ever want her again. But later, as Lorca, he couldn't afford to have her arising from the ashes of his lurid past, with that face, and lousing up his new goody-goody image, not to mention his election." I gave her back the photo and watched her slip it into the envelope. "So now we know why he turned his wreckers loose on you when somebody tipped you off to the name 'Swallow.' Let's go visit Mr. Velo."

We arrived at the tall waterfront building right on time and a sun-burned young man in a very flowery sports shirt, worn over very white pants, came forward to help us out of the taxi and steer us to the private elevator at the rear of the lobby, which took us straight up to the penthouse.

There were a couple of men at the door, also dressed in a casual way, but their attitude was not quite so casual. One of them followed along behind us as our tanned young guide led us through the gleaming apartment and out onto the sun roof, where a very brown old man awaited us in a wheelchair under a green plastic awning that shaded a table set for three. The man who had followed us hurried past and whispered in the old man's ear.

I said, "If it's the gun that's bothering him, you're welcome to it, Mr. Velo. I've been assigned to protect the lady; but I'm sure she's quite safe here."

I opened my jacket invitingly; but the old man shook his head quickly. "They only do what they are told to do," he said. He waved the man away and the young guide as well. When we were alone, he said, "You're Helm? Also known as Eric, ha! From W, ha! So many tricks and codes and ciphers, like little boys playing Blackbeard the Pirate. And the little newspaper girl who is so tough; my soldiers were impressed and they don't impress easily. Come here, girl." Eleanor stepped forward, and the old man reached up and touched the faint scar on her lip with a bony brown finger. "They said you'd taken a beating, but I see it's better now. I was glad I could help. That was not a nice thing. You would like something to drink? You, Helm?"

A buzzard, Eleanor had said, but she'd gotten the wrong bird. This was not a scavenger but a predator, a very old and very dangerous predator, a totally different bird of prey from the aristocratic lady hawk I'd once known. The body was shrunken inside the light loose slacks and shirt that looked almost like pajamas, and the face was skull-like under the leathery brown skin; but the menace was still there in the fierce hooked nose and the hooded brown eyes that watched and weighed without a hint of senility. We had our drinks, brought us by a statuesque golden blonde in very snug violet trousers, worn so low that the suspense was almost unbearable. Her breasts were restrained, if you'll excuse a bit of exaggeration, by a rudimentary violet brassiere that obviously wasn't up to the job. We talked about the flight we'd had across the Gulf Stream, and the

178

fine weather, and the sailboats out on the water we could see from the penthouse patio, and the sportfishing boat Velo still owned but didn't get out on anymore, doctor's orders.

"Ha, that doctor," he said. "One day soon I will tell the boys to put me on the boat and strap me in the fighting chair and raise for me the biggest marlin in the world, and when I have killed myself fighting that big fish they must cut it loose with my thanks. Ha, these doctors who want to keep us all living after the machinery is no good any more. There are too many people in the world; the least they can do is arrange for the old ones like me to self-destruct comfortably when the time comes and make room for the new ones. But the big fish will do the job for me. Not a bad way to go, ha! Now we eat, and then we talk business. Help me with the chair, girl. Not you, Helm. I prefer to be pushed around by the pretty ladies, ha!"

It was an act, he was doing his moribund-old-man routine and watching us carefully meanwhile and making up his mind: there was no doubt in my mind that he had a pretty good idea what I'd come for. The blonde served us, teetering on five-inch heels, and it was hard to decide if the inadequate brassiere was going to give up the unequal struggle before, or after, the precarious pants fell down around the ankles. I saw Eleanor watching me with that prim, disapproving look women always get watching a man reacting in a perfectly normal way to perfectly normal age-old stimuli, without which reaction the race would long since have become extinct. The blonde made an unnecessarily intimate business of pouring my coffee, and one of her elaborately madeup eyes winked its incredible lashes at me, letting me know that there was a real girl—mischievous and perhaps a bit malicious—inside the efficient decorative robot.

"So," Giuseppe Velo said. "That will be all, my dear. Leave the coffee, we'll help ourselves. All right, Helm. What is it you want from old Seppi Velo?"

"Manuel Sapio," I said.

CHAPTER 20

THE silence went on for quite a while after I'd spoken. Velo stared at me hard across the table with those hooded eyes. Abruptly, as if dismissing me and the nonsense I'd just spoken, he switched his attention to Eleanor, addressing her politely,

"We are supposed to be evil men, living for nothing but evil, Miss Brand," he murmured. "Selling young ladies into white slavery. Teaching school children the delights of marijuana and cocaine and heroin. Intimidating innocent storekeepers and poor downtrodden prostitutes and robbing them of their hard-earned wages. If we play golf, it's only to arrange a wicked political deal on the course. If we go skiing, it's only to hold a secret meeting at the lodge with our fellow gangsters and racketeers. If we go fishing, it's merely to scout out that area of ocean or river for a future drug delivery."

When he paused, Eleanor said, "Are you saying that you're terribly misunderstood, Mr. Velo?"

He smiled thinly. "Not exactly, my dear; but it does not seem to occur to anyone that evil men require relaxation just as much as good men, and often participate in sports simply because they need and enjoy them. Evil is very hard work, Miss Brand, and requires just as much concentration as good." He turned his cold brown gaze on me. "Considerable money and effort have been invested in the man you call Sapio, who now calls himself Lorca."

"I know," I said. "That's why I've come to you, sir."

"I control nothing any longer," he said. "I have little influence. I'm only an old man sitting on a rooftop waiting

180

to die. But I know that much is expected from this Lorca, now that he has attained such a favorable position."

I said, "Mr. Velo, you had better tell your associates—former associates if you prefer—that they are going to lose Senator Lorca very soon."

Velo's eyes narrowed. "You are taking him out? A United States Senator?" When I didn't speak, he asked curiously, "How do you know this patio is safe? There could be a microphone in that vase of flowers."

I grinned. "Hell, I brought my own reporter, Mr. Velo. She's sitting right there beside you. To hell with your mikes. Just tell her what you want printed and she'll print it for you. Right, Elly?" After a moment, I said, "That is, assuming that you care to have the whole of Lorca's recent record published. When you hear it, I rather doubt that you will."

He studied me carefully across the table, and nodded slowly. "So, let me hear it."

It took a while. I took him clear back to that seaside bluff in Mexico where I'd last seen Sapio—Lorca apparently dead, and brought him up to the present by easy stages. When I had finished, Eleanor rose and refilled the coffee cups—well, hers and mine. Velo said he wasn't really supposed to have had even one; he'd certainly better not have two. As Eleanor sat down again, he tapped his fingers thoughtfully on the glass-topped table.

"You haven't mentioned the thing that happened to Miss Brand," he said. "Those were Lorca's men. We checked afterward, in case there should be complaints. But no complaints were made."

I said, "Miss Brand's difficulty was not an agency affair. Anyway, she found her own solution with your help. And I haven't mentioned a girl named Arlette Swallow, either, who had her pretty face brutally reconstructed by Senator Lorca back in his Sapio incarnation; and was recently killed along with her brother to keep the story quiet. Justice is not our business, sir. As my chief likes to say, we can't take care of every sonofabitch just because he's a sonofabitch, it's too hard to know where to draw the line.

But Lorca has turned this thing into a matter of survival, us or him."

"You have no proof."

"For a court of law, no. But then it isn't his lawyers he's using against us."

"So what do you want from old Seppi Velo?"

I said, "My instructions are to solve the Lorca problem discreetly. Will I be allowed to do that, sir? Or will your friends and associates in whatever you call your extensive organization these days insist on trying to protect their investment in this man?"

The hooded brown eyes regarded me steadily across the table. "If they do, what happens?"

I shook my head. "Let's not go into that, Mr. Velo," I said. "You've checked me out; you know the kind of agency that's behind me; you can figure it out. I don't want to say anything that can be construed as a threat, sir."

He smiled faintly. "The most effective threat of all, ha!" He glanced at Eleanor. "I like this man of yours. He is polite and he speaks well. But I think he overestimates my resources."

I said, "There's one more thing. I think the Lorca investment will eventually turn sour, anyway. You might suggest that to your friends."

"Explain yourself."

I said, "Consider, sir, here's a man who's achieved a powerful political office. With a little work, pulling a few political strings, he could probably destroy us in a perfectly legal manner, cutting our appropriations to nothing, or simply having us legislated out of existence. Yet he resorts to murder and blackmail instead, risking everything he's achieved for you and for himself. Why?"

Velo said softly, "That clumsy bully-boy with a hole in his head has never achieved anything for me. I advised against trying to make use of him; I could not believe that a little money and a few hypocritical words could sell a gorilla like that to the American people, even with a good public relations firm on the job; proof that old Velo is hopelessly out of date. Lorca was expertly packaged and

182

sold, and the people loved buying him. Him and his scar and his mystic, purifying experience, not to mention his loud-mouthed anti-crime crusade. So I am not in a very good position to recommend that he should be abandoned now." The old man frowned. "Why do you think he takes the risk?"

"Political deals take time," I said, "particularly for a newcomer to Washington not yet firmly entrenched in his office. I think the operation wasn't wholly successful, Mr. Velo, even with divine intervention or whatever Lorca likes to call it. I think he was all right for a while, sure, maybe even exaggerating his weak arm and his speech impediment for effect; but I have a hunch that now something upstairs is going wrong again and he knows it. Why would he be in such a hurry to pay off old scores if he didn't know his time was, shall we say, kind of limited? Ask your friends if they really want to go out on a limb for a guy who may not be functioning effectively very much longer, regardless of what action we take."

Velo sat there frowning thoughtfully after I'd finished. At last he pressed a hidden button and the girl in the low-slung violet pants appeared.

"I'll use the inside phone, Wanda," he said. "Then you can clear away this mess and see that our guests are comfortable while they wait."

We watched him being rolled out of sight inside the penthouse; then Eleanor rose and walked to the edge of the roof, looking out over the beach and the water. I went to the bar near the door to make myself a drink but the blonde, Wanda, returning, forestalled me, asked what I wanted, and mixed it for me. A very obliging girl. When I went to stand beside Eleanor, she didn't look at me. When I asked if she wanted a drink, she shook her head, still not looking at me.

"Doghouse day," I said. "If I can stand it for breakfast, I guess I can stand it for lunch. Ah, well, if she's jealous that must mean she loves me."

Eleanor glanced at me sharply. "Jealous? Of that . . . that manikin?"

"Shh, not so loud. She's bigger than you and she looks in good shape. I bet she could take you."

"Yes, she certainly makes no secret of her shape!" Then there was a small, stifled sound and I glanced at her quickly, thinking I'd heard a sob, but realizing belatedly that what I'd really heard was a giggle. "God, I sound stupid, don't I?" Eleanor murmured. "It's just that girls like that, so sleek and beautiful, so arrogantly sure of how beautiful they are, give me an awful inferiority complex. Dumb!" After a moment she said, "You're being very polite all of a sudden, Mr. Wild Bill Hickok. What happened to the Wild West act?" She mimicked my words. "No, Mr. Velo, sir, I don't want to say anything that can possibly be construed as a threat, please, sir."

I said, "Hell, you've got to tailor your performance to your audience. This is no mush-head from the OFS. If I started acting tough with this guy he'd make me prove it. And I don't in the least mind bucking Bennett and his boys after the games they tried to play; but I'd rather not go up against the whole damned syndicate or Unione Whatsisname or whatever the hell they call it, not if I can avoid it by a little simple hypocritical politeness."

Velo was on the phone for better than half an hour; then Wanda, who'd kept herself busy clearing the table and tidying the bar, received a signal of some kind and disappeared. Shortly, she came back shoving the wheelchair. She rolled Velo up to where we'd settled in some beach-type furniture in the shade of the plastic awning.

"All right, my dear, run along," he said. "I don't want to be bothered with any calls or anything, understand?" After she'd left, he said, "They're checking. You have this much in your favor: they don't think much of his risking the reputation as a reformed citizen they went to a great deal of trouble to build for him, just for a private vengeance." He smiled thinly. "Of course, it's only your word so far; a little proof would help. And it's not that anybody minds a little vengeance, you understand. It's in the blood; and it keeps people from getting out of line, knowing that if you step on somebody's toes too hard he'll come back and cut yours off with an axe. But it's not supposed to interfere with important business like this, particularly not if it involves us with a government agency, one we make a point of steering clear of. So they're checking. But they say there's nothing to your medical theory. They're kept informed, of course. The man's in practically perfect health, considering."

"Informed," I said. "Who informs them, Lorca himself?"

Velo glanced at Eleanor. "Smart, isn't he?" he said, and looked back to me. "The question did come up. No, the information comes from other sources as well; but it was suggested that even the medical profession isn't completely incorruptible. That's being checked also. There will have to be some high level discussion—"

He stopped as the blonde came up and paused by the wheelchair, waiting for Velo's attention. He turned his head. "What is it?"

"There's a call for—"

The brown, predatory old face turned suddenly vicious. "You dumb broad, I told you I didn't want to be bothered with any calls. Listen when I talk or comes it a fat lip."

The blonde's lovely face was impassive and her voice was expressionless. "You old goat, you told me *you* didn't want to be bothered. You didn't tell me *he* didn't want to be bothered." She jerked her head toward me.

Velo frowned. "The call is for? . . ."

"Helm. That's his name, isn't it?"

Velo looked at me, still frowning, and I said, "We didn't announce our visit here, but we didn't make it a big secret, either. We came from the airport in a taxi. I didn't check for a tail in all that traffic, since I figured it wasn't likely I'd lead anybody to you you couldn't handle, Mr. Velo."

"So take your call. Show him the phone, Wanda."

The old man's voice was remote and uninterested. I rose, but the girl gave me a small signal with her hand, asking me to wait. She stepped over and kissed Giuseppe Velo lightly on his leathery brown skull. He glanced up with an odd mixture of guilt and relief on his predatory face; I realized suddenly how old he really was. He reached out

185

and gave her an affectionate pat behind, and they were friends again.

As I crossed the patio beside the girl, matching her healthy, high-heeled stride, I said, "It must be interesting."

"Don't knock it," she said. "I'd spend a year working in a hospital to earn what he pays me in a week. He's not a bad old guy."

"He's a very bad old guy," I said.

Her bare golden shoulders moved minutely. "Well, maybe that's what keeps it interesting. There's the phone."

I picked it up and waited for the sound of her high heels to die away. "Helm here," I said.

"The Sacred Earth Protective Force," said a woman's voice I'd never heard before.

"What about it?"

"Are you interested?"

"I might be," I said. "What will it cost me?"

"Three bullets," said the voice. It was low and husky, with a faint masculine quality that bothered me; and I remembered that a woman with a deep and husky contralto voice had called a certain Roger Elliot and told him his hard-drinking wife was playing around with Bob Devine, leading to the latter's violent demise. The voice went on, "One for each of them. Go to. . . ."

I made her repeat the address. "Who are you?" I asked.

There was a laugh and the line went dead. I put the phone down, went out to say goodbye to my host and thank him for an excellent and entertaining lunch.

CHAPTER 21

BENNETT made it the subject of a full-dress council of war, of course. If we'd been the only outfit involved, I would simply have got in touch with Mac for some quick instructions if I could—generally he's easy enough to catch and, as it turned out, we caught him at the airport just before he took off for Washington. But if he'd been unavailable I'd have figured out what he probably wanted me to do about what I'd just heard over the phone, and done it. No problem. I've worked for him long enough to know how his mind operates; and conveniently enough, mine just happens to operate very much like it. Whether we are that way because we've worked together so long, or whether we've worked together so long because we are that way, is something for the philosophers to figure out after they solve the one about the chicken and the egg.

But with the OFS involved, the formalities had to be observed; and the whole deal got as complicated as a mideastern peace conference. We wound up high up in a Miami hotel in another hospitality suite practically indistinguishable from the one in which we'd held our last conference in Nassau. Bennett brought along his whole honor guard: Lawson, the heavyset man who didn't like me much because I'd been instrumental in making him shoot his partner, the two gofers I'd first seen guarding the door, and handsome brainless Warren Peterson whom he seemed to have adopted as a pet.

Our side wasn't quite as badly outnumbered as it had been on the previous occasion; we'd been reinforced by Brent, our standby man in Miami. I figured Mac had brought him along for his local knowledge; but it was possible that Brent was also present to show Mr. Bennett that we did have nice, polite, well-behaved young men on the payroll, as well as rude and unreasonable old campaigners like me.

"Velo!" Bennett said sharply after we'd all settled down and he'd been given the background information. "You say your man got an anonymous phone call while he was visiting the old Don himself, that senile Mafia crook? What was Helm doing there, anyway?"

Mac asked mildly, "Isn't that slightly beside the point?"

"I think it's very much to the point," Bennett said. "It

187

establishes, or otherwise, the credibility of the information." He gave me a hard look. "And of the informant."

It was time for the old whipsaw act again, and I got up and said wearily to Eleanor, "Here we go again." I looked at the three Bennett men sitting together in a corner of the room. "Anybody want to play Horatius At The Bridge today? No? Come on, Elly, let's blow."

"Matt."

I turned sharply on Mac. "I said it wasn't any use letting the OFS in on it, didn't I? To hell with interdepartmental cooperation; we can handle it. The dame called us, not him. Tell him I was there to get our monthly cut of the Florida heroin business and let's go out and do some work. We're wasting time. I've got to get up to New York and pick up our take in the numbers racket there, remember? And then there's all that prostitution money out on the Coast. I've got a busy collection schedule and all this horsing around isn't doing it any good."

"Matt, Mr. Bennett wasn't suggesting—"

"Well, he's got a damned funny way of not-suggesting it. I suppose in his refeened line of work he associates with nobody but presidents and popes."

Bennett stirred and started to speak, but Warren Peterson, sitting near him, spoke up abruptly, "You'll notice that this agent who claims to have Miss Brand's welfare so much at heart is going to drag her along now as he sticks his head into a nest of dangerous terrorists."

He was kind of pitiful, and I never forget or really forgive anybody who's pointed a gun at me—in our real world, unlike his movie-and-TV dream-world, somebody who points a gun at you is somebody who's demonstrating his perfect willingness to kill you—but I had to admit that his criticism was valid.

Eleanor said quickly, "I'd like to see him try to leave me behind! This is *my* story, remember?"

We didn't need this argument, and I said a bit sharply, "It may be your story to write with a typewriter, but that doesn't mean you get to shoot it with a gun. The man's right."

Hurt and angry, she started to protest further, but Mac broke in, "Please sit down, Matt. Have you a theory to explain why your anonymous caller chose to get in touch with you at Velo's apartment?"

I made a show of hesitating, shrugged, and seated myself once more. "Maybe she wanted to let me know that Big Sister, whoever she is, had her eye on me—me, and presumably Miss Brand. That she could reach us anywhere, even at Seppi Velo's unlisted number. A threat and a brag at the same time."

Bennett asked, "Did you recognize the voice?"

I shook my head. "Feminine but muffled, maybe by a handkerchief." To hell with him, let him chase sopranos while we were tracking down contraltos. "I'd never heard it before in my life," I said. Well, that much was true.

Mac, who'd had my full report, did not set the record straight; nor did he help us speculate about who the mystery woman might be. Instead, he changed the subject by introducing Brent as the local boy who'd just been checking on the address I'd been given. Bennett had a sour look on his face as he listened. He obviously felt that with his agency's greater resources he could have done a better job of casing the joint, or having it cased; he disliked having to rely on this freckle-faced young errand boy of Mac's. But Mac, while informing him of the gist of the message I'd received, had carefully refrained from giving him the essential details. Interdepartmental cooperation.

"It's a beatup old houseboat on a canal south of town," Brent said. "A bunch of hippies, or whatever they call them nowadays, who pay some token rent to the guy who owns the rickety dock. A kind of run-down industrial area. The canal's pretty well silted in so you can't get anything big in there any longer; they probably couldn't get the old bucket out even if they could fire up the stern drives, but judging by the weeds on the props they haven't been turned for several years. Probably rusted solid by now. They get power for the lights and air conditioner, the refrigerator, maybe the stove, through an extension cord to an outlet on the dock. Right now there are three living on board, two men and a girl. The girl seems to have a small income, enough to keep the menage operating. She's a pale, down-trodden-looking little blonde who might be pretty if she'd take a bath and wash her hair. I caught a glimpse of her, driving by. The younger man was with her. He's a cheerful-looking butterball type who, I'm told, does a bit of boat-repair work around the marinas to help out. The older one, who didn't seem to be around today—at least he didn't show—is supposed to be thin, dark, bearded, and intense-looking. He is supposed to have been involved in a mari-juana run a while back, maybe more, but you can say that of fifty percent of the waterfront population of Florida. The court turned him loose on some technicality. There's speculation locally about who does what with what to whom on board, if you know what I mean."

Bennett said sourly, "A cautious reconnaissance was ordered, not an investigation in depth. If these are the people we want, they'll be gone the minute they hear somebody's been around asking a lot of questions about them."

Brent shook his head. "I only drove past once, and watched a little from good cover; I wasn't seen. As for the rest, well, I have a little boat of my own and I like poking around the backwater marinas of the city. There's a small one a bit farther down where the canal is still maintained, that I've visited before. I just dropped in on the manager and bought him a beer while I arranged for dockage for my boat for next weekend. He's a chatty old party; he thinks those immoral pot-freaks upstream give the neigh-borhood a bad name; and he's happy to tell you all the bad things he knows about them and a few he doesn't."

I said, "Three dropouts on a broken-down houseboat doesn't seem like quite the sinister pirate crew we're look-ing for, capable of destroying half a dozen ocean-going ships in a way nobody's quite figured out yet." I glanced at Bennett. "Have you had any further instructions from the Sacred Earth people about how the money's to be paid? And are you going to pay it?"

He said stiffly, "If we can apprehend them without payment, the question will not arise, will it? And you're over-looking the fact that at least one of the trio has been involved in drug smuggling. That means . . ."

I didn't listen to any more of that. I could have written the script for him. They've got this mastermind-of-crime routine they trot out whenever anybody pushes the drug button. The fact that the older hippie's name had once been mentioned in connection with a drug offense meant, to Bennett, that the guy was Fu Manchu in disguise with a fleet of speedy smuggling craft at his disposal, all easily convertible to torpedo boats or mine layers or laser ships or death ray carriers. . . . The trouble was, I told myself grimly, that I didn't like that houseboat at all. I was al-lergic to houseboats. I'd had very bad luck with house-boats. I'd barely made it alive out of one up in Canada—well, Mac had mentioned that incident at our previous conference—and it had been on another houseboat right here in Florida, over near the Everglades on the West Coast, that Martha Devine, Martha Borden as she then was, and I had escaped death by very little. Old Home Week. I smelled danger. I smelled death. Fuck all house-boats. This one was a trap, I could feel it. But whose trap, set for whom?

"Tonight," Bennett was saying, speaking to Mac now. "We can, of course, handle it perfectly well by ourselves if you'll give us the address; but I suppose you'll want a representative along. . . ."

He stopped as a knock came on the door and a woman's voice spoke my name. That brought me the attention of everyone in the room except Mac who, as I did, recognized the voice immediately. It was not the husky contralto voice of the mysterious, informative stranger; it was a voice we both knew very well. I glanced at Eleanor, who should have recognized it too. I realized that she had, but that she was studying my reaction to it for some reason.

I rose and went to the door, waving aside the Bennett contingent that had automatically organized itself into a defensive formation to cover the opening. I turned the knob and looked out at the dark-haired girl standing in the hall. She smiled a little when she saw me. The remembered smile did funny things inside me. She was wearing a crisp white summer suit and her legs were bare but nicely tanned, and her white pumps had high slim heels that made her look taller and more lady-like than the image I'd been carrying in my mind, of a barefoot girl in a loose striped robe. I told myself I didn't really believe in ESP; but it was odd, wasn't it, that I should have been thinking of Martha Devine only moments before?

"Is Daddy here?" Martha asked. She'd always had a fine disregard of security and protocol; she might have been the self-assured daughter of the chairman of the board, any old board, or the president of the company, any old company. "I called Washington and they said I'd find you here, but they weren't quite sure if you'd managed to catch him before he got on the plane back north."

Then I saw her look past me and notice Eleanor Brand inside the room. Her lips tightened as she remembered the betrayal she'd endured at the other girl's hands.

I said hastily, "Yes, he's here. Come on in and meet all the nice people."

Mr. Bennett of the OFS thought it was a hell of a sloppy way to run a top-secret conference, with young ladies dropping in casually to ask for their daddies.

CHAPTER 22

THERE were four of us in the car; and even though it was a large sedan of the old-fashioned kind America used to love but can't afford to feed any longer, you could hardly see the men for the guns. I wouldn't have been surprised to bruise my shin on a bazooka or bust an elbow on a trench mortar. Certainly there were submachine guns —machine pistols if you prefer—coming out of our ears, complete with spare magazines galore. It seemed a pity, while we were in the mood and had the equipment, that we couldn't take over the Kremlin and remodel it more to our liking, or at least pay a visit to Havana and persuade Castro to straighten up and fly right. . . .

Earlier, Mac had taken off for the airport with Martha, leaving us to thrash out the details. The plan that had been decided upon after much technical discussion was very simple, as all great plans are. Since I was the gent with the most experience, and a fire-breathing gladiator to boot, I could have the honor of being the guy who marched up to the front door—actually it's aft on a houseboat—and told the terrorist miscreants to come out with their hands up, while Bennett's three men covered all possible exits. Bennett didn't put it quite that way, he kept pointing out that his boys were quite capable of handling this minor chore unaided, but if I insisted on coming along they might as well, he said, make use of my well-advertised talents. Unless I preferred to play a less risky role, of course. And, of course, he didn't really expect any resistance, but he made a point of planning for all eventualities.

After the battle plans had been made, I spoke briefly with Brent while the others were dealing out arms and ammunition.

"Here you are," he said, and I took the small flat automatic pistol he handed me and slipped it into my left sock. Those .25s aren't good for much; but as somebody once said, nobody really wants to be shot with anything, even a .25, and sometimes that can be a deciding factor if things go critical unexpectedly and you've lost your main battery or shot it empty. I was wearing rubber-soled shoes, dark pants, and a black turtleneck that would have been too hot for the climate if we were going to operate in sunshine, but we weren't. Evening was already well advanced by this time. Brent said, "There's a car for you in the marina parking lot, in case you should need transportation of your own. Small white Toyota pickup. Nobody notices an extra little truck in a place like that. Here's the key. Anything else you'd like to know?"

"Cover?" I said.

"Plenty. It was an industrial park that never got off the ground, so to speak. Empty lots with weeds and brush and trash. Some empty buildings; some that were never finished."

"The canal?"

"A jungle along the banks."

"Actual depth?"

"It was supposed to be dredged to twelve feet for barge traffic; I doubt they ever made it. Less than half that now, only a couple-three feet in spots I'd guess; and it's full of junk, blocks of concrete, old cars, you name it."

"Your job is Eleanor Brand," I said. "I know you haven't been trained for the bodyguard bit, but do the best you can. It's probably better than I could do at the moment. I'm in the doghouse there but good; I suppose because of the way I slapped her down when she wanted to come along."

"At least Bennett had sense enough to agree with you on that, publicity hound though he is. Well, take care. . . ."

I had said something appropriate, and joined Task Force Sacred Earth, or however Bennett had it down for the record; and now we were approaching the target area, in a rather dismal part of the city I'd never seen before—but then, I'm hardly an expert on Miami. I thought of Eleanor Brand and her hostile attitude and hoped she'd get over it and, at least, not give Brent too hard a time, watching over her. I thought of Martha Devine and the nice way she'd smiled at me when I opened the door; but then she smiled nicely at lots of people. To hell with Martha Devine. I'd exorcised Martha Devine, I told myself, by sleeping with another, handsomer lady, now dead by her own hand; and somebody would pay for that eventually, but not tonight. Tonight we were chasing dangerous political activists and sinister drug fiends in whom I had no faith whatsoever.

"Drive by the boat once," Lawson said, sitting beside me. "Don't slow down. Eyes front, I'll do the looking."

As senior officers, Lawson and I had the rear of the

command car. The man whose name I'd once heard in Nassau, Burdette, was in the right front seat; and the driver was the youngest soldier in our army; a slight, dark-haired kid named Ellershaw. He had a bad case of nerves, I noticed. He was yawning a lot, as if sleepy, a dead giveaway; but he drove all right. Burdette; short, square, and sandy, looked like a good steady man who might actually know what he was doing; but he had things on his mind, too. Lawson, beside me, was jumpy as hell; almost jumpy enough to forget how much he hated me for how bad I'd made him look more than once. Almost, but not quite. Some task force, I reflected sourly. If they practically crapped in their pants going up against three unwashed hippies, one a girl, it would be sad to see them tackling something or somebody truly dangerous.

As we drove past, I was aware, without turning my head that way, of the lighted windows of the houseboat, a fairly large vessel of its kind, fiberglass construction, once white but badly streaked and weathered now, with a topside steering station sheltered by a tattered white awning—Bimini tops, I think they're called. The dock against which the craft lay had been a massive affair designed for heavy commercial barges, but half of it had fallen into the canal, leaving stumps of pilings sticking out of the dark water like broken black teeth. There was a small Ford station wagon, badly battered, with the fancy phony-wood decoration half-peeled off, parked above the dock on the gravel area between the street and the sea wall. I caught a snatch of music as we passed, something loud with a heavy beat.

"Turn left up ahead," Lawson said. "Those warehouses or whatever they are. Find a place to park out of sight over there. Ready, Helm?"

"As ready as I'll ever be," I said. "Are you sure this trip is necessary?"

Reluctance is always diplomatic at this point in the proceedings. Nobody loves an eager hero.

"You wanted to come. We didn't ask you."

So much for diplomacy. Young Ellershaw found a slot between two dark cinder-block structures, both with

195

broken windows speaking of desertion; he slid the sedan into it. We piled out. The weapons of the three-man submachine gun squad gleamed wickedly in the dark. I hadn't been offered one of the rat-a-tat machines, but I wasn't brooding about it. As far as I'm concerned, they're for people who can't shoot, and figure they'll let ten inaccurate bullets try to do the job of one accurate one. Well, sometimes it works; but even so, it seems wasteful.

"Give us time to get set," Lawson said.

"Take all the time you want," I said. "Where I come from, the watchword is mañana."

"To hell with mañana. Give us fifteen minutes and move in."

I peered at the luminous dial of my watch. "Fifteen minutes. Your wish is my command, Señor."

He made a growling sound in his throat and moved off with his cohorts. I remembered, as I often do in such circumstances, the general who said he could deal with his enemies, but God would have to save him from his allies. I couldn't remember his name. It was quiet in the alley once the soft footsteps died away; the distant rumble of the city barely reached this place. A car went by on the street or drive that followed the canal; I saw Lawson and Company duck back against the buildings and wait for it to get clear; then they were gone from sight.

I went the other way, around the rear of the warehouses. I swung wide across the vacant lot beyond, slipping from a clump of brush to an old car body to a dented white refrigerator somebody'd had no further use for. I reached the road well over a hundred yards downstream—well, toward the mouth of the canal, wherever it finally joined the Miami River or Biscayne Bay or the Straits of Florida or whatever, call it east to keep it simple. I moved a little farther east where the drive curved slightly, putting me out of sight of the houseboat and anybody near it as I slipped across the pavement and fought my way into the bushes bordering the canal. A jungle, Brent had said. I couldn't tell you what the bushes were, maybe mangroves. A midnight botanist I'm not.

Then I was in the water wondering about snakes and alligators. It didn't seem like a promising area for sharks, but barracuda came to mind; and I'd read a piece in the paper about pet-shop piranha that had been released somewhere in Florida and were finding the ecology very much to their liking. There had also been mention of a walking catfish; but I figured I was man enough to handle a catfish, ashore or afloat. This detour was not in the battle plan; and it was, of course, a stupid damned business. Probably I'd return from the wars soaked and dirty and ridiculous while the rest of the conquering army marched home dry and clean, laughing uproariously at my sorry state; but agents who worry about making fools of themselves don't last very long. I'd be everlastingly damned, Bennett or no Bennett, if I walked up to a door to which I'd been sent by an anonymous phone call without making at least a small attempt to find out something about the people behind that door.

Moving very slowly to avoid splashing, I fought my way along the bank under the tough overhanging foliage. I had a pitched battle with a boa constrictor that turned out to be a discarded tire, and I barked my shin on something hard and rectangular and submerged that could have been another discarded refrigerator. I thought of clear blue tropical waters and white beaches. I thought of Eleanor Brand and rather regretted not letting her come and get a first-hand taste of the wet and muddy delights of a secret agent's life. The trouble with that was the screwball girl would probably have had a wonderful time sloshing along this mucky canal behind me, making notes in her waterproof notebook all the way. But it was just as well that Bennett had, unexpectedly, backed me up when I told her she had to stay home and play with her dolls, the only time he'd ever agreed with me on anything. . . .

I stopped. The white houseboat was less than fifty yards ahead of me now, with the black shape of the dock almost level with the upper deck at this stage of the tide, if they had tides in Miami. I thought they did, but I didn't really know. There were a great many things I didn't know, of varying degrees of importance; but the most important at the moment, I realized suddenly, was that I didn't know why a confirmed publicity seeker like Mr. Bennett of the OFS had been unwilling, tonight, to let a journalist accompany this expedition and record in deathless prose his organization's triumph over the forces of evil and terrorism. Brent had already noted this phenomenon casually, but I'd been thinking of other things and let it pass. And then, I reflected grimly, there was also the very interesting fact that, to the best of my recollection, neither Mac nor I had actually insisted on my coming along. Bennett had simply assumed we'd insist; or he'd pretended to assume it. . . . The thought that came into my mind was fairly incredible; but I'd survived in the business longer than most, and I hadn't done it by dismissing the incredible anymore than by avoiding the ridiculous.

I drew a long breath and moved forward again very cautiously. A small night breeze had come up, sending ripples across the canal that helped to hide the water I disturbed as I moved, and the small splashing sounds I couldn't avoid making. Then the dock was above me and I slipped between the black pilings and paused in the darkness beyond. Here the thump-thump music was louder and I could move more quickly without fear of being heard. I saw that the occupants of the houseboat had constructed a clumsy ladder to help them reach the deck from the dock above. It was a contraption of rough two-by-fours spiked together inaccurately by somebody who took no pride in his carpentry. I made my way there, finding the water quite deep where the houseboat lay; I had to swim a cautious stroke or two to reach the ladder. I raised myself slowly and cautiously, grateful for the loud music that covered the sound of water draining from my clothes.

Two rungs above deck level, I could peer through the ladder, straight into the big deckhouse window opposite. It had been broken at one time, perhaps by a casual rock pitched from the shore by a passing vandal. Thin, transparent plastic had been taped over it, but this had ripped and now hung in shreds that stirred faintly in the breeze, letting the music—and presumably the air conditioning Brent had mentioned—escape almost unobstructed. I had a pretty good view of the interior of the deckhouse and it was an intriguing sight. It was the first time in my life that I'd seen a boat carpeted with money.

There were bills everywhere, like dead leaves in autumn. They littered the shabby sofa, the scarred table, and the two armchairs with their torn upholstery, not to mention the threadbare indoor–outdoor carpeting. There were even bills on the stove and sink of the galley visible in the far corner of the deckhouse. In the middle of the floor sat a small, rather pretty girl with a moderately dirty face and stringy blond hair. She was wearing an elaborate and obviously new and expensive cream-colored satin negligee, lavishly trimmed with light, coffee-colored lace—ecru is the word that comes back from a long-ago brush with fashion photography. The inadequate fastenings of the garment made it obvious that she was wearing nothing else. She had a rather nice little body. She was holding a plastic champagne glass, the kind that comes in two pieces, stem and bowl, and you stick them together. With her free hand, she was tossing bills into the air from a sizeable suitcase that was full of them, and laughing happily as they fluttered down around her and on her. She tossed a handful playfully at somebody I couldn't see.

Abruptly, the music came to an end; a moment later there was a sharp sound that made me wipe my hand on the wet stuff of my turtleneck and get a fresh grip on my revolver. A man came into sight holding a foaming champagne bottle with which he refilled the girl's glass. She made a helpless gesture toward her shining negligee as the stuff fizzed over.

"Oh, dear, I'm getting it all spotty," I heard her say.

"Forget it, you'll have a closet full of them where we're going. I just brought you a small sample of the beautiful life so you could try it out. But now you'd better get your clothes back on. You can't travel like that, although it would be nice."

He was the older one who'd been described to us, the

one Brent hadn't actually seen, on the tall side, dark, with a neat, pointed, devilish little beard that contrasted oddly with his ragged denim shirt and grimy jeans. He waved the bottle invitingly, and the third sinister member of this deadly terrorist gang came into sight: a plump boy, also in jeans, who had no beard, simply because he hadn't managed one yet. Only a feeble blond fuzz decorated the lower part of his chubby face.

The girl said uneasily, "Are you . . . are you sure it's safe now?"

The dark one said, "Hell, the tricky pickup I worked out went slick as silk; and I let things cool off for several days before I came back, didn't I? Nobody followed me here, I'm sure of that." He grinned. "Well, kiddies, let's disband the Sacred Earth Protective Force. Jeez, I still can't really believe anybody'd be a sucker enough to hand over all this lovely loot on a wild yarn like that." He shook his head incredulously. "Well, it beats smuggling pot, you've got to admit that."

"I thought you were crazy when you started it," the girl said. She giggled. "You were crazy all right, crazy like a fox."

The plump boy asked, "But . . . who *really* sank all those ships, have you any idea?"

The bearded one shook his head sharply. "Don't know and don't want to know. People who sink ships are dangerous." He glanced at the bottle, poured judicious amounts of champagne into the glasses that were held out to him, and finished the rest by putting the bottle to his lips, wiping his mouth afterward. "You know, I could make a habit of this stuff," he said. "Well, who's to stop me now? Drink up and let's gather up our tax-free wealth, split this dismal scene and go join the idle rich."

It was time and past time; twenty-five minutes had passed since I'd left the car. Well, a little waiting wouldn't hurt the creeps in the bushes, or wherever they were hiding, holding their cute little stutter-guns in their sweaty little hands. I drew a long breath, eased myself out of the water, and swung myself around the ladder to put a foot on the houseboat's rail, transferring my weight to it very slowly. Even a large boat will react noticeably to a couple of hundred pounds landing suddenly on deck. Easing myself down at last, I scuttled below the window, straightened up, and moved swiftly around the corner of the deckhouse to the aft-facing door. I rapped on it hard with my gun barrel.

"Office of Federal Security," I said loudly. "This boat is surrounded. Come out with your hands up."

Then I took two quick strides to the rail away form the shore and vaulted it, dropping into the canal feet first. Even so, I wasn't quite fast enough. The first submachine gun burst was smashing into the door before I'd finished speaking; if I hadn't already been in rapid motion sideways, it would have riddled me. As it was, one of the nasty little 9mm slugs burned my arm before I got clear. I could hear all three rat-a-tat guns chattering and racketing behind me as I hit the water. It sounded like World War III on a busy day.

No wonder Bennett's boys had been a trifle nervous, riding into action in the same car with the gent—well, one of the gents, and ladies—they were planning to kill. And no wonder Bennett hadn't wanted a sharp-eyed lady reporter along to watch the massacre.

CHAPTER 23

I'D gone in feet first remembering Brent's report of old car bodies and hunks of concrete and two-to-three-foot shoals; but there was plenty of water where I hit. I must have gone down at least eight feet before my feet touched bottom, a rather soft and unpleasant bottom with which I didn't want to associate any longer than I had to. On the other hand, I reminded myself, there was a certain amount of unpleasantness awaiting me on top, also. I got myself turned around and struck out underwater in the direction of the houseboat, the shadow of which—if shadow is the proper word where gunfire is concerned—seemed to be the safest place for the moment. Those little jacketed sub-machine gun bullets have considerable penetration, and they'd certainly make a sieve of the deckhouse, but I didn't really think they could penetrate both the deckhouse and the heavier hull at the plunging angle they were being fired.

Surfacing cautiously, I winced as a bullet screamed overhead with the nasty wavering sound of a ricochet, or a projectile that's been deformed and destabilized by passing through something moderately solid. There were splashes in the water beyond me, but none close in where I'd come up. But the guns were still going. It didn't seem possible that anything could be left intact at the focus of all that firing; but there was still a glow of light inside the deckhouse. Apparently all the electric bulbs had not been shattered in there. Even in the dark, I could see that the sides of the superstructure facing me were torn and splintered by emerging bullets. The windows were all smashed. It was lucky that nobody'd ever tried taking that cheapo tub to sea, I reflected, lightly as it seemed to have been constructed, with what seemed to be ordinary window glass, for God's sake, instead of the much stronger stuff normally specified for marine use. Well, houseboats weren't made for open water and big seas, but still. . . .

Okay. So Mr. Bennett, with his knee-jerk anti-terrorist reactions, had been played for a fool by a bright young hippie with a beard, who presumably, after reading of the *Fairfax Constellation* incident and realizing its connection with the other sinkings, had sent threatening ransom notes to various shipping firms in the name of an activist group with a crazy title; but they've all got crazy titles these days. Symbionese Liberation Army, for God's sake! The companies had naturally gotten in touch with the Office of

Federal Security. The head of that august organization had advised paying up, undoubtedly with the intention of trapping or tracing whoever came for the money; but apparently the kid with the Mephistopheles whiskers had been too smart for him, setting up a very tricky drop, as he'd said, and getting clean away with the money.

All this must have happened, I realized, before I'd encountered Bennett's men in my room in the hotel in Nassau. It explained why Bennett had been so desperate to have Eleanor to himself that he'd even been prepared to take her from another agency at gunpoint. He'd hoped to retrieve the situation with the data she could give him, or he thought she could give him—I had a hunch that, without Mac's intervention, and mine, she'd have had a very hard time at his hands. He'd known that she'd been working on the case for weeks; he'd undoubtedly convinced himself that she must have come across something he could use, and to hell with freedom of the press. His career and reputation were on the line. He was, at the very least, the man who'd advised payment and then lost the payment. It seemed likely that by this time the dreadful suspicion had crossed his mind that he'd been suckered into paying off the wrong man and the wrong gang.

Total ruin stared him in the face; and then I'd gotten that phone call telling him where he could strike with at least a possibility of getting back the money and saving himself and his organization from public disgrace. But the people who'd tricked him could obviously not be allowed to survive. He could not afford to have them describing happily, in court, how easily they'd conned the director of the OFS out of a million bucks of other people's money. Hell, if that happened, they might even go free on a nationwide wave of laughter at the agency's expense. Something was needed to discredit them, like, say, a dead body brutally murdered by those vicious young terrorist criminals when they were cornered like the rats they were— after which a massacre could take place quite justifiably. But what dead body? Obviously it should be a dead government body. And what more suitable defunct governmental torso could be found than that of the loudmouthed jerk, who'd bluffed Mr. Bennett into backing down shamefully in the presence of his men. . . .

Suddenly the guns were silent. I heard the distant rattle of a magazine being removed and replaced somewhere on shore, and the soft voice of the sandy man, Burdette, "That's enough, you trigger-happy young punk. Hold your fire."

It was time to drift silently away before they boarded the houseboat and started examining the canal beyond for potential targets; but a movement caught my eye. Something had stirred at one of the shot-out windows. Incredibly, somebody was still alive in the bullet-riddled hulk. Slowly two heads appeared, not just one: the blond head of the girl and the dark head of the whiskered man. Well, it was a good demonstration of what you can accomplish by spraying a lot of lead around haphazardly—and what you can't. The man was behind the girl, steadying her, urging her on. There was blood on his face.

"Easy now," I heard him whisper. "Go straight over the side, slip out of that glamor-rag, leave it floating for them to shoot at, and swim under water as far as you can. . ."

"Elmer?" Her voice was thin with shock, but there was more to her than I'd thought; she could still remember her friends.

"Elmer's dead. When I say go—"

"You?"

"Right behind you, baby. Now go!"

They rose together, the man knocking away some broken glass with his bare hand to clear the way for her, freeing her long garment when it snagged, boosting her into the opening with, I could see, the last of his strength. He wasn't going anywhere and he knew it; he was just holding himself together by sheer willpower long enough to get her away.

Then the deckhouse door slid open and a machine pistol opened up. I saw the bearded man deliberately interpose his dying body between his small blond lady and this new hail of death; but in a moment he fell away and left her helplessly balanced on the sill. Her body jerked sharply several times as she clung there. There was enough light that I could see the shocked and unbelieving expression on her pretty face. A little blood trickled from the corner of her mouth and she made a vague attempt to wipe it away with her sleeve; then her lips parted and a thick dark torrent poured down the front of the beautiful robe her boyfriend had bought her to introduce her to the rich and beautiful life. She teetered there a moment longer, and let go, and fell back out of sight.

Well, people who try to find Eldorado in other people's bank accounts can't complain too loudly when they get caught. Still, the kids hadn't really hurt anybody, except in the pocketbook. Although I'm a fairly violent guy myself and perhaps should feel otherwise, I make a very sharp distinction between muscle crimes and brain crimes, or, if you prefer, crimes of violence and so-called white-collar crimes. Endangering a man's life is one thing; endangering his money is, I feel, a considerably less heinous offense. Hell, as long as they leave you with life and health, you can always go out and make more money. It's when they kill or cripple you that things get serious. These young folks hadn't inflicted any physical damage on anybody. The savage retribution that had struck them seemed like, if you'll pardon the word, overkill.

But it was no time for sentimental reflections. If you play with rough people, rough things happen to you. I eased myself forward along the houseboat's side and waited in the shadow of the blunt overhanging bow. I'd barely established myself there when the vessel rocked noticeably in response to the weight of the other two joining Lawson on board. I knew it was Lawson who'd hit the door and done the final shooting because I'd heard his voice back there right afterward telling the others it was okay to come in now. After a little, I heard stumbling footsteps and violent retching sounds; that was young Ellershaw losing his dinner over the rail after discovering that firing at live targets wasn't quite the same as practicing on the OFS range. The other two came out on deck.

"As soon as he stops puking," I heard Lawson say, "take him ashore and spread out and find that guy and take care of him. Dammit, I had him right in my sights, but he moved too fast. . . ."

"No."

"What did you say?"

"You heard me," Burdette replied coolly. "I don't go into heavy brush after wounded grizzlies, and I don't prowl vacant lots at night after a guy like that, particularly not after I've helped try to kill him. Hell, the man's a pro. He's out there right now waiting for us. I'm not taking a green kid—and I do mean green, look at him—and playing tag with that character in the dark. You want Mr. Helm, you go chase him yourself."

"Listen, we've got to—"

"You got to. I don't got to. Now if you want to rearrange things slightly on board, make them look better for our side, stick guns in people's hands and such before we call in the police, give the orders. But suicide orders I don't take, and I'm not letting the kid go out there, either. He's an okay kid except he gets a bit excited, and you're not sending him out to get killed by a professional manhunter he can't begin to handle. You feel brave, you try it. I'm a yellow-bellied coward and I'm staying right here. And I'm not even staying here very long if you don't make up your cottonpicking mind."

"You'll hear about this, Burdette!"

"That's right, I'll hear about it. Dead men don't hear so good."

"Actually, Helm's probably long gone by this time. Hell, he knows he's outgunned; he didn't have anything on him but a lousy little thirty-eight."

"Go ahead, talk yourself into it. You're not talking me into it, or the kid here. And if you want us to help you rig that mess inside so it looks a little more convincing, you'd better tell us how you want it done before the stuff congeals. Or before somebody sends some cops to investigate the goddamned Battle of Miami." There was a little pause, and I heard Burdette speaking in a different, gentler voice,

206

"Come on, Sonny. If you're going to shoot at them, you're going to have to learn to look at them."

They moved inside where I couldn't hear them. I paddled gently toward the dock and found myself a spot where a big piling gave me protection and a crossbeam gave me something to stand on. I waited. Eventually, having put his gang to work, Lawson came. They never learn, particularly the ones with fancy gold badges. Well, that wasn't quite right. Burdette had learned; he knew. But this one couldn't conceive of the possibility that there were people around who could get tired of having revolvers and submachine guns waved their way, and even fired their way, by wonderful, important Mr. Lawson. He'd had two cracks at me and that was enough. Besides, a dead body was still needed, badly, and I wasn't about to offer mine.

His thick figure came around the deckhouse, heading for the ladder. He heaved himself up and reached up to lay his weapon on the dock above so he'd have both hands free to climb with. It was really very unsporting of me. He didn't have a chance, any more than the girl in the deckhouse window had had a chance. I just leaned over a bit for a clear target and shot him four times in the body, through the ladder. It was wasteful, one bullet would probably have done the job, two would have been perfectly adequate insurance, but I wanted to be absolutely certain and, besides, I was curious about whether or not the cartridges would all fire after the way they'd been submerged. But they do very well with ammunition these days.

He clung there for a despairing second or two after the last shot, like the dying hippie girl; then he tumbled limply back onto the deck. I pitched the weapon down there and watched it slide along the deck and come to rest against the motionless body. A moment later, young Ellershaw came charging around the deckhouse, submachine gun ready; but Burdette was close behind him, and clamped a strong hand on his shoulder as he prepared to spray the neighborhood with unaimed fire.

"Easy, Sonny."

"But he shot Mr. Lawson! He can't have gone far!"

Burdette was leaning over the body. He rose holding the revolver—my revolver, but we don't carry weapons that can be traced. Burdette didn't look toward the dock at all, but his voice was loud and clear as he said, "It's too damned bad, but at least we've got us a nice corpse with the bullet holes in front. I wasn't looking forward to arguing that little detail with the medical examiner, the way it was originally set up. And we've even got a gun to match the holes. Come on, Junior, lend a hand and let's fix the pretty picture so we can report to Mr. Godalmighty Bennett how his fine upstanding agent died heroically at the hands of those murderous activists. . . ."

I slipped away while they were taking care of it. It was a long hike along the canal to the marina Brent had told me about; and several times I had to dive for cover as police cars went by, heading for the scene of the crime at last. The little pickup truck was parked with some other cars in the marina lot and I attracted no attention getting it away. When I'd put a safe distance behind me, I stopped at a gas station, closed at that hour, and used the public phone there. I hadn't expected to catch Brent himself, since he'd been assigned to watch over Eleanor Brand; but he was supposed to have somebody covering the phone in his absence. I was totally unprepared for hearing Martha Devine's voice.

"I thought you were in Washington by this time," I said.

"Who said I was going to Washington? I just went to the airport to see Daddy off; then I . . . Matt."

Her voice warned me. "Trouble?"

"Yes. Your friend, Mr. Brent's been hurt and he wanted to be sure you came to the hospital as soon as you could. He said . . . he said for you to shoot your way in if you had to, but he *had* to see you right away."

Assorted fears went through my mind very quickly. "You don't know. . . ."

"I know very little, Matt. Just that the poor boy wants you badly; he insisted on my coming here to wait for your call so I could make you understand it was very important."

"How the hell did you get mixed up in? . . . Never mind. What hospital?"

"St. Margaret's." She gave me the address. "I'll meet you at the information desk. . . . Oh, Matt."

"What?"

"Don't be too hard on him. I'm sure he did his best."

CHAPTER 24

You learn to turn it off. There was absolutely no point in my wearing out the brain cells as I drove by, wondering how badly Brent was hurt or what was happening to Eleanor Brand in his absence. That information would be forthcoming in due time. Speculating about it beforehand could gain me nothing.

One unpleasant subject that I had to consider right away, however, was the possibility that I, like Bennett, had been played for a sucker. Rather belatedly, I was beginning to realize that, if the anonymous telephone lady with the husky voice had merely wanted to direct Bennett's attention to those grubby kids calling themselves the Sacred Earth Protective Force, she could have called Bennett directly. Why had she brought me into it at all? Unless she knew Bennett's reputation well enough to know that he'd never have shared the dangerous information with us if it had been given to him alone. He'd have managed without us somehow.

The way she'd done it, however, through me, she could be fairly certain that, having received the address and dutifully passed it on as interdepartmental cooperation required, I'd very probably take a part in the ensuing action, meaning that I would, at least for a little while, be unavailable for bodyguard duty. The job of watching over Eleanor Brand would temporarily devolve upon somebody else. It was likely that, lulled by the total lack of activity to date—after all, the only threat to Eleanor's well-being since I'd been watching over her had been Bennett's own abortive action—we would not go to the trouble of hastily importing another experienced senior agent, of whom we don't have an unlimited number, for a mere evening's protection of a lady who seemed to be in no real danger at the moment. We'd simply make do with what we had at hand.

So we—to hell with we, I— had sent an untrained boy to do a man's bodyguard job while I went off to swim in dark canals for reasons that were beginning to seem less and less compelling. Well, it's hard to do a good job of kicking yourself while driving a car; and the undersized Japanese pickup had all the bad habits of any unloaded truck with no weight on the rear wheels. Pushing it hard, I had to handle it carefully so I wouldn't lose it; even then, it took me longer than it should have to reach the hospital. Martha was waiting when I got there, sitting on an upholstered backless bench facing the information desk.

She got up as I approached and gave me a curious look, reminding me that I was no shining example of immaculate sartorial splendor; but what the hell, my clothes had dried and I'd brushed off most of the mud, and these informal days it's the guy with the crease in his pants who looks conspicuous.

"Are you all right?" Martha asked.

I nodded. "How is he?"

"Not really critical, but he won't let them do anything, give him anything, until he talks to you. He's afraid they'll put him out."

"Where do we go?"

She said, "The doctor just went up. He said if you arrived, sit tight; he'll be right back."

"Sure." I hesitated. "Do you know where Eleanor Brand is?"

"Elly?" Martha frowned, surprised. "No, I have no idea, why should I? I haven't seen her since this afternoon." Her lips tightened. "After the way she abused my girlish trust a while back, we're not exactly friends, remember? Why do you ask?"

"Brent was supposed to be keeping an eye on her for us. We thought she might be in danger."

"It couldn't happen to a nicer person." Martha threw a wry grin my way. "Don't mind me; I'm just being bitchy. But Brent didn't tell me that." She sounded mildly resentful.

I grinned. "He probably wasn't sure how much you were supposed to know, even if you were the boss's daughter. What happened, anyway?"

She drew a long breath to prepare herself, and launched into the recital, "After seeing Daddy off, I went into one of the airport restaurants—well, kind of a bar, actually—and had a drink; then I remembered I hadn't eaten anything since I left New Mexico this morning. You can't eat that plastic stuff they hand you on airplanes nowadays. The bar girl said I could have dinner right there in the booth; but of course it took practically forever. They had to bring it all from the real restaurant next door, and they didn't break their necks working at it. But I didn't really mind. Daddy had given me a number to call so I could find out how . . . how your expedition had turned out before I went to bed; but I knew it was too early for that. So I had a slow brandy afterward; and suddenly there was your friend, Brent, at the bar. I waved and he came over, but I must say he didn't seem very pleased to see me. Kind of preoccupied. Not very flattering; but he did say, when I asked, that he had a car and would be happy to give me a ride to my hotel and save me a taxi. Well, he could hardly say anything else. They jumped us in the airport parking lot." She hesitated. "I . . . wasn't much use, Matt. In fact, I was totally useless, just a damned helpless movie ingenue cowering back against the cars while her escort. . . . It happened so fast!"

"How many?" I asked.

"Two. Young. Black. One came from nowhere and

snatched my purse; and when I cried out and Brent grabbed him, the other jumped out from behind the cars and hit Brent on the head with something. Brent fell down and the one with my purse turned around and kicked him a couple of times. Then the big one reached down and hit him again with whatever it was and they ran off. . . ." After a moment, she went on, "The police found my bag almost right away, only a little distance off, with only the money missing. They think it was just an ordinary mugging, but it wasn't, was it?"

"Probably not."

"After seeing him safe in the ambulance, I drove his car to his place—he'd given me the keys—to wait for your call as I'd promised him. There was another man there, the backup man, Brent had called him; and he was very suspicious of me. He insisted on confirming my identity with Washington before he'd let me near the phone."

"As he damned well should have," I said. "Did Brent tell you what he was doing at the airport?"

"He said . . ." She frowned with the effort of remembering. "He said he'd been seeing somebody off and . . . and making arrangements to follow them. Elly?"

I shrugged. "It's a guess. What the hell is that doctor doing?"

"Matt."

"Yes."

"What's his name?" she asked.

I frowned. "Who, the doctor? How the hell would I. . . . Oh, Brent? Something flossy, Michael, I think. Michael Brent. Why?"

"He . . . seems like a very nice boy, too nice to be mixed up in Daddy's dirty games. And yours."

She sounded a bit patronizing, the very experienced, very grownup, widow-lady in the smart white suit, Mrs. Robert Devine, looking down condescendingly upon the children at their foolish play. Her disapproval of her parent's activities and mine didn't bother me, I was hardened to that; but I was tempted to point out to her that the boy she was referring to was a promising member of a respected law firm; and that she wasn't so damned ancient herself. But the woman behind the information desk was trying to catch our attention.

"Dr. Levine just called," she said. "You can go up now."

The doctor was waiting for us when we got off the elevator, a rather small man with a white coat, a brown face, a big nose and intelligent, compassionate brown eyes.

"I hope this is really important," he said.

I asked, "What's the damage, Doctor?"

"That's what we want to determine, but the patient refuses to cooperate until . . . we do know that a couple of ribs are broken. There were two blows to the cranium, one fairly severe. We are concerned about the possibility of a fracture. . . . Make it as quick as you can, please. I wouldn't allow it at all, but he did keep saying it was important, and a disturbed mental state can be as damaging as a little delay. So help him get it off his mind, whatever it is, but please don't take any longer than absolutely necessary."

I nodded, and went inside first, impolite, followed by Martha and Dr. Levine, polite. Brent was lying in the bed with his eyes closed. His freckles showed very clearly on his pale face. His head was bandaged; and under the hospital gown, his chest was obviously strapped up tightly. The doctors love doing that to you, and it doesn't do a damned bit of good that I've ever discovered. The ribs will heal in their own good time, strapped or unstrapped; and all you can do is grit your teeth and wait for it to happen. When you can laugh and cough without hurting, you know you're cured. But I guess the medical profession doesn't feel it's doing its duty if it isn't doing something, even if it's hot and uncomfortable and useless. Brent opened his eyes and licked his lips.

"Sorry," he whispered. "I loused it up."

"Never mind that," I said. "Where did Brand go?"

"Back to the Bahamas. She got a phone call. She went back to talk to somebody named Einar Kettleman who . . ."

"I know who Kettleman is. Where?"

"Same hospital in Nassau. He'd been picked up at sea by a fisherman and brought to one of the Out Islands first. . . ."

"Never mind, I can get all that elsewhere. How'd she get away from you?"

"She was mad at us, at you, for not letting her go with you. She told me to . . . go fly my kite. She said she was tired of having us . . . us government creeps hanging around her. She said . . . by this time obviously no real danger . . . Warren Peterson could do all the bodyguarding needed. I was to tell you . . . tell you goodbye and . . . chuck you, Farley. Sorry, but that's what she said. They had tickets, she and Peterson. Commercial flight. I couldn't get any. Great bodyguard, couldn't get on the damned flight, all full up. Couldn't reach Delman, off on a job somewhere. . . ."

"Delman?"

"Murray Delman, the charter pilot who . . ."

"Sure, go on."

"Left word. He'll be back and ready to go again oh-three-hundred. Flight all cleared. Called Fred, he'll pick Brand up and watch over her after she lands in Nassau, until relieved. Best I could do. Sorry made such a mess of . . ."

"You did okay," I said. "You did fine. Now just relax and let the doctor . . ."

"No! Don't go!" There was a breathless urgency in his voice. "That's not all. What I really wanted to tell you. . . . Should have reported this afternoon, but everybody so busy and I thought we'd have plenty of time later. Investigation. Down in the Keys, remember?"

"I remember, but can't it wait?"

"Not wait. Now. Serena Lorca."

"What?"

"The Lorca girl. Serena. They call her Rina. Lorca has a fishing boat, big job, twin Detroit diesels. All those hard Mafia types down here have big chrome-plated sportfishermen, good for secret meetings with the boys. And girls. And good for the ego. Sometimes they even catch some fish. But Lorca's daughter likes sailboats better. A lot better. That's what . . . what Captain Harriet Robinson discovered: Rina loves sailboats so much she's bought four of them—five now—in the past two years. Five good-sized cruising sailboats, at least a quarter of a million bucks' worth, even secondhand, the way she got them. Bought but not sold. No record of sale anywhere. Interesting?"

"Very interesting," I said. "Give me Rina."

"Serena Lorca, daughter, twenty-two, five-four, one-thirty-five, short dark hair, brown eyes. . . . Supposed to be good sailor but lost a boat offshore couple-three years ago, cruising with a friend. *Tumbleweed*, thirty-footer, sloop rig, built by . . . built by . . . forget. That one daddy bought new for her. Oh, it was Parsons' Boatyard, Lauderdale, remember now."

I said, "Never mind. Eleanor told me about that accident."

"No, listen!" Brent's voice was insistent. "Storm, dismasted. Girlfriend knocked overboard by falling spar, couldn't save. Mast, lying in water alongside, smashed through hull like battering ram in heavy seas before she could cut it free, working alone. Picked up in life raft after five days adrift, bad condition, hospital, psychiatric treatment. Phony."

"What?"

Brent licked his lips. "It's a phony, Matt. 'The fallen mast smashed through the hull like a battering ram in the heavy seas.' That's what she told reporters. Only she got it word for word out of an old magazine article. I remembered reading the story. I dug out the magazine; I keep them. It's at my place, along with a list of the boats she's bought. Story's about a guy who lost his boat and wife in a storm off Cape Mendocino, California. Serena cribbed practically every detail right out of the article. And I back-checked the weather records at the time, no storm. Squall, maybe; there could have been a local squall, they come and go. But it didn't blow hard enough or long enough to raise any heavy seas the whole time she was out there. Think about it."

"Good work," I said. The doctor was getting fidgety off to my right. "Give me the girlfriend who was lost."

215

"Ann Bergerson. Eighteen at the time of her death, couple of years younger than Serena. Data incomplete; but tall, slim, blond, and beautiful is what it says so far."

"Where's Serena now?"

"Sorry, don't know. Working on it when . . . she took off two days ago in her latest sailboat, *Jamboree*, forty-foot ex-racer, built sixty-nine, masthead sloop converted to slightly cut-down cutter rig. I wanted to check with you before getting official help to locate her. Daddy's fifty-foot sport-fisherman's gone, too; it always goes when the sailboats go. Why? You guess, my head is tired. *Ser–Jan*. Ugh, hate those stuck-together cutie-pie names! Serena and Janine. Lorca named that gold-plated fishing machine after his daughter and wife, very touching, like a sentimental shark. . . ."

Dr. Levine was moving forward now. I said quickly, "That's a hell of a fine job of research, amigo. Anything else?"

"No, I guess. . . . Yes, one thing. Gun you gave Brand."

"Peterson's gun, actually."

"Yes, but couldn't take on commercial flight, through scanners, asked me to hold. Car, glove compartment. She said to tell you. . . ."

"I know," I said, "Chuck you, Farley."

"Now you really must leave," the doctor said, and we left.

CHAPTER 25

Downstairs I stopped at a pay phone in the lobby and called the Miami contact number again, Brent's number, this time getting a male voice I didn't recognize. We went through the standard identification routines and he connected me with Nassau, after some delay.

"Fred was ready for them at the airport," said the pleasant female voice with whom I was familiar. "No report since."

"He's been advised that the subject has turned uncooperative?" I asked.

"Yes. And she knows him, which makes it more difficult, but he's traded cabs with another driver and will try to stay out of sight." There was a sound that might have been a throaty chuckle. "Of course, one black boy do look much like another in the dark, Massa Eric."

It was the first time, on this assignment at least, that she'd said anything human and unofficial, or indicative of her race. I hadn't given it much thought. I'd been more concerned about the distinct impression I'd gotten, from her cool and businesslike telephone manner, that in the undeclared feud between Fred and me she'd picked a side, and it wasn't mine. But apparently a slight thaw had set in.

"What about one black girl?" I asked.

"No comment. I'se a respectable married woman, sah." The phony-darky accent vanished. "Instructions?"

"I'll be there before daylight to take over, but I'll have to know where. When he checks in, tell him to keep checking in as often as possible."

"Noted. Anything else?"

"Yes. Tell him to keep his head down. They laid for Brent and he's in the hospital here, condition uncertain. The party's getting rough. Extreme caution."

"I . . . will pass it along as soon as I can. Extreme caution."

The little worried hesitation made the picture very clear. I thought it would be nice if I had at my disposal a great worldwide organization manned by nothing but tough professionals, preferably unmarried and unattached, instead of willing but untrained half-time heroes like Brent and Fred. But it was no time for handing out greasy, insincere reassurances to the worried dependents.

"I'll need a hotel room," I said. "Oh, and check if a

sailing yacht called *Jamboree* or a motor yacht called *Ser–Jan* or both are in the harbor. I'll call when I get in. Eric out."

After a little silence, the male voice came on, "Are you finished with Nassau, sir?"

"Finished," I said. "Give me your name again."

"Maestas. Backup. That's spelled Em-aye. . . ."

"I've lived in New Mexico; I know the Spanish spellings," I said. Another goddamned amateur, eager and respectful; and I'd trade a bushel of them for one tough, reluctant, snotty old pro I wouldn't have to feel responsible for.

"May I ask about Brent, sir?"

I said, "There's only one man we normally 'sir' around here and I'm not him. Brent's alive and talking, doesn't look too bad, but the medical verdict isn't in yet." I frowned. "He said he had a list of five boats lying around there. Can you find it?"

"Right here. . . ." He bit off the "sir." Well, at least he knew the word and wasn't too proud to use it, a point in his favor. There are a lot of proud dead men around. "Do you want me to read it to you?"

"Yes."

They call boats the damndest things. I made him go through the list a second time, and repeated it back to make sure I had it right, although I couldn't see any immediate use for the information.

When I was through, Maestas said, "Question."

"Yes?"

"There was a . . . a young lady in here throwing her weight around; said Brent had sent her. I checked her out with Washington and they said okay, but I'd like to clear it with you. Is she for real?"

I glanced toward Martha, sitting on the waiting bench nearby, trying not to look impatient. I grinned.

"She's for real," I said. For some reason I thought of a girl called Serena Lorca, whom I'd never seen. I said, "Life would be a lot simpler if people would stop producing strong-minded daughters, Maestas; particularly important people. But not nearly as much fun."

When I hung up the phone, Martha got up and patted her dark hair and smoothed down her white suit. I waited for her to join me and we headed out the door. Before crossing the street to the hospital parking lot, I stopped, stooped, and palmed the .25 auto I was still wearing in my sock, just in case they thought they had a good thing going for them in parking lots. I'd stripped the little monster hastily, earlier, and wiped it clean with a wrung-out handkerchief before reassembling it; but as wet and muddy as it had been, I wasn't counting on it to function reliably even if the ammunition fired. Still, it might scare somebody long enough for me to say boo, or kick them in the balls or something. But nobody bothered us. Although it was a clear night, the parking-lot lights made the stars look far away. I remembered a night not too long ago, back in Santa Fe, visiting the same girl who now walked crisply beside me on her high heels, when the stars had seemed much closer. But this was Miami, Florida, with ratty-looking palm trees rustling in the warm breeze off the Gulf Stream.

Martha unlocked the driver's door of the racy-looking Datsun I remembered Brent chauffeuring me around in, down in the Keys. She got in, reached over to unlock the far door, opened the glove compartment and brought out the revolver Brent had just told us about.

"I suppose you'll want this," she said, giving it to me. "Who's Einar Kettleman?"

"A seaman who was on the bridge of a tanker called *Fairfax Constellation* when it was sunk off the Bahamas recently by a mysterious explosion. There was a young officer on watch, too, but he was murdered before he could answer all the questions Elly wanted to ask him. She's undoubtedly hoping to get the answers she wants from Kettleman."

"And the fact that she may get him murdered, too, couldn't concern her less." Martha's voice was tart.

I said, "I'm not too worried about her getting Kettleman into trouble. What bothers me is the possibility of Kettle-

219

man getting her into trouble. If he's actually alive, or even if he isn't."

"Oh, you think it may be just a trick to get her. . ."

"They've peeled away her protection very nicely, haven't they?" I said grimly when Martha stopped. "First, I'm sent off to chase terrorists, and then Brent is put out of action. Meanwhile, she's lured out of the country by a fancy story, true or false, with an escort who barely knows one end of a gun from another; and doesn't have a gun, anyway. I've got his piece right here." I glanced at the revolver, checked the loads, tucked the weapon into my waistband, and pulled my sweater over it. I stuck the .25 back into my sock. Two-gun Helm. I glanced at my watch. "Well, I'd better get into some halfway respectable clothes and pack my suitcase and head for the airport. . . ."

"I'll drive you," Martha said.

"I've got wheels of a sort right over there. Thanks just the same."

"You can leave it and get somebody to pick it up, can't you?"

I glanced at her. After a moment, I shrugged. "Sure, if you don't mind taxiing me around."

"What else would I be doing except catching up with my jet-lag? Get in." After we'd driven for a while, she said carefully, "I guess you've gotten to know Elly Brand pretty well by this time."

I said, "Cut it out, Martha. You're a big girl now and this is the tired tail end of the twentieth century. If you want to know if I've been to bed with her, ask." When she didn't speak, I said, "The answer, ma'am, is negative. And if you're wondering why we're protecting her in spite of the kind of stuff she's been writing about us, I think we kind of touched on that in Santa Fe. Use your brains and you'll realize the kind of stuff she's been writing about us is exactly why we have to keep her alive if we can. She's not making it easy."

Martha was looking straight ahead as she drove, employing the sports car clutch and gearbox with considerable skill but a little too much emphasis. Even in the darkness of the car I could see that her face was pink. Her voice was quite soft when she spoke.

"My God, was I that obvious?"

"Pretty obvious," I said. "But don't give me too much credit for my pure relationship with the lady; there were circumstances that made it advisable. Normally I probably wouldn't have been all that strong-minded. She's rather an attractive person when you get to know her."

"Attractive!"

"You're letting your prejudice get the better of you," I said. "If Eleanor Brand is so damned unattractive, how did it happen that she was your friend for years, until you learned what a ruthless and single-minded person she really is when the chips are down?"

Martha said stiffly, "I consider loyalty very important, Matt."

"Sure, but loyalty to what, a person or a profession? Try putting me on that spot, sweetheart, and see how fast I throw you to the wolves."

She laughed abruptly, triumphantly. "That's what you say now, but when you were on that spot once, years ago, you didn't."

There was a little silence. She was perfectly right, of course. Once on that long-ago assignment that had brought us together, when I should have been shooting a rifle at somebody totally different, I'd picked off a man who was about to kill her instead, jeopardizing the whole mission so that I'd had to scramble like hell to retrieve it. Just as she had once compromised her sturdy humanitarian principles to save my life, as well as her own. You might think it would cancel out, one life for another, even-steven, but it doesn't work that way. A bond remains.

Martha spoke quietly, looking straight ahead through the windshield. "You haven't asked me what I'm doing in Miami, Matt."

I glanced at her. "What are you doing in Miami, Mrs. Devine?"

"I'm looking for a man."

I said deliberately, "It's a big city. There are lots of them around. Any particular man?"

"Character named Helm," she said. "Totally undesirable. Roving eye, itchy trigger finger. Does perfectly horrible things. You did a perfectly horrible thing tonight, didn't you, my dear?"

"That's right," I said. "Perfectly horrible."

"I can always tell by your eyes. There's a bleak look they get. I'm not asking about it; I don't want to know. The only trouble is . . ." She stopped and swallowed hard. "The only trouble is, this perfectly dreadful creature is . . . kind of nice sometimes; and I've known him a long time. And when he goes away, I kind of miss him. In fact, I find I miss him very much, now that I don't . . . don't have a man around the house any longer. So I thought that if I came here and saw him again, maybe even talked with him a little, I'd know . . ."

Her voice stopped. I heard her make a small sniffing sound. She gave each rear-view mirror a careful look, switched on the turn signal, pulled the Datsun to the curb, and set the hand brake. Then she took a Kleenex out of her purse and blew her nose.

"I don't know what the hell there is to cry about," she said. "I guess I'm making kind of a spectacle of myself, aren't I? I was going to be very calm and sensible about this, Matt. I was going to discuss it with you very intelligently. So what do I do? I act like a jealous bitch, first, and then I break into helpless tears." She drew a ragged breath. "All I can say is that the house was damned lonely after you left and I kept wishing you—we—hadn't been so damned respectful of my new-made widowhood. If we hadn't, if we'd just said to hell with propriety that night, I think we'd have got something settled, one way or another, don't you?"

I said, "Well, it was certainly on my mind."

She smiled faintly. "Yes, I could see what you were thinking; and I liked having you think it. But then you started having noble afterthoughts, didn't you, about how the poor girl had made one mistake and you were going to keep her from making another?" She made a quick gesture. "Oh, I knew you thought Bob was a mistake, for me. You liked him, he was your friend, but you thought I was . . . too good for him, really. You've even gotten a silly notion I'm too good for you. Well, just stop idealizing me, my dear. Remember that talk we had about wolves and cocker spaniels. You've spoiled me for the spaniel-men; isn't it about time you stood still for the consequences?" She drew another long, uneven breath. When I didn't speak, she went on, "Well, I seem to have got it out after a fashion, what I wanted to say. I just wanted you to know; you don't have to commit yourself tonight. I know what you're thinking." She grinned abruptly. "You're thinking: oh, Jesus, what a time the dame picks for a gripping love scene, with the plane warming up on the field! Well, at least you're a gentleman; you haven't looked at your watch once."

Then we were laughing and she leaned over and kissed me lightly before letting off the hand brake and putting the Datsun into gear. Three hours later, with no hint of dawn in the sky ahead, the silent moustached pilot whose name I'd finally learned, Murray Delman, set me down on Providence Island without speaking and handed me my suitcase without saying goodbye.

CHAPTER 26

INSIDE the airport building I found a telephone and made my arrival call, identifying myself as required, although our girl in Nassau ought to know my voice by now. Somewhat to my disappointment—you like to maintain friendly relations with the troops—her voice was remote and businesslike again as if we'd never kidded each other

223

even a little: perhaps she was regretting her momentary lapse into informality. Perhaps she'd been lonely in the middle of the night; but it was getting close to morning now.

"Reservation: Paradise Towers Hotel as before," she said curtly.

"Check."

"The yacht *Jamboree* has not yet been located. The yacht *Ser–Jan* is here in Nassau, berthed in the Islander Marina just above the bridge."

"Check. Any word from Fred?"

"I was coming to that." Her voice reproved me for my impatience. "The subject has made contact with Fred voluntarily. She says she has obtained information she must discuss with you at once. She has interviewed Einar Kettleman."

"Where do we meet?"

"Warren Peterson will take you to her. He should be at the airport by now. Rental sedan, green intermediate, make unspecified."

"I bet he just loves playing chauffeur for me, fond as he is of me," I said. "What's the matter with Fred and his borrowed cab?"

"It was decided that Fred had better accompany Brand, since he has a gun and some experience in using it."

"Accompany her where? What the hell is our screwball girl reporter up to now?"

"I believe she's following up some of Kettleman's information. Peterson will brief you as you drive. Over and out."

I stood for a moment staring at the telephone grimly, before hanging it up. *Over and out*, for God's sake. It never had been proper radio procedure, but the movies had used it so often nobody really questioned it. Even if the guy who was listening knew better, he just assumed you didn't. To us it was the big red light and the siren and the warning rockets. No wonder the girl had turned formal again. *Over and out*. It meant grab a life jacket and head for the boats, Buster, the lousy ship is sinking. I drew a deep breath. Another long, damned day, and night; but if I'd wanted a simple and quiet life I could undoubtedly have gotten a job as night watchman somewhere, with my experience. It occurred to me that Martha would probably think that was great, although she might prefer a slightly more respectable occupation that didn't involve my wearing a gun at all. But it was no time to be thinking about Martha Borden, who'd become Martha Devine, and now seemed to be toying with the notion of becoming Martha Helm; and I could muster a few arguments in favor of the idea, myself. . . .

The sedan that pulled to the curb when I came outside was green all right, and I could see why the make was unspecified. It was one of the anonymous middle-sized conveyances Detroit keeps producing stubbornly, instead of the little ones people really want to buy these days. I suspect that, where this car is concerned, the manufacturers have secretly consolidated their facilities for the sake of efficiency and economy, using a single assembly line that turns out Chryslers on Monday, Fords on Tuesday and Wednesday, and General Motors products on Thursday and Friday, just changing the trademarks and radiator grills accordingly. I remembered the old days when you could really tell the difference, when a Ford man wouldn't associate with a Chevrolet man and neither one would bother to spit on a Plymouth aficionado; but nowadays we're all driving Datsuns or Toyotas, or Mercedes or VWs anyway, while we wait for the U.S. industry to get its finger out. And these thoughts were all totally irrelevant, too, of course, just like Martha Devine; but there really wasn't anything to think about that I wanted to think about. I tossed my suitcase into the back seat and got in front with the driver.

"Where are we going?" I asked.

Peterson took us away with a flourish that was wasted on a family sedan. I mean, yanking the lever of an automatic transmission dramatically into DRIVE isn't nearly as impressive as working your way expertly through the gears of a five-speed box.

"Islander Marina," he said. "They went over to see a boat that's docked there, to find out who's on board."

"A fifty-footer called *Ser–Jan*, I suppose," I said sourly, and he nodded. "What the hell steered you there?" I asked.

"Well, you did, really," he said a bit maliciously. "I mean, all we had was a story about a mysterious power-boat about that size; and then we talked to your agent, who'd been following us. Elly insisted on getting in touch with you after we'd heard what Kettleman had to say. The black boy checked home base to see where you were, and his wife said you were on your way. She also mentioned that you'd been inquiring about just such a boat and she'd located it right here in Nassau. . . . Well, you know how Elly is when she's on the trail of a story. Wild horses couldn't have stopped her from going over and taking a peek at the damned boat while she waited for you to arrive."

"Fred ought to learn to keep his mouth shut about official business," I said. "But I wouldn't call him a black boy where he can hear you."

"Well, anyway, she should be safe with him, he has a gun," Peterson said, unimpressed. "I had to leave mine in Miami."

I didn't tell him I had his well-traveled revolver under my belt; he was enough of a menace unarmed. "Just what did that Kettleman guy tell Elly, anyway?"

Peterson hesitated; then he shrugged and said, "A hell of a story, is what he told us. He said the ship ran down a sailboat and the whole world blew up."

I frowned. "Go over that again, slowly. Are you saying that Kettleman told you—told Elly—that the *Fairfax Constellation* was involved in a collision with a sailing yacht? The third mate with the oddball name, Jurgen Hinkampf, never mentioned a collision to her, or anybody else, as far as I know."

"Well, would he?" Peterson was scornful of my stupidity. "Think, fella. I mean, he was responsible, right? It was his ship and his watch. Was he going to announce to the world that he'd been writing a letter to his girl or something and his seaman-assistant had been taking a snooze or something while that goddam great tanker was crashing along on autopilot with nobody looking—and running down a yacht in the dark? Hell, it would have meant Hinkampf's career right there; and probably a court trial and prison as well. But nobody on board had seen that goddam sailboat except him and Kettleman, and he thought Kettleman was dead, so he just kept quiet about it."

I said, "Tell me about the collision. What's Kettleman's story?"

Peterson moved his muscular shoulders in another shrug. "Well, normally you'd hardly call it a collision from the tanker's standpoint; a big ship like that would go right over an ordinary yacht without anybody on board noticing a thing—like a loaded semi squashing a bug on the freeway —except that Kettleman just happened to remember that he was supposed to be on watch. He got up and took a casual look through the bridge windows as they smashed along at fourteen knots; and there, dead ahead of the ship, were the weak running lights and the dim little white sails of the yacht. He yelled for the officer, the third mate, who came running; but it was too late. There was nothing they could do. Those things take three or four miles to stop— hell, the really big ones take eight or nine—and they even take a good part of a mile to just start turning after you crank the steering wheel hard over. So the two of them just stood there frozen, out on the wing of the bridge, watching those little sails disappear under the bow, expecting maybe to feel a tiny jar or crunch and suddenly . . . KABOOM! The whole works went up like that volcano, Mt. St. Helens. Kettleman was blown clear off the bridge into the water and left behind—the ship was still doing thirteen or fourteen knots, of course, even if it had just been blasted wide open forward—but he found a hatch cover that had gotten blown overboard at the same time and crawled onto that. He saw the ship finally come to a stop a couple of miles away, sinking by the bow and burning like a torch."

227

When he paused, I asked, "What was that you were saying about a motorboat?"

Peterson made an irritable gesture. "Don't rush me, fella! Let me tell it, huh? Naturally, Kettleman tried to paddle toward the ship, hoping at least one of the lifeboats had gotten launched and would pick him up. Then he heard a distant roaring sound and looked around to see a big sportfisherman coming up fast—throwing a bow wave like a destroyer, Kettleman said. There was a funny thing, it was running without lights, he said; just the spidery superstructure against the sky and the black shadow of the hull and that white bow wave. But he didn't think too much about that at the time; he was just waiting for it to get close enough for him to attract its attention. He thought, of course, that it was racing to the rescue of the burning ship and would pass right by him. Instead, it slowed down before it got to him and circled around as if it was looking for something. Kettleman saw a light winking in the water, and the boat stopped and took something aboard. Kettleman said it was big and black and shiny; he thought it was a man in a wet suit. Then the sportfisherman swung around and roared back the way it had come, leaving the ship to sink and the crew to drown. Kettleman was pretty bitter about that. He kept drifting farther and farther away. In the morning, when the official rescue craft arrived on the scene, he could see them on the horizon but they never saw him. Two days later a fisherman almost ran him down, and got him aboard, and took him to a little village on one of the outlying cays of the Bahamas. Communications were lousy and it was almost a week before arrangements could be made to have him moved to Nassau for better treatment of his burns."

It was an interesting story, but at the moment the most interesting thing about it, to me, was that Mr. Warren Peterson, who didn't like me at all, would bother to tell it to me in such minute and loving detail. Even if Eleanor had asked him to bring me up to date as we drove, in order to save time, I'd have expected a brief and surly synopsis instead of this lengthy saga of the sea that had now brought us clear through the city of Nassau proper and onto the bridge that led across the harbor to Paradise Island. Peterson stopped to pay the toll. As we came off the bridge I asked him to pull into the first likely parking spot for a moment. The warning I'd been given was still very clear in my mind: *Over and out*. I'd been doing some careful thinking.

"Look," I said, "I don't know what the hell we'll be running up against, but everything indicates that the people on that sportfishing boat aren't very nice. So I guess you'd better have this back."

I held out the Colt .38 Special with the four-inch barrel. There was a moment of suspense as he took it and looked at it, recognizing it; then he tucked it away and said sulkily, "It took you a while to get around to mentioning you had it, fella."

I said, "We didn't have a hell of a lot of fun the last time you had it, fella."

"Okay, okay, so maybe I was a little hasty when we first met up in Elly's hotel room. You got one, too?"

I showed him the pipsqueak .25. "If they don't just die laughing at the gun maybe I can tickle them to death with the bullets," I said. "Well, let's hope we won't need all the firepower. Let's go see what Elly and Fred have been up to that they shouldn't."

Peterson started the car again and soon turned onto a curving park-like drive that swung gracefully through the trees to a parking lot overlooking a small marina. The basin was tiny compared to the giant installations popular in the States, but the boats it sheltered were big and flashy. There were several expensive sportfishermen with long outriggers that looked like sailboat masts complete with rigging, and tall tuna towers that looked like oil derricks. I remembered fishing out West as a boy. My equipment had consisted of a pair of patched rubber boots and a battered fly rod. These characters seemed to be going at it the hard way—at least the expensive way—but, hell, it's not for me to tell somebody else how to get his kicks. Or her kicks.

"There's the taxi," Peterson whispered. "Looks like your Freddie-boy is waiting for us. I don't see Elly."

I said, "Hell, the brash way she operates, she probably got herself invited aboard for a breakfast interview. Which boat?"

"Number three from the sea wall, over on the right. The one with the dark blue hull."

I studied the craft for a moment, seeing no lights in the cabin and no signs of life on board. I said, "Okay, park on this side where we're not so conspicuous, and we'll slip across and hear what Fred has to say."

The lot was not very big and it was considerably less than half full of cars. The taxi Peterson had pointed out to me—another anonymous medium-sized American sedan—was parked facing the water, giving Fred a good view of the basin below. As I started across the paved open space with Peterson close behind me, I noted that a hint of dawn was visible through the trees to my left; but the boats below were dark and the cars around us were dark. There was no breeze and nothing moved; and Fred still hadn't looked around. Okay. *Over and out*. Reaching the taxi, I knocked on the door on the driver's side, and got no reaction. I did what was expected of me: I grabbed the door handle and opened the door, and Fred's body spilled out limply onto the pavement of the parking lot. I gave the gasp of shock and horror appropriate to the occasion, recoiling sharply. Something touched me in the back.

"Drop the gun," Peterson said behind me. "Drop it and raise your hands. Sorry about this, fella, but I had to make the deal. I give them you and they give me Elly, right? Thanks for making it easier by returning my gun."

"What happened to Fred?"

"Your black boy tried to reach the phone to tell his wife to warn you, regardless of their threats. He fought so hard they had to use a knife. . . . Stand still! I told you to drop that gun. . . ."

He was still talking as I turned around and shot him with the .25. I was aware that we were no longer alone in the parking lot. Shadowy figures were closing in, but first things first. Warren Peterson was looking at me, startled and reproachful: once more I was breaking all the rules he'd learned from the silver screen. He'd pointed a gun at me, that symbol of power, that magic wand, again he'd pointed a gun at me, and I still hadn't done what he'd told me to do. The TV formula just wasn't working at all and he was very distressed about it.

Then the dreadful truth dawned on him that he was being shot at, hell he was being shot, and he was holding a gun. He was supposed to be shooting back. In fact, he was supposed to have started shooting when I first turned, before that first shocking little bullet went into him. Now my second bullet hit him and at last he made an effort to aim his .38 my way—re-aim it my way—but it was too late now and his heart really wasn't in it. One of the no-kill kids. My third bullet struck him and he went down, dropping the powerful weapon he'd never fired.

After three, the little .25 remembered it had been swimming and jammed; but where I'd put them, three would be enough. It's not really a toy, even though it looks like one. They were closing in on me now. I turned and heaved the jammed pistol at one, and another one sapped me expertly from behind.

CHAPTER 27

SHE was a square brown girl with short black hair. She looked oddly fuzzy around the edges; but careful consideration inclined me to the theory that it was my vision that was fuzzy, not the girl. At first glance she seemed like just a sturdy, rather attractive, tomboy type, the kind who'll take you on and probably beat you at any sport you choose; but you'll have to run her down with dogs to put a dress and high heels on her—and then she'll deck you with a hard right to the jaw if, in an amorous moment, you try to get them off her, later; because she hasn't quite discovered, yet, what being a girl is all about.

But at second glance, it became apparent that this husky young woman belonged in the special category of those who'd made the earthshaking discovery, all right, but hadn't liked it. She had an athletic, well-shaped body, deep-breasted and full-hipped, obviously in very good condition. Her face was handsome, too, deeply and smoothly tanned with good features, good enough to survive and even thrive in the company of the short mannish hairdo, if there is such a thing as a mannish hairdo these unisex days. She was wearing white tennis shoes, the kind with the deathgrip yachting soles; white sailcloth shorts that weren't so snug you couldn't stand it; and one of the elastic tops, strapless, that look like giant, glorified Ace bandages. This one was red and made her bare shoulders look very brown and strong. Her bare legs were brown and strong, too. I had a particularly good view of them since I was lying on the floor—excuse me, cabin sole—at her feet.

I thought about it for a moment and decided that if there was a cabin sole there had to be a cabin, and if there was a cabin there had to be a boat. Very good reasoning, Helm. Intelligence seems to be returning. Now that you've gotten yourself located on a boat, can you figure out how to get yourself off it? With the person you came here to liberate, of course; assuming she's somewhere around?

But that was rushing it. For the moment it was enough to know that I was on a boat, a powerful motorboat by the sound and vibration and, yes, the boat was under way. I also knew, from Brent's description and the snapshots in the Lorca file I'd finally got around to studying on the plane, that the muscular young lady standing over me was Miss Serena Lorca, daughter of Senator George Winfield Lorca, also known in days past as Manuel Sapio or Kid Sapio or The Sapper. And I remembered with a sudden pang of regret and guilt that I had lost somebody of importance. I had lost a guy named Fred, who'd died fighting on my behalf, and now we'd never settle that old disagreement between us. . . .

"Can you sit up?"

It was the deep female voice I'd heard once before over the phone, in Giuseppe Velo's penthouse. It seemed like a lot of voice for so young a girl. Not trusting my own voice yet, I nodded, but that was a mistake, reminding me that I'd recently been hit on the head with a sap or kindred object.

"There's a man right behind you with a gun," Serena Lorca said. "Don't try anything. You've already shown what a hell of a violent macho type you are; don't overdo it."

She reached down and grabbed my arm and helped me up to the port settee against which I'd been lying. I had to cling to her for a moment to steady myself against the motion of the boat, almost getting myself blasted by the automatic pistol—9mm Browning Hi-Power, or reasonable facsimile thereof—held by the gent braced in the doorway that led out into the cockpit. Whatever a doorway is called on a boat. He was a husky, swarthy specimen in clean white pants and a blue-and-white-striped jersey. Looking around, I discovered that I hadn't been lying in the cabin at all, to be technical about it, but in the deckhouse, with glass all around. It was a pretty fancy deckhouse with lots of teak, including a bar and table, elegantly upholstered settees, and wall-to-wall carpeting that had to be the indoor–outdoor stuff, since it was on a boat, but didn't look it. There was no steering station down here, I noted. Somebody must be driving the bucket from up on the flying bridge. One up there and two down here made three, so far. It isn't necessary to be a mathematical genius in this business, I told myself proudly, but it helps.

We seemed to be at sea with no land in sight. It was a fine sunny day with a light breeze. The sun was well up in the sky; the morning was well advanced. Or the afternoon hadn't progressed very far yet. Of course it didn't even have to be the same day. Well, when I felt strong enough to look at my watch I'd find out, if it was still running.

Serena Lorca said, "If you're worrying about how long you've been out, don't. You weren't hit that hard. You started coming around almost right away, but I didn't want to be bothered with you for a while, so I just gave you a hypo of some stuff we found in your suitcase. Injection A. Four hours almost to the minute, right?"

"How did you know which one?" I asked. "Assuming that you cared."

"The girl told me. After I pointed out that if she didn't let me know which one was harmless I'd just grab the first one handy and let you take your chances. One in three, correct? The other two kill, she said." Serena Lorca jerked her head toward the boat's bow. "And the answer to the next question is that she's locked up forward in good shape." She added with a hint of malice I didn't like, "Well, pretty good shape."

She'd freed herself from my grasp, with some signs of distaste. Stepping back now, balancing herself easily as the deck lurched under her feet, she gave a couple of touches to her crisp black hair and a pull to her elasticized bodice. The instinctive femininity of the movements seemed a little strange under the circumstances. She was a striking young woman if you like them compact and muscular; but she was obviously off limits, sexually speaking.

I always find it disturbing, which I suppose proves what an old-fashioned square I really am. I've explored the man–woman relationship, as Eleanor Brand liked to point out, with considerable interest and enjoyment; but I don't really know what this man–man and woman–woman stuff is all about. I suppose it's a gap in my education; but as long as it exists I can't help resenting, slightly, a good-looking girl who's completely unattainable. I don't mean happily married—somebody else attained that one even if it wasn't me—I mean quite out of bounds for the whole male sex. It seems a waste, even if the lady's having her fun in other ways. Of course, that's the selfish masculine way of looking at it.

I became aware that Serena Lorca was watching me, her lip curling in an arrogant, contemptuous manner; the girl knew exactly what I was thinking. I reminded myself that her sexual attitudes were, after all, none of my business. I looked away at the white wake running straight toward the empty horizon astern.

"Don't get your hopes up," the girl said. "There's nobody chasing us yet."

"Neatest trick of the week," I said. "Three shots and two dead bodies and nobody cares?"

She laughed shortly. "That little gun of yours didn't make hardly any more noise than a back-firing motorcycle; and they've got lots of motorcycles in Nassau. There wasn't much blood in the parking lot and we mopped it up a bit; in the taxi, too. And we had a couple of funerals at sea while you were out. Nobody'll ever see those corpus-delictuses again, not with fifty-pound pigs of lead wired to the ankles. The Northeast Providence Channel goes down a thousand fathoms around here." She frowned, watching me. "Now you tell me, what's that black girl of yours going to do?"

"What black girl? . . . Oh." I shrugged. "She'll call Washington and do what she's told."

"And Washington? What will they do?"

I shrugged. "Who the hell knows what they'll do, ever?" I grimaced. "It was a simple bodyguard assignment, they didn't want the Brand woman embarrassing us by getting herself killed right now, but then she got difficult and the way things are, maybe they'll just write her off and me, too."

"What about the Shitfuzz?" Serena Lorca asked. "Do you think they'll be notified?"

"The what?"

She grimaced. "You know. The Kapok Kops. The Pot Pigs. They used to spend their time worrying about life preservers and drugs, but now it's our crappers that are a matter of life and death. You'd think a Service that claims a lot of proud traditions would draw the line at investigating a bunch of stinking boat toilets, but I expect pretty soon they'll have us all taking down our pants when they come aboard so they can inspect where it comes out of as well as where it goes into. . . ."

I grinned. It never fails these days, when you're with yachtsmen of any kind. Just the thought of the idiot EPA regulations for seagoing plumbing will set them off. It made the girl seem more human and sympathetic, despite everything I knew about her.

"You don't have to worry about the Coast Guard," I said. "This is a very discreet operation, no uniforms invited."

She frowned suspiciously. "Meaning that the helicopters are already airborne and you want to keep us feeling safe and happy until they get here."

I shook my head. "There are very good reasons why the Coast Guard won't be called, or the Navy or the Marines, either."

"What reasons?"

I hesitated. "Tell me something first. Peterson rattled off a crazy story about the way that ship sank, the *Fairfax Constellation*. I know it was just something you fed him to pass along to me; you wanted him to have a plausible story to tell me so I'd think they really had interviewed Einar Kettleman, and so I wouldn't suspect he was leading me into a trap to save Miss Brand. But how much truth was there in that yarn, anyway?"

She studied me for a moment unblinkingly. "How much do you think?"

I said, "Well, I don't believe Kettleman was blown off any ship's bridge; his officer, Hinkampf, described the explosion quite differently. And I don't believe Kettleman saw a lot of stuff while he was floating around on a hatch cover—I'm not much of a nautical expert, but floating wooden hatch covers went out with Captain Horatio Hornblower, didn't they? They're heavy steel nowadays and it takes a big steam winch to pick one up. In fact, I don't believe in Einar Kettleman at all; I think he's just a bunch of nice white bones on the ocean floor picked clean

236

by the fish. Otherwise it was a very interesting and convincing yarn."

She hesitated. "What has all this to do with whether or not the Crap Cops are coming?"

"Everything," I said. "Because you just think you sank that ship. . . . It was you, wasn't it? I figure the big shiny black thing that was picked up after the explosion by the mysterious motorboat without lights—I suppose this boat right here—wasn't a man in a wet suit after all. It was a woman in a wet suit. You."

Serena Lorca said, "Well, if you went to the address I told you, and saw those grubby kids, you know they never sank anything but themselves, in a sea of hash. The Sacred Earth Protective Force, for Christ's sake! Just another bunch of parasites trying to cash in on . . . on somebody else's work."

"Oh, no," I said. "Oh, no indeed, lady. That's where you're so wrong. You don't realize that that great law-enforcement agency, the Office of Federal Security, in a brilliant display of investigative genius, has just triumphantly tracked the terrorist evildoers to their sinister lair and recovered the extorted loot after a desperate gun battle in which one heroic agent died and the vicious political activists all met the violent ends they so richly deserved."

Serena Lorca was staring at me, aghast and incredulous. "Oh, Jesus! You've got to be kidding, Helm!"

I said, "Hell, I was almost elected to be the heroic agent who got heroically killed. In fact I was elected but I refused to serve; I got another guy to volunteer for the honor. Well, he didn't know he was volunteering, but it amounted to the same thing." I rubbed my bullet-nicked arm reminiscently.

She licked her lips. "But goddamn it, that bunch of freaked-out space cadets would have peed in their crummy jeans at the sight of a gun. Not that it would have made much difference to the way they smelled." She looked at me. "You mean, that smooth government bastard at the

237

head of that outfit—what's his name, Bennett?—sent a bunch of his guys to deliberately massacre . . ."

I said, "He couldn't afford to take them alive, could he? Not alive and telling everybody how they'd played him for a sucker with a terrorist fairy tale, a million dollars' worth."

Serena Lorca drew a long breath and said, "Well, I didn't really mean to set them up for a hit. Three hits." Her voice hardened. "Not that it matters. Nobody asked them to butt in, the greedy little creeps."

"It was the oldest one who did all the thinking; the other two just went along for the ride." I glanced at her curiously. "How did you find them?"

She shrugged. "They used pot, didn't they? They used other stuff; they had to get it somewhere, didn't they? One of them even made a couple of runs for us. The organization keeps track of people like that, and notices when they start acting funny, it could mean trouble. All I had to do was ask a few questions around, when I heard somebody was trying to hold up the shipping companies for a lot of money . . ."

"Heard how?"

"Who's asking the questions around here, anyway?" she demanded with sudden anger. Then she shrugged. "Naturally we've got connections along the waterfront; we hear what's going on." She frowned. "And I still don't see what the hell all this has to do with whether or not your people are going to alert the Shit-and-Piss Police."

I said, "Concentrate and it will become clear to you. The case is solved, solved, solved. Get it? You don't think Bennett is going to ask the Coast Guard to sail out and unsolve it for him, do you? And leave him standing there with egg on his face and four dead bodies to explain? Right now the last thing in the world he wants is to find out, or have other people find out, what's really been happening out here on the ocean. He's just sweating it out, hoping that nobody ever does find out; and particularly that the Mad Ship-Sinker never strikes again. Or Mr. Bennett's name will be Mister Mud." I shook my head. "Oh, no. No matter what he knows about you by this time, he's not going to send anybody after you or let anybody be sent if he can help it. Not even if it means sacrificing an unimportant operative from another agency and an insignificant girl journalist. Hell, if he sent somebody, they might catch you and then where would he be?"

"But you don't work for this Bennett guy, really."

I shrugged. "What difference does that make? You know the OFS; they're the takeover boys in spades. When you work with them, you do it their way or else. My chief hasn't held his job all these years by bucking a big agency like that." Please excuse me, sir, I said silently.

Serena Lorca frowned at me. "But you don't really think much of this Bennett character, right?"

"Now what would give you that idea?" I asked. She was driving at something, and I didn't know what it was; I just hoped this was the attitude she wanted from me. "I mean, all the guy ever did was set me up for murder and then let me be kidnaped without doing a damned thing about it, if that's the way he's handling it, and I'll bet on it. So why wouldn't I love him like a brother?"

She smiled faintly. It had been the right answer, although I had no idea why. But it would presumably become clear eventually, if I lived that long. She studied me carefully for several seconds; then she turned away from me and picked up a large red canvas purse from the opposite settee, and groped inside. She brought out a small photograph, apparently a color Polaroid shot, which she gently slipped out of its protective plastic sleeve and held out to me.

"This is what it's all about," she said in an odd voice. "Do you know who she is?"

I took the picture. For all its small size it was a very good portrait of a very beautiful young girl with blond hair that was so wonderfully pale and silky you could hardly believe it. It was worn quite long. The girl had delicate features and large blue eyes. I got the impression that there hadn't been a great deal behind those big eyes, but that was a lot to read from a photograph.

I dredged up a name Brent had mentioned. "Ann Bergerson?"

"Yes," Serena Lorca said. "Ann. My Ann. She was so young, so lovely, you can see how lovely she was, and they smashed her down and threw her into the cold ocean and drowned her. That great ship crashing through the dark without anybody looking. I turned on the strobe, I even fired a flare, but they kept right on coming; and *Tumbleweed* just wouldn't go to windward fast enough against that chop, even with the motor running. And afterward, the hull all broken and sinking and the mast down, and her blood on the deck where it had hit her, but she wasn't there. I looked and looked, all that night I looked, all the next day, rowing search patterns in that damned rubber dinghy, but I never found her. *Now* do you understand why I have to hunt them down and kill them as they killed her?" She didn't wait for my answer, but snatched the picture back and said to the man with the gun, "Put him with the other one. Stay where you can see the door. Arturo will watch the foredeck hatch from the bridge; he's got a gun up there." She started to make her way out into the cockpit, and stopped. "Helm."

"Yes?"

She stared at me for a moment. I was beginning to realize that this was a girl who stared at everything, in the weird, intent way some nuts have. It doesn't necessarily mean they're studying what they're looking at harder than other people; in fact they may not be seeing it at all.

But her voice was quite sensible when she spoke, "I'm not going to kill you or the girl; that's not the plan. Not unless you make me. Believe it. So don't do anything hasty, please."

Then she slipped outside and turned to mount the ladder to the flying bridge. The goon poked me with his gun, which was a hopeful sign. The gun-pokers are generally pretty easy; but it was too early yet. I had to think about Serena Lorca's promise; I didn't know for sure how many were on board; and I didn't know the situation forward. I

240

let myself be nudged and goosed down into the main cabin, all well-oiled teak except for the stainless stuff in the galley where a wiry, gray-haired man was cooking something. Number four.

I let myself be urged past the galley and up to a closed teak door in the bow. Another nudge with the gun muzzle indicated that I was supposed to open it. When I did, a hard shove sent me forward to stumble over a plastic bucket that was wedged into the small floor space between two bunks that met in a vee. The door slammed shut behind me.

There was a small girl huddled face down on the starboard vee-berth. I recognized the short-sleeved navy sweater and the white linen slacks and the high-heeled blue sandals. I'd been seriously worried about her ever since Serena Lorca had felt obliged to revise, slightly and maliciously, her report on the swell condition of the prisoner up forward; but the stench in the little wedge-shaped cabin was reassuring. If it was only *that*, it was nothing to worry about.

"Elly," I said, touching her shoulder.

She shrugged my hand away miserably. "Go away!" she moaned. "Oh, God, I'm sick as a dog. Go away, damn you! Oh, Jesus, if there's any way of being uglier and crummier and more revolting, little Elly will find it every time. . . . Oh, Christ, here I go again!"

I moved aside hastily to allow her access to the bucket. It wasn't very nice of me, the girl was suffering, but I found myself grinning anyway. Miss Eleanor Brand was at it again, tearing herself down as usual. It was kind of like coming home.

CHAPTER 28

I was proudly told as a boy that the family had descended, on one side at least, from seafaring Viking rovers who weren't, subsequent research informed me, very nice guys. Well, I know a wealthy lady out West who's very proud of an ancestral horse-thief she wouldn't dream of letting in the house if he were to appear in the bewhiskered, tobacco-chewing flesh. I can't say I've inherited any great nautical capabilities from those ancient Norse pirates; but they do seem to have bequeathed me a fairly rugged digestion, which stood me in good stead now. As the big sportfisherman pounded along toward an unknown destination, the motion in the cramped bow stateroom was violent and the vomit-stink was unpleasant; but I found myself unaffected except for a slight queasiness, perhaps because I'd had no chance to partake of nourishment since the day before.

Well, the first job, obviously, was to clean up the joint. When Eleanor indicated that she was through regurgitating for the moment, I picked up the bucket, knocked on the door, waited a bit, and opened it cautiously. Our jailer was braced in the narrow passageway outside, gun ready.

"What the hell do you want?" he demanded suspiciously.

"What's your name?" I asked.

He started to tell me it was none of my damned business, but shrugged instead. "Giulio," he said.

It's always easier to establish a useful relationship of mutual respect and confidence if you know and use the name. "Okay, Giulio," I said, "where do I dump this?"

"Use the head. No, the door to port. And be damned careful, Government Man."

242

"I'm always careful, Giulio."

It was a small, gleaming cubicle and it seemed a shame to defile it, but I got the bucket emptied and washed out, getting water from the shower, since the bucket wouldn't fit into the diminutive washbasin. Then I couldn't figure out how to work the nautical potty. I'd been shipmates with the kind you pump with a lever, but this was a much more elegant and complicated apparatus, presumably electrical in nature. I stuck my head out cautiously.

"How do I flush this cottonpicking thing?"

Giulio grimaced. "You've got to turn on the fancy electronic shit-eater, first. The macerator—chlorinator button, MC to you. When you get the green light, hit the flush button, F, and you're in business. And when the bastard goes on strike, or leaks crap all over the boat, or runs the batteries down, you call the EPA and they come running to fix it for you. Haha. Funny story."

"What's the other button for, with the red light?" I asked.

"That tells you you're out of shit-eating gunk and you've got to give it another dose before it will work. Hit R for refill to set it up, but you won't need to. It was recharged before we shoved off. Mr. Lorca likes us to keep his boat ready to go." His eyes narrowed. "Quit stalling and get it done, if you're going to do it."

I set up the right combination on the master computer and the smelly stuff was sucked smoothly out of the bowl, to be purified and sterilized to government specifications before being pumped overboard. Fascinating. It made me feel all warm inside to know that this part of the world's oceans was safe from our pollution; you never know how much harm one small girl's puke is going to do. Pretty soon, we'll have diapers on all the whales and porpoises and be in great shape.

I washed my hands, got a clean towel, and a washcloth and dampened that, and went back in there and rolled her, protesting weakly, over on her back so I could work on her, washing her face and cleaning off her sweater where she'd messed it a little. She lay there exhausted by her convulsive illness, eyes closed; and I found that her pale

243

little monkey-face did funny things to me. I'd been worried about her, badly worried. I was very happy to have caught up with her before anything more serious than seasickness had happened to her; and I wasn't about to try to figure out how I reconciled my feeling for this girl with my feeling for Martha Devine. Or, for that matter, my feeling for Harriet Robinson, who'd died. But, obviously, what I needed was a burnoose, a camel, a sheikhdom, and a harem. Maybe two camels. Eleanor's eyes opened.

"Hi," she whispered.

"Dumb," I said. "What did you want to go running off for, anyway? Like a little girl pouting because the big boys wouldn't let her play football with them. Dumb."

"How . . . how did you get here?"

I said, "You first. How did they catch you?"

She shrugged. "We took a taxi from the airport and told him to take us to the hospital. I didn't expect to get in to see Kettleman at that hour, but at least I could find out if he was really there. Only, after we'd driven for a little, the cab driver simply slammed on the brakes very hard, so hard that we both wound up on the floor of the back seat. Before we could pick ourselves up there were guns at both rear windows. The girl was there. She's kind of a weirdo, isn't she? A man, she called him Giulio, got in the front seat with a gun and we drove along some more and there was a car crash behind us; and pretty soon they brought your man Fred and put him in with us. He'd been following us but they'd laid for him and run him off the road. They took us to the boat, this boat, and wanted Fred to call in—there was a phone connection to the dock—but he wouldn't give them the number."

I said, "But the call was made."

She licked her lips. "Yes. I gave them the number, the one you'd told me. Remember? I'm sorry, Matt, but they were going to hurt him, maim him, very badly. There was a little gray-haired man with a funny French accent, they called him Robert; but he had a knife and he wasn't funny at all. I couldn't bear . . . anyway, the call was made, and Warren was ordered to talk to the woman at the other end who was apparently Fred's wife, telling her that her phone was tapped, which was obviously a lie; I mean, if they hadn't known the number how could they have tapped it? But they told Warren to tell her exactly what to say to you, the girl did; and what would happen to all of us, Fred particularly, if she tried to warn you in any way—they'd be listening. Only Fred broke loose and tried to reach the phone, to tell her something, and the man called Robert stuck the knife into him. . . . The girl gave him hell afterward, but then it was too late. Matt?"

"Yes?"

"Was I . . . was I wrong to give them the number? Did I help kill him?"

I shook my head. "I don't think it made a damned bit of difference, Elly."

"Thanks for saying that," she whispered. "I'll try to believe it. Now it's your turn; how did you get here?"

I told her. It took a while. When I'd finished she didn't say anything for a while, thinking it over. I was happy to see that the greenish tinge was fading from her face; apparently she was over the worst of it. At last she pushed herself to a sitting position and swung her feet over the edge of the starboard bunk, facing me as I sat on the edge of the port bunk.

"I'm hardly in a position to criticize, am I?" she said quietly.

"You mean Warren?"

She nodded. "Disregarding the question of the telephone number, Fred was there on account of me; he died on account of me. If I hadn't charged off to Nassau like that. . . . Well, never mind. But with that on my conscience, I'm not really qualified to take a high moral stand. . . . I just don't understand why you had to kill Warren."

I said, "I could say he was asking for it. I ran a considerable risk to disarm him once. How many times do I have to gamble my life for a gun-waving slob who keeps coming at me? I told you once to keep him in line or lose him. Well, you lost him."

245

She shook her head quickly. "That's not a satisfactory answer, Matt. You must have had a better reason for killing him than the mere fact that he disregarded a rather arrogant warning you'd given him once, through me."

I said, "It wasn't the reason, but it left me with no obligation to worry about his health; I'd given him all the breaks he had coming. I gave him the gun to test him. What I did was a sign of trust and confidence; if I was willing to give him back his gun that meant I was willing to let bygones be bygones and work with him to save you, didn't it? But he didn't respond to my gesture of confidence by taking me into his confidence and telling me what the problem was and asking my help to solve it. Obviously he didn't want to work with me to save you; he wanted to do it all himself, at my expense. There just wasn't any reasonable hope of making it a cooperative venture; he hated my guts and was almost as eager to make me look bad, as he was to save you. And so we come to the final reason for giving him that gun—to keep his little hands busy. If he hadn't had that toy to play with he'd have jumped me from behind with some *yah-yah, huh-huh* karate or judo stuff, wouldn't he?"

"Well, he *did* know—"

"Sure. Those big-biceps boys are always cracking bricks with the edges of their hands. It had the advantage of making my capture look very good indeed. Very spectacular and dramatic."

"She . . . the Lorca girl, had promised Warren that if he delivered you she'd let me go."

"She just promised me that she won't kill us, that's not the plan. I was happy to hear it; but I don't think we need to take her promises or plans too seriously."

"Matt, I didn't . . . I mean, I tried to argue with him, to stop him. I told him I didn't want to be . . . be set free at that price."

I grinned, and reached out to touch her cheek. "What happened to the ruthless little bitch who'd sacrifice anybody for a story?"

246

She wasn't quite comfortable with my touch. She said stubbornly, "I still don't think you should have shot him."

I said, "Suppose I'd put it up to you, Elly. Suppose I'd told you your life was at stake and you had to pick one man to take this boat ride with you and help you make it home again alive if possible. Over here we have the dossier of Mr. Warren Peterson; training, experience, general batting average in times of stress. Over here, Mr. Matthew Helm. Just making your decision on the cold official data, leaving personalities out of it entirely, which one would you have picked to give you the best possible chance of surviving your impending ordeal?" I shrugged. "It seems to me that I made the only choice possible on the record."

She licked her lips and said, "You really are an arrogant and self-satisfied bastard, aren't you, darling? . . . Matt!"

"What?"

She was regarding me oddly. "I'm kind of stupid this morning; I must have thrown up my brains along with my dinner. I didn't realize. . . ."

"What didn't you realize, girl reporter?"

"Why, you deliberately let yourself. . . . you let them capture you on *purpose*!"

"Well, how the hell else was I going to find you in a hurry?" I asked irritably. "There wasn't time to call out the cops; and a bunch of clumsy guys in uniform poking around carelessly could have got you killed. I figured it was safer to work it from inside; I just had to *get* inside, and that was the logical way. Look, let me get these goddamned wet towels out of here, they're stinking up the place. . . ."

Again, I gave plenty of warning before opening the door, disregarding whatever Eleanor was saying to my back. Giulio was alert outside. He told me about the built-in laundry basket in the head compartment and I dumped my damp burden there.

"How's the little lady?" he asked when I emerged.

"She'll live," I said. I glanced at the gun in his hand. "Well, for a while, at least."

247

He said, "If Miss Lorca says you're not going to die, you're not going to die."

"You mean she's got The Power?" I asked. "Immortality at her fingertips? It should be worth a lot of money."

"You know what I mean. Nobody's going to hurt you if you don't get antsy, is what I mean. I don't know what the hell she wants you for, but it's not that." He glanced aloft, toward the flying bridge. "She's a hell of a little sailor. I can't figure it."

"Why?"

"Well, you know," he said awkwardly. "We all figured it would be a non-stop panic party when the boss told us she'd be running this boat from time to time as well as her own, and we had to take her orders and keep our mouths shut. I mean, a dame for a skipper is bad enough, and a young dame is worse, but her being a dyke like that, you know what I mean." He made the old limp-wrist gesture. "I mean, you know, it takes guts to take a boat offshore, you never know what you're going to hit out there."

"Or what's going to hit you," I said, watching him. I saw his dark, rather handsome, face close up; he wasn't going to discuss that subject. To reassure him I went on smoothly, if a bit pedantically, "That's just a myth, you know. Hell, the old Greeks took homosexuals for granted; and their armies were full of them. At the Battle of Cheroneia, the Thebans had a whole regiment of them. Well, the Macedonians attacked and the Athenians on the left broke and ran, and the center was smashed, but the Sacred Band of Thebes on the right stood firm; they died where they stood, all three hundred of them, each man beside his lover or whatever the hell you call it. Nobody figured it had anything to do with courage back in those days."

He eyed me suspiciously, obviously wondering what my sexual predilections were. "Sounds like you know a lot about it."

I grinned. "No, I just read historical novels." I sniffed. "Smells good, just like food. But maybe she's not going to kill us outright, she's just going to starve us to death. . . ."

He had me check on Eleanor who said she didn't want

248

anything to eat, God no! He was pretty cautious about getting me back into the deckhouse, seated at the table; and about watching me while I ate. The food was very good. The cook's name was Robert and he had a funny French accent. He was a wiry little man with gray hair, as I've said. The description fit the man who'd tortured and killed Fred. It seemed likely that he'd taken this seagoing job because his knife work had gotten him into trouble on land; and, while I was grateful for the excellent meal, I thought it would be nice to do something about Robert some day if it wouldn't interfere with more important duties. . . .

We spent the afternoon resting on our bunks. Toward evening we heard somebody yell, "Sail Ho!" up above. Half an hour later, the door opened and we were ushered aft into the cockpit and helped aboard the single-masted sailboat that lay alongside, rolling heavily in the long Atlantic swells. The name painted large on the flanks of the vessel, racing fashion, was *Jamboree*; Miss Lorca's fifth sailboat, according to Brent, in the two years since her beautiful young friend had died.

I hoped the present yacht was not scheduled to go the way of the previous four; but it wasn't much of a hope.

CHAPTER 29

WHEN a sailboat heels to starboard it's on the port tack, and when it heels to port it's on the starboard tack, don't ask me why. It was starboard tack now as we headed out into the Atlantic in a freshening southeasterly breeze. Eleanor and I had the bow stateroom again with a pair of vee-berths very similar to those on the powerboat we'd just left; but there the resemblance ended—except for the constant factor of the bucket. It was a smaller and darker prison without any portlights in the side of the boat, just a transparent hatch above through which we could look up at the two, taut, triangular sails forward, jib and forestaysail, if I remembered my nautical nomenclature correctly. The mainsail, my salty memories told me, was the big one aft, outside our range of easy vision.

Perhaps because of the sailboat's lesser speed, the motion was not as sharp and jerky as the sportfisherman's had been; in scientific terms the period of oscillation was longer, and the amplitude was greater. Every so often the whole boat would drop right out from under us coming off a wave and leave us airborne until we caught up with our mattresses again as they were still going down, or met them coming back up. With the hatch closed against the flying spray that lashed the foredeck, it was warm and stuffy in the tilted fifteen degrees to port, give or take ten, and it wasn't the most comfortable detention cell I'd known; and I'd known a few.

Eleanor held out for about half an hour after we were under way again. Then it hit her again, but her spasms were getting pretty unproductive now. There really wasn't much for me to get rid of, but it seemed advisable to maintain the useful image of the poor suffering young lady and the patient loyal gentleman looking after her conscientiously, so I made the pilgrimage to the head whenever she gave me an excuse. Giulio had accompanied us to this new boat, complete with Browning 9mm; but we had a fine relationship now, Giulio and I, two big strong men bound together by their noble, and rather patronizing, concern for a little woman's weakness.

There had been two men sailing *Jamboree* when we boarded her. One of them was now asleep on a bunk tucked away up behind the leeward of the two settees that faced each other across the teak table in the main cabin, preferably known, I believe, as the main saloon—not salon, unless you're a sissified ad-writer who doesn't know any better. There was another, similar berth up to windward. Still another bunk, I'd noted as I came below, was located to starboard alongside the galley aft, almost under the main hatch that led to the cockpit. It was a quarter berth, running back alongside the engine under the cockpit seats. You used the head of it for a seat when working at the chart table. Apparently this bunk was reserved for Serena Lorca as skipper and navigator; her shoes and purse were on it. She was now barefoot on deck sailing the boat with the assistance of the second crew member. I gathered that Giulio was not expected to assist in the working of the ship. Strictly a powerboat man with a sideline in muscle, he'd been brought along to function as guard and jailer only.

The head compartment on this boat was in the same location as on *Ser–Jan*, to port just aft of our pie-shaped prison cell in the bow. It was smaller, with no separate shower facilities. A grating and drain in the floor, and a fixture above, indicated that you were expected to keep yourself clean on board by using the whole compartment as your shower stall and to hell with what else got wet in there. The washbasin was even more rudimentary than that on the big sportfisherman; and the principal plumbing device was a slightly smaller version of the same electric toilet, equipped with the same elaborate console, displaying the same green and red lights and push-button controls. Well, at least I wouldn't have to be checked out on it again; I'd already soloed on that general model. The installation seemed to be brand new. When I mentioned this to Giulio, he made a gesture of disgust.

"Christ, the head that was in there was perfectly good, but she's an older boat, built before the crapper law went into effect, so Miss Lorca had to rip it all out and spend a couple of grand to make it legal."

"Yes," I said, "I can see how she might not want to do anything illegal."

"Get the hell back in there where you belong," he snapped, but there was no real anger in his voice.

It was getting quite dark by now but the electric lights in

251

our cell were in functioning order—I'd checked—one over each bunk. I turned mine on. This brought some shouts from the deck and a pounding on the door.

"Switch it off, how the hell can they see to steer with all that light shining up on the headsails?"

"Sorry, lights off."

I hit the switch again, and lay in the dark listening to the rushing, splashing sounds of the boat going through the water. It seemed unnatural, but kind of pleasant, to be moving along briskly without any motor noise or vibration. Looking up through the transparent plastic hatch, beaded with spray, I could see the sails overhead weakly defined by the colored running lights—apparently, whatever Serena Lorca had in mind, it did not involve illegal invisibility for her boat. The picture was clear: she was avenging her dead lover just as her daddy was avenging the hole in his head. Only the final details of her revenge remained to be explained; and instinct told me she intended to explain them to us before long. The trouble with being a master criminal is that if you're a good one, and keep your mouth shut as you should, nobody knows how great you are. Most of them can't stand that forever. They want their genius admired by somebody. I had a strong hunch we'd been elected to admire Miss Lorca's.

"Matt." Eleanor's voice reached me faintly through the noise of the boat's progress.

"How's it going down there?" I asked.

She had the secure berth down to leeward, while I was clinging to the precarious one up to windward. There was a canvas contraption I could raise to keep me in place up there, but I preferred not to immobilize myself to that extent.

"Matt!"

There was sudden panic in her voice; I realized she hadn't heard my response for the boat sounds. I eased myself out of my bunk and, avoiding the everlasting bucket on the floor, got myself sitting on the edge of hers, and found her shoulder in the dark. Her hand found mine, gripped it convulsively for a moment, and released it.

"Oh, God, I'm such a scared and puny thing!" she breathed.

"That's right," I said. "And ugly and spoiled. Don't forget ugly and spoiled."

"Damn you, Matthew Helm! . . ." I heard her giggle in the dark: "Very well, Dr. Helmstein. Very vel. Ve vill zee shock treatment permit, in moderation. But I'm really kind of a mess, aren't I? God, I've been sick! Do you know that it's worse throwing up when you haven't anything to throw? Do I smell too bad?"

"A little sour," I said judiciously. "Not unbearable."

"Sorry about that. I mean, if I were really nauseating, you could . . . you could grit your teeth and hold me without being, well, overstimulated by this smelly repulsive creature in your arms."

From her, it was as much of a plea for comfort and reassurance as I was likely to get. It was also, I realized, a rather brave breakthrough, considering what had been done to her once and how it had left her. Of course, she was drawing a clear line between what would be permissible and what wouldn't if I did accept her suggestion; but the fact that she could make it at all was an encouraging sign.

I said carefully, "You'd better let me get over on the low side. That way I won't land on you and squash you when the boat tosses us playfully. . . . Ouch, what the hell was that?"

"I'm sorry, did I get you with my heel?"

I said, "My God, do you still have those spikes on? You'd better fire that male nurse of yours. Let me . . ."

"Never mind."

"High heels are frowned on, on shipboard, ma'am."

"To hell with that," she said. "Did you ever get stomped by a high-heeled lady, Matt? I mean, really perforated? A determined gal can do a lot of damage with her heels in a pinch; so let them think I'm just too damned miserable to know, or care, that I'm in bed with my shoes on." Later, as we lay side by side, I could feel her fighting it; me, my closeness, trying to maintain a discreet measure

253

of separation between us, but the motion of the boat was against her, settling us as firmly together at the lower side of the slanting bunk as tamped tobacco into a pipe. Gradually I felt her rigid body relax against me. She whispered, "This isn't very fair to you, is it, Matt? But I'd rather you wouldn't. . . . I don't think I can yet. . . . I just need, well, company."

I won't claim I wasn't aware of the small warm body in my arms and didn't react to it at all. For some perverse reason I found myself remembering another night of gentlemanly frustration I'd endured not too long ago with a different lady, although with separate bedrooms the conditions hadn't been nearly so intimate. But it didn't seem advisable to share the memory with my present companion.

I said, "I'll try to control my raging lust, Miss Brand."

"Tell me about Martha," she said.

It took me completely by surprise, although I'd just been thinking of Martha Devine. It's never safe to discount ESP, particularly when a man and a woman are sharing the same bed, or bunk, even with all their clothes on.

"What about Martha?" I asked.

"What did she want, popping up in Miami like that, unexpectedly?" Eleanor asked. "I mean, it was obvious you weren't expecting her and neither was her father. You were both very surprised to see her."

"Hell, I don't know what she wanted," I said. "Ask my chief, she's his daughter."

"You're a liar, darling," she said.

"That's right," I said. "I'm a liar."

There was a little silence. "All right," she said quietly. "I'm a nosy snoop and it's none of my goddamned business, right?"

"Right," I said.

"Do you love her, Matt?"

"Sure," I said. "Hell, according to you I love fifty percent of the human race. The female fifty percent. Why should poor Martha be the lone exception?"

There was another pause. "Well, all right, tell me what

happened on your midnight expedition with the OFS task force." There was a slight edge to her voice. "If that isn't classified, too."

I said, "I'm sorry, but it is. At least, it's not for publication. If you really want to know, I'll tell you; but it'll have to be strictly off the record. Word of honor and all that crap." After a little, I went on, "As a matter of fact, I'll probably wind up having to ask you to forget this whole crazy business, sinking ships and all."

I felt her stiffen against me. "Matt, you're crazy! I wouldn't kill a story for the President of the United States!"

I said, "Hell, I wouldn't kill a story for the President of the United States, either. But it's not the Chief Executive who's asking you."

"And . . . and if I don't, what happens?"

I said, "Go to hell, doll. It was a request. If you want me to, I'll say please. No coercion, no sanctions. It's entirely up to you. I merely expressed a wish, okay?"

She was silent for a little; then she said stiffly, "Tell me about your midnight excursion. Off the record." I told her. When I was through she said, "You're not a very nice person, are you, Matt?"

"I keep trying," I said. "Somehow it always seems to go wrong. Sorry."

She said, "Well, it's obvious why you're trying to shut me up. You don't want the truth about these sinkings to come out because your precious Mr. Bennett has already, by this time, explained them publicly in a very different way, and you don't want me showing him up for a liar, a murderous liar." When I didn't say anything, she asked, "Why?"

"Why what?"

"Why are you protecting him? Why not let me write the truth and show him up for the shit he is?"

I said, "Who's stopping you? All I'm asking is a personal favor, no threats or menaces uttered or implied. Nobody's *stopping* you. You're free to do as you please, assuming that you live long enough to learn the whole truth out here, and get back to write it; and I'll do my best to see that you do. That's still my primary job. Bennett is strictly peripheral."

I felt her make an impatient gesture in the dark. "Bennett certainly wouldn't ask any favors for you."

"I don't have to be a shit just because he is."

"Why?" she demanded. "You still haven't told me why!"

I said, "Well, it's really your fault."

"Mine!"

"Look, girl reporter," I said, "you're already raising hell with the U.S. Government for employing a bunch of homicidal jerks like me, correct? Well, your last piece was on Bob Devine, but your next one is on me. There's nothing I can do about that. You've told me it's even beyond your control by now; it's in the works; so we're just going to have to weather that storm as best we can. All we can do is try to keep you from getting killed so we won't be blamed for that, too." I drew a long breath. "Okay, you're raising hell and that's your business, but goddamn it, can't I ask you in a friendly way to take it a little easy for a while? Don't clobber the poor damned OFS with this new thing before Washington has had time to catch its breath from the way you've blasted us. Sure, Bennett is a revolving sonofabitch and he's got some other rotary bastards working for him; but there are a lot of good men in that outfit. Although your experience with them may make it hard for you to believe, they do a lot of good work. You're not going to bring those larcenous kids back to life no matter what you write, are you? If Bennett's still around a couple of years from now, fine, go after him with my blessing. Use what I told you tonight, even. Permission granted. But right now you've made enough trouble, to be blunt about it, and I'm asking you to take a little rest from your journalistic hell-raising. Give us a little rest, please. Let it all cool down a bit before you light the publicity fires again."

There was a long silence. At last her voice came out of the noisy darkness, "What's a revolving sonofabitch?"

"A guy who looks like an SOB any way you turn him."

"I haven't heard you say any nice things about the OFS before."

"I probably wouldn't go around saying nice things about my brother, either, if I had a brother. He'd probably be an infuriating stuffed shirt with a dull nine-to-five job and I'd consider him a total loss—until an occasion arose when I'd have to remember that, as the old saying goes, blood is thicker than water."

"Mr. Bennett is hardly your brother."

"Don't be too sure. At least his man Burdette is my brother and that kid Burdette was trying to break in safely is my kid brother. We're all members of the same big happy squabbling and bickering governmental family and we're all in more or less the same line of work, most of us for the same reasons."

"What reasons, Matt? I've always wondered."

"Oh, Jesus," I said. "Now she wants my philosophy of life! Well, there are a lot of reasons, and one is that there are some people who just aren't happy unless they're being shot at occasionally and getting to shoot back. You don't have to understand that. It's a dirty little secret these safety-minded and supposedly nonviolent days, but just take it as a fact. There are the manhunters who get their kicks out of tracking down what's been called, and is, the most dangerous game on earth. There are the do-gooders who want to fix up the world according to their own ideas and ideals; you find those everywhere, even in our business. And there are the power-hungry gents who get their jollies from carrying guns and commanding men who carry guns. There are lots of other motives, not all nice, maybe none of them nice, but there's one motive we've all—well, most of us— had in common at one time or another, although some of us keep forgetting it."

"What's that, Matt?"

I said irritably, "Well, it may not be the best damned country in the world, although I haven't seen a better, but it's the only damned country we've got. Now for Christ's sake, let's get some sleep. It's been a long day and I have a hunch tomorrow isn't going to be any shorter."

257

CHAPTER 30

THE whole thing was a little unreal, I thought the following morning as I took the place indicated by Giulio on the settee at the low leeward side of the main cabin table, with Eleanor beside me. It was the most comfortable place at the table, like a reclining chair reclined—as a matter of fact I'd sat there earlier to eat breakfast under Giulio's supervision—but it immobilized me almost as effectively as if I'd been tied hand and foot. The table was a large drop-leaf affair, leaves up now, firmly secured to the cabin sole with the great aluminum mast coming up through the middle of it. It wasn't going anywhere. There was no chance of my dumping it into Giulio's lap, for instance, like John Wayne cleaning out a Western saloon; and with Eleanor blocking the way out on one side and that massive item of teak furniture filling most of the cabin, I could never hope to fight my way uphill against the heel of the boat to get at him.

But such hostile thoughts seemed almost wicked under the circumstances. After all, since we'd put to sea, our captors had all been just as nice to us as they could be. Nobody'd slugged us or kicked us or even spoken harshly to us. We'd suffered no mistreatment at all, and no hardships—except for those unavoidable on a yacht under way. My only possible complaint was that Giulio wasn't half the cook the Frenchman, Robert, had been back on *Ser-Jan.* My breakfast coffee had been weak and my eggs badly overdone. Considering other captivities I'd endured, a little unreal.

Serena's first words only heightened the atmosphere of unreality. She was very polite and gracious, "I want to

258

thank you," she said. "I want to thank you both for taking me at my word."

There were, of course, certain flaws in this civilized and well-mannered atmosphere. While the cabin itself was quite respectable with its oiled teak and comfortable upholstery, the occupants were no longer quite so respectable. My own slacks and sports shirt were getting pretty limp and I needed a shave. Eleanor had washed her face and combed her hair, and her dark sweater was moderately durable, but her nice linen slacks looked fairly disreputable and slept-in by this time. Giulio needed a razor even worse than I did, being darker; and his natty boating uniform was kind of wrinkled and grubby. Serena's short hairdo was undisturbed and her red bodice was performing its elastic duties as efficiently as ever; but her white shorts weren't quite as crisp and immaculate as they had been, and I'd noticed when she came down the companionway steps that her bare feet were dirty. Well, I guess the sharp white flannels and natty blue blazer are no longer part of the yachting scene.

I heard one of the men on deck speak to the other; the ratcheting sound of a winch followed, as one of the sails was trimmed. Serena was still speaking, sitting above us on the high side of the slanting cabin table with Giulio and his gun beside her—another uncivilized blemish on this friendly boating picture.

"I know you're an experienced professional," she said to me, "and I was very much afraid you'd seize some opportunity to attempt a violent escape with Miss Brand. Well," she added with a glance at Giulio, who'd stirred, "what you thought was an opportunity. Giulio is fairly experienced, too. But, please, I don't want to threaten or challenge you in any way. You're here because I need you; and I need you alive. No harm is going to come to you, either of you. Please believe me."

It sounded good, it sounded very reassuring, but I couldn't help watching her eyes. They still did not behave like normal eyes, casually glancing from this to that; they simply stared at what she told them to stare at until she told them to stare at something else, sometimes nothing at all.

Watching those disconcerting brown eyes, wondering how much real sanity was behind them despite her elaborate courtesy, I almost missed the much more important signal that showed for an instant in Giulio's eyes when she assured us that no harm would come to us: just a brief flicker of expression, half-evil and half-amused, that betrayed the truth. It was a chilling thing. It warned me that I'd almost made the kind of mistake you don't survive, the mistake of overconfidence, of underestimating the enemy, the old-pro mistake of thinking you're so damned smart and tough nobody can outwit you, nobody can touch you. Suddenly I realized that this ordinary-looking waterfront thug in his sailor pants and jersey, carelessly brandishing his 9mm Browning like an amateur, had been playing with me just as I'd been playing with him—establishing a nice atmosphere of mutual respect, even a kind of friendship, while he waited for the moment to kill.

I forced myself to keep looking where I was looking; if I glanced his way, he'd know I knew. I said to the girl, "Well, it's nice to hear."

She nodded to me and said to Eleanor, "I'm about to give you your story, Miss Brand, the story you've been working on so hard. To start with, I'm sure you'll both be interested in knowing that you're sitting on top of a sizeable charge of powerful explosive." She smiled at our expressions. "Oh, don't worry. It's totally stable. As a matter of fact, it was built into the boat right after I bought it while I was making other changes, some required by recent changes in the law. It's practically part of the boat; it's fiberglassed into the hull, way down in the bilge, where nobody can possibly find it without tearing the boat apart. And it's no danger to anyone until the fuse is armed a certain way."

"How?" I asked.

She shook her head. "I won't tell you that. The person who knows how to arm it, knows how to disarm it; and there's no need for you to know that."

I shrugged. "Okay, what kind of a fuse?"

She hesitated, and spoke obliquely, "I'm not going to tell you any more about the explosive. First, because it's got a complicated technical name I can't even remember; and second, because if you know what it is, you may be able to trace where it came from, and I don't want to get anybody who helped me into trouble. As for the fuse, that was kind of a problem. A practical problem, but also a moral problem."

Eleanor stirred. "Moral? That's an odd word to use in this connection, Miss Lorca."

Serena Lorca's face hardened. She said coldly, "Not at all. You see, I didn't want to kill the lousy bastards myself, Miss Brand, so I couldn't use a remote-control firing device where I had to push the button. That wasn't the idea. I wanted the fucking sons of bitches to kill themselves." She drew a deep breath and gave a nervous pull to her bodice and spoke precisely, "The practical aspects were quite challenging. You've just spent a night on a sailboat under way; you can see that any kind of impact device is out of the question. The charge would explode the first time the boat fell off a wave hard. The same is true of any detonator depending upon the attitude of the vessel. Sailboats assume all kinds of insane attitudes without being involved in collisions; being knocked flat by a squall is all in a day's work."

"Proximity?" I said.

She nodded. "I believe proximity fuses were used on torpedoes way back in World War II. Since then, of course, a lot of missiles have had them. I can't tell you much about this particular type of fuse except that we—somebody—picked up half a dozen as military surplus through an illicit-arms dealer who . . . well, never mind that. They were adapted for me by one of my father's . . . well, by a specialist in that line. They're set to go off within thirty feet of any large metallic object. That's fair enough, I think. After all, the fuse is buried in the middle of the boat. Any large steel power vessel that comes within thirty feet of the center of a forty-foot sailing vessel at sea is certainly not obeying the law of the sea that requires her to keep clear. COLREGS 18-a-iv. I didn't feel obliged to handicap myself by requiring a direct hit."

Eleanor said, "I should have guessed. You got the idea out of a book, and I think I know the book."

"Book, hell!" the black-haired girl said harshly. "There isn't an offshore sailor alive who hasn't dodged one of those great, arrogant, mechanical monsters out at sea and wished to God he had something to shoot back with. I thought of something like that, something big I could fire at the bridge and blast the bastards—a bazooka or something—but this way is better. This way it's up to them. If they obey the law and steer clear, they're safe. If they keep coming and ignore the lousy sailboat as a lot of them do—to hell with it, it's just a crummy little yacht, let it get out of the way if it can—or if they simply don't bother to watch out for it at all, why then they're dead and it couldn't happen to a nicer bunch of seagoing assassins."

Eleanor said, "It seems to me you're condemning the whole crew of a ship to death for the carelessness of a couple of men on the bridge."

"Don't be too sure it's carelessness. Those big ship people just think they own the damned ocean, laws or no laws," Serena said. "And if the engineers and motor men didn't make the vessel go, it wouldn't run people down, would it? If they're going to operate their lousy engines and move twenty or fifty or a couple of hundred thousand tons of metal and cargo through the water at twelve to twenty knots, knowing what kind of homicidal clowns are steering it topside, then they're just as responsible for what it hits as the creeps up on deck. Tell the Jews they should have let Eichmann go because he was only taking orders!" She drew another long breath and hauled at her bodice again, although it still seemed to be doing its job pretty adequately. "All right. I won't go into the actual details, because you've both heard about the *Fairfax Constellation* sinking, so you've got the general idea. The story I told that man, Peterson, was pretty accurate except for some dramatic flourishes. All that's left is to give you your press

262

kits. You'll note I've supplied waterproof envelopes for them. I promised you wouldn't get killed; I didn't promise you wouldn't get wet, although it depends a little on the weather." She turned her unblinking stare on Eleanor. "But as a journalist, you should be willing to put up with a wet ride in a rubber boat in order to witness the deadly Bermuda Triangle in action. It *was* the Bermuda Triangle you were investigating, wasn't it, Miss Brand?"

She slid two plastic envelopes down the slanting, heaving table. Eleanor hesitated before opening hers.

"Press kit?"

"Well, this *is* a press conference, isn't it, Miss Brand?" the black-haired girl said. "I'm giving you the background material for the demonstration you'll be witnessing as soon as I can arrange it. I'm sure you've attended many such preliminary conferences. I hope I'm conducting this one properly; I don't have your experience."

I'd already opened my envelope. The paper inside was a lengthy signed statement, really a confession covering all her recent activities. There was a list of four ships, each with a date, a geographical position, and the name and description of a yacht—presumably the sailing mine or torpedo that had been employed in sinking it. It was quite an absorbing document. After a little, Eleanor looked up.

"This list is incomplete," she said.

Serena shook her head. "Maybe you're thinking of the *Bonaventura* off Cape Sable. We've never operated that far north. She was carrying a load of illegal munitions, some fairly old and perhaps deteriorated. Or perhaps somebody didn't want those weapons arriving at their destination. There was an explosion of undetermined origin, well aft, and the whole ship went up. Naturally, the owners didn't want to admit the illegal nature of the cargo, so they did their best to add their ship to the list of mystery-sinkings; but the information is in the hands of the proper authorities by now."

Eleanor was watching her carefully. "What about the *Zeta President* that went down in the Caribbean south of the Mona Passage?"

"You've done your homework," Serena Lorca said approvingly. "But Zeta Shipping, Incorporated, is in financial trouble; you might say they're ship-poor. Overextended. They paid some of the crew considerable money to scuttle the poor old *President* for the insurance in such a way that it would look like another. . . ." She stopped. Her hands had closed into angry fists, but she spoke in even tones, "The insurance company has been given the evidence and is pressing charges. And then, of course, there were those bright, pot-smoking kids who were going to become millionaires at my expense. . . . Everybody trying to get free rides on my coattails, and nobody, nobody realizing what I'm trying to prove, what I'm trying to do out here! I promised my beautiful Ann that night, that terrible night when she disappeared forever and I thought I was going to die, too; I promised her that I'd live long enough to—"

"Miz Lorca!" The call came from the cockpit.

Serena Lorca was silent for a moment and I saw her throat work; but when she spoke her voice was normal again.

"Yes, Henry?"

"We got us a ship off to starboard on a crossing course, ma'am."

"Coming." Rising and sliding out from under the big table, she gave us a thin smile. "Maybe we'll have our little press demonstration sooner than I expected. Watch them, Giulio."

She took an instrument from a bracket on the bulkhead above the chart table. It looked like a good-sized compass with a pistol grip and sighting vanes. She climbed halfway up the companionway ladder and turned to stand there facing forward; we could only see the lower part of her body. Minutes passed; then she came back down and hung up the sighting compass again, shaking her head.

"Container ship, passing well ahead; the bearing's drawing forward. Well, I prefer to hunt at night, anyway." She seated herself and regarded us for a moment. "You see, I don't cheat. Maybe I could have started the motor and gained enough speed to put *Jamboree* across his course, but I don't work that way. For one thing, it would have been legally wrong. With the motor going, we become a power-driven vessel under the law, even if we have the sails up; we'd have no more rights than he does, and coming from starboard he'd have the right of way. No, I play fair. I don't make it hard for them to avoid me, if they try at all. And I make it very easy for them to see me if they're looking. I carry a large radar reflector; and at night my running lights are much more powerful than the law really requires; as a matter of fact, I replaced all of *Jamboree*'s at considerable expense. I give them every advantage I can; I don't even arm the fuses in fog or bad weather when somebody could make an honest mistake. I'm not even breaking the law very much, really. Perhaps I should have a bureaucratic permit for the explosives and maybe fly a red flag or something to show I'm carrying dangerous cargo, but do you really think it would make any difference? If they can't take the trouble to notice and avoid an eighteen-ton sailboat with eight hundred square feet of sail on a sixty-foot mast, do you think they're going to see a lousy little eighteen-inch red flag?" She paused, and went on, "Well, any questions?"

I asked, "What does the Senator think about all this?"

"He's paying for it; what do you think he thinks about it?" Serena Lorca stared at me unblinkingly. "Of course, I'm doing something for him in return."

"Like murder," I said.

"You're thinking of the slinky glamor-blonde on the West Coast?" She shrugged. "I told you, I made somebody a promise, an important promise. Important to me. I'll do whatever I have to do to keep faith with the dead and—speaking of murder—to show the whole world the kind of giant murder conspiracy that exists out here on the ocean. That's more important than one dead Hollywood blonde and her squalling brat." Her voice was quite even. "As for your macho friend who got shotgunned, he should have been more careful where he exercised his machismo. And your handsome lady down in the Keys was, after all, a fugitive from justice; she couldn't have expected it not to catch up with her eventually, particularly when she started sticking her aristocratic nose where it didn't belong. But there's one thing for which I take no responsibility . . . Miss Brand."

"Yes?" Eleanor said.

"I want to tell you I had nothing to do with . . . with what happened to you." Serena Lorca licked her lips. "Believe me, I wouldn't help inflict *that* on any woman. Those orders came from . . . from somebody else."

After a little pause, I said, "So you made a deal with your dad, you scratch my vengeance and I'll scratch yours."

"Vengeance? I call it justice," she said coldly. Then she grimaced and said, "Well, that's getting pretty heavy, isn't it? Let's take it the way it happened. I had enough money, with the insurance from *Tumbleweed*, to buy one second-hand boat and prepare it. I was only thinking in terms of one . . . one run at that time. No backup vessel. I wasn't in very good shape; I'd kind of flipped floating around out there alone in that rubber dinghy after . . . after losing everything. I was just out of that place where they were supposed to put my head on straight again. I didn't really care if I came back or not, just so I got one of the murdering monsters. I wanted to hear the bastards screaming, burning; I wanted to see them jumping into the sea all on fire. I dreamed about it at night. Hell, I still do. Have you ever *hated* anybody, Mr. Helm?"

I said, "It's a luxury we don't permit ourselves."

She laughed scornfully as if she didn't believe me; and maybe she was right not to. She went on, "So I had the boat, the first one—that was the little ketch *Barbara* on your list—but, of course, I had to have technical advice; I don't even know how to set off a stick of dynamite. And the stuff I needed wasn't available on the open market. I suppose I should have expected that one of the men I approached secretly would know who I was and check with my father. There was a . . . confrontation."

"I'll bet," I said.

She shrugged. "Yes. Of course, I'm not much of a credit

to the family even when I'm not messing with high explosives. I'm sure he's gone to a lot of trouble to cover up my little . . . idiosyncrasy. We'd kind of broken off diplomatic relations several years ago when he first learned about it. He told me I turned his stomach and I reminded him that . . . that his stomach hadn't always been so delicate. Anyway, he came storming down to the yard where I was working on the boat, asking what the hell I was up to now. When I told him, he laughed."

There was a space of silence, except for the creaking boat sounds and the murmur of quiet conversation from the cockpit.

"He laughed!" Serena Lorca said softly. "It was the last thing in the world I expected, that he should throw back his head—with that scar and the dramatic white streak in his hair that I'm sure comes partly out of a bottle—and laugh and laugh as if he'd heard the funniest thing in the world. Then he put his arm around my shoulders and squeezed me affectionately; the first time he'd touched me in years. 'Rina!' he said. 'Little Rina, a chip off the old block after all! Going to blow them all to hell for what they did to you and your pretty friend, eh! That's the spirit!' You'd have thought I'd won a scholarship or a beauty contest or something." There was contempt in her voice, but there was a wistfulness, too; perhaps she was thinking of the parental approval she'd gotten too late and for the wrong reasons. She cleared her throat. "Then he asked if I didn't have a drink around that half-pint ship of mine; and we sat down and had a beer apiece in the middle of all the tools and sawdust; a real father–daughter scene like never before. He said thoughtfully, 'You know, Little Rina, there are a few people I've been wanting to blow to hell for what they did to me,' and he touched the scar on his head. He said, 'Only I've got to step pretty careful these days; they've got their eyes on me. But not on you, baby, not on you. Maybe we can work out a deal, eh?' "

Eleanor looked up, frowning. "What did he mean? Who had their eyes on him?"

Serena Lorca frowned at the interruption. I cut in before

she could speak, "Hell, you were there when I discussed it with Velo, Elly. The syndicate has spent a lot of money to put Lorca where he is. It's only natural they'd try to keep him in line to protect their investment."

Serena nodded. "And my father isn't the kind of man who likes to be told what to do, or what not to do. He'd been brooding about you and your organization for a long time, ever since he was hauled out of Mexico almost dead like that. It had gotten to be an obsession with him. But he was smart enough to know that if he used his own men, his own organization, to hit back at you, if he'd run around making the necessary arrangements himself, the word would have been sure to reach the top that he was endangering everything by a stupid vendetta against the U.S. government. But who's going to pay much attention to what his oddball daughter's up to, as long as she doesn't flaunt her offbeat sexual preferences before the great American public?"

"So you made the deal?" I said.

She nodded again. "Of course, knowing him, I knew he'd stick to the bargain only as long as it suited him and no longer. But that might be long enough for the whole big project I'd had in mind, and had given up because I didn't have the resources. So I asked him, 'Who do I kill?' He laughed that big laugh of his and said, 'Well, suppose you start with a dame out in L.A. named Hendrickson, Roberta Hendrickson. Call it a test, eh? Do a good job there and you can write your own ticket, all the boats you want, all the help you need.' So I did." She said it quite without emphasis, as if she'd merely obliged her daddy by picking up his suit from the cleaners on the way home. She smiled. "As you said, Mr. Helm, we kind of traded vengeances, all in the family. I did the legwork for his revenge, and he paid the bills for mine."

Jamboree came off a wave and landed with a crash that would certainly have triggered an impact fuse if one had been set. Eleanor was thrown against me. I felt her hand find mine for reassurance and squeeze it briefly, before she pushed herself upright again. I knew how she felt. I found Miss Lorca a bit scary, myself.

I said, "Of course you know I didn't shoot your dad, Miss Lorca. As a matter of fact, I eventually took care of the man who did shoot him."

She shrugged. "You set him up for it, whether you meant to or not. And you made fools of him and his men that night in Mexico." She shook her head quickly. "Don't expect him to be reasonable about it, after all that time in the hospital. Somebody had to pay for everything he'd suffered, everything he'd endured; and you and your government friends were elected." She turned her eyes fully on me. "And don't expect me to be reasonable, either, Mr. Helm."

"You said your dad didn't dare use his own men," I said. I jerked my head toward Giulio. "But he's here."

She said, "Giulio is waterfront, not syndicate. He goes with the boat, right, Giulio? That goes for the two on *Ser—Jan* and for Henry and Adam, topside. They're all men who've worked on Daddy's boats at one time or another. They have nothing to do with the rackets."

Eleanor was studying the list she'd been given. She looked up and asked, "How do you explain that in none of the reports concerning these four sinkings has there been a single mention of a sailboat being sighted in the vicinity?"

Serena Lorca laughed harshly. "You know the answer to that as well as I do. Oh, I've been seen, all right, my boats have been seen; but what ship's officer is going to admit, or allow his crew to admit if he can possibly prevent it, that he's such a nautical slob that he runs down little sailboats way out in the middle of the ocean where there's all the room in the world for him to avoid them as the law demands? Hell, it isn't even any real trouble; all it takes is a twist of the autopilot knob, no sweat. It's not like a modern sailing vessel with vangs and preventers that have to be cast off and sails that have to be trimmed and maybe even a giant spinnaker that has to be brought down or a big genoa that has to be tacked before any significant change of

269

course can be made. The old square-riggers were even tougher to maneuver. That's why the law was written that way in the first place."

Eleanor was frowning doubtfully. "You really believe that they're keeping quiet deliberately—"

The black-haired girl snorted. "By now there's at least a handful of officers and seamen around who know perfectly well that they hit a booby-trapped sailboat. But they're damned well not going to jeopardize their careers and risk going to prison for criminal negligence by admitting what really happened; they're happy to leave it as a great mystery of the sea. And maybe others are beginning to suspect the truth, but they're not going to talk, either."

"Why not?" Eleanor demanded.

"What, criticize the professional conduct of their noble nautical colleagues? No, indeed, they're going to stick together like incompetent surgeons concealing each other's botched operations. I told you it was a giant murder conspiracy. I'll make a bet with you, Miss Brand. I'll bet that when the whole story does come out, there'll be a great scream of protest from the shipping industry at how terrible I was to put my loaded sailboats out there for them to hit, and not one word about how unseamanlike and illegal they were to hit them. That's where you come in. Write it! Tell them! Tell everybody that all I did was to sail back and forth across the steamer lanes as I had a perfect right to do. As Ann and I did in poor harmless *Tumbleweed*. All I've done is even the odds; I'm no longer totally helpless as I was that night. I've got a few pounds of explosives to give me a fighting chance against all those tons of machinery. I told you, I play fair. I don't hunt them down. They hunt me down. If they don't like what they find waiting for them at the end of the trail, that's just too damned bad."

There was a period of silence as we contemplated the girl's paranoid vision of an ocean full of enormous enemies and of herself as a shining Joan of Arc doing battle with these great, evil dragons of the sea. Serena Lorca gave that nervous tug to her bodice once more.

"I can see you don't really believe me," she said to

Eleanor. "But you have the facts on paper, signed by me. I want you to tell the American people, all the people, the truth about these arrogant incompetents shoving their great steel homicide weapons blindly across the oceans without the slightest concern for the small sailing craft that have just as much right to be out there as they have. But I'm not asking you to take my word for it, I'm going to show you. You'll get a chance to see what it's really like. It's the story you've been after, isn't it? Write it!" Abruptly, she turned to Giulio. "Give me that other gun, please."

"Miss Lorca—"

"It's all right; I know how to use it. I'll watch Helm. You take Miss Brand topside and let her see everything she needs to; she ought to know a little about how a sailboat works to write her story. Henry can answer any technical questions she wants to ask."

Reluctantly, Giulio reached down and produced a revolver that looked familiar—Warren Peterson's weapon, or one just like it. Serena checked the loads and snapped the cylinder back into place; when she turned the muzzle toward me, the gray lead noses of the bullets visible in the chambers on either side of the frame informed me it was still loaded.

Eleanor obeyed the jerky command of Giulio's firearm, and slid out from under the table. She made her way through the galley and up the companionway out of sight, followed by her escort. I remained facing Serena Lorca.

She watched me in her intent, disconcerting way. "I think you have some questions you didn't want to ask in front of him," she said.

"Two," I said. "First, if what you really want is publicity for your seagoing operation, why did you have Jurgen Hinkampf murdered before he could spill the beans? Seems to me that's exactly what you're after, the confession of one of the ships' officers involved."

She frowned. "Hinkampf? Oh, the young mate on that last tanker. . . . I wasn't in Nassau when it happened, but they told me he died of his burns. Murdered?"

Her attitude was convincing. I said, "He was smothered

271

to death in his hospital bed before he could break down and tell Eleanor exactly what he'd seen the night his ship went down. Do I gather that somebody's covering up for you that you don't know about, giving you protection that you don't want?"

She laughed shortly. "The protection is hardly for me, Mr. Helm. I didn't know about Hinkampf, but I had a pretty good idea. My father never made a straight deal in his life. He's making certain that now that I've given him the revenge he wants—well, most of it, and the rest will be taken care of as soon as Giulio takes care of you, if you let him—I don't also give him the publicity he doesn't want. For the sake of what I could do for him, he was willing to risk financing a few anonymous forays; maybe I gave him the idea that I'd do my best to keep them anonymous." Her smile was crooked. "But now that he has no further use for me and realizes what I'm *really* after, he's about to terminate our agreement, as the saying goes, unilaterally. Giulio's here to see to that, too. To see to me right along with you. Only I don't think he knows I'm aware of it." She stared at me intently. "I know the way to beat him, one way. I hope you have a way, too, so you can help Miss Brand get clear with her story. Later, this gun will be in the second drawer of the galley dresser, right under the flatware. I can't give it to you now because you'd try to use it prematurely, before I finish what I have to do. But if things go wrong for me, you'll find it there." She frowned at me. "You had another question."

I said, "You promised Peterson that Eleanor would be set free if he did what you said. And you promised me that we wouldn't be killed."

She laughed. "Well, she will be turned loose eventually, as far as I'm concerned. I have every intention of setting her free; I want her free. And I have no intention of killing you; I hope you live a long, long time. Maybe I just didn't word my promises quite as precisely as I should have, Mr. Helm." Suddenly the odd brown eyes focused intently on my face. "But you know you can't believe a word a crazy girl tells you. What was it you called me, the Mad Ship-Sinker of the Atlantic?"

Chapter 31

It was almost a relief to be once more locked up in our little triangular prison cell—well, it didn't quite come to a point up forward, terminating instead in a small bulkhead beyond which, presumably, was stowage space in the bow for the anchor rope or chain. And the door didn't really lock, but Giulio and his Browning, waiting outside, made a pretty good substitute for bars and bolts.

Eleanor seated herself on the port berth and looked up and started to speak, but found herself suddenly, ridiculously, overbalanced and thrown backward across the bunk, legs waving helplessly, as *Jamboree*'s bow came crashing down. She'd forgotten how much more violent the motion was here up forward. I reached down and retrieved her, bringing her back up to a sitting position and steadying her as she rubbed the back of her head, which had borne the brunt of the impact.

"Okay?" I asked.

She shrugged. "I wouldn't go *that* far. I'm very scared, I need a bath very badly, I wouldn't mind some clean clothes and I still get a little queasy now and then. I wouldn't say I was exactly *okay*. But there don't seem to be any soft spots in my skull, if that's what you're asking."

I grinned. "Good girl," I said, and leaned down to kiss her lightly on top of the head.

It was just a casual friendly gesture, or it was meant to be; but it turned out to be a serious miscalculation. Suddenly she was looking up at me gravely, questioningly; and I found myself very much aware of the expressive shape of

273

her mouth and thinking that, if kissing was to be done, I could have picked a better target. And if anything was less relevant at the moment than the sweet curve of a lady's lips, I'd have to scratch hard to find it, imprisoned as I was in a plunging pie-shaped cell with an armed killer beyond the door and a substantial charge of high explosive under the floor, whatever the hell you called it on a boat. Sole. But I knew suddenly that I wasn't going to spend another night holding this girl in a chaste brotherly embrace, no matter how lonely she might be or what her psychological difficulties might be. You can ask only so much of the iron self-control for which we grim undercover operatives are noted.

I turned away and got the pillow off my bunk and wedged it, along with hers, behind her to prevent her from repeating her undignified trip to leeward. Then I seated myself facing her with my feet against her bunk to keep me from being pitched into her lap.

"Report, Brand," I said. "Give me the topside picture. Weapons first. Incidentally, there are some knives in the galley, including a couple of good big ones; and that .38 is supposed to find a home in the second drawer down if Miss Lorca keeps her word. I wouldn't bet either way; but you might keep it in mind."

Eleanor nodded. "There's a shotgun in the cockpit," she said. "Held in place near the wheel by some shock cord. Rather short barrel. Like a police riot gun."

I glanced at the hatch overhead. "That means that even if we can get that thing open—and it doesn't seem to be locked in any way, just dogged down normally against the spray—we'll get our heads blown off the minute we stick them out of there. What kind of a shotgun? Single-barrel or double?"

"I think it's what's known as a pump-action gun. One barrel with a magazine tube underneath and a sliding wooden handle."

"Probably five or six shells, then, if it isn't plugged to three for legal hunting, and that's not likely. They'd have

274

removed the magazine plug when they sawed off the barrel. Go on."

"The man called Henry wears a sheath knife, but it seems to have a funny blunt point; I wouldn't think it would make much of a weapon, not for stabbing, anyway."

"A sailor's rigging knife. What about Henry?"

"Big. Tough, I'd say, but not really mean, if you know what I mean."

"A fighter perhaps, but not really a killer?"

"Something like that. The other man, Adam, carries a real weapon, kind of a dagger with a very fancy sheath and grip. Six-inch blade?"

"Ugh," I said. "Sounds like a custom fighting knife; let's hope it didn't come with a book of instructions. What about Adam?"

"Not quite as tall as Henry, but I'd say the same weight. Broad and muscular. Black; and I'm afraid he's working at it. I didn't like the way he looked at me; and not because I'm a woman. A lot of hate there, Matt."

"Well, they've got cause, I suppose; but it doesn't make it any easier. Any other weapons?"

She shook her head. "That's all I saw, except Giulio's gun, of course."

I said, "You're not thinking, girl reporter. It's a sailing ship, it ought to have some belaying pins and marline spikes and stuff lying around, oughtn't it?"

She laughed. "I'm afraid you're behind the times. This isn't an old-fashioned square-rigger. No belaying pins. But there were some hefty handles for cranking the winches, steel, about a foot long. Maybe even fifteen inches, I couldn't tell. Two in plastic sheaths in the cockpit and two on the mast. A long boathook, at least nine feet, lashed to the deck, port side. A big aluminum pole secured to starboard—spinnaker pole? But it's five or six inches thick and over twenty feet long, so it would make a pretty awkward weapon—even for Hercules. A big anchor on the forward deck, marked forty-five pounds. A life raft, marked six-man, in a plastic case fastened to the cabin just behind the mast, with some kind of a rescue beacon mounted in a clip beside it." She frowned, visualizing the deck as she had seen it. "Oh, I almost forgot, there's no tender on deck—if that's what you call a real dinghy of wood or fiberglass—but we're towing a good-sized rubber boat behind us now. Giulio called it a Zodiac. It's two fat rubber tubes joined together at the bow and coming to separate points aft, with a wooden transom between them for the outboard motor. Wooden floor. No seats except for a kind of box to hold the gas tank."

"Was there a motor?"

"Not mounted on the Zodiac, but there was one stored on a bracket on the stern rail. Marked twenty-five horsepower."

I said, "Very good report, Brand. He really gave you the guided tour. Now I'll let you lay it all out for us. I think we've got all the necessary information. Pretend there's a ship approaching. The attack is ordered. Write us the script."

She thought for a moment. "Well, first of all, the Lorca girl is going to check the approaching target with that sighting compass of hers. Giulio called it a hand-bearing compass, because you hold it in your hand to get the bearings. She's going to want to make sure it's really on a collision course or close to it. And then—" She frowned, working it out in her head. "Then Serena's got to get rid of her crew, doesn't she? She won't need them for the final run-in, and they haven't got the motive she has for taking the risk. That must be what the Zodiac is for. The two men—I suppose up to now she only had the two on board—unload into that. She gets on the radio and alerts the sportfisherman that's trailing along just over the horizon somewhere. She sails on alone, leaving the Zodiac behind. She says she won't turn on the sailboat's motor because that's cheating; but I'm sure she'll fiddle with the sails and rudder enough to bring about a collision if it's at all possible. Unless the ship really changes course to avoid her. I think she's sincere about that. If they show that their lookouts are on the job, and that they're willing to take appropriate action to steer clear, she won't make it difficult for them." Eleanor grimaced. "Of course, she seems to think the ocean's just crawling with baddies, but she must be exaggerating. The freighter I sailed on when I was starting on this story was handled quite competently as far as I could judge, and there's no reason to think it was an exception."

I said, "We got to keep in mind that the girl's kind of paranoid on the subject. It does seem unlikely that the average commercial vessel is handled as negligently or illegally as she seems to think."

Eleanor said, "Of course, she's got reason to be prejudiced. We've got to remember that her first boat *was* sunk and her girlfriend *was* killed. It must have been a very traumatic experience."

I shook my head. "That's not the point, Elly. The point is that her current demonstration, as she calls it, probably isn't going to work on the first ship that comes along, or even the second. They'll avoid her in time. Chances are, she'll have to make runs at several vessels before she finds the slob ship she wants, that'll come straight in for the kill all lawless and careless. So we've got to be prepared for a number of different possibilities."

Eleanor said, "Actually there are three possibilities, aren't there? First: Serena dumps her crew and sails toward Collision Point X, but the target dutifully dodges in plenty of time and nothing happens. In this case, I suppose, she just gives the abort signal to *Ser–Jan* and sails back to pick up the Zodiac and crew. Second possibility: she sails for Point X as before, but has time to pull on her rubber suit and set the autopilot and drop overboard. She can't stay with the sailboat too long, or she'll be too close to the explosion when it happens. But either the ship manages to turn aside at the last moment, or she's misjudged her trajectories; again nothing happens. In that case, presumably, the Zodiac comes buzzing along to pick her out of the water. They chase after the big boat—I suppose that outboard is fast enough to run down a sailboat—and scramble back aboard. *Abort repeat abort.*"

I said, "She's taking a chance there. Finding a swimmer in the middle of the ocean isn't easy. But, of course, she does have a second line of defense. If the Zodiac misses her or the outboard conks out so they can't catch the sailboat, there's still the sportfisherman coming along to pick up the pieces. Even so they must use some kind of electronic locating devices, with a directional receiver on board *Ser–Jan*."

Eleanor nodded. "Possibility three," she went on. "Everything goes like clockwork and the sailboat and the ship meet at X. BOOM! *Ser–Jan* comes roaring up, gathers up the crew, and maybe even retrieves the Zodiac for future use. It then picks up Miss Lorca paddling around in her wet suit like in the description she gave Peterson, and she heads back to the U.S. to buy another secondhand sailboat."

I said, "Well, one thing is clear. She wasn't kidding when she said she preferred to work at night; she was probably just bluffing earlier, trying to give us a little scare, when she let us think she might go into action in the middle of the day. Obviously, even if there's a ship around so negligent that it'll run down a sailboat in broad daylight, she can only pull off her routine safely in the dark. Otherwise, sooner or later, a survivor is bound to report seeing a big, private powerboat that ran away and left people to drown; and there'll be a big stink and a careful investigation. But at night a boat, even a sizeable boat, is pretty invisible without lights."

"Another thing," Eleanor said, "there isn't going to be another secondhand sailboat this time. Giulio made it pretty clear, talking to me, that this is her last run. Daddy's turning off the money hose."

I nodded grimly. "She knows that. She's just hoping Giulio will let her complete this final attack, demonstration, however you want to refer to it, before he makes his move. The only question in my mind is, why he hasn't moved already? There can be only one answer to that. He doesn't trust Henry and Adam all the way."

Eleanor frowned. "I don't understand. If it's a question

of getting rid of us, against her wishes—and I suppose he's working for the father and not the daughter—you can't hope that those two men will help us, regardless of what she says. After all, they are Lorca's men."

I said, "I wasn't thinking of us."

Her eyes were wide and dark. "If you're thinking what I think you're thinking, that's pretty horrible."

"Horrible or not, she's expecting it," I said. "Giulio's here to clean up. Everything. No loose ends. She knows it and she's got some kind of an answer, some kind of a defense—she just hinted at it. I can't see how it can be anything but the two men with whom she's been sailing, even if they were originally planted on her by her pop." After a moment, Eleanor not speaking, I said, "Boat people can be funny. I've dealt with them before. Those three, Serena and her crew, have covered a lot of sea miles together, and shared a lot of dangers. And a gutsy girl like that, obviously a hell of a sailor in spite of her quirks, is going to command loyalty in some strange and unexpected places."

Eleanor licked her lips. "Maybe I'm being naive, but I can't really believe that her own father would—"

I said, "Hell, I can believe anything of Lorca, and you should, too. The girl has already had one bad boating accident; why shouldn't she have another that she doesn't survive? Cold-bloodedly speaking, now that she's served his purpose, Lorca's much better off without her. He'll look a lot better to the voters as the grieving parent of a lost girl sailor—it'll get him sympathy that's money in the bank —than as the papa of a practicing pervert, as some people like to call it, or of a notorious lady pirate, or terrorist or whatever's the right name for what she's doing out here. Dead, she's a help. Alive, she's nothing but a menace to Lorca's ambitions, particularly now that she's frustrated enough to want real publicity for her weirdo seagoing crusade. Do you think Lorca's got the slightest intention of letting her get it? If he thought she was that screwy, he'd never have dealt with her in the first place. Publicity for her seagoing activities, involving him, would not only ruin him politically, it would get his syndicate sponsors very, very angry with him. And they're not nice people to have mad at you, even if you're as powerful as Mister Lorca." I shook my head. "He took a big risk to get his revenge with her help. Now that that's all taken care of, or will be as soon as Giulio eliminates me, he's making sure there'll be no awkward kickbacks. Afterward, he can put his poor drowned daughter's picture on his desk for a nice sentimental touch that'll impress his visitors, and lean back and enjoy being the respectable and popular and powerful Senator George Winfield Lorca, all accounts closed."

Eleanor said, "I'm being silly." Her voice was suddenly hard. "Why should I be shocked at anything people do to each other after all the time I've spent in this writing racket? But what does this mean to us, Matt?"

"It means that Giulio's going to have to play his hand very carefully here," I said. "He knows he's outnumbered on this boat. Oh, as far as we're concerned, he can do anything he likes, and probably nobody'll interfere. Serena may want to, but she knows that Henry and Adam aren't going to stick their necks out for us, even if she asks them. But the minute Giulio reveals his hostile intentions toward her, he'll have her crew to deal with. Therefore, I suspect that as long as we're docile and don't cause Giulio any trouble, he'll just save us alive until he can make one big clean sweep of everything; and for that he'll need reinforcements. But he can't call up his pals on *Ser–Jan* without a good excuse or Serena'll guess what he's up to and maybe do something drastic before the sportfisherman arrives. Maybe Giulio can handle Henry and Adam alone, not to mention Serena and you and me, but why do it the hard way?" I grimaced. "So I think we'll all continue to be good friends, smiling and happy, until Serena makes her first run tonight and the other boat is summoned in the normal course of business. Arturo's probably been told that's the signal and he's to come right in, ignoring any cancellations or aborts. So that's got to be our signal, too, and we'd better think about what we're going to do." I studied her for a little, remembering something. I said,

"You don't happen to have that little two-bladed stockman's knife on you, by any chance?"

There was a lengthy silence. At last Eleanor murmured, "Ooooh, that's scary! Clairvoyance, Mr. Helm?" When I didn't speak, she went on, "By some chance I do. How did you guess?"

I said, "You're a smart girl. Even though you were mad at me, you must have known you were doing a stupid thing when you left our protection to run off to the Bahamas like that. I couldn't see you entrusting your safety entirely to that helpless dope, Peterson. You must have given some thought to how you might defend yourself if you had to. And you told me last night you were sticking to those ridiculous spike-heeled sandals through thick and thin just on the off-chance you'd get a chance to use them in a manner for which they were not intended. Well, if your mind was running along those channels, I couldn't see you leaving that knife in your purse, the first thing that would be taken away from you if somebody grabbed you." I looked her over critically. There was something in her pocket, I saw, but it didn't have the right shape for a knife. "Where?" I asked.

She grinned abruptly; her nice, wide monkey grin. "I'm glad it doesn't show. It's down inside my panty hose. Very intimate and, I might add, a bit uncomfortable. But Serena didn't spot it when she patted me up and down after we were caught."

"Accessible?"

"You've got to be kidding." She laughed. "You either go in from the top of my pants and grope way down the front of me in a most embarrassing way, or you unzip me and perform a quick Caesarean section on my best tights. Well, hell, they've got a couple of runs in them already." She shook her head. "No, it's not readily accessible, but it was the best I could do."

I regarded her for a moment, wanting to tell her that the best she could do was a hell of a lot better than most girls could have, or would have, done under the circumstances. However, it would have sounded patronizing; and she wasn't anybody it was safe to patronize, so confident in some respects, so insecure in others.

Instead I said absently, "I didn't know panty hose were standard equipment with pants. It seems redundant." I grinned. "But it explains something that's been bugging me."

"What's been bugging you, Mr. Helm?" she asked warily.

I said, "I promised to report as the data came in, remember? We've already checked out the shoulders, and it's agreed that the legs and ankles are okay. Well, when you were walking out to the plane ahead of me the other day, I took the opportunity to do a little further research, and I'm pleased to state that, in my opinion, you have a very passable little ass, Miss Brand. A nice, smooth, seamless little ass."

She drew in her breath sharply and started to say something angry and stopped. I saw her grin faintly instead. "Thank you, Mr. Helm," she said, "but at the moment I feel my ass is fairly irrelevant, don't you? And this discussion, fascinating though it is, doesn't help get us back home with Serena Lorca's story, which you're not going to let me publish anyway. Here, you might as well keep this, since it's no good to me."

She dug the plastic envelope she'd been given, folded, out of the snug pocket of her slacks. Suddenly the atmosphere of our little stateroom—prison had lost its warm friendliness. I took the envelope and tucked it away.

"Thanks," I said. "I appreciate it, Elly."

"Just don't ask me why I'm doing it, because I'd hate to have to figure out an answer." Her voice was cold. "And I hope your friend, Bennett, appreciates it too, but it isn't very likely, is it? Can a man like that appreciate anything? And you aren't a bit welcome, either of you." She drew a ragged breath. "Do you want the knife, too?"

"No, it's better with you," I said. There was nothing to be accomplished by offering condolences for her lost story, or apologies for asking her to give it up, so I went on briskly, "I have a hunch we may wind up having to cut

282

ourselves free of some rope or tape eventually. Giulio's probably going to drop the easygoing act when it's served his purpose, and tie us up for easy management. I've got a trick cutting gadget hid out, too; but it's nice to know you're holding something in reserve." I hesitated. "Elly."

"Yes?" Her voice was stiff.

"I really do appreciate the favor."

She said coldly, "It was that patriotic guff that really got me, I guess. How can a girl refuse anything to a man who can shovel crap like that?"

"Sure," I said. It was time to change the subject, past time, and I asked, "Elly, do you remember the last time you used that knife?"

There was a little silence before she spoke, "It's hard to forget, but why should I remember it?"

I said carefully, "Because the girl who did that is the girl I want beside me when the break comes tonight, if it is tonight." She didn't speak. After a moment, I went on, "I don't want you to have the wrong idea about what comes next. Forget everything you ever saw on TV or in the movies. It doesn't really work like that."

"What do you mean, Matt?"

I said, "Well, in a movie or TV show we'd be carefully plotting our escape, wouldn't we? We'd be thinking of ways of breaking out of this cabin, of overpowering the opposition and tying the boys and girls all up in neat little packages, of summoning help by radio to get us off this floating bomb. Wouldn't we? We'd be thinking very hard about saving our precious lives, but preferably with a minimum of bloodshed, being the nice TV hero and heroine we are. Right?"

Her tongue touched her lips. Her hostility had faded. She was watching me closely. "Go on, Matt."

"That's dream stuff," I said. "Nice TV heroes and heroines don't just finish last, they finish dead. I am going to let you into a secret that I don't often share with anyone, particularly a delicate young woman. The basic principle of escaping, Miss Brand, is that there is no problem in

283

escaping, none whatever, if everyone who's in a position to prevent you from escaping has been killed. Do you follow me, Miss Brand?"

She licked her lips. "Go on."

I said, "To turn a corny phrase, baby, we go for the throats, not the boats. Never mind that Giulio's been reasonably polite to us, to date. Never mind that Serena's a poor unbalanced girl from an unfortunate family situation. Never mind that Henry may be a hell of a sailor and even a reasonable guy in his salty way, and that Adam's attitude is understandable, considering his racial background, and that Robert on the other boat is a hell of a cook, even if he's a bit too rapid with a knife, and Arturo may have something to be said in his favor also, although I don't happen to know what it is. We just forget all that. *You* just forget all that. Can you?"

She drew a long breath. "I don't know. It seems . . . a little drastic."

I nodded. "It's a normal reaction. I've met it before. On a recent assignment I had to stop in the middle of the great breakout scene to argue with a tender young lady who thought I was being too hard on the poor guards who got in our way." I shrugged. "Okay, it makes it tougher, but if that's the way you feel, I'll do it all myself, or try. I just thought that, since you were willing to get blood on your knuckles once for reasons you considered adequate, this time with your life at stake you might be willing to get your pinkies a little gory again. But—"

"Matt, shut up!" When I looked at her, her face was pale. "Don't talk so much. I just said it was drastic, that's all. I didn't say I wouldn't do it. But you'd better be specific."

"Specific," I said sourly. "Okay, if that's what you want. Stop me if I get too rough for you. Here's specific: if you get a chance to use that knife, it must go in all the way, low, edge up, and rip upward until it hits bone. Then you step back fast and let the guts spill out. If you get a chance to swing one of those winch handles you described, there should be brains on it when you stop swinging. Forget all

284

about trying to escape. Escape will take care of itself, later. As long as there's one of them standing, moving, even twitching slightly, you keep after him and to hell with escape. Too damned many people, thinking about getting away instead of concentrating on the job at hand, have been killed at the last moment by somebody they chivalrously refrained from finishing off when they had the chance, TV fashion. I don't want to die because you were too sensitive to give somebody who was still wiggling another bash on the head, and he managed to reach a gun before he died." I looked at her bleakly. "Are you still with me, girl reporter?"

She swallowed. "Go on."

"That's by way of general psychological preparation," I said. "Specifically, I want you to concentrate on Serena. It's not nice in the sense that she kind of favors our side against Giulio, if only to get her story out, but we know the story's not going to get out if I can help it, so to hell with that. Remind yourself that she callously killed a pleasant young married woman and her child just to get support for this seagoing crusade of hers, not to mention a few other nasty stunts she pulled for her daddy. The girl's a monomaniac and now she's bound she's going to use this last sailing torpedo of hers for the purpose for which it was intended. We simply can't take a chance of leaving her loose and trying to reason with her later. If she isn't attended to, we could easily wind up with another blown-up ship at the bottom of the Atlantic." I waited but Eleanor was silent. I went on, "So stay near her whenever you possibly can. Go for her when the action starts. She's bigger than you and stronger, but I'm hoping that all she'll be expecting from a nice little landlubber like you is the usual hair-pulling, face-scratching, dress-ripping, shin-kicking ceremony that passes for a girlish fight. If you drive right in with the idea that you're really going to smash her, put her out for good, not just muss her hairdo and spoil her clothes and her looks a bit, you stand a chance of catching her by surprise. Objections?"

As I stopped talking, we heard Henry's voice call out on deck, "Ship off the port bow, ma'am."

"Coming." Presently, waiting in silence, listening, we heard the husky voice of Serena Lorca, also on deck now. "Ease sheets. Bear off. He's passing well clear but we don't want him close enough to wonder why we're towing a tender way offshore where it would normally be stowed. But we might as well put the motor on the Zodiac as soon as he's out of sight." We heard her laugh pleasantly. "I think this weather's going to hold for us. We'll have a good night for hunting."

Eleanor was looking at me. "No objections, Matt," she said quietly. "I don't want any more sailors to die, or their ships, either. As you say, it's too bad in a way, but she's got to be stopped no matter what justification she thinks she has for what she's doing."

"Yes," I said. "Unfortunately, we probably won't be able to prevent her from taking one more shot at it. We'll just have to hope that first shot is a miss."

CHAPTER 32

LYING in our bunks, that were separated aft but joined up forward where the cabin narrowed, we watched daylight fade from the hatch above, with our heads apart and our feet together. The wind had apparently lightened a bit; the boat's angle of heel was smaller and I had no trouble remaining in my berth to windward. I didn't know what my cellmate was thinking and I didn't ask. I found myself wondering how Martha Devine would have reacted to my detailed instructions for disemboweling a man; but the simple fact was that I wouldn't have given them to

Martha, even though she'd once come through for me—
and for herself—in a pinch, a rather tight pinch. But she
was not as tough-minded a girl as this one, which was
really nothing against her. Or for Eleanor Brand. They
were simply different people-models, designed to function
well under different operating conditions.

It was hard to imagine Martha, for instance, avenging
herself as directly and crudely on a pair of rapists, as
Eleanor had done. To be sure, Martha had once considered
punishing the other girl for a certain betrayal, but I had a
hunch she'd been very glad when I'd relieved her of the self-
imposed obligation. I suspected that she would never have
carried her plan to a truly lethal conclusion, although she
might have gone far enough to embarrass us. If she'd really
been serious about the project she wouldn't have given it
up so easily. On the other hand, Eleanor would never have
dreamed of marrying a crippled warrior out of the hospital
and making a comfortable home for him. Unlike Martha,
she was not a comfortable, homemaking kind of a girl. . . .

Above us, the boat's running lights went on, tinting the
sails overhead with red and green. The spray had dried,
and there was salt crusted on the transparent plastic hatch,
our window to the darkening sky. It was no time to be
thinking of Martha Devine, who'd come halfway across a
continent to offer herself to me. She was looking as much
for relief from the loneliness of widowhood, I guessed, as
for an old excitement we'd once found together. But there
was really nothing else left to think about. All the heavy
thinking required here had already been done. You can
drive yourself nuts trying to figure out in advance all the
permutations and combinations you may encounter; better
just to establish a few guidelines to follow and figure on
taking it as it comes. Over the boat sounds, I heard movement in the cabin aft, approaching.

"Here we go," I said, sitting up and swinging my legs off
the bunk.

"I haven't said thanks," Eleanor said. "I haven't forgotten that you're here because of me, Matt. Thanks."

I said, "You might consider having a recurrence of your

recent ailment at a suitable moment, if you don't mind making a bit of a spectacle of yourself."

"All right."

There was a rap on the door. "Helm."

"I'll see if he's in," I said. "Whom shall I say is calling?"

"Come out careful," Giulio's voice said, unamused. "Very careful. The lady stays until she's told."

I looked down at Eleanor as I rose, and reached down to brush her cheek lightly with my knuckles. She turned her head and gave me a straight and steady look, the meaning of which I couldn't interpret. Perhaps her waiting thoughts had been running close to mine; perhaps she was telling me it was time I got my women sorted out before somebody got badly hurt. But this was really not the time for solving the complicated problems of my love life or, for that matter, of hers. Although they did keep intruding.

"Easy," Giulio said as I emerged. "Take it very easy now, friend."

The party was over and it was time to do the dishes. There had been a number of occasions when I could have tried to take him with some hope of success, although he could have been simply teasing me, testing me. I knew regrets for those lost opportunities, if that was what they had been, because he was giving me no opening now, backing cautiously ahead of me down the short, narrow passage between the head compartment to port and a bank of lockers, contents unknown, to starboard. He stepped aside when he reached the lighted main saloon, where the leaves of the big table had been lowered to make more room. He gestured to me to move past him.

The black man I hadn't gotten a good look at before, Adam, stood braced against the chart table with the shotgun at the ready. The knife on his hip was, as I'd guessed from Eleanor's description, a custom job; and if I'd thought it was important, I could probably have dredged up the name of the knife-maker. You don't generally invest in personalized cutlery like that unless you know how to use it.

Adam was in jeans and an old work shirt from which

the sleeves had been ripped. It was unbuttoned to the waist, so the first impression was more of gleaming black arms and chest than of faded blue cloth. The shotgun was a Winchester 12-gauge pump with the barrel sawed off just ahead of the magazine tube, as Eleanor had indicated. The shells were probably loaded with 00 Buck although, of course, I couldn't see that. Somewhat smaller buckshot, with more projectiles to the load, producing a denser shot pattern —as the man who'd shot Bob Devine had known. The ordinary guy with homicide in mind just goes for the shotgun ammo with the biggest, ugliest lead balls in it and feels happy. And there's no doubt that 00 Buck will render a man quite dead enough under most circumstances.

Serena Lorca, a remote and preoccupied look on her tanned and handsome face, was leaning against the galley counter with a roll of silvery tape in her hand: duct tape or air-conditioner tape, two inches wide, immensely strong and adhesive, nowadays used for emergency repairs everywhere, apparently even on boats. She looked at Giulio.

"Front or back?" she asked.

He hesitated, quite aware that a man with hands taped behind him is somewhat more helpless than a man with hands taped in front. Then he shrugged.

"Front," he said reluctantly. "Otherwise we'll have to carry them up and down these damned ladders. . . . Hold your hands out, Helm. Wrists together." He watched the tape being applied. Serena did not look at my face as she worked; she seemed to be living in a distant world of her own. When he was satisfied with her labors, Giulio nodded to her, and said to me, "Now get down there to leeward and take the place you had before. . . . Watch him, Adam."

I had to admire Giulio, turning his back casually on a shotgun in the hands of the black man whom, if my estimate of the situation was correct, he did not trust and probably intended to kill, along with Henry, along with Serena and Eleanor and me, as soon as reinforcements were available. But he showed no signs of uneasiness as he made his way forward. A few minutes later Eleanor had been fetched, taped, and planted beside me on the port settee where the slant of the ship would inhibit any hasty action we might consider—not that any such action was likely to be effective with our wrists bound.

Giulio studied us thoughtfully. He said, "We'll be turning out the cabin lights now so they can see better topside, but that shiny tape shows up good in the dark, so don't even think of messing with it, either of you. . . . All right, Adam. That does it. Secure that blunderbuss in the cockpit where you got it so it doesn't slide around and go off and kill somebody."

"Well, I'd better get on deck, too," Serena said after the black man had disappeared. She did not look at Eleanor or me. I realized that we were a part of her crusade that no longer interested her; she had more exciting things to think about. It was opening day of the ship-hunting season. She turned her faraway eyes on Giulio. "Just one more," she whispered. "Stay with me a little longer, Giulio. Just give me this one more and I'll be satisfied, like I promised Daddy. Ann will be satisfied."

"Good hunting," Giulio said; but as she disappeared into the darkness above he looked at us and tapped his head significantly, reminding us that he might be a dangerous fellow, and he might have a gun, but he wasn't as nutty as some people around. Then he reached for a switch and the cabin went dark. "Just make yourselves comfortable," his voice said. "We could be here a long time. We chased the screwball dame around the ocean for two weeks once—I was on the backup boat, thank God—and picked her out of the water five times, not to mention several times that number of early-aborts, before she got one to come in right."

I said, "That makes you about as screwy as she is, doesn't it?"

I saw his shoulders move in a shrug, up on the weather side of the saloon. The Browning was a dull gleam in the dark. "Mr. Lorca says do it, I do it." After a moment he went on, "But maybe you've got the wrong idea. She's a nut, but we're not *against* it, understand? It's not just the pretty-sailboat-fairies who feel that way. Hell, there isn't a real waterman in the country who hasn't had to cut loose everything and run like hell when one of those king-sized motherfuckers came crashing through. To hell with your right-of-way and whatever fishing or trawling gear you had out." Giulio laughed harshly. "Saw a big freighter come into Port Everglades with holes all over the glass of her bridge. A fisherman they almost ran down got mad and emptied a thirty-thirty shark rifle at them. No, don't kid yourself, friend; we've got nothing against what she's doing. We've had a lot of good clean fun, all of us, helping her play this fancy game, kind of a bullfight, like. Big bastards think they own the fucking ocean. No, we don't mind a bit what she's doing; it's just that we can't let her make trouble for Mr. Lorca, doing it."

It was a rather shocking revelation, uncovering hostilities and antagonisms at sea that, as a practicing landlubber, I'd never dreamed existed. If I'd thought about it at all, I guess I'd assumed that little-boat seamen just kind of admired and envied all the big, beautiful ships cruising by. I'd accepted Serena Lorca's burning hate unthinkingly as the wild aberration of a lone, unbalanced individual avenging a personal loss. It hadn't occurred to me that others on the water might hold the same general attitude, if less intensely. It answered the question that had been at the back of my mind, about how Lorca could have gotten five salty characters to help his daughter on her outlandish expeditions and keep their mouths shut. But with that much free-floating hatred around, it would have been no problem. Apparently, small-boat seamen all, they'd thought it a great big joke to help turn a well-financed lady maniac loose on the lousy big-ship industry. They'd jumped at the chance.

I felt Eleanor sitting beside me quite still, clearly as startled and intrigued by this grim vision of the maritime world as I was. Then she stirred slightly.

"Matt," she said faintly. "Oh, goddamn it, Matt, I think I'm getting sick again."

Giulio heard her. "To hell with that!" he snapped. "Do you think I'm stupid or something? You're getting no free trips to the head, girlie. If you've really got to puke just spread your feet and put it on the floor. Or do it on your shoes for all I care."

"But I. . . . Oh, God!" She doubled up, hugging herself.

"And you're not lying down cosily with your pretty little head in his lap and chewing his wrists free, so forget it." Giulio hesitated. "But if it makes you feel better to lie down the other way, if you aren't faking, okay. But keep those hands where I can see them."

"All . . . right," she gasped weakly. "Thanks . . . maybe if I just lie real still. . . ."

She curled up on the settee beside me in the foetal position, emitting a small moan of misery from time to time. I didn't let myself wonder if she was overdoing it, or had gone into her act prematurely; the suggestion had been mine, but the execution was entirely up to her. . . .

"Ship off the starboard beam!"

That was the voice of sharp-eyed Henry, topside. We could hear Serena changing position up there, although her bare feet did not make much noise. The silence ran on for what seemed like a very long time; then she dropped down into the cabin and switched on the red light over the chart table. She drew some hasty lines on a pad of oddly ruled paper and made a sound of disgust, switching off the light.

"Passing astern," I heard her say as she hauled herself back up the ladder. "No way we can slow down enough to intercept. Carry on."

I heard Giulio snort in the darkness of the cabin. I heard his voice, "I told you it was going to be a long night."

It was.

Chapter 33

THE next ship didn't come along until some time in the early morning hours. Serena had shoved my watch well up under my shirt-sleeve to tape me, so I had no way of telling time. It had been a long wait, but night was still black at the cabin ports and the stars were still bright over the main hatch. Eleanor was still curled up unhappily on the settee cushion beside me. She didn't stir for the cry of the lookout—Adam this time—or the soft thumping of Serena's feet on the companionway ladder, or the sudden red glow of the chart table light. She didn't even react immediately to Serena's triumphant call,

"We got us a live one! Adam, get forward and get that working jib down and give me the big genoa. I'll need just about another knot of speed; but if he doesn't change course, we've got him cold." She reached for the microphone of the radio above the chart table and spoke into it, "Scramble I repeat scramble."

The radio spoke back, "Scramble received. Position?"

Lacking Robert's French accent, that would be the voice of Arturo, whom I'd never met, since he'd lived on *Ser—Jan's* bridge all the time I'd spent on board the sportfisherman. Serena switched on a bulky electronic instrument of some kind next to the radio, fiddled with it for a little, and read off a latitude and longitude. Apparently the picturesque old-fashioned sextant is a thing of the past. The radio repeated the numbers back to her.

"Check. Activating homers," Serena said into the mike. She turned her head to call to the cockpit, "Okay, Henry, hit those buttons."

Henry's voice said, after a moment, "Switch one."

The radio said, "Unit one transmitting."

"Switch two."

The radio said, "Homer two transmitting. Reception clear. Good luck. Out."

Serena replaced the microphone, turned off her instruments and the red light, and swung herself up on deck in agile fashion. Eleanor moved at last beside me. She fell back helplessly as her bound hands betrayed her. I didn't try to help her. I could see Giulio, very alert, across the cabin. A forty-foot boat has a maximum beam of around twelve feet, and the pilot berths outboard took up some room, so the range could hardly be called excessive. He was a shadowy pale figure in his white sailor pants and light jersey; and I could see the glint of the steady weapon he held. He'd be on hair-trigger now, psychologically cocked and ready, expecting a last-minute break. It was no time for reckless chivalry. Eleanor succeeded in getting herself upright unassisted, and made a clumsy thing of pushing her untidy hair out of her face.

"How do you feel?" I asked her to remind her, if she needed reminding, that she wasn't supposed to be feeling very well.

"Awful," she said in convincingly miserable tones. "I still feel perfectly ghastly. Oh, God, I'm so sick and headachy I could die!" Then she swallowed hard; I could hear her throat work. "I guess . . . I guess that wasn't exactly the right thing to say, was it? Matt?"

"Yes."

"I'm so sorry I got you into this. We're not going to make it, are we? I don't believe a word that woman says." After a little, she asked, "Does *it* . . . hurt very much?"

"The last few times I died it was practically painless," I said.

"Damn you, don't make fun of . . . Matt, is it true that when *it* happens you . . . dirty yourself disgustingly right afterward?"

"Sure," I said. "Everything relaxes and it all comes out in your pants."

"I can't bear to think of it," she said. "I don't mind everything going black so much, but I can't bear the thought of people seeing me all messy like that."

It was a hell of a conversation, but it was a conversation, and one was needed. I said callously, "What do you care? You won't be there to be embarrassed by your own repulsive condition."

"That helps," she said bitterly. "Oh, that really helps! Gee, thanks lots, you really know how to comfort a girl. . . ."

"All right, Giulio, send them up." Serena's head showed in the hatchway, a dark shape against the stars. "Make it snappy now. We haven't got all night."

"Here comes the dame," Giulio said, giving Eleanor a sharp signal with the gun. To me, he said, "You get behind her and steady her as she climbs; and don't you get any smart-ass ideas, either of you. Like putting on a big clumsy act just because you're taped like that. No phony falls. If you let her tumble back on us, Helm, I'll just step back and empty this piece into both of you; and it holds fourteen, including the one up the pipe."

It was a little tricky, but it was a slanting ladder, actually a small, steep, wooden staircase; and only five steps high. I put my shoulders against Eleanor's rear to support and steady her as, climbing, she had to release her first hand hold and reach higher up. Then Serena had her by the bound wrists and was hauling her out.

With my greater height, I just reached up and felt my right hand grabbed. I walked right up out of there, steadied by the black-haired girl's muscular grip. A sudden yank might have unbalanced her, although she was pretty well braced; but the stunt would have got me nothing but a collection of nasty little metal-jacketed 9mm slugs in the back. They put hard coats on them so they won't get malformed and jam in the clattering actions of the automatics and submachine guns. It's also a gesture toward the so-called rules of civilized warfare—and that means they don't expand when they hit, like the softer all-lead revolver slugs; but any size hole in me, even 9mm unexpanded, is too big as far as I'm concerned.

I waited in the cockpit, aware of Giulio climbing up to join us cautiously. I was also aware that Eleanor, despite her abject air of illness and defeat, was staying close to Serena as instructed, and that Adam was way up forward putting on a big jib in the place of a small one. Another ghost of an opportunity had slipped by while Giulio was emerging from the cabin; but Henry was right there at the wheel with the 12-gauge Winchester pump within easy reach, and instinct told me it wasn't time yet. But if you pass up too many borderline chances you may wind up with no chances at all.

"Ready forward," Adam called.

"Run it up," Serena commanded, and turned to glance at Eleanor. "You can hold a line, even like that, can't you? When I give it to you and tell you to pull, you lean into it and pull like hell."

There was a great deal of noisy flapping forward as the big sail was hoisted, and Serena started hauling in a good-sized rope, hand over hand—the jib sheet, if my nautical terminology is correct. Then the strain got too much for her as the sail grew taut and she threw three quick turns around a large stainless steel winch mounted on the port side of the cockpit—there was a matching one to starboard —and grabbed one of the handles Eleanor had mentioned. She clapped it into the socket in the top of the winch and started cranking hard with one hand while pulling with the other. Finally that got too tough, and she passed the line to Eleanor.

"Now, *pull!*" She cranked with both hands, leaning over to watch the sail. "That does it. Okay, I've got it."

She cleated the sheet. Straightening up, she dropped the winch handle back into its plastic cockpit holster and made the usual instinctive gesture toward hauling up her stretchy bodice. I looked around and saw the ship at last. It was far out toward the horizon, approaching from starboard; and it was not a very impressive or frightening sight, just a small pattern of pretty lights on the dark ocean, well off the bow. There were two white lights, the range lights, with the one to the left, forward, lower than the one to the right, aft. Under the latter was a small red glow: the port sidelight. The green one to starboard would, of course, be obscured from this angle. Confusing the picture was a cluster of weaker, yellowish lights that had to be the deckhouse windows.

Jamboree was well heeled over and roaring right along now with the big genoa jib up and pulling hard. She was proudly showing her racing origins as she headed for Point X, still far ahead, where the courses of the two vessels would intersect. Even without sighting over compasses and drawing lines on oddball graph paper, I could see that it was going to be close when she got there. Very close.

Serena stepped over to the big steering wheel. "I'll take her now, Henry. Get the Zodiac alongside. I'll slow her with a luff when you're ready to load. . . . Oh, don't forget your homer."

A black wet suit was laid out on one of the cockpit seats—but looking at it more closely, I saw that it was not really the type of close-fitting suit the active surfers and scuba divers employ under chilly conditions. This was a real survival suit; a thick, heavy, all-encompassing flotation garment with hood and feet like a baby's sleeper. I'd heard of them, but I'd never seen one before. Attached to it were a couple of items of equipment. In the dark I could identify a signaling light of some kind, but I did not recognize the small rectangular orange box beside it. Another, somewhat larger, box the same color was not attached to the suit. When Henry picked it up, I saw the gleaming tip of what seemed to be an antenna that could be extended and, presumably, had been extended for the operational test I'd just heard. Homer. Well, actually, I'd been bright enough to guess that the reference had been to a homing device, not a Greek poet. Superior intelligence is, of course, a prerequisite for this racket; but if I were truly smart, I asked myself, would I be here? But that's what you always ask yourself when things get a little tight.

Then the rubber boat was alongside and Serena was

turning us into the wind. The sails were flapping and *Jamboree* was losing way and rising to an even keel. A gate had been opened in the starboard lifelines and a folding ladder had been dropped over the side. Henry, a dry sandy man, taller and leaner than Adam just as Eleanor had described him, in dungarees with, at his hip, the sailorknife she'd mentioned, dropped down the ladder first, followed by the black man who'd returned from the bow. Henry seated himself near the motor but Adam remained standing, steadying himself by a grip on the ladder, waiting to receive Eleanor. At Giulio's command she moved to the rail, turned her back to the water, got to her knees, and groped for the ladder with her foot. Finding it, she eased herself downward, clinging to a lifeline stanchion with her bound hands. Adam caught her around the waist as she came within his reach, and swung her back and down into the Zodiac. A moment later he had his fancy custom knife out of its sheath, its edge at her throat.

"All right, Helm," Giulio said. "You see how it is. One false move from you. . . . Now get down there!"

It was childish, of course. It made me feel old and cynical to realize that there were still people around who'd use that tired old routine against us. Under normal circumstances, it would have meant nothing to me if I'd seen the opportunity for which I was waiting. It could not have been allowed to mean anything to me. We're not supposed to be deflected from our duties by the mere fact that stray young ladies may get slightly dead; we don't play that game at all. It's tough, but that's the way the standing orders read. Too many people think they have the world by the tail, these days, if they can just point a knife or a gun at a warm body, any warm body.

Nowadays, they'll give you a jet airplane complete with pilot, crew, and pretty stewardesses—excuse me, flight attendants—if you can just manage to threaten the wellbeing of somebody, somehow. They'll even throw in a million bucks or two to make you happy. Mac long ago came to the conclusion that an organization like ours could not afford to operate in this benevolent manner. The in-

298

structions went out: *no mission to be jeopardized for hostages of any description.* In other words, we're just supposed to plug away at our jobs and let the bodies, amateur or professional, involved or uninvolved, innocent or guilty, fall where they may. The theory is that our missions are supposed to be reasonably important to the national welfare, and almost invariably involve some loss of life anyway; why should a hostage's life be treated as more valuable than anybody else's?

So, under ordinary circumstances, I'd have been duty bound to ignore the fact that this was a bright and attractive girl whom I liked and respected. My normal assignment did not include the preservation of bright and attractive girls—but this abnormal assignment, fortunately, did. In fact, my current mission was specifically concerned with keeping Miss Eleanor Brand alive, thank God. For once I did not have *that* grim choice to make; the choice that was supposed to be no choice at all.

I descended obediently into the Zodiac and took my place beside her on the wooden floorboards forward. There was only one seat, the box near the stern that presumably concealed the gas tank for the outboard motor, and Henry had that. Some water had splashed into the boat and was washing around in the bottom. I felt it wet the rear of my slacks coldly as I sat down. I decided that even with a survival suit, even this far south in this mild season, paddling around neck-deep in that stuff was something I'd leave to Serena if I could, without envy. I watched Giulio descend the ladder backward and turn to sit down facing us. He winced as the water soaked through his sailor pants, but the Browning did not falter. Adam sheathed the knife and Eleanor, released, turned toward me miserably and buried her head in my shoulder. Above us, Serena threw off the lines that held the Zodiac alongside. As we fell away from the sailboat's side, she hauled up the ladder and returned to the steering wheel. The big boat heeled sharply as the sails stopped slatting and filled; then *Jamboree* was pulling away, gaining speed rapidly and leaving us bobbing there on the dark ocean.

I glanced around and saw the ship again, closer and larger now. I could make out the dim, white shape of the superstructure, and even the ghostly outline of the black hull. It seemed to be a freighter with the deckhouse amidships. The red running light gleamed like a bloodshot eye. *Jamboree*, racing eagerly toward the meeting point ahead, was represented by a single white stern light, low, and, at the masthead, a red light over a green telling the world that this was a sailboat with certain rights at sea. The masthead lights, I knew, were not mandatory. Apparently Serena was serious about playing this deadly game of hers according to her own notions of fairness. . . .

Eleanor moaned with sudden distress. "Oh, God, Matt, this crazy jiggling little boat! Now I'm *really* getting sick. . . ."

As she tried to turn around, Giulio said sharply, "Cut it out. None of that thrashing around!"

I shrugged elaborately. "Okay, if you want it sloshing around in the bottom of the boat with us."

He hesitated. "Well, all right, but slow and careful, and I mean *careful*."

I helped Eleanor turn, and boosted her up over the fat rubber tube until she had a clear shot at the water. Her thin little sweater had ridden up behind. I got a good, if awkward, grip on the exposed waistband of her slacks to keep her from going headfirst into the sea. There was some loud, agonized, and very convincing retching and gasping. A sharp unpleasant odor reached me, scaring me a little. If she was genuinely and disablingly ill, it was time for me to take action on my own. I didn't know if, under Giulio's sharp eyes, I could get at the trick belt buckle we're issued, but I would have to try. Eleanor slid back down onto the floorboards and huddled there in the bilge water, spent, lying half across my lap, groaning feebly. I saw Giulio start to speak, to order her to move away from me, and check himself. I guess the whiff of bona fide vomit had convinced him of her total helplessness. . . .

"Christ, will you look at that fool girl!"

It was Henry's voice, and he was not looking at Eleanor

at all. He was staring into the darkness toward where *Jamboree* was already just a distant, slanting, three-light pattern decorating a dim sloping triangle of sail. The figure at the wheel was still discernible; her white shorts made a small reference point somewhat brighter than the sails.

Adam said, puzzled, "Hell, she hasn't suited up yet. What the fuck does she think she's doing? She's running out of time; the bastard's coming up fast."

Henry didn't seem to hear. His voice was pleading, "Don't do it, Missy! Goddamn it, you get in that survival suit and get the hell off that sailing bomb! You don't have to do it like that just because it's the last. . . ."

"You mean the screwball butch is doing a kamikaze?"

That was Giulio's voice, but nobody answered him. I realized that I had just learned Serena Lorca's defense against Giulio's plans for her destruction. She didn't have to worry about them, she could laugh at them, even, because she fully intended to destroy herself. This time she was simply going to stay on her self-propelled bomb and guide it home with her own hands.

The two light patterns were still well separated, but they had begun to close with frightening speed. We could see the luminous white wave at the ship's bow and hear the faraway rumble of its engine as it rushed toward its secret rendezvous with death. And much closer, almost in my lap, I heard the tiny sound of a zipper being opened, and then the faint whispering noise of something being torn as the girl huddled across my lap went for the little knife she'd hidden in a very intimate location. I suppose I should have had an automatic masculine reaction to the thought of a lady deliberately ripping open her fragile nylon underwear to expose herself in that particular area; but I'll have to admit that I was more concerned with the question of how she was going to get a folding knife unfolded with her wrists tightly bound, which I suppose says something unfavorable about my virility. I heard the faint zipper-sound again. Good girl. She had what she wanted and she wasn't going to risk any awkward questions about why she was suddenly appearing in public with her fly open.

A sudden snarling noise made me look around. Henry had started the outboard motor.

"What the hell do you think you're doing?" Giulio snapped.

"We can't let her. . . . We've got to stop her!"

"Goddamn it, shut it off!"

"But—"

"I said off!" The gun's threat left me as the weapon was directed aft. "Jesus, you can't stop her, all you can do is get us blown up with her! Shut it down or I'll—"

The outboard went silent, as a sharp knife blade nicked my wrist. Eleanor must have had more slack in her bonds than I'd hoped. I'd expected to have to help her, but she'd got it open by herself. She made a faint sound of apology for hurting me, which wasn't so bright; but I'd have been an unappreciative bastard to criticize her now. She was doing fine. She was doing great. I felt the blade working under my wrists. The tape relaxed its firm grip somewhat, although it remained stuck in place. Then the open knife was put into my fingers and I managed to draw a little blood from her, too, before I got it working in the right place at the right angle. . . .

Henry's voice spoke sharply, "He's turning, he's trying to turn. He's seen her!" He was staring at the lights ahead, now approaching each other fast as the courses converged. "Come on, you lousy lubber, it's about time you woke up on that fancy bridge; now get that wheel hard over. . . ."

I used the sound of his voice to cover the click of the closing knife, which I'd slipped into my pants pocket. It was smaller than I'd expected, smaller than I'd hoped; it really wasn't enough of a weapon for either of us to rely on. On the other hand, it couldn't be left lying in the boat to betray us, and pocket-bulges are less noticeable on gents than on ladies. Then there was only to keep the wrists close together so the cut tape wouldn't fall away prematurely; and to watch the sea drama unfolding across the black water. Even Eleanor allowed herself to raise her head and show a dull interest.

"Back her down!" Henry was still issuing orders. "Hard

302

astern, goddamn it; is everybody asleep down in that fucking engine room? Tack now, Missy! You're too close to go
overboard now, the blast would kill you in the water; but if
you bring her around fast, maybe you can still. . . . Tack
and cut that lousy arming switch. You don't want to die
like that, a nice young lady like you. . . ."

I watched with what might be called an ambivalent attitude. On the one hand, I didn't want another ship sunk,
not only for the ship's sake, but because this was supposed
to be a discreet operation all around, and another sinking
would blow everything wide open. But on the other hand,
I've never been sold on keeping people alive who want to
be dead in this crowded world; it doesn't seem quite fair to
people who appreciate living and could use the extra space
to do it in.

It was now clear that Serena Lorca had been heading for
this toward the start. She'd planned just a single suicide
mission but her father had given her the opportunity to
exact a greater revenge than she'd hoped for and she'd
accepted his offer. Now the job was finished and she was
going to wind up the operation exactly as she'd planned
from the start and rejoin her beautiful Ann in heaven, if
her beliefs inclined that way. At least she'd avoid all the
inevitable ugly hassles that came next; she'd go out clean,
vengeance accomplished.

The ship was beginning to swing now, turning toward us
to pass astern of the crossing sailboat. We could see the
space between the range lights diminish slowly, gradually
foreshortened by the changing angle. There was a distant
vibrating roaring sound over there; the enormous power
plant had been reversed at last. *Jamboree*'s attitude did not
change at all. I felt Eleanor's fingers grip my arm tightly as
the two light patterns came together over there.

In the Zodiac, nobody spoke, awaiting the unbearable
burst of light, the deafening clap of sound. Then, for a
moment, there was only one set of lights visible on the
dark ocean, those of the freighter. There was time to wonder if perhaps the fuse had failed and *Jamboree* had simply
gone down silently under the ship's bow. . . .

"There she is!"

Henry's voice was hoarse with emotion. We watched the red, green, and white sailboat lights appear again beyond the stern of the ship, the great bulk of which had briefly hidden them from view.

CHAPTER 34

THE sailboat's lights worked their way back toward us, directed by the big waterproof flashlight Adam shone that way from time to time. The outboard motor was running and Henry was steering to meet Serena's vessel, but he had to take it easy with a load of five passengers. There was some sea running and already we'd gotten thoroughly soaked as the blunt Zodiac bulled its way through the crests and butted them high enough for the wind to blow aboard. The level of the little lake in which we sat was rising; not dangerous in a rubber boat that would continue to float if filled to the top, but not exactly comfortable, either. I remembered Serena saying that she might possibly preserve our lives, but she certainly wouldn't guarantee our dryness.

The receding tanker was again merely a pretty cluster of twinkling lights off near the horizon. The officers on the bridge had probably, by now, even stopped swearing at the crazy little yacht that had forced them to take violent evasive action. Henry and Adam were discussing the weird idiosyncrasies of their employer. Henry thought she was a gutsy but messed-up kid who ought to be under the care of a good shrink, if there was such a thing. Adam thought she was a crazy bitch and who the hell cared what happened to a dame who fucked dames except that kind of dame?

They almost got into a fight about it, and lapsed at last into sulky silence.

Then *Jamboree* was tacking to leeward to us and shooting up to us, her sails breaking into thunderous flapping as Serena cast off the sheets—I caught a glimpse of her in the light of the binnacle and she had a pale destroyed look, as befitted a girl who'd sailed deliberately up to the gates of death only to have them close in her face. Of course, the impression was undoubtedly helped by the ghastly red color of the compass light. Henry laid us alongside the ladder that had been lowered again. Giulio, closest to the bow, tossed Serena the Zodiac's painter left-handed; and she gave it a couple of hasty turns around a cleat.

Came the old hostage gambit again, with a switch. Giulio aimed the big Browning directly at me and spoke to Eleanor,

"Up you go. No tricks or I'll blow a hole right through him."

Eleanor nodded dumbly, still sticking to her misery act. She made her way across the Zodiac and stepped up onto the big rubber float. Teetering there uncertainly, she made a grab for the stanchion she'd held before and hauled herself painfully up the ladder. I was very glad I'd stuck her little knife into my own pocket. Even in the darkness her drenched, clinging white slacks would have revealed any foreign object clearly. I noticed that she remembered to hold her wrists close together so as not to dislodge the tape or betray its sabotaged condition; just the same, I was happy that Serena, waiting above, wasn't her usual sharp-eyed self. She was still just going through the motions of being alive after deliberately offering herself up to a loud and violent death. Giulio followed Eleanor's upward progress warily without really shifting his attention, or his gun, from me. He waited until she'd dragged herself up to a kneeling position on *Jamboree*'s rail and, at last, managed to stand up on the deck beside Serena, breathless and dripping.

Serena seemed to shake herself a little, waking up to the present. "Okay, she's up. You can send up the man. . . ."

Giulio rammed the automatic into his pants, rose, turned, and jumped for the ladder. He pulled himself up a step and reached far out for the cleat that held the Zodiac's bow line, to cast it off. His intention was obvious. On *Jamboree* he had only two girls to deal with, one supposedly bound. He was turning loose the rubber boat holding three men, one supposedly bound, the other two armed only with knives. With his own pistol, and the shotgun that awaited him in the sailboat's cockpit, he should have no trouble keeping the girls under control or disposing of them quickly; then he could easily hold off the Zodiac until *Ser–Jan* came up to help him take care of it.

I ripped my hands free—there was a sickening moment when a strand of tape that had escaped the knife threatened to be too tough to break—and dove across the rubber boat, reaching for the ladder. I felt the Zodiac, freed, slide out from under me and skitter away as I got a precarious hold too far down. I dangled there for an instant with ocean up to my knees; then I got my feet against the sailboat's side and started walking up it like a monkey up a palm tree. A foot lashed out and grazed my head, but I could only duck and thank God that boat shoes are rubber-soled; I needed both hands for hanging on. The jointed ladder was bucking and swaying under the antics of two active men. I got a toehold on the bottom rung at last and tried to grab one of Giulio's ankles, but he kicked at me again and hauled himself onto the deck above and rolled over and came to his feet up there. He was dragging the gun from his waistband, and there was no way I could possibly reach him in time. . . .

Serena screamed. It was a pure shrill howl of total agony. Giulio wasn't quite pro-caliber after all; he couldn't help a glance that way. I heaved myself over the rail and lunged at his legs. Bringing the gun to bear again, he stepped back quickly to avoid me, forgetting where he was. His heel caught in the cockpit coaming and he tumbled backward into the well of the cockpit beyond. I had a glimpse of the two girls locked in battle. For a husky young woman of her offbeat sexual persuasion, Serena

306

fought in an oddly feminine manner, one hand tearing at her opponent's sweater, the other yanking at her hair; and she was sobbing loudly as she fought. The smaller girl was battling in grim silence. She seemed to be doing okay, even though she was overmatched; it was up to me to do as well.

But Giulio, disarmed and half-stunned by his fall, was no real problem. I simply grabbed the heavy winch handle I'd seen Serena use and beat in his skull with a single blow as he rose before me in a half-dazed manner. When you feel everything give under the club like that, you know there's no need to strike again. Serena screamed again, another high, cracking, uncontrolled shriek of pain. I glanced that way and saw that the two struggling figures had parted company. The smaller girl had been thrown off and the larger one was staring down at a bare foot covered with blood in the middle of which I could discern, even in the dark, a strange object that didn't belong there: the broken-off high heel of a woman's sandal. It had been driven clear through the foot like a spearhead. Obviously, the first scream had come with the original impalement; the second had been elicited by the agonizing wrench as Eleanor fell, leaving part of her sandal firmly lodged in the flesh and bone of Serena's foot.

An ugly expression of rage replaced the incredulity on Serena's face. She took a limping step toward her small opponent, who was just regaining her feet.

"Elly, catch!" I called, and threw the winch handle.

There was more light now, enough so Eleanor could see the steel crank coming. She grabbed it out of the air. I had no more time for her problems. Over the sound of the loudly flapping sails, I could hear that Henry had gotten the outboard going. I couldn't see the Zodiac anywhere; that meant it was somewhere off to leeward of all that loose canvas—well, dacron—and I knew that Henry would be using that blind spot to come to the rescue of his screwball lady skipper, whom he'd heard yelling with pain. Prepare to repel boarders. I rolled Giulio's body aside, hauled the shotgun out from under the retaining shock cords and wasted one shell pumping the action to make certain that it was working and that there was a round up the spout. There was. Apparently they'd been optimistic enough to store the weapon like that. Well, there are people who put their trust in gun safeties, and people who don't. The latter generally live longer.

I started forward to meet the attack, and checked myself. A sawed-off shotgun is strictly a close-up weapon. If Henry and Adam saw me waiting at the rail with the Winchester, they could sheer off and be out of range in a moment. Maybe I could put enough holes into the Zodiac to sink it, and maybe I couldn't. And maybe they couldn't swim a stroke, but maybe they were the original fishmen of Florida. It was all too damned uncertain and I still had *Ser–Jan* to cope with. I had to get rid of these two permanently before the big powerboat came up. I couldn't have them maneuvering around at a safe distance, in or out of the water, waiting to attack me from behind or simply joining forces with Arturo and Robert. The four of them, all together on the bigger, faster, and more maneuverable sportfisherman, probably with plenty of weapons on board, would be more than I could hope to deal with.

I ducked back down into the cockpit, therefore, waiting. Serena cried out again; for a tough lesbian lady she certainly made a lot of female-type noises. Glancing that way, I saw that she was staggering back with blood streaming down her face. The determined, disheveled figure of my little old combat buddy was moving in with the winch handle raised for another blow; then Serena, half-stunned and retreating blindly, fell back into the main companionway, caught herself for a moment, lost her hold and tumbled down out of sight. Eleanor dove down after her.

I was relieved to have her off the deck, because the outboard motor had stopped. I crouched down and waited. Adam was pretty good and pretty silent, but not silent enough. I could hear him coming, even with all the boat noises. When I rose up with the shotgun, he was just passing the aft end of the cabin, but it was not Adam I wanted —well, not first. When you're trying for a double on ducks, you take the distant bird first; that's the one that can get away. The close bird, to hell with that; you've got all the time in the world to take care of that. Of course, ducks don't generally come at you with custom knives.

I looked past Adam, now starting his rush, and there was Henry as I'd hoped, just advancing, crouched, under the great dancing spar of the main boom. I centered him and fired, pumped the action, swung on Adam and caught him in the middle of his headlong dive at me; but he was dead when he hit me, with a hole in his chest you wouldn't believe. I picked myself up and drew a long breath that wasn't, I'll admit, quite as steady as it might have been. I set the push-button safety of the shotgun. I found the loaded shell I'd ejected into the bottom of the cockpit. Working very systematically and not thinking at all, I wiped the blood off of it, using Adam's shirt, and fed it into the magazine, giving me three or four remaining, depending on how they'd had it loaded in the first place. I didn't take time to look. Unloading a magazine-type shotgun to count the rounds isn't a simple process; one reason why some people still like the old-fashioned double-barreled jobs where you can see exactly what you've got simply by opening the gun.

The firearms drill had steadied me. I looked up at last and saw Eleanor in the main hatchway, very pale, clinging there helplessly with her sweater torn off one shoulder, her hair wildly tangled and the bloody winch handle in one hand.

"I . . . couldn't." Her throat worked. "S-she's unconscious and I just c-couldn't. Oh, God, Matt, I never before. . . . I just went k-kind of c-crazy, I gu-gu-guess." Then the tears started rolling down her face.

I drew a long breath. I stepped over there, past Adam and Giulio or what was left of them, and slapped her hard.

"For Christ's sake!" I said contemptuously. "I thought you were the little girl who cut big guys' balls off just for fun." When she made no response, staring up at me with wide, wet eyes, I asked, "Can you shoot a shotgun?"

"I . . . I've shot a little s-s-s . . ." She licked her lips and tried again. "Skeet."

"Well, these aren't light skeet loads in this cannon," I said. "These are heavy buckshot loads and kick a lot harder. You've got to hold the gun tight to your shoulder and put your face tight against the stock. If you're all locked together tightly in one piece, gun and you, it won't hurt you; it'll just shove you back a little way. But if you hold it loosely and give it a running start at you, you can get badly bumped. Got that?"

When she nodded, I took the winch handle from her and put it back where it belonged. I took her by the arm, helped her out of the companionway, and led her forward, past Henry who didn't look very good, having taken most of a load of buckshot in the face. A clump of pellets that had missed him had done some damage to the big, flapping sail beyond, the genoa jib, shooting the lower rear corner—clew, if you must be nautical—right off it. It occurred to me to look for the Zodiac, but it was nowhere to be seen; apparently they hadn't taken time to secure it and it had drifted away into the night. Forward of the mast, I lay the shotgun down on the side deck, against the cabin trunk.

"You'll be lying sprawled on top of that," I said. "You'll be dead, understand? They'll bring Ser–Jan alongside to starboard, the other side; they have to approach from windward because of the boom and sails blowing out the other way. Now remember this—whichever one of them is at your end of the boat, their boat, the sportfisherman, he's yours. I'll take the other one from aft. Say they lay her alongside bow to bow, Robert is on the foredeck to handle the lines, and Arturo is up on the flying bridge. You take Robert and I'll take Arturo. On the other hand, if Robert works out of the cockpit, aft, he's mine. You get Arturo up on the bridge. We can't afford to waste time and ammo shooting at the same target, at least not until one of them is down. We've got to get them both and we've got to get them fast. You lie perfectly still until you hear somebody shoot; until then, you're dead. When the firing starts, you get up, clear to your feet. It takes a lot of practice to mount a heavy shotgun properly from any other position, so don't try. Get on your feet, brace a knee against the cabin if you like, get the gun shouldered right, get the muzzle on the target nearest to you, and pull the trigger. I'm shoving the safety to off so you won't have to worry about that—forget the safety. Just get to your feet, shoulder the gun well, aim carefully, and shoot. Then pump the action—this sliding handle here—and keep shooting until there's nothing left to shoot at."

There was a little silence. She licked her lips once more, watching me steadily. "I don't . . . like men who go around slapping girls, Matt."

"I know," I said. "But right now, you're not supposed to like me. You're just supposed to snap out of whatever wingding you were throwing and do what I tell you, for both our sakes. Okay? Now lie down and play dead."

She hesitated, small and stubborn. "All right, but I do think you . . . ought to apologize, really."

I said, "Yes, you're perfectly right. I'm very sorry I slapped you, Elly. Will you please forgive me?"

She looked at me gravely for a long moment. Then she nodded and lay down on the deck at the side of the low cabin, on top of the shotgun.

"Like this?"

I moved one of her legs a little. "That's very good . . . Elly."

"Yes?"

"I really am sorry. I'm glad you forgive me. Good luck."

"Good luck, Matt."

Returning to the cockpit, I looked around, but by now it was that funny dawn half-light in which you seem to have some visibility, but you can't really see anything. But there was an uneasy murmur of sound out there that didn't belong to *Jamboree*'s splashing hull, or creaking gear or ever-flapping sails.

I took a quick look around the cockpit, but Giulio's Browning was nowhere to be seen and I had a growing feeling of urgency. I ducked down into the cabin instead of spending more time searching for it. Serena was lying

311

sprawled on her back down there with considerable blood around both ends of her—the whole boat was lousy with blood—but she seemed to be breathing. I hoped she wouldn't come to and cause trouble at the wrong moment, but I sensed that I didn't have time to tie her. I yanked open the second drawer of the galley dresser and the .38 revolver was there as she'd promised; the gun that had once belonged to Peterson, defunct. There was, I reflected, getting to be quite an accumulation of defuncts in this operation.

I grabbed the weapon, checked the loads, and returned to the deck. The sound of powerful engines was now quite distinct. I didn't take time to locate the source; I merely draped myself untidily across the bridge deck just aft of the main hatch, face down, with my gun hand under me. Just another body, I hoped, added to the two already in the cockpit, and the two sprawled along the side deck to port. Just a ship of death with blood running from the drains or, if you must be nautical, scuppers.

They came in cautiously. I heard the diesels stop some distance off. The voice I'd heard over the radio, Arturo's voice, called out,

"Hey, Miss Lorca! Giulio. *Jamboree* ahoy!" A pause. "Hand me those seven-by-fifties. . . . My God! Jesus Everloving Christ! Take a look at that, will you? That must have been the shooting we heard. It's a fucking slaughterhouse!"

"Tout mort?"

"We'll have to see if they're all toot mort."

"I will go forward for the ropes—"

"You'll go aft for the ropes, Frenchy. I'm not bringing the bow in there. I want it clear, so I can blast off in a hurry, in case . . . I'll swing the stern in. You be ready in the cockpit to take a line out; I'll lay you right in close. You have your gun handy?"

"Oui, I have the pistol. And the knife."

"Don't make the jump until we're sure; somebody could be playing cute over there."

"I will be prepared."

312

"Hang out some fenders first, port side. No sense beating up the damned boats."

Lying there, I reflected that it was a gamble; but then it usually is. But there was no possible way I could avoid exposing myself to enemy fire here; I'd simply have to hope it missed. In my favor was the fact that shooting from one heaving boat at a target on another heaving boat is quite an exercise in marksmanship, since the pistol—and I hoped they had nothing else—is a fairly inaccurate weapon at the best of times. There was more on my side. The modern theory has it that the one-hand gun is really a two-hand gun. They all learn it that way now, and they're never really happy unless they can clap that second paw around a gunbutt that was originally designed only for single occupancy. Well, it's been proven that somewhat better shooting can be done that way—when the shooter has his feet firmly planted on solid ground. When the whole world is heaving and pitching and rolling, however, the gent who learned how to master a pistol waving uncertainly at the end of an unsupported arm has a certain edge, since he never expects to deal with a steady target or a steady gun, anyway. At least I hoped so, since that was the way I'd learned. And an edged-weapons specialist like Robert very often scorns the use of noisier implements and is not very good with them. Anyway, it was a reassuring theory. . . .

The soft, rubber-fendered bump of boat against boat came before I expected it. I wasn't ready. You're never really ready to be shot at. I reared up and a pistol blasted in my face and missed. I put two bullets into Robert's chest at five yards' range—hey, Fred, here's your boy—and he collapsed into the sportfisherman's cockpit. I swung the revolver left and up, toward *Ser-Jan*'s high flying bridge. I saw Arturo up there, saw his gun jerk and heard the report; and something hit me hard in the left thigh, throwing my shot off. Then the shotgun thundered up forward. Arturo staggered. I fired and thought I had a solid hit. The heavy Winchester blasted again. The man up on the flying bridge stumbled toward the engine controls; he had his hands on them when he was struck simultaneously by my

313

next bullet and the third blast of buckshot. He fell, still clinging to the black-knobbed levers up there. . . .

There was a sharp, snarling sound from the big twin diesels. *Ser–Jan* seemed to hesitate; then she lunged astern, giving the sailboat a glancing blow, and slid away backward at steadily increasing speed—Arturo must have hauled the controls to full reverse as he fell. I watched the big yacht recede in that strange, backward fashion for longer than there was any sense in; so a boat was sailing backwards, so what? I looked down dully and found my left pantleg bloody, and a small hole to port and one to starboard—since we were being so goddamn nautical. A foot higher and he'd have got me in the ass. Well, at least it had gone clear through instead of sticking around inside to make trouble. And while it seemed too bad to be wounded at the very end of all the action, I didn't dream of complaining. After all, it hadn't perforated a lot of meat, it had hit no bones, and it seemed to have cut no major arteries. Hell, I was alive, wasn't I? Maybe there's nobody supervising, helping, maybe it's all dumb luck, but if The Watchers should exist out there, somewhere, I'd be a fool to antagonize Them by displaying ingratitude.

I took out a soggy handkerchief and tied it around my thigh to check the bleeding a little. I limped forward to find the little girl sitting on the cabin with the shotgun on her knees. I took it from her and shucked the remaining shell out of it—apparently they'd had it loaded with six—and dropped it into my pocket, noting that it was 00 Buck, as I'd guessed. When she looked up, I was shocked to see that her face was smeared with blood; although I didn't know why a little more gore should shock me.

"Elly, what? . . ."

She sniffed and drew the back of her hand across her nose, streaking her face even worse. "Don't get excited, it's just a dumb nosebleed," she said. "That stupid gun jumped so much I couldn't hold it tight, and the recoil slammed my thumb right into my nose." She looked down and said softly, "I never killed anybody before. It feels so strange."

I said, "I know. But remember what I told you once.

314

There are people and there are enemies. That one wasn't people. The way you could tell, he was shooting at us."

"That's . . . just words, isn't it?" After a moment, still not looking at me, she asked, "Did we *have* to do it?"

"No, not really," I said. "Not if we were willing to let Serena sink another ship. Not if we were willing to let them kill us."

She licked her lips. "It's so very ugly, isn't it?" She looked up at last, and drew a long breath. "And I think I'm being so very silly. Matt?"

"What?"

She was looking down at her knees again. "I'm sorry," she said. "I know it doesn't help much, but I'm sorry, sorry, sorry."

"For what, for God's sake?"

"Don't be nice. You know what. I just did everything all wrong. . . . Oh, God, you're hurt!"

"Just a flesh wound, as we say in the trade."

"Please don't try to pretend," she said breathlessly. "I know what you're thinking; what you've got to be thinking. First, I. . . I couldn't hit her again, even though you'd given me explicit instructions. Then I went into hysterics so you had to slap some sense into me—my God, you'd think I was a silly kid instead of a grownup professional woman. It took me forever to get up and get that big gun lined up, so long that he had time to shoot you; and I couldn't even hold it right and got a bloody nose and it served me right and . . . and . . . oh, yes, that ghastly business at the start."

"What ghastly business at the start?"

"You know, that perfectly awful conversation. I'd been lying there all night just thinking what it would be like to die, be killed. I guess I was really pretty scared. Suddenly, I heard myself talking all that horrible, tasteless nonsense about . . . about how you mess yourself when you. . . . I'm sorry, Matt. I did try, I did my best, but I wasn't very good, was I?"

I stared at her helplessly. I knew there was absolutely nothing to be gained by telling her how very good she'd been—well, by the standards of the world in which I operated. There was, of course, another world that disapproved of young ladies who spiked people with high heels, clubbed them with winch handles, and blasted them with shotguns. I'd met young ladies from that world and I'd almost died for their fine humanitarian impulses. It was a revelation to encounter a female person bright enough to accept the face of violence, and brave enough to cope with it. But I couldn't tell her that. There was only one thing about herself she liked: she was rather proud of her professional attainments. As for the rest, she was that crummy little Elly Brand, ugly and spoiled and useless; and nobody was going to persuade her otherwise.

"Elly—"

"It's all right," she said calmly, "I said you didn't have to pretend. Now I think we'd better take a look at that hole in your leg, don't you? And see about that . . . that girl downstairs, only you say below on a boat, don't you?"

"Elly," I said, and looked at her streaked, small, stubborn face, and gave up. "Oh, hell," I said irritably. "No, let's get the sails down first, before a storm comes up or something. Anyway, I'm getting tired of listening to them flapping. But you'd better take a quick look at Serena and wrap some tape around her if she looks about to come to, while I'm trying to figure out all these ropes and cleats. . . . What is it?"

She was staring at something beyond me. "Look, it's coming back! It's going to run us down!"

I turned quickly. There was the sportfisherman, still in reverse gear, diesels still cranking out somewhere in the neighborhood of a thousand horsepower. She'd made a wide circle and now, as Eleanor had said, she was rushing straight at us, backward, rolling up a great wall of water with her blunt stern. I glanced around hastily. The sheet that controlled the big genoa jib had been blown away by buckshot, but the mainsail was still operative if things hadn't gotten too tangled; and there was a possibility of starting the auxiliary motor if I could figure out the controls. . . .

"Matt, look!"

I turned back to *Ser–Jan* and realized belatedly that there was something wrong with her attitude. The bow seemed higher than I remembered; the stern lower. Suddenly, I realized that the big yacht was sinking. There may be high-sterned powerboats that can survive backing at full throttle in the open ocean, but sportfishermen have low cockpits aft for fighting the fish and reaching over with the gaff. There were scuppers back there to drain the water out, of course, but even if they functioned with the boat crashing backward—and they might even operate in reverse at this speed, to let the water in—they could not possibly cope with the whole sea pouring over the transom, filling the cockpit and rushing forward into the deckhouse and cabin.

I felt Eleanor find my hand and grip it tightly. It was obvious now that we were in no danger; *Ser–Jan* was not going to reach us. Even as we watched, the stern sank lower and became totally submerged. Then the weight of the flying bridge and tuna tower took charge of the now unstable, half-filled hull, and the big yacht rolled over on her side and sank.

We saw Arturo's body float free of the bridge momentarily, before the suction pulled it down. We never did see what happened to Robert.

CHAPTER 35

I hadn't really let myself think beyond the actual break. I guess I'd vaguely imagined that once everything was under control, if it worked out that way, I'd simply push some kind of *Mission-Completed* button and watch the cleanup troops arrive within the hour to patch up the wounded, bury the dead, and take over all decisions and responsibilities; but, of course, it didn't work that way. For one thing, there wasn't any button. The only radio on board was the short-range VHF that Serena had used for ship-to-ship communication, good for about thirty miles. The last marked position on her chart showed the Bahamas, the nearest land, to be almost two hundred miles to the west.

For another thing, when the troops arrived—if they did arrive—I wanted to be sure they'd been briefed to keep their mouths shut about what they found; not an easy thing to arrange over the air, even if I could make contact with the U.S. It occurred to me that we weren't sinking, or even seriously incapacitated. Hell, Columbus had found America. Leif Ericson had found America. An Irish monk named Brendan was supposed to have found America. Why couldn't I? Once ashore I could drop the whole tricky problem in Mac's lap and wash my hands of it.

"What about the EPIRB?" Eleanor asked.

"What's an EPIRB?"

"That rescue beacon mounted next to the life raft, top-side," she said. "I told you about it, remember? Giulio said it was called an Emergency Position Indicating Radio Beacon, EPIRB for short. It's kind of like those little homers they were using, only bigger and more powerful. When your boat sinks, you just turn it on and it makes a noise on a couple of aircraft emergency frequencies and a jet flying over reports you to the Coast Guard."

I said, "First you need a jet flying over."

"It's good for a couple of hundred miles, Giulio said. The plane doesn't have to be right overhead. A lot of planes fly across the ocean."

"And then you've got to want the Coast Guard," I said. "I'm not sure I do. At least, not until I've alerted somebody at home to lean on them a little first. Otherwise, we're going to have too much publicity about the blood-stained murder yacht they picked up at sea loaded with corpses and explosives."

Eleanor hesitated. She spoke without looking at me. "You're not going to be able to keep it quiet, Matt. Not now. Not as long as *she's* alive." I didn't say anything, and Eleanor went on, speaking carefully, "You wanted me to kill her, didn't you?"

I said, "It did occur to me that it would be convenient. And to be cold-blooded about it, no real hurt to her—considering how she feels and what's in store for her ashore."

"And what it would do to me, having that on my conscience, too; that didn't matter a bit?"

I looked at her for a moment. "I said it occurred to me it would be convenient, if it happened that way. Am I supposed to close my eyes to the possibilities, Miss Brand? I did not say that I arranged it that way deliberately."

"But you—"

"I aimed you at the only opponent against whom you had a ghost of a chance," I said. "And I psyched you up to make the most of that chance. Hell, you weigh what, a hundred and ten, a hundred and fifteen? And you get your exercise doing what, punching the keys of a typewriter? And do you think you'd have lasted five seconds against a girl twenty pounds heavier, in practically Olympic condition, if you hadn't gone straight in for the kill like I told you? Look what you actually accomplished. You hurt her foot rather badly, you put a little crease in her scalp, and then you got lucky and she fell down a hatch and knocked herself out. Considering the weight you were giving away, that was a hell of a performance, but it was a pretty close decision, wasn't it? How do you think you'd have made out if you'd been hampered by a lot of sentimental reservations? Hell, that young Amazon lady would have wrung you out and hung you up to dry."

Eleanor was silent for a moment; then she nodded reluctantly. "All right. I'm sorry; I was wrong." She wasn't looking at me. She continued not to look at me as she said, still speaking very carefully, "But, of course, you can still fix it. Her. Repair the lousy job I goofed."

We were relaxing with a couple of stiff drinks in the main saloon, which had been cleaned up after serving as a field hospital—even Eleanor had a couple of Band-Aids on

319

her wrists where I'd nicked her, freeing her. Serena was lying on the leeward settee, literally bandaged head and foot. She still had not regained consciousness, but my amateur examination had indicated that the pupils of her eyes were of equal size and that there were no significant dents in her skull. We'd snipped away the matted hair and covered the scalp laceration as well as we could, considering the limitations of *Jamboree*'s first-aid kit. We'd gotten the thing out of her foot—a pair of pliers had been needed, and she'd been lucky to be unconscious—and packed and wrapped the foot, using up most of what was left of our one small roll of two-inch sterile gauze. This, after cleaning and bandaging the holes in my leg, which Eleanor had insisted on doing first. Now we sat side by side, regarding the girl across the cabin, aware of the dead men still on deck, of the sails we'd lowered that should be lashed down more securely, and of the other untidy gear and rigging that should be attended to up there. Without sails up, *Jamboree* was rolling heavily in the long Atlantic swells.

"That's right," I said agreeably. "Why didn't you think of it before we went to all the trouble of patching her up? But, gee, you're perfectly right, she's got to be eliminated. I guess I'd better get at it. What method do you suggest? Cutting her throat would be kind of messy after we've just mopped the place up, and she seems to have a pretty hard head. . . . Hey, I know, I'll just use a pillow like they did with that young guy in the hospital. If you'll excuse me, I'll just put one over her face and sit on her for a few minutes."

"Matt, stop it."

I glanced at her. "It was your suggestion. What's the matter, are you chickening out?"

She licked her lips. "Don't make fun of me. I never know. . . . I mean, you *do* kill people."

"So do you, now," I said, and saw her wince. Then I said, "To save the world from total annihilation, yes, I might consider it. Even just to preserve the United States of America from an overwhelming sneak attack, yes, I might consider it. But for a small intramural matter involving Mr. Pompous Jackass Bennett, forget it. If he wants

320

any helpless ladies murdered—any more helpless ladies murdered—he can murder them himself. Up to a point, I'll do my best to keep his antics quiet for the sake of the government of which I'm a part. I'll even make fine patriotic speeches on the subject, but what you suggest is getting a long way past that point. My real job here is to bring you back alive; the rest is strictly incidental." I grimaced. "Now I think I need one more drink before tackling the burial detail. Then we'll figure out how to start that auxiliary motor. I don't know much about sailing, but I have run a powerboat from time to time. If you don't mind, I think we'll just make a stab at finding our way back to civilization by ourselves."

"Civilization, and people who'll help you hush it all up." But she was smiling a little as she said it.

"And people who'll help me hush it all up as much as it can be hushed with the girl alive," I agreed, holding out my glass to be refilled.

On deck, we were careful and methodical as befitted a pair of landlubbers stuck in the middle of the ocean on a boat they didn't know how to handle. The sun was well up now and it was a bright clear day. We cleaned up the decks, and the less said about that the better. We got the shot-torn genoa off and bagged and put away in the sail locker under the cockpit seat. We furled the mainsail, lashed it to the boom and secured the boom. We did the same for the smaller forestaysail, forward, which had a little boom of its own. Eleanor, smaller and unwounded, got up in the narrow bow again and tied the working jib—over which the genoa had been set—to the protective stainless railing up there, so it wouldn't be blown overboard. Then we found the motor manual and read it carefully. We started the motor and, after it had warmed up for a little, with water spitting out of the exhaust as it was supposed to, and all instruments registering properly, we put it in gear. It ran for about a minute and came to a groaning, shuddering halt.

I tried it again, and it ran well in neutral, but stalled the instant it was put into gear. Finally Eleanor, who'd glanced down the side, beckoned me to the port rail and pointed down. I limped over there and saw a bar-taut rope leading down and aft, disappearing under the boat: the trailing genoa sheet I'd shot off, now neatly and tightly wrapped around our propeller. . . .

Half an hour later I caught Eleanor as she stumbled off the boarding ladder. She was shivering violently, naked except for a strap around her waist to which was attached Adam's fancy knife-sheath, empty.

"I'm sorry," she gasped as I wrapped a towel around her. "I'm just no damn g-good down there, and it's like hacking at iron, and I lost the stupid knife." She seemed to read my mind, because she looked up sharply and said, "And don't you *dare* get another knife and try it yourself, with that hole in your leg! If you get s-sick or infected or something. . . . What the hell are you looking at? Anybody'd think you never saw a nude lady before, Mr. Helm; and it isn't as if she were particularly attractive, pale green and all over goosebumps. Throw me those pants, will you? God, you wouldn't know they started out as an eighty-dollar pair of slacks!"

"Elly," I said.

"Now the sweater, please. I certainly don't have much luck with sweaters, do I? I wonder if this flossy yacht has a safety pin on board."

"Elly," I said.

She said, "I'm just so goddamned *useless*. Can't even cut a lousy piece of rope."

"Elly," I said.

She looked at me in a strange, blind way. Then she was sobbing in my arms and I held her and told her what a fine and brave and lovely girl she was, and she didn't believe a word of it, but the sobbing stopped. I pushed the towel-touseled damp hair back from her face and kissed her gently, and then not so gently. I felt her start to respond, and hesitate as if shocked and surprised at herself, and then yield herself fully to the kiss. Suddenly, we both knew that something that had been broken was mended, something that had been badly hurt was healed.

At last she turned her face away and pressed her forehead against my shoulder. "Oh, my dear," she breathed. "However did *that* happen?"

"Don't ask," I said. "What's your pleasure, ma'am?"

She shook her head minutely. "Not here," she whispered. "Not now. It's too soon after. . . . Unless you . . ."

"Your wish is my command."

"You're a very patient man."

"When something is worth waiting for," I said. "Well, so much for that. Let's get some sail on this barge. I was checked out on sailboats—small sailboats—about a hundred years ago. We had a boat course just for us spooks at the Naval Academy that included a little bit of everything. I've forgotten most of it, of course, but it can't be all that tough, considering the people who do it. I mean, they don't all look like geniuses to me. . . ."

Two instruments made it easy. The first was the boat speedometer, labeled a knotmeter. Once the sails were up, all I had to do was experiment until I got the highest possible reading on the dial, indicating that our windy power plant was operating at maximum efficiency. Soon the general principles of this means of propulsion returned to me; but I was still surprised at how far the sails should be let out. You'd think the harder you hauled them in, the faster the boat would go, but it definitely didn't work like that.

The second life-saving gadget was the fancy Loran navigation apparatus I'd seen Serena using. Once I'd figured out the instruction manual, there was nothing to it—just twiddle a few knobs and there were the latitude and longitude at a glance. How to be an instant navigator. The charts were no problem, of course; I'd dealt with nautical charts before in the line of business. I laid out a course north of the Bahamas that gave the nasty-looking reefs up there a wide berth. By evening, things were pretty well under control. If it had not been for Serena, and the hole in my leg, I would have enjoyed myself thoroughly, learning how to manage a big handsome boat while basking in the admiration of a small pretty girl.

But the other girl was a nagging worry. I had no idea what was going on in her mind. She had taken up residence in the forward cabin where we'd been kept, and she seemed to be in a kind of zombie state that was as much a reaction, I thought, to her frustrated suicide attempt as to the knockout blow she'd received. There were a lot of unpredictable forces trapped inside that handsome, bandaged, young head—I had to keep reminding myself that the girl was still in her early twenties. I would have been happier if she'd been tied hand and foot, but with a forty-foot boat to sail, ignorant as we were, we simply had no time to look after her. So Miss Lorca was left free to find her way to bathroom and galley as her metabolism indicated. As for my bullet wound, it made sitting painful; and you do a lot of sitting on a sailboat.

Nevertheless, it was an interesting experience—if a little intimidating—after darkness fell and there was nothing to be seen but the glow of the running lights, the compass light, the stars overhead, and the dim horizon. We'd figured out how to work the automatic pilot, so there was really not much to do but watch and let *Jamboree* sail herself. We took turns sleeping on the cockpit cushions. Shortly after midnight, Eleanor woke me to show me a ship's lights in the distance, but they passed far astern.

Near morning, the stars disappeared in a large sector to the west, and lightning began to flash in the black area. I woke Eleanor and we fumbled all the sails down, finishing just as it started to rain. We made a dash for the cabin as all hell broke loose. Eleanor joined me on the main cabin settee after checking all the ports and hatches. She reported that Serena was asleep or pretending. We sat there holding hands like scared children while the rain sluiced down and the lightning blazed and the thunder crashed and the wind screamed in the rigging, while *Jamboree* rolled and pitched in a crazy manner. I guess we were both just waiting for the hull to break wide open and water to start pouring in, but nothing happened. After about an hour the storm simply stopped. We stuck our heads out the main hatch, cautiously, and found weak daylight. The boat was washed clean of the last traces of the battle that had taken place on board.

The squall had killed the wind, so there was nothing to be gained by re-setting the sails at the moment. After Eleanor had cooked us a good breakfast, however, we ran them all up and tried to work our way west and somewhat north, using the vagrant breezes that never lasted long enough to really get her going. I decided that there was, after all, something to be said for the internal combustion engine. I left Eleanor in charge and went below for another navigation check, which showed that we hadn't moved much since the last one. I poured myself a cup of coffee and wished my leg would stop aching, reminding myself again that the bullet could easily have damaged some part of me for which I had much greater affection than the back of my thigh. Sorry Fellows. Didn't mean to seem ungrateful. But how about a little wind if You've got some to spare? . . .

"Matt, you'd better come up here." Eleanor's voice was calm enough, but I knew she wouldn't ask me to haul my damaged limb up that ladder just to light one of the cigarettes she'd found to keep her company during the long night watches. When I stuck my head out the hatch, she pointed. "What about that?"

The ship was a small gray smudge on the northern horizon. I got out the binoculars to examine it, climbing up into the cockpit for a better view. Before I could see more than that the vessel was heading our way, I heard a husky laugh behind and below me.

"Congratulations, you've got a live one," Serena's deep voice said. "Good luck, kiddies."

She was standing in the hatchway watching the distant ship. She had a battered, rakish look with the clumsy bandage on her head, but her tanned face was no longer gray and her eyes had come to life. Seeing me looking, she made the usual unnecessary gesture of tugging up her unsupported bodice, rather grubby by this time, like her shorts.

I said, "Hell, you can't tell yet—"

325

"The masts are in line," she said calmly. "The bearing isn't drawing aft and it isn't drawing forward; I've been watching through the porthole. And you've messed up my engine and you're not going anywhere without any wind, so it's strictly up to him. You can hope he hasn't stepped out for breakfast, leaving it all to Iron Mike or Electronic Eddie. You'll know in about ten minutes. Like I said, rotsa ruck."

She started to step down. I asked quickly, "Any advice, Miss Lorca?"

She stopped and looked back at me. "Why the hell should I give you advice? You know what I want, what I really want. To hell with the public relations bit; that was just a cute wrinkle I thought up to make them sweat, make Daddy sweat." She grinned maliciously. "Miss Lorca will await developments in her private stateroom. If we don't meet again, it's been a pleasure, I'm sure. I'll be so happy to know that you learned what it's really like. Maybe then you'll understand—if only for a few seconds."

She disappeared below. I glanced at Eleanor and saw that the ugly question that had come into my mind had also entered hers. I really should have tied the girl up and to hell with whether or not she starved or wet the bed because we didn't have time for her. I eased myself painfully down the ladder and limped forward, opening the door to the little bow cabin. Serena had already stretched out on the starboard bunk that had been mine for a while. She was studying her bandaged foot. She spoke without turning her head.

"You're really quite good, Helm," she said. "How did you get that little girl to fight like that? She hurt me so damned badly at the start that I never really. . . . Screaming and sobbing like a little kid. I'm not like that, really. It was just such a ghastly surprise, that sudden excruciating pain. . . ."

I said, "The arming switch for the proximity fuse. Where is it?"

She turned slowly to look up at me. "Do you really think I'll tell you?"

"Is it turned on?"

"Of course."

I said, "But you turned it off after that last abortive run. You wouldn't have sailed back to pick us up with the fuse still armed. So you must have gone to it just now, after you saw this ship coming. It can't be too hard to get at. Where?" She didn't speak. I said, "You've proved you don't like pain very much, Serena. Don't make me work you over. You just think Elly hurt you. You haven't seen anything yet. Or felt it."

It's not something I enjoy doing; but sometimes it has to be done. Even if I hadn't cared what happened to the oncoming ship, I wasn't going to have Eleanor killed by this vengeance-happy girl, not to mention the fact that I also preferred to go on living as long as possible. And even if the present ship was no real threat—I couldn't quite bring myself to believe that there was any danger of it running us down in broad daylight—I wasn't about to sail around in a boat that could erupt like a volcano any time a large chunk of steel came near it. I had to get that circuit broken before I got into more crowded waters. I might as well get the job done right now.

I had her wrists before she realized what I intended, but she was a hell of a strong girl and I couldn't keep her pinned down. She slammed a knee into my injured leg quite deliberately and I felt sickness go through me. All the time I was aware that, out in another world from this tiny cabin filled with grunts and gasps and moans, there was a ship approaching rapidly. . . . Well, two could play that game. I threw my whole weight on top of her and kicked out three times before I found the bandaged foot. Her breath went out in a silent scream and she went slack under me.

I became suddenly aware that the disaster she'd been at such pains to prevent for so long had finally occurred during our struggle. The elastic bodice had slipped clear to her waist, just a wide red belt now, leaving her breasts uncovered. They were very fine, brown and firm and wonderfully shaped. I was suddenly very much aware of her, and of my own automatic reaction to her—Gentleman Helm, the solicitous chap who cleaned up after distressed young ladies, comforted them chastely, and refused to take any advantage of them seemed to have gone off somewhere. I knew that she was aware of my awareness, and of her own semi-nudity. Something odd happened in her eyes: she seemed to leave me abruptly for another dimension. There was a period of silence, and the voice that broke it was not the husky contralto I knew.

"Daddy, you're making me all *bare* and it isn't *nice*!" It was a high girl–child voice. "Oh, no, you really mustn't *do* that again, Daddy, *please* not that thing that hurts. . . ."

Then her eyes found mine once more. Suddenly they were quite adult and sane; and she knew what she had said and what she had betrayed. And we both knew that I'd found the leverage I needed. I didn't have to twist any arms or break any fingers. All I had to do was unbutton and unzip her shorts and yank them off with whatever she wore underneath and pretend, just pretend, to do the thing that came next. Rather than run the slightest risk of being subjected to that dreadful thing men did, that had happened to her as a little girl, she would tell everything she knew. . . .

I drew a long breath. After all, it was not, as I'd told Eleanor, as if the fate of the world were at stake. I mean, it was only a question of Eleanor and me and a lousy ship and a few dozen crummy sailors; nothing of any real importance. I released her, she went for me wildly and I used a short hard blow to the jaw to knock her cold. I got the hell out of there and ran right into the loose swinging door of the bathroom—head if you prefer—as I stumbled into the narrow corridor outside. I slammed it aside in a panicky way, fleeing that place; and it jumped right back at me. I got control of myself and started to close it very gently and firmly so it would stay closed, and stopped.

Inside the little cubicle, on the fancy control console of the fancy john, a red light glowed.

Okay, so somebody had used the can, and the last of the

shit-eating compound, as Giulio had called it, had gotten used up, and now the refill light was on. . . . But who'd been in here since I'd performed my morning duties? Not Eleanor. Not I. And Serena had not had time to indulge in any serious processes of elimination between the time I'd been called on deck and the time she'd made her appearance at the main hatch. The apparatus hadn't been operated, anyway. You could hear it flush all over the boat, particularly on a calm day like this. And while the boat was being rebuilt, and the new head was installed according to law, all kinds of strange hookups could have been made. Who'd think of explosives and danger in connection with the controls of a fancy marine toilet?

"Matt!" There was urgency in Eleanor's voice.

"Coming," I called.

"It isn't turning. It isn't changing course at all!"

"Coming."

I pushed the button and the red light went out. I hurried aft and found the big main switch for all the boat's electricity and turned that off, too, although it was probably a waste of time. She would have had a special, direct circuit run that would not be spotted if somebody had to check out the regular wiring.

"Matt, please!"

I forced my bad leg, throbbing painfully from Serena's blow—she'd started it bleeding again—to take me up the companionway ladder. I stopped halfway out, shocked at what I saw. I mean, I have after all, as they say, looked death in the eye a few times in my life. I've stared into the muzzles of rifles of various calibers, pistols ranging all the way up to .44 and .45 Magnum, and shotguns single and double. I'd always thought that for real menace there was nothing to beat the twin muzzles of a double-barreled large-bore shotgun. But the thing that was bearing down on us was death in the double-king-sized package, blind and remorseless; thirty or forty thousand tons of tanker rumbling toward us across the calm sea, close enough now that we could hear the roar of the bulbous bow splitting the water.

329

I noticed that the ship was riding high, heading south, empty except for ballast, presumably to pick up a cargo in Aruba or Venezuela.

Slowly, because there was no hurry now—there was obviously nothing to be done—I stepped out into the cockpit and went to stand beside Eleanor at the wheel, putting an arm around her. She felt small and firm and warm and I realized that I was very fond of her.

"I think I got it. Keep your fingers crossed," I said.

She nodded, staring at the onrushing ship. "But he's *got* to see us!" she protested. "What's the matter with the idiot, is he blind?"

I said, "Hell, he's doing the ship's accounts, or writing up the log or something. He doesn't care. It won't hurt him a bit." A slow rage was growing inside me. "Like Giulio said, big bastards think they own the fucking ocean."

"Should we . . . jump?"

I thought about it and shook my head. "Ride it out on the boat. Hang on tight. Maybe we'll be washed aside or something. What the hell chance have we got in the water, anyway, way out here over a hundred miles offshore, even if we don't get sucked into his propeller?"

It was very close now, towering above us. *Jamboree* lay almost still on the glassy ocean, sails slack. It seemed idiotic that there was nothing to do. I had a belated thought of the radio, but if he wasn't looking it seemed unlikely he'd be listening—and it was too late for him to avoid us anyway. I thought of the shotgun below with one shell left, and the revolver with three. I regretted the Browning with fourteen, but I'd never found that; it must have gone overboard. It would have been a pleasure to at least leave the bastard a few bullet holes to remember us by. But there was no time for that now.

"Matt," Eleanor said.

"What?"

"You're a nice guy. I've been wanting to tell you."

"Don't take a vote on the subject. You'd lose. But I like you, too. In a moment, we're going to lie down in the

330

bottom of the cockpit and hug that steering wheel post or whatever you call it. . . ."

I stopped. *Jamboree*'s forward hatch was opening. We saw the hands first, and then the bandaged dark head, and the whole girl as she heaved herself out and sat on the edge of the hatch for a moment, staring at the onrushing tanker that was now blotting out a large sector of the northern sky. She scrambled up and ran, limping, for something on the side deck—the boathook. It seemed like a stupid reaction, as if all those tons of metal could be fended off by a lousy little boathook, for God's sake!

I could see now the way it was going to be. The bow was not going to hit us, not quite, and there was a chance we'd be pushed clear by the great white Niagara of water foaming off the weird-looking bulb they have up there. At least we were lying pretty well, not crosswise, presenting the smallest target possible, facing the immense murder weapon aimed at us. Serena had taken up a position on the forward deck, port side, with the boathook in her hands. . .

Then it was on top of us, and the towering bow went by terrifyingly close. The sides were black and rusty and there was a lot of red bottom paint showing, not in very good condition. The name was *Elmo Trader*. I thought I would undoubtedly remember that name as long as I lived; but under the circumstances, the memory cells might not have the chance to retain it very long. Serena moved.

I saw her step forward as *Jamboree* lifted to the roaring bow wave. She raised the long boathook over her head with both hands, holding it poised and balanced as she watched the ship's side approach—we were not going to be shoved clear after all, not far enough clear. There were endless miles of ship still to come; and the high wall of steel was coming inexorably closer. Serena braced herself. I could see now what she had in mind. She was not going to fend the monster off. She'd forgotten all about blowing it up. She was simply going to kill it. She was Captain Ahab driving the lance into the back of the great white whale. She was the cave woman fighting beside her mate, plunging

331

the stone-tipped spear into the heart of the charging mastodon. I saw her arch her body and strike with all her strength, just as *Jamboree*, having rolled wildly away from the ship, rolled back.

The mast swung into the passing wall of steel. The rigging caught on something high up there and was ripped away as if the heavy stainless wire and thick aluminum spars were mere strings and toothpicks. I threw myself down into the bottom of the cockpit well with Eleanor and locked an arm around the steering standard. Rigging wires were still snapping with loud twanging sounds, or ripping their attachment points out of the fiberglass hull. I heard a heavy metal object, torn loose, scream through the air above us with the wavering sound of a ricocheting bullet. Then the whole boat jolted violently as the hull made smashing contact with the ship's side, scraping and slamming and pounding along the rusty plates. I heard the beat of the great propeller, like a giant heart, gradually getting closer. It went by, an enormous wave threw *Jamboree* on her beam ends, drenched us in the cockpit and it was over, it was past.

I lifted myself cautiously. The ship was pulling away. It showed no signs of stopping. *Elmo Trader*, Monrovia, was lettered across the receding stern.

"*Elmo Trader*." I didn't recognize the voice that spoke. I knew now what had motivated Serena Lorca, and I thought she'd really had hold of a swell idea; but not being a sailor, I'd have to tackle it in a slightly different fashion. "Have fun, *Elmo Trader* of Monrovia," I whispered. "Enjoy. Until the people start falling dead in the streets." I swallowed hard. "I'm going to get those bastards, Elly. I'm going to get every last incompetent slob of them. I'm going to take leave and hunt them all down one by one; hell I've got a vacation coming. I'm going to start with the grease monkeys and cook's helpers and work up. By the time I get to the lousy sleepwalking captain he'll be changing his pants and reaching for the booze every time somebody slams a door. He'll know it's coming and I'll make sure he knows why. . . ."

"Matt."

I looked at her blankly. "What?"

"Matt, the boat is sinking. We'd better get that life raft over and activate the EPIRB." When I looked around, coming out of my berserk seizure and remembering something, someone, Eleanor shook her head. "No. She's gone."

Late the following day the Coast Guard found us. I was feverish by that time; the hole in my leg was going bad. I remembered that Serena had referred to them contemptuously as the Crap Cops or something, but I was very happy to see the lean white ship with the orange stripe. All that bothered me was what the hell I was going to tell everybody. It turned out that I didn't have to worry. As they lifted me aboard I found Brent bending over me, giving me the small private signal that indicated that everything was under control. He had a funny patch of bandage in his red hair, I noticed; a souvenir of his airport-parking-lot experience. The strangest thing was that Martha Devine was with him. After looking at me for a moment with an expression I found puzzling—what did she have to feel guilty about, anyway?—she turned quickly to speak to Eleanor, who was being wrapped in a gray blanket.

I couldn't figure all that; but I didn't have to. The cleanup troops had arrived.

CHAPTER 36

GIUSEPPE VELO'S improbable blond companion was wearing a snug blue satin jumpsuit that covered her from neck to wrists, and from neck to ankles, without a wrinkle. It was totally unadorned except for a big gold zipper down the front with a big gold ring on it, and her name embroidered in neat gold script where a breast pocket might have been: *Wanda*. She led me out onto the penthouse sundeck where the old man lay in one of the long chairs with nothing on but a pair of white shorts. He looked like a scaly brown lizard that had died and dried out in the desert sun. He sat up when she spoke to him and looked at the cane I was using to support part of my weight as I stood there.

"Looks like you didn't jump fast enough, ha!" he said.

"You should see the other guy, sir," I said.

"You have something you want me to read?"

"Yes, sir," I said.

I took it out and gave it to him. He snapped his fingers and the girl in the shiny jumpsuit produced a pair of heavy horn-rimmed glasses, which he set on his beaky nose, very carefully. There was silence while he read. I would have liked to sit down, but I wasn't going to ask any personal favors of Giuseppe Velo. But it had been a bad one after all, considering the relatively minor nature of the wound— they'd had to go in and dig out scraps of this and flakes of that and put drains in. I hadn't reacted properly to this antibiotic so they'd had to try that one; and after everything going right for a while, everything had gone wrong for a while. Well, you can't expect Them, assuming that They do exist, to spend all Their time looking after you. Velo looked up at last.

"I'd like a copy of this. When are you planning to break the story?"

I shook my head. "We are not planning to break the story, and we are not passing out copies. This is not a blackmail threat, Mr. Velo. I can tell you in confidence that, for reasons that don't concern you, this confession will not be used against Lorca, no matter what."

"Then why waste my time with it?" He smiled thinly. "I see. You want old Seppi to pass the word along."

I nodded. "I thought you and your associates would like to know what kind of a crazy man you've been spending good money on. Ask your friends if they really want to keep propping up a figurehead guy who'll risk everything by playing games like this behind their backs; and who may not be useful too much longer, anyway."

Velo said, "We never did find anything wrong with his health. All our sources say he's made a practically perfect recovery against all expectations, ha!"

I said, "Maybe you didn't tap the right sources, Mr. Velo."

The hooded eyes studied me bleakly for a long time; then the skull-head nodded abruptly. "Nobody listens to old Seppi Velo anymore. But I'll pass the information along, for what it's worth."

"Thank you, Mr. Velo."

"Are you seeing him soon?"

"I have an appointment with Mr. Lorca at four o'clock."

"It should be something to see," he said, watching me closely. "You're a goddamned mealymouthed hypocrite, Helm."

I said, "That's the best kind to be, Mr. Velo."

"Get the hell out of here."

At the door, the girl in satin said, "He likes you. He wouldn't call you names if he didn't like you."

"You just made my day, Wanda," I said.

A taxi took me to the same Miami hotel as before, and an elevator took me to the floor on which the hospitality suite was located; but I had to walk down the hall to the door all by myself. Well, it was about time I learned how. Outside the door was a neat young man I didn't know. Inside the door was an older, sloppier man I did know—Burdette, who'd been along on the Great Houseboat Raid in the course of which his colleague Lawson had died at the hands of some dirty blackmailing terrorists. Official version. He showed me no hostility; but no friendship, either. We both knew how Lawson had really died, and you don't buddy up to a guy who's killed one of yours, no matter what kind of a slob he happened to be. At the other end of the room, just as if nothing had changed in the time that passed, were Mac and Bennett, the latter with the same cropped head but uneasy, angry eyes.

"I hope you're feeling better," Mac said to me.

335

"It's good to be up and around," I said.

"Mr. Bennett wanted to see you. I think he wishes to apologize for a certain misunderstanding."

"Misunderstanding," I said. "Yes, sir."

Bennett said, "I'm sorry, Helm. It was . . . a mistake. I'm sorry."

Mac said, "I think Mr. Bennett also wishes to express his appreciation of, and his thanks for, certain services you seem to have rendered him in the course of your latest assignment."

Bennett said, "Thank you, Helm. I'm very. . . ." He choked on it, but he got it out. "I'm very grateful."

Mac said smoothly, "I'm sure Mr. Helm is pleased to have been able to help, and entertains no hard feelings for the unfortunate incident. We won't take up any more of you time, Bennett."

We watched him go out, followed by his escort. Mac said softly, "Down, Rover."

"Yes, sir," I said. "Down. Yes, sir."

"About that ship you wanted located, with the names and addresses of her crew. I hope you have reconsidered that foolishness."

"Big bastards think they own the fucking ocean," I said. I grimaced. "Okay, I'm over it. Forget it."

"Mr. Warren Peterson seems to have gone fishing on a yacht that seems to have gone missing. Very unfortunate for him, and for his friends and family, who have been making inquiries." Mac studied my face for a moment. "I assume that was necessary, Eric."

"It seemed so at the time, sir."

"I'd call it borderline, myself," he said. "But the judgment of the agent on the spot governs, as long as that judgment seems to be reliable. A successful operation is generally considered evidence of reliability, so we'll leave it at that."

It was a gentle, if you want to call it that, reminder that berserk retaliation schemes and personal vendettas were frowned upon.

336

"Yes, sir," I said.

"And we have Miss Brand under light surveillance, for safety's sake. Her safety. The Bellton Hotel, New York. No hostile attentions of any kind reported." Mac studied me for a moment and went on carefully, "After the experiences you shared, one would think she would keep in touch with you."

He didn't often display curiosity, but I could see that he wondered if perhaps I'd made a too-heavy pass at the girl when she was under my protection out there at sea, or just repelled her by too-violent efforts on her behalf. I couldn't help him out. I was wondering myself.

I said, "Yes, one would certainly think so, wouldn't one?"

He smiled almost imperceptibly and said, "Well, if you feel competent to wrap it up, Eric, I think it's about time."

"Yes, sir," I said.

The Lorca winter residence in Miami—officially, of course, he lived much farther north—was the same kind of instant waterfront I'd seen down in the Keys: a dredged, well-bulkheaded canal with boats tied up conveniently at the bottoms of green manicured lawns. The house was not as big as I'd expected, but it had a great deal of glass that would, I thought, create problems during a hurricane. But then, he wouldn't be in residence here during the hot hurricane season. I told the taxi to wait and I told the man who opened the door—who acted like a movie butler but looked as if he could use a knife if he had to—that the Senator was expecting me.

He led me through an elaborate living room with a glass wall into what was apparently the Master's Study. There were guns and heads on the walls. I don't have a great deal of faith in anyone who makes a big point of not having guns around and not killing anything—with a can of Raid in the kitchen and raw steer meat in the freezer—but I have even less faith in anyone who fakes the sporting bit and buys the stuff at auction. Lorca was sitting at the big desk and pretending to be working hard at something. He kept right at it. The butler-type indicated a chair and left me to observe the great man at his labors.

I had to hand it to him. He'd accomplished a lot in the way of self-improvement since I'd last seen him down in Mexico, when he'd impressed me as merely a well-dressed meaty thug with a few more brains than most. His long hospital ordeal had fined him down; he looked lean and hard and almost handsome. I would use the word distinguished if I'd ever figured out exactly what it meant. There was a kind of intensity about him that he hadn't had before. And, of course, there was the scar and the dramatic streak of white in the black hair. He was wearing the pants of a summer suit and a white dress shirt without a tie, sleeves rolled up loosely. The jacket and tie were draped over the arm of the naugahyde sofa against the wall—apparently the butler-type's duties did not extend to hanging things up neatly. I noticed that Lorca did everything very much right-handed, using the left only to hold things down clumsily so the right could operate on them.

"Long time," he said at last, looking up. "How many years, Helm?"

But I wasn't there to indulge in happy reminiscences. I rose and passed his daughter's confession across the desk and went back to my chair to let him read it. Finished, he shoved it back toward me irritably.

"You're bluffing," he said. "You won't use that. The speedboat thing, how are you really going to prove it was done on my instructions, and not just because a crazy girl thought it might please her daddy? And she made an anonymous phone call and sent an anonymous letter and fed some information to a reporter, big deal. In the big thing, her own thing, the ship thing, maybe you can trace some of the money she used to me, but you've still got to prove I knew what it was being used for. And you can't afford to open that can of worms, can you, considering that the official explanation. . . ." He stopped. After a moment he went on as if nothing had happened. "The

338

official terrorist explanation for that has already gotten a lot of publicity. You can't afford. . . ." He stopped again, and waited, and went on, "You can't afford to change it now."

"That's official," I said. "I'm here unofficially. Seppi Velo has read that. He's consulting some people you know better than I. We should be getting their reaction pretty soon. You have two things to worry about. One, that they won't like what you've done in the past. Two, that they won't like what we'll do in the future. Because they know that with that much provocation we'll keep after you until we get you, Lorca, and they can't be sure just how many people we'll manage to involve before we bring you down as a matter of self-preservation." I shook my head. "I won't venture to guess which way they'll jump. But in the meantime, let me offer my deepest sympathy."

He frowned. "For my daughter? For Serena? You think I give a damn about the girl after she did *that* to me?" His left hand made an awkward gesture toward the incriminating confession on the desk.

"And what did you do to her?" I asked.

His eyes stared at me across the desk. "Never mind my. . . ." Pause. "Never mind my daughter. Sympathy for what?"

"It's too damn bad," I said. "It was a brave effort, Senator, and although I have reason not to like you, I certainly admire the way you fought your way back after what happened to you, but. . . ."

His eyes were narrow. "What the hell are you trying to say?"

I rose again, picked up the confession, and dropped another piece of paper on the desk. "Of course, you'd try to keep it secret as long as possible, I understand that. Progressive deterioration is not a nice thought, is it? Of course, it's all described in the proper medical terms there, but that's what it amounts to. You must have known it would have to come out sooner or later."

He looked down for a moment, reading, and lifted his

head abruptly and glared at me. "That's a god . . . a goddam lie! A lousy medical fake! There's nothing wrong with. . . ."

The telephone rang. He swept it toward him with his clumsy left arm, and picked it up with his right hand.

"Who? Yes, of course I'll talk to. . . . Yes, this is. . . . What?" He glanced at me sharply as he listened. Seppi Velo's timing had been very good; but it was not Seppi's old-man voice rattling the earpiece of the phone. I saw sudden perspiration appear on Lorca's forehead. "But it's all f-finished. . . ." He beat on the desk with his good hand in anger at the disability that prevented him from expressing himself fluently. "It's all finished and forgotten," he protested, with a glance at me that showed it was far from finished and forgotten. "It was something I had to do but it's done, all over. Just because some busybody government snoops. . . . Just because old Seppi's hated me for years. . . . You can't throw away everything we've. . . ." He was silent, listening. He licked his lips. He spoke very quietly when he spoke again, "Yes, I understand. Yes, I know what's expected. No, if that's the decision, of course, I. . . . No. Yes. Yes, I understand what must be done. I understand very well. Yes."

He put the phone down gently with his right hand and swept the set aside with the left arm and sat there for a moment looking straight ahead.

"You bastard!" he whispered. "There's not a goddamned thing wrong with my health! If it hadn't been for that, for the goddamned suspicions you'd planted, they wouldn't have let the other stuff bother them."

I took out the long-barreled Colt Woodsman I'd brought along, and laid it gently on the desk. "A present from a lady, Lorca," I said. "She used it very effectively, so I know it'll do a good job for you. And considering that medical report, which I assure you will stand up as well as it has to, everybody'll understand. You won't even have to write a note. Goodbye, Senator."

There was a very cold place in the middle of my back as I walked out of the room; but I didn't think he could jack

340

the single .22 Long Rifle Hollowpoint cartridge, that was down in the clip, up into the chamber fast enough. It's a two-handed job, and he didn't quite have two hands to work with. But he would make it eventually, I was sure, or find another gun fully loaded. He would not dispute the verdict that had been handed down, the sentence that had been imposed, they hardly ever do. They know there's no appeal, simply a choice between hard and easy, and mostly they prefer it easy.

The small muffled crack that I heard as the taxi drove away let me know that he had managed to use the .22, Harriet Robinson's gun. I told myself that he'd had it coming many times over. I told myself that alive he'd been a serious threat to the well-being of the nation I served. I told myself it was a good job discreetly performed, according to instructions. I told myself that if I kept saying that long enough maybe eventually I'd start feeling good about it. . . .

The Bellton Hotel was small and inconspicuous outside, some distance away from the main New York action; and inside it was a quiet and pleasant place. The gray-haired woman at the desk said that Miss Brand was indeed in her room, which I knew. After using the house telephone, she informed me that Miss Brand would see me, which I hadn't known, not for sure, not after the strange way she'd disappeared without explanations or farewells. Room 512. I rode up in the tiny elevator and the door was ajar when I got there. I knocked anyway. The voice I remembered very well, although it was not as distinctive as some I'd heard recently, told me to come in.

She was standing by the dresser lighting a cigarette. She was not, of course, the bedraggled stringy-haired little castaway I'd last seen, barefoot, wearing only a torn blue sweater pinned at the shoulder, and grimy white slacks rolled to the knees. This was a respectable professional woman in a neat blue linen suit and a white silk shirt open at the throat. Her nylons were very smooth, and her blue pumps had very high heels. Her hair was combed very

341

smooth, too, in the businesslike way I remembered. There was a bare hint of lipstick on her mouth. But her nose still showed little pinky signs of having peeled recently.

The funny thing was, I couldn't really see her clearly. I recalled looking at a very small picture once and finding certain flaws in the face it represented. I remembered meeting a smallish girl in a hotel room and considering that her appearance was pretty good in some respects but not so good in others. But that critical faculty seemed to have deserted me. All I saw when I looked at her was Elly Brand; and there wasn't any way I wanted her changed. She was fine the way she was.

"It's considered polite to say goodbye when you go away," I said, closing the door behind me.

"I waited around until they told me you were going to be all right," she said. She glanced at the cane. "Are you . . . is it really all right?"

"It's supposed to be, eventually," I said. "You're kind of erratic, aren't you, Elly? Taking off to the Bahamas like that. Taking off to New York like that. The impulse girl." I looked at her hard. "An odd thing about those impulses, doll. They always seem to hit you when Martha Devine shows up. A very strong positive correlation, as we statisticians say. I had plenty of time to put it through the mental computer, lying in that damn hospital bed. After running all the calculations and computation, I came to the conclusion that you didn't really light out for Nassau like a spoiled little girl just because the big boys wouldn't let you go on a nice raid with them."

She said, "Why did you come here, Matt? The job is finished, isn't it? I saw on TV that Senator George Winfield Lorca shot himself yesterday on account of bad health. So I should be in no more danger from him; and the daughter is dead, too. So aren't you wasting your valuable time here?"

I said, "Do you get mad at every guy who gets an infected leg, or does the guy's name have to be Helm?"

She said, "I'm not mad at you. I'm mad at myself, because I've been doing some very strange things—that's

342

what I came up here for—and I don't really know why I'm doing them. I mean, I'm the nasty, ruthless little girl who never lets sentiment or friendship stand in her professional way, aren't I? So I've thrown away all my research on one story just because . . . because somebody asked me to in a nice way; and now I've made my editor withdraw another that was just about to go into the works, and without even being asked!"

I looked at her for a moment. "I thought you told me it was much too late to cancel—"

She said irritably, "Why the hell don't you sit down? It makes me dizzy to watch you holding yourself up with that dumb stick." After I'd limped to a chair, and she'd seated herself facing me, she placed an ashtray on the floor by her feet and blew smoke my way. "Naturally I'd tell you that. That was back when I was afraid of you, remember? I was afraid that if you thought I could do it, you'd try to force me to do it, somehow. But you didn't." She grimaced. "So in the end I did it myself, stupid me."

"Why, Elly?"

She drew a long ragged breath. "Because the story was all wrong, dammit!" she snapped. "Because you weren't at all the way I'd written you. How could I let it be published when I knew it had no resemblance to . . . to the man who deliberately let himself be captured in order to look after me? Who listened patiently to my endless sad stories about my dreadful sad experiences, and cleaned up my messes, and never once took advantage of. . . . Not to mention saving my life. A real Gold Star Agent, Angel Division!" She glared at me. "You must be very proud of yourself, Matt. It was really a lovely job of gaining the lady's confidence and respect and then having the sense to let her draw her own conclusions and make her own decisions, no coercion or persuasion at all. A real fine con job. Well, it worked. The ship story won't be written. The other series is being withdrawn, costing me a lot of money and some professional standing. I don't know why the hell I'm doing it, but I'm doing it. Maybe you can thank Bob Devine and the way I felt when I thought I'd got him killed because of

343

my single-minded devotion to my profession. Maybe . . . maybe I just don't want to risk the way I'd feel if I'd heard you'd been killed, knowing that I'd spend the rest of my life wondering if it had happened because of something I'd written about you." She rammed the cigarette angrily into the ashtray. "But why are you wasting your time here? I tell you, it's all taken care of. The personal touch is no longer needed, Mr. Helm; and don't you have . . . have engagements elsewhere?"

I said deliberately, "Martha is marrying Michael Brent, our red-haired young man in Miami. But I have a hunch he's not going to be doing that for us very much longer."

I heard Eleanor's breath catch. Her face looked suddenly pale and shocked. "I . . . I don't understand. I thought. . . ."

"I know what you thought," I said. "And it was true up to a point. She did come out from New Mexico to see me with some idea of. . . . Well, we go back a number of years and she was pretty lonely."

Martha licked her lips. "She loved you! And you loved her. I could see that so plainly when you opened the door of the suite that day in Miami, and suddenly saw her standing there in the hall. That's why I left like that. I'd done something pretty nasty to her once in the line of business, as you know. I owed her something, like getting myself the hell out of the way so there'd be nothing to interfere. . . ."

"Giving her a clear field," I said. "Noble. Nothing a man loves like being passed from woman to woman like a box of chocolate candy."

"It wasn't like that!" Eleanor protested. "It was on your face when you saw her. She meant a lot to you, too. And I was just a job and somebody for whom you . . . had a certain sympathy. Because of what had happened to me. I was damned if I was going to hang around and trade on that, Matt. I just complicated things for the two of you by being there. So I got the hell out of the way. Twice." Suddenly she was angry in a strange, perverse way. "What's the matter with the dumb girl, anyway? Is she really going to marry that . . . that freckled little boy?"

I said, "It's the best thing that could happen to her. Marry that freckled little boy and raise a brood of freckled little kids and forget all about violent guys like Bob Devine and me. And Brent's not so damned little, really. He's a good man, a very good man for her, and I'm very happy for her."

"I'll just bet you are! Don't forget, I saw your face when she popped up unexpectedly like that. You looked like a man just getting a good view of the Promised Land."

I looked at her for a moment, sitting there tense and angry like a small, fierce predator. And the strange thing, the marvelous thing, was that she was angry not because some other woman had got her claws into me, but because that other woman had been too stupid to appreciate me, and had rejected me. I felt very humble. It was more than I had any right to expect.

I swallowed the thing in my throat and said gently, "Elly, guys like me are always dreaming of a vine-covered cottage to come back to and a nice girl like Martha to put into it. It's a pretty dream, but in real life it's damned hard on the nice girl like Martha. And she had enough sense of self-preservation to see it at last, and grab a good steady guy who could give her the kind of life she really wanted, and I'm very glad she did." I cleared my throat. "So much for Martha. Nice girl, Martha. Nice guy, Mike Brent. Now can we talk about something else? Or somebody else?"

Her eyes were steady on my face. "Like whom?"

"Give me a drink," I said, "and I'll probably think of somebody."

I did.